Stealing Some Time

STEALING SOME TIME

Volume 1

Parts I and II

Mark Ian Kendrick

iUniverse, Inc.
New York Lincoln Shanghai

Stealing Some Time
Volume 1

Copyright © 2003 by Mark Ian Kendrick

All rights reserved. No part of this book may be used or reproduced by any means, graphic, electronic, or mechanical, including photocopying, recording, taping or by any information storage retrieval system without the written permission of the publisher except in the case of brief quotations embodied in critical articles and reviews.

iUniverse books may be ordered through booksellers or by contacting:

iUniverse
2021 Pine Lake Road, Suite 100
Lincoln, NE 68512
www.iuniverse.com
1-800-Authors (1-800-288-4677)

ISBN-13: 978-0-595-27672-1
ISBN-10: 0-595-27672-5

Printed in the United States of America

Contents

Part I: World Without You

Prologue	3
Chapter 1	11
Chapter 2	33
Chapter 3	53
Chapter 4	78
Chapter 5	86
Chapter 6	92
Chapter 7	98
Chapter 8	106
Chapter 9	113
Chapter 10	119
Chapter 11	126
Chapter 12	132
Chapter 13	140

Part II: Chance Encounter

Chapter 14	149

Chapter 15 158

Chapter 16 170

Chapter 17 177

Chapter 18 187

Chapter 19 197

Chapter 20 202

Chapter 21 221

Chapter 22 233

Chapter 23 248

Chapter 24 253

Chapter 25 259

About the Author 265

Acknowledgement

To Glenn,
who provided invaluable editing,
and who continues to put up with
my restless imagination.

And, to Les, my long ago (and long lost) mentor,
who taught me to think differently about everything.

PART I:
World Without You

*"Sometimes a goodbye is more difficult
when it's said to someone
you should never have said hello to
in the first place."*

—Uncle Martin,
from the 1960s
My Favorite Martian
TV series.

Prologue

Ten-year old Kallen Deshara was listening intently. He loved it when Mrs. Drabus read to them in class. Today was a special day, too. Fourth grade was when everyone learned about the Great Climate Change.

Behind Mrs. Drabus was a large vidscreen. Displayed in brilliant colors was an animated Dymaxion projection map of the world. Its icosahedron shape unfolded, then reassembled into its original shape in a slow moving loop. As she started speaking, the rotation stopped, zoomed in, and at the same time the map unfolded to the particular continent or country she was talking about.

"The world was barely one hundred and fifty years past the Little Ice Age when the weather patterns started gyrating wildly," she said. "It starting in 2087 when summer failed to come to parts of Europe and Asia. During that first year of cold, many expected harvests failed, causing severe economic hardship.

"Following that year, winter was the mildest ever recorded in those regions. Then for seven more years, the world saw progressively higher average yearly temperatures than before. Starting in 2092, winters as they had been known for centuries all around the world were almost a non-event.

"All that time, as the average yearly global temperature steadily rose, the polar ice caps had been melting. It was first noticed a long time before that, but many people kept altering the data or simply said it wasn't true. Toward the end of the century it was impossible to ignore. Over the next ten years, coastlines became more and more altered as the polar ice melted more rapidly than ever before. Hurricanes, typhoons and cyclones—the name depending on what part of the world you lived in—became more and more frequent, and much more deadly than ever before. Cities that dotted shorelines were regularly flooded. Huge public works projects were designed to stave off as much damage as possible. In more places than not, it just didn't work, mostly because the money ran out. Hundreds of millions of people's homes and livelihoods disappeared in a spiral of escalating catastrophes. The economic and property damage the changing climate left in its wake was unimaginable.

"In many areas great dust storms blew away the last bits of topsoil in lands that had been farmed for centuries. In forested areas, uncontrollable wildfires became commonplace and were even set by people who drew pleasure in seeing things burn. Huge migrations of people moved from country to country seeking new permanent homes when theirs were no longer habitable.

"Class, what was that era called?"

Kallen raised his hand, wiggling it to get her attention.

"Kallen."

"The First Wave," he said with a smile. Everyone had heard of the First Wave, but never in this much detail.

"The First Wave. Good," Mrs. Drabus said. "The First Wave is marked from the years 2087 through 2102 inclusive." Several children keyed those dates in to their lesson PADs.

She walked to the other side of the room as she continued to read from her text. It read like literature so that it would keep their attention. She read it with dramatic flourish to keep it, too. It was close to lunch and the kids were getting restless.

"The beginning of the Second Wave has been traditionally marked by the disappearance of the last remnants of the rainforest in Central Africa, South America, and in tropical Asia during the first decade of the 22nd century. The average yearly temperature along the equatorial region was just too high to sustain them anymore. Africa became a continent-wide desert as the Sahara and the Kalahari connected for the first time in recorded history. But the desert didn't stop after it had taken out that continent. Like a cancer, it grew. Sand blew into the surrounding oceans and across the skies to other continents. In fits and starts, the rest of the deserts around the world were also expanding as the heat continued unabated. When the oceans could no longer sustain even the most meager fisheries, entire populations that hadn't already felt the loss of land-based agriculture became history.

"The changing climate had, oddly enough, been good to the North American Midwest. During the First and Second Wave, North America had record harvests. That was when our agriculture was exclusively aboveground. There were once hectare and hectares of fields all topside!"

Kallen was amazed. *Fields of kamut and amaranth growing topside?* It was difficult to imagine.

"The vast Ogallala Aquifer that sustained the Midwest hadn't yet been emptied. Depleted in some areas, yes. But not empty like today. In fact, it rained a lot. Imagine that, class—rain in the Great Central Desert!

"Because of the certainty of rain, the Midwest managed to sustain record harvests. So, while the other continents felt the negative affects of the Great Climate Change, North America was not as badly affected. The rest of the world looked to our ancestors to feed those who remained. It was difficult, since all the old seaports were no longer available for grain transportation. But they found a way.

"The Third Wave commenced in 2119, the year the rains ended. The disadvantage of an incredibly long growing season was finally felt. No one was prepared for that. Lack of rain caused the harvests in most of North America to fail, despite the aquifer. The failures lasted for three years."

Kallen keyed in that date, too. There would be an exam on all of this later.

"There was a decent year in 2123. But nature didn't design the aquifer to be pumped out like that. In fact, it was emptied in a single season. The great heat that had long burned the rest of the world had come to stay.

"The Great Central Desert first appeared in the sandy western part of what was once called Nebraska in 2131. It spread east and north and quickly engulfed the entire Great Plains. In just over a decade that region that had once been spared finally received the blistering heat and drought that the rest of the world had already known. The desert eventually bisected North America from the Gulf Coast to the Arctic Ocean."

She looked back at the vidscreen with her kids. Images had been cycling by. There were pictures of dry baked earth, empty bowl-shaped lakebeds, dams with no water behind them, people migrating by the hundreds out of devastated cities, smoke rising into the air from burning cities. Some of the students squirmed in their seats. It was chilling. Frightening to all. Even terrifying to some of them.

"So, the Third Wave," she said, "which is now historically marked as starting in the year 2124, awakened the Great Central Desert after shutting down the world's food supply.

"Little was recorded about the years shortly after the beginning of the Third Wave, mostly because of the massive number of deaths by starvation and lack of water, and the horrible riots and killings by angry mobs. Over the next two decades, hundreds of millions of people died all over the world as a result of losing that last large farming region. Of course, the loss of that farmland led to the total collapse of our economy and ultimately to the collapse of almost every organized government in the world.

"It took almost three generations, but the three countries that once existed in North America consolidated along geographical lines and became two politically isolated nations. What was left of the Eastern seaboard states of the old United States, the un-flooded eastern provinces of Canada, and the remaining populated areas in northeastern Canada became known the United Canadian Territories—the UCT.

"Great waves of refugees came to our western shore. Some came from Australia, which had long since become a burning continental desert. Many came from coastal Asian countries. There were Pacific Islanders whose atolls vanished beneath the relentless Pacific waves. And there were others, mostly from countries along the Pacific Rim.

"Much of the population of the northern Mexican states had long since migrated north to the Sierras, the Rockies, or the formerly temperate forested areas of the North American Pacific coast. All of the diverse cultures that came to our shores eventually assimilated into our society. A huge consolidation of the peoples and cultures that lived in the westernmost Pacific states, the Rocky Mountain States, Alyeska, British Columbia, and Yukon all became known as the North American Alliance, the NAA. Our country.

"That political reorganization took over a hundred years to accomplish. But what happened long before that, class?" Mrs. Drabus asked.

Kallen knew the answer, but he'd already raised his hand too many times. Too bad. This particular subject was one he knew a lot about.

"The pipelines?" Tem asked.

"Correct." The screen zoomed in to a region centering on the western shore of Lake Michigan.

"Just as it is now, the one limiting factor for everyone during all those changes had been water. Obtaining steady supplies of drinkable water had become difficult more than a century before the First Wave. Thanks to our ancestors, more than a decade before the First Wave began a grand public works project was completed: the pipeline that drew water from Lake Michigan and delivered it to the thirsty West. It was built just north of a city called Chicago. From there it ran southwest. It took years to build, was entirely downside, and spanned the width of the Great Central Desert. But that was before it became burning hot.

"Shortly after that pipeline was completed, the grandest pipeline project in history was started. That one originated from Lake Superior near Duluth, Minnesota. It was completed and water was flowing through it only six months before the First Wave began."

Kallen knew all about that pipeline. In fact, on one of the walls of his father's office was a large map of the region. A distinct red line traced its path as it ran from the Duluth pumping station and spanned the entire width of the Great Central Desert. It was buried downside, too, within secure concrete casements.

"A huge pumping station was built to push the water through and bring it out west. It was three times the size of the one on Lake Michigan. Does anyone remember when the Lake Michigan pipeline was shut down?"

Letan raised her hand. Mrs. Drabus called on her.

"2262."

"The newer pumping station drew water from the much bigger and deeper Lake Superior and sent it out west, too. And as we all know, Lake Superior also belongs to the UCT. They told us we couldn't draw water from there. After a war with them many, many years ago over water rights, we were allowed to keep the water flowing from that single pipeline. To this day, we still draw water from it."

Kallen just smiled. He was from a proud family of two generations of watermen. His grandfather and father had dedicated their lives at that work.

She stopped her lecture when the bell rang.

"You may go."

As her kids filed out to the lunchroom, Mrs. Drabus pressed a button on her monitor panel. The maps disappeared from the vidscreen. She didn't get a chance to tell her fourth graders the rest of the story. Actually, she was unaware of virtually all of it anyway.

Mrs. Drabus barely knew anything about the re-pumping station in Fort Morgan, Colorado. She was only peripherally aware of its strategic importance to the North American Alliance. Due to Fort Morgan's location within what became known as the Great Central Desert, it was now a hot, dusty NAA military outpost. Three smaller pipelines distributed the water from that station to the northwest, almost due west across the mountains, and southwestward.

Centuries ago, when the re-pumping station was first built, it was a pleasant place to live and work. Today it was only home to pump engineers, a handful of support personnel, and several platoons of Black Guard who were security for the downside installation. The Black Guard also flew reconnaissance along the pipeline's path across the vast burning expanse, monitored topside conditions, and generally making sure the pipeline stayed safe. Much further east, Black Guard, and military regulars were stationed on a large base adjacent to the Duluth pumping station. Being so far from NAA territory, the Duluth pumping station was a lonely outpost.

The Black Guard had originated as National Guard and Marines. Centuries before, while cities burned and riots were a weekly occurrence; the two services were merged to form a more mobile tactical force. Complete with a new name, the Black Guard were used to quell strikes and looting. Later they were used to stop rebellion. In due course, they became a full-fledged military division. Platoons of Black Guard troops had been stationed all over the NAA for more than two centuries. They kept the order, protected the public and the local water supplies, and kept everyone in line. Officially, they were security troops. But the public was aware that they were more than that. The Black Guard listened for dissenters. They determined who was seditious. They made sure everyone was 'happy'. Code, of course, for towing the line.

Although generally despised, the elite Black Guard recruited thousands of men and women. In return, they were given luxuries not traditionally associated with military service. That was one of the prime incentives. Because of that, Black Guard were prized for their loyalty. The only way in was after one had been drafted into the more traditional services, then underwent a rigorous background check and further training.

Both the NAA and the UCT required mandatory military service for all men and women starting at age eighteen. One of the NAA's primary military objectives was the protection of scarce water resources. Since both countries had been permanently armed nations for generations, military bases dotted their landscapes. Thus, mandatory conscription and the liberal use of force. But only the NAA had Black Guard.

Although technology flourished—despite the havoc wrecked all over the planet due to radically changed climates—many disciplines, once the hallmark of modern civilization, ceased to exist. Aerospace, incredibly expensive to maintain, had ceased to be a priority. Satellites that once circled the earth by the hundreds had long since burned up on reentry. Healthcare changed and only the wealthiest had access to the best doctors. Genetic engineering was shifted to modify food products only, but eventually was no longer funded. Natural and manmade cavern systems were used to grow huge hydroponics gardens powered by sunlight piped in via fiber optic bundles.

Eventually, due to the need to conserve energy and protect themselves from the constant burning sun, the West moved the majority of their production facilities and habitation underground. In Kallen's time, the majority of the population, except those who lived in the northernmost climes, lived and worked meters below the surface—called downside—in vast interconnected neighborhoods, towns, and business centers.

Other technological disciplines grew and continued to change. The melding of photonic and electronic technologies became known as photronics. Photronic devices needed photronic software, and it eventually became the programming language embedded in everything from clothing to hovercars. In a limited economy, photronics was an easy technology to sustain. Forced to shift resources due to energy scarcity wind, solar and hydrogen sources had replaced fossil fuels centuries ago in the NAA.

Improvements to fuel cells had continued almost unimpeded, too. They were used in many personal photronic devices. Super-efficient solar cell technology and wind turbines also helped energize most of the NAA.

In the three and a half or so centuries since the beginning of the Great Climate Change, civilization, which had taken over six thousand years to build, had been severely curtailed. But when pressed to the limit, humans are remarkably inventive.

Traditional energy sources aside, in 2380 an innovative energy cell design was rediscovered after having been lost for centuries. The concept? Quantum nucleonic energy. Quantum nucleonic energy utilized pulses of highly charged particles in an extremely small space to produce power. Fuelled by an irradiated nickel-hafnium isotope, this miniature radioactive cell was unlike any other energy source. Extremely lightweight, fully shielded, yet incredibly powerful, it produced no radioactive by-products, and all without fission or fusion. It became known as a q-cell. This high density energy generation technology revolutionized almost every industry. Within five years, tiny powerful batteries utilizing the new technology were put into commercial use.

The seemingly inexhaustible energy that a q-cell produced caused a cascade effect in the inventive process with regard to the photronic technologies industries. Utilizing a q-cell, a portable photronic-based product had an effective life of up to fifty years. Research money poured into the industry.

The infusion of those funds led to the development of the graviton generator. The generator created the first true anti-gravity field. Within a dozen years, the first working hovercars became available to the general public. In fact, the entire transportation industry got a much-needed boost.

And another centuries old technology was rediscovered late in the 24th century as the past was culled from ruins. Spidersteel. Genetically engineered from spider silk, one of the strongest materials known had once been mass produced. Shortly after the formula for its manufacture was rediscovered, its synthesis was begun once again. Ultimately a method was developed whereby it could be mass produced for a new era.

By 2389 the NAA economy was rebounding after so long in the doldrums.

Although technology progressed, water remained the constant limiting factor in daily life, keeping populations from expanding or civilization from completely rebuilding. Indeed, since the dawn of Man, water had always determined the course of a civilization. In fact, the economy rebounded so mightily that huge domes were constructed over open water reservoirs, using spidersteel beams. It was even discovered that the reason the pipeline from Lake Superior never cracked or failed was because they had been made of spidersteel.

Thin sheets of valicant, which was its rolled form of spidersteel, was the skin that covered the support beams that arched over the large lakes and reservoirs all over North America to prevent evaporation. Public works projects, employing thousands, helped run waterdome operations, helped maintain local pipelines, and oversaw the reclamation of water. In fact, decades before Kallen was born, all sizeable rivers had been piped and redirected to reservoirs, sealed caverns, and aquifers. Eventually, not a single river worth bothering with on the entire continent had been left un-piped.

Desperate times had required desperate measures.

The classroom story of the Great Climate Change was taught to every grade schooler in the North American Alliance. Today, that included Kallen. But, as in all ages, history lessons don't tell the whole story. In fact, sometimes they don't tell the right one at all.

History wasn't the only thing Kallen discovered to be different from what he'd been taught. In fact, young Kallen Deshara had no idea he would become one of the most important figures ever to shape the course of civilization, and thus, go down in history himself.

Chapter 1

Friday, June 11, 2477

Summer temperatures usually arrived at Denali Air Station Recruit Camp in Alyeska long before daylight became its constant companion. Eighteen-year old Kallen Jahn Deshara arrived on Friday evening, exactly one week after graduating from high school. This was the first time he'd been this far away from his hometown and he was both excited and anxious. He was toward the back of the hoverbus that held sixty-four other eighteen and nineteen-year old boys. After the ten kilometer ride from the hoverport to the recruit camp, he had his toes stepped on multiple times as everyone dashed out the door to the designated area in front of the gate.

Immediately, their ears were assaulted by yelling drill instructors. "Don't look at me!" "Keep your mouth shut!" "Stand up straight!" The routine heard by recruits for centuries.

Kallen stood in line, his sandy brown hair noticeable because of the blond ends waving in the warm breeze. His 1.83 meter frame stood as much to attention as he could muster. His lean seventy-four kilo weight completely motionless. Despite the commotion that threatened to break his concentration at any second, his deep green eyes were fixed on the dead center of the back of the head of the boy in front of him.

The view surrounding the recruit station was breathtaking. The mountains here were higher and far more rugged than the ones that graced the skyline back home. The temperature was wonderful, too, almost chilly in comparison to what he was used to this time of year. But what was most surprising was that he saw dozens and dozens of topside buildings, and people walking around like they didn't have a care in the world! He wasn't prepared to see everything designed to be completely topside. Already it looked like his life would be quite a bit different for a while.

Tiago Sandoval, 1.92 meters tall, a lean eighty-two kilos, coffee-brown skin, black hair, and dark brown eyes, was from the Oregon Domain. He had lived his entire life some three hundred kilometers west of New Meadows. The two had never met before. He stood directly behind Kallen, his eyes focused directly at the center of the back of Kallen's head, trying to look as innocent as possible and trying to keep from being yelled at. It wasn't working. Drill instructors know that an innocent look means nothing.

Eventually, they were ushered through the gates and soon enough their three-month training began.

Tiago, with his thick shiny dark hair, his green-tinged brown eyes, and light-brown complexion enamored Kallen more than any boy he'd ever met before. Kallen's hometown was an almost homogeneous mix of European stock, of which Kallen's family was no exception. Tiago, on the other hand, was totally different, since he had Central American roots. Within a week Kallen and Tiago became buddies.

Eighteen years of age like Kallen, Tiago had a certain mystery about him that, at first, Kallen was unable to properly define. But, like himself, Tiago was there because he had to be. It was the law. Everyone knew that at eighteen or nineteen they would be serving at least five years in the National Ground Patrol, the Air Defense Force, or the Coastal Marine Observers. Later, some would even opt to join the Black Guard.

As the weeks passed, Kallen became mesmerized with Tiago's ability to concentrate on the tasks put to him, his easy-going nature, his unbelievable smile, and with something he didn't want to admit at first: his fascination with Tiago's gorgeous body. No one else in his entire platoon came even close to Tiago in that respect. Just being near him made Kallen feel emotion about to burst out of his chest.

It wasn't until his second month in boot camp that Kallen finally admitted he was gay. Up until that time he thought his secret fascination for males was an odd quirk. It was because of Tiago that he came to terms with what he'd been suppressing all this time. Alone on night watch gave one time to think. Kallen's turn came around every eighth day. It was during his fifth rotation that he let himself be overwhelmed with the fact that he was totally sexually attracted to Tiago.

Before, when he let the feelings come up, he had always carefully, calmly, and deliberately suppressed them. He noticed that here in boot camp he couldn't suppress them at all—despite the rumor that some sort of chemical had been put in their food to keep them from getting aroused. It certainly wasn't working on him.

Here, it was impossible to deny what was true about himself. Not while being surrounded by nothing but other boys, most of whom were getting stronger each day, filling out where it counted, losing the last remnants of baby fat, oozing pure testosterone with every yell, every precision movement. And the aroma of over five dozen hard bodies entering the showers en masse was something Kallen couldn't put out of his mind even when he was dead tired at the end of a day.

Yet none of them, not one, mesmerized him like Tiago did.

On that fateful night, he stopped by Tiago's rack and stared at his sleeping face less than two meters away, traced the outline of his body under the thin blanket with his eyes, and danced them over his short beautiful shiny black hair. As Kallen's erection grew, he realized he'd been fighting something that had always been in his heart.

Unfortunately, military service and a gay orientation remained incompatible in the eyes of command. He realized that he had no choice but to keep it hidden. He was barely eight weeks into a five year stint in the military. He had to stay quiet about it at all costs, for fear of jeopardizing his future.

As the weeks wore on, Kallen fantasized even more about Tiago. It was getting difficult to contain himself with how he felt.

Perhaps it was his toothy smile that gripped Kallen the most. After all, it covered a great deal of his face. Maybe it was the way he looked in his standard issue low cut t-shirt and tight shorts, with his hairless dark arms and legs drenched with sweat after their workouts. Maybe it was the way he looked in nothing but skivvies when he stood at the end of his bunk waiting for nightly inspection. Perhaps it was his wonderfully proportioned body which he saw almost everyday in the showers.

Kallen's bunk was directly opposite his and one over. He had a perfect view of Tiago's faultless pecs, his perfectly rounded deltoids, and his nicely developed triceps as they stood at attention at the end of their bunks. Tiago wasn't overly muscular, just taut and firm. He had become Kallen's ultimate fantasy boy in the flesh.

And he was always just out of reach.

How he was going to break the news to his girlfriend once he returned home?

Despite his attempts over the last couple of years, and despite having a steady girlfriend, Kallen was still a virgin. His first attempt to become a non-virgin was at the party at Bayla's house. They were both sixteen. They were having such a good time that no one thought it strange when Tal sat back on the recliner and Bayla sat on top of him. She didn't just sit on him, she laid back on him. Tal put his arms around her middle. Kallen was having fun, too, so stretched out on top of her on his back. He knew it was the only time he'd ever be able to be that close to Tal. Tal had reached up and put his arms around Kallen's middle, sandwiching them all together. Kallen slid off the pile as fast as he could since he got an almost instant erection just from Tal's hands holding onto his sides. After he got off them, Bayla turned over. With her and Tal face to face, they started making out, thinking no one would care. But Kallen wished it was him making out with Tal. He razzed them until they stopped.

Later, Kallen went upstairs and made out with the much-inebriated Bayla, too. But it was a ruse. He was doing it only because her lips had touched Tal's. Every second he had his mouth against hers he thought about Tal's lips against hers earlier. When his saliva mixed with hers, he only thought about Tal's having done so less than an hour ago.

Kallen tried and tried to get her to go all the way with her. But she refused to let him cross that line with her. Crushed, Kallen gave up. It was weird enough feeling that he could somehow absorb some sort of 'essence of Tal' by being with her.

Months later, after that failed attempt, he tried to lose his virginity twice with Ylana from his junior chemistry class. Both times he lost his erection just before he entered her. They weren't going out, so when he stopped hitting on her she was probably glad he wasn't pursuing her anymore. That's what he told himself.

One month into his senior year, Naya Sommercorn became his first actual girlfriend. He managed to put aside what he considered his annoying attraction to boys for long enough to focus his attention on her. Kallen was well-aware of how socially unacceptable his obsession with other males was becoming. It was taboo to express affection the way he was inclined. His peers were viscerally opposed to even the concept. They were merely a reflection of the prevailing cultural norms.

With the two other girls his advances had been forced awkward teenage attempts at intimacy. But Naya was different. She was sweet, charming, and cute, and was very interested in him. So, he had asked her out. At the time, it was the right thing to do since he really wanted a girlfriend. Naya was attractive, although unassuming about it. She continued to be charming after they started dating. He was relieved he felt comfortable enough to be with her. He loved her soft skin and lips, and everything else about her actually. Her only drawback? Her insistence that the Holy Mormon-Methodist Church was correct in saying that sex before marriage was wrong. At first, he was exasperated at her insistence in not letting him consummate their relationship, then relieved about it as his unrelenting attraction to his male friends continued to intrude into his fantasies, daydreams, and wet dreams.

Regardless, after his initial nervous first attempts, they ended up doing virtually everything else sexually except outright intercourse. Kallen found himself surprised at how easy it was to get her to respond to him and how easy it was to respond to her, too. Unfortunately, there was a price to pay. No intercourse. Her one holdout seemed absurd. He wondered if her god truly appreciated the distinction between intercourse and a blowjob. It seemed to him she was getting by the 'no sex before marriage' rule purely on a technicality.

Kallen had developed an odd sort of way to sustain sexual interest in her. Odd because he was sure no other guys did what he did in his head. Every time they got naked together he fantasized about Obin, Tal (who had gotten even better looking as the year went on), or Kemp mostly, with him. Kemp, with his upturned nose and his short fingers was his favorite fantasy. Yet, Kallen continually pushed away the complete implication of what he was imagining. After all, Naya was his *girl*friend. Although he was never one hundred percent present when they were intimate, he never questioned his loyalty to her.

He found it humorous about Naya's church teachings on sexuality (his family wasn't all that religious). Heck, here they were having almost routine sex—just not intercourse, vaginal or anal—and she was constantly telling him how important her virginity was. Right. How silly was *that*?

Kallen was sure that his sexual allegiance would totally shift to girls one day. When, he wasn't sure. He wondered if it took any other boys this long.

It took being in boot camp to totally understand why he never made that transition.

More quickly than Kallen realized, a full twelve weeks and three days went by since he'd left New Meadows. It was finally graduation day from boot camp. Kallen and Tiago, along with four others, had received a meritorious promotion to E-2 for their outstanding achievements and physical endurance. For the last several weeks Kallen had been encouraging Tiago to come visit him back home.

No longer Airmen Recruits, Airmen First Class Deshara and Sandoval stood in front of the huge Air Defense Force flag that was painted on the wall of the graduation hall. Their parents were busy taking photos. Finally, the handshakes, hugs, and photo ops were over. Their parents were occupied near the refreshment bar.

"So, what'd they say?" Kallen asked, eager to know if he would be allowed a visit.

"They said no problemo."

"Wicked hot!" Kallen exclaimed.

"Wicked hot!" Tiago echoed. At that, they both yelled out their platoon slogan, more of a guttural exclamation than anything else.

Standing before him in his crisp graduation blues, at the far edge of adolescence, Tiago was, like himself, filled with excitement about their new phase in life. What was even more exciting was that Tiago's parents had okayed his visit to see Kallen for two weeks before they both went off to their respective duty stations, Kallen to Vancouver for operations training and Tiago to Monterrey for intelligence.

Kallen was breathless with anticipation. Finally, away from the watchful eyes of their drill instructors, he'd have Tiago all to himself—for a while, at least.

It was late evening when the Deshara family arrived back home. From the window of the commercial air transport, Kallen could easily see the waterdome. This was only the third time he'd seen it from the air. Kallen mused about that. His grandfather had worked his entire adult life on the Payette River pipeline crew. The pipeline meandered from the south to the lake in McCall, Idaho, which was the county seat near New Meadows. Kallen's father Tannert was one of the senior engineers who worked for the Payette Lake Waterdome Authority. The immense waterdome covered the entire lake, containing their precious water reserves. Kallen might just be the third generation to join them, but hadn't decided just yet.

Kallen had been a star pupil since he was in junior high. At an early age, his father encouraged him to develop his interest in the one subject he was enamored with since he could walk. Photronics.

When Kallen was eleven, he was repairing test equipment at his father's shop at the waterdome. Tannert had him work all summer (not all day, of course) to keep their hydronics equipment in top operating condition. There was no central authority in scripting photronic software. Completely open-source, it could be pieced together by anyone smart enough to understand the object-oriented code sequences. Kallen was that smart. His precocious aptitude for it made him invaluable.

When the chief engineer was reviewing bills from the maintenance organization that normally did that type of work, and found the sum to be far less than expected, he investigated. When he found out that the reason was Kallen, it got a lot of attention. Tannert's eleven-year old boy could script photronic code that well?

From there, Kallen progressed to more sophisticated equipment. By the time he was thirteen, he was familiar with three foundational operating systems, five software codebases used in waterdome operations, and had optimized the water quality database on their development server. His father couldn't have been more proud, except for the time he was caught attempting to break encryption codes and punch through the firewall to the NAA I-net.

No one accessed the NAA I-net without proper authorization. That little adventure got him reprimanded by the head of the Engineering department. Mr. Deshara's boss wasn't keen on the possibility of having Black Guard in his waterdome investigating the incident. It was bad enough that security was assigned to them by a local Black Guard unit. The whole experience was an eye opener for young Kallen. He learned to keep some of his activities a closely guarded secret.

Little did he know how important that secrecy that would become for the rest of his life.

Naya was waiting for Kallen in his family's living room when he arrived home from the hoverport. Neighbors, his great-aunt, some of his cousins, and other friends from school were there, too. Naya hadn't entered basic training yet, but would be in a few short weeks. Everyone was allowed to defer their entry into the service for up to a year. Kallen hadn't delayed his.

Kallen stepped inside, looking forward to the crowd of friends and family. She ran up to him and gave him a tight hug. "Finally, you're home!" she exclaimed.

"It's good to see you in person again," Kallen responded, knowing it wasn't quite true. It wasn't just his time away that made him feel awkward. He was no longer the Kallen who left three months ago. It wasn't because of his training either. He wasn't the Kallen she thought she knew. He wasn't the same Kallen he thought he knew either. And now, Naya seemed like a complete stranger. He was hardly sure why she was in his house since most of his thoughts were focused on when Tiago would arrive.

As they hugged, his stomach tightened. At first, he thought he'd poked himself on something sharp. When he pulled away from her, he inspected himself. Satisfied he hadn't gotten stabbed by a belt buckle or something he wondered what had just happened. That was the first time he felt the funny gnawing pain in his stomach. The pain that accompanied him, on and off, from that day on.

She brushed the top of his head with her hand. "Do they always have to cut it so short?"

He smiled, despite how his stomach was protesting, and ran his fingertips over it a couple of times. He lowered his head and tried to poke her with the spiky locks. She playfully pushed him away and proceeded to take him to his bedroom by the hand. The rest of his family and friends were in the kitchen or had spilled out into the covered porch with refreshments and snacks, not realizing the two of them had disappeared.

His bedroom door was locked. Kallen and Naya were the sole occupants. They had spent the first several minutes holding each other and kissing. Now she was on her knees in front of him after he sat on the edge of his bed. His trousers and skivvies were down to his ankles. She was kissing him again and fondling him at the same time. Despite his erection from the moment he locked the door he noticed how he had to force himself to feel affectionate back with her. She slowly kissed her way down his chest, to his navel, then to his crotch where she skillfully took him in her mouth.

It took a lot longer than normal for him to finish, despite the danger of being caught. After all, there were over a dozen people in the house. He was sure that after his three months of celibacy (he was only able to beat off twice in boot camp) he would have been a loaded cannon. It wasn't so.

Luckily, just as they heard the knock on the door, his belt was buckled once again and he had his finger on the open button. No one else knew what had transpired as they quickly made their way back to the festivities and celebrated his new status.

Tiago arrived a couple of days later at the New Meadows hoverbus terminal. He knew all about Kallen's girlfriend. Kallen had talked about her often. He had even been in the booth with Kallen and watched two short vids she had sent while they were in boot camp.

Kallen talked like he was straight and acted the part almost perfectly, but Tiago knew better. It was, after all, an act. Outwardly, Kallen had all the signs of liking girls, but from the start Tiago had had his suspicions. For starters, Kallen was the biggest flirt he had ever met. He wasn't sure if Kallen knew the reality of what he was doing when they interacted, but Tiago was definitely sure that the object of his desire was making his way out of the closet. Tiago had come out to himself only six months before they first met. He had never had sex with anyone. He had never even kissed a girl before in an affectionate way. He hoped all of that would end before his trip was over.

The Deshara house was entirely downside except for the monolithic dome that broached the surface. Most of the homes in New Meadows were similar in design. Entire neighborhoods were completely downside except for a highly-insulated dome-shaped upper level. That's where the solar light bundles were affixed which brought much of their light to the sub-surface levels. Egress to the surface could be found there, too, as well as most of the utilities, the garage, and their covered porch area.

The Waterdome Authority was generous with their salaries. The Deshara home had two bedrooms and slightly over two hundred thirty square meters of living space on three sublevels. Spacious as homes went. Kallen was an only child, so an extra bedroom had never been a priority. Originally, it was assumed Tiago would sleep in the den but Kallen insisted that the blow-up air mattress would be put in his bedroom. Tiago tried not to look visibly excited when he discovered their sleeping arrangement.

That first night, the two boys talked long into the night about boot camp, life in New Meadows, and the newfound respect they were getting now that the mantle of airman was a part of their lives. Slowly, Tiago steered the conversation to Naya.

"So, did you guys do it?" He wasn't sure why Kallen had been avoiding the topic.

"Of course. She did me within an hour after I got back."

"Are you kidding?

"I swear." The invisible hand started squeezing his stomach again.

"You lucky fuck."

"I wouldn't call it lucky." Kallen felt like he was going to vomit now.

Tiago didn't notice Kallen's distress. "Why not?"

Kallen looked away. "It's not like the real thing, you know."

"Huh?"

Kallen made a fist and placed it on his crotch. He pumped air a couple of times while he grinned. "You know, the 'real thing'."

Tiago threw his head back and laughed. The extent of his sexual contact had been only with himself since he had been alive, and now Kallen was telling him anything else wasn't the 'real thing'. "I sure could go for something other than the 'real thing'. At least once." He had an exasperated sound to his voice, which Kallen clearly heard.

"You're a virgin?"

"I-I lied. I've never done it before."

"Hmm. Maybe we can change that while you're here."

"Maybe we can," Tiago replied with genuine interest. He gazed into Kallen's eyes. He hadn't been so bold before, but the venue required it.

Kallen fell back on the bed. His heart pounded, his pulse raced. *Was that a come on?* He desperately wanted to know for sure. His face became beet red at the embarrassment of thinking about Tiago that way in the isolation of his bedroom. He waded through the pain in his stomach. Once he composed himself he noticed that their conversation and the tone of their friendship had somehow shifted. Being completely unfamiliar with the uncharted territory he'd suddenly found himself in made it difficult for him to know where he was.

Tiago knew exactly where they were. He could see it on Kallen's face. Hadn't he just turned as red as a second degree sunburn? He could even tell from how Kallen's tone of voice had changed. And Kallen kept looking at his crotch ever so often, something he only did on rare occasions before. Tiago had been keeping count. Tonight, Kallen had looked nine times.

Tiago moved the sheet over just a bit so that his tight white skivvies would be plainly visible against his dark skin. There. Kallen looked again. *That's ten times now*, Tiago counted. Kallen was an easy tease. He loved being able to do that—all innocently—or so it appeared.

But Kallen couldn't find the bravery he so desperately desired. Soon enough, his profuse yawning led him to call lights out.

The excitement about being alone with Kallen kept Tiago from falling asleep for over an hour.

The next morning Kallen drove them to the waterdome. Due to his previous employment there, and the influence of his father, Kallen had an un-expired access card that was encoded for restricted areas of the interior. Tiago had seen other waterdomes since they littered the landscape all over the NAA. But he'd never been inside one before. The Payette Lake one was large enough to have a visitor center.

Kallen parked his mother's hovercar in the lot next to the administration building. Behind it, high above them, the gleaming white dome covering reflected the morning sunlight.

Tiago slid his sunglasses down over his eyes. "It's huge!"

"It's the biggest one in the region. My dad's been an engineer here since before I was born." They weren't going to see his dad right away. Kallen wanted to take Tiago to the usual touristy sections of the dome first. He pointed to an igloo-like domed entranceway off to their left. "We sign in over here." They headed over to the visitor's entrance which was under a broad sun-shaded walkway. On weekends, tourists could be seen pouring out of hoverbuses that were parked in the lot. Today, since it was during the week, there was only a single empty tourist hoverbus nearby.

Kallen waited for Tiago to get his visitors pass. Kallen's previous employment card still gave him all the access he needed, so he didn't need one of his own. The administrative official took a digital snapshot of Tiago, did the required security checks, and handed him his card. The official shook Kallen's hand, since she had known him for years, then congratulated them for their recent graduation from boot camp.

They went down a long interior corridor. A guard at the end of it scanned their cards then allowed them through thick metal doors. Once inside, the humidity tripled.

The visitor's group was off to the left and consisted of only eight people. The guide was ushering them into a room where they showed the informational vid before starting the actual tour. Kallen led Tiago in the opposite direction up an escalator built along the inside of the dome. Once up to the second level, they had a good view across the entire lake.

Tiago pulled off his sunglasses and placed them in one of his pants pockets. Standing at the railing, he looked out over the water. It was unbelievable. This much drinkable water all in one place (after being filtered and processed, of course)! Tiago had lived his life well inland and had only seen the ocean twice. Most of the potable water for his region was piped in from one of the dozens of desalination plants that dotted the Pacific Coast. Supplemental water was purchased from smaller nearby covered reservoirs or pumped from deep wells. None of the reservoirs had internal escalators, and none of the watermen had authority to allow visitors inside.

Tiago looked down at the calm water. "Have you ever been in it?"

"I've waded out to my knees a couple of times—unauthorized, of course. I've been *on* it in the boats we use to monitor water quality. They're launched from over there." He pointed to his right. "They usually just send out automated ones. But occasionally we would go out and take a manual sample."

"It sucks that you can't dive right into it, huh?" Tiago wasn't afraid of heights, nor of the water.

"I can't even imagine." Kallen wasn't afraid of being up so high either. It had just never occurred to him to swim to their water supply!

Kallen gripped the railing next to Tiago, thinking about the word he'd just used. *Suck. I'd love to suck him. I'd love to have him suck me!*

The feeling of Naya's mouth on him two days before Tiago had arrived was still on his mind. A spark of a thought grew into a bonfire almost instantly. He realized right there that before Tiago left New Meadows he would never again be intimate with Naya Sommercorn.

It was while the bonfire was burning at its greatest intensity that he slowly moved his left hand until his little finger just barely touched Tiago's. It seemed that the whole world was filled with the sound of his heart pounding in his chest and the feeling of the tiny bit of Tiago's flesh that touched his. *God, it would be so easy to put my hand on top of his.* As he thought about doing it, his stomach tightened, making him exhale loudly. Instead of doing it, Kallen place his hand across his middle.

Kallen's sudden movement caused Tiago to divert his attention from below. "Something wrong?"

"My stomach. Been bothering me lately." Finally, it loosened up. He pointed to the next escalator. "Onward."

They continued up several more levels. As they progressed, the air became warmer, but not overpoweringly so. Tiago wondered why, then spied an elaborate fan and ductwork system. There were louvers that opened and closed in a slow progression along the top of the dome. Nearly lost in the network of overhead beams, they seemed to take advantage of outside breezes, venting the hottest air and creating circulation inside the dome. It was as if they were inside an organic structure, what with all the subtle motion above them.

They reached the sixth level, feeling a breeze ever so often. It was pleasant up here, although somewhat more humid than Tiago cared for. This level was along the junction of several thick spidersteel beams. Kallen pointed to the left. "That door leads to one of the sensor rooms. The dome is covered with different types of them so they'll know if there's a puncture," he pointed up, "or a leak. Power conduits run though the room, too." Kallen held up his card. "I have clearance. We can look inside one."

From this height a rocky peninsula that nearly bisected the lake was plainly visible, as was the far shoreline to the south. Tiago moved toward the railing, tentatively at first, but once he was sure it was secure he leaned over and looked down. It was exhilarating being up this high.

Kallen looked down the escalator, then upward. There was no one else up this far. *We're alone. I could do it now. If I could get past my fear, everything will change. I am bigger than my fear. I am!*

He watched Tiago lean over the railing. Without a pause, he stepped up behind him and wrapped his arms around Tiago's chest. "Don't move!" He was almost not believing he had done it.

Tiago's sudden lurch against the metal barrier startled him. "Fuck!" he yelped. His hands tightly gripping the railing, he pushed backward against Kallen's body. At the same time, Kallen loosened his tight grip yet kept his arms around Tiago's chest. Tiago twirled around, still surrounded by Kallen's arms. Their faces were only centimeters from each other. Tiago's eyes were mesmerizing.

Tiago wanted him as badly as did he. Kallen knew it now. No more delays.

Kallen's breathing became rapid and shallow. He slowly moved his hands to Tiago's shoulders. It seemed that everything was suddenly, and quite mysteriously, shining in brilliant colors. Tiago's skin took on a sheen he'd never noticed before. He could see beautiful striations of brown and brilliant green in the Central American ancestry of Tiago's eyes, the long dark eyelashes, and the dot on his left earlobe—the black spot that he could swear said 'lick here' in microprint. The water below them was a dark blue sapphire.

"Your girlfriend," Tiago whispered. Or did he ask it?

Kallen shook his head. "Shhh," he quietly said.

Both of them closed their eyes and kissed. Tiago's lips were the softest cushions he'd ever felt. Tiago's breath, hot against his, was the nuclear fire that lit the sun. Tiago's tongue was the tasty flesh he'd always craved, and now had.

Kallen pulled back after the kiss and touched the card on the lanyard around his neck with his trembling hand. He pointed to the door.

Tiago swallowed noticeably, then rapidly nodded. Before he could move, Kallen pressed against him again. Each could feel the other's hardness at their groins as they kissed, slowly this time, with their tongues exploring deeply inside each other's mouths. It was a dizzying feeling, especially this high up. Kallen ran his hand through Tiago's thick dark, albeit short, hair. He thought he'd lose all control with that simple act and stopped. He nuzzled the top of Tiago's head and breathed in deeply. "You smell so good," he said in a barely audible whisper. He grasped Tiago's warm hand and went to the door, waving his passcard by the sensor. The door immediately unlocked.

There were a dozen sensor hub rooms along the inside surface of the dome. Kallen was familiar with this particular one. He had come here many times to find some private time alone when his teenage hormones were working overtime. Although the room reminded him of sex, he'd never brought Naya up here. Now that he'd thought about it, although she'd come to meet him in the dome four or five times while they were dating, he realized he'd never even kissed her in this building. He was about to do much more than that with Tiago.

Both of them were simultaneously excited at their forbidden pleasure and scared of being caught. Yet it seemed that Tiago couldn't remove his shirt fast enough. In seconds both were bare-chested, their erections pressing tightly against zippers, their hands exploring each other's shoulders, arms, nipples, and lats as they passionately kissed.

Kallen dropped to his knees and tentatively touched the hard mound at Tiago's crotch. He could feel Tiago's thick legs shaking. He could feel the warmth of Tiago's body so near his face and reveled in his masculine stature. He pressed his cheek against the hardness hidden only millimeters behind thin fabric. He tilted his head and opened his mouth so he could press his lips against its full length. Done with that, he reached up and unbuttoned Tiago's pants, then unzipped them. He slowly pulled them down, revealing black civilian underwear straining against the relentless pressure of his impossibly hard penis. He grasped the waistband with both hands and pulled them to Tiago's ankles. The faint aroma of his genitals wafted under Kallen's nose, making Kallen even more light-headed than he already was. Kallen's hands slowly, tentatively explored the curve of Tiago's hard buttocks, touched his rapidly tightening scrotum, and lightly stroked his rock hard shaft. He waited no longer as he took Tiago's upward-curved hardness into his mouth.

Breathless, Tiago thought he would melt from excitement. Less than ten seconds later he did. Kallen gagged, then swallowed. He didn't care. The moment had finally arrived. He was too busy feeling satisfied that he had a penis in his mouth.

He used his tongue to caress Tiago's penis, then sucked everything out that he could get. It was well over a minute before he even thought about removing his lips from the still-hard, still-pulsating penis. He planted several kisses on the dark head. As he pulled back, a glistening strand of semen followed him. He licked it from the air and the wispy filament disappeared. He stood; un-cinched his pants and pulled them and his underwear to his shoes. It was as if his penis had been replaced by a bar of titanium-reinforced spidersteel.

Tiago had finally come down from his orgasmic high. He grasped Kallen's penis, alternating with both hands, feeling the full length of it, then cupped his scrotum and slowly caressed his balls. Still erect, as if they'd just started, Tiago dropped to his knees, moistened his lips, and began. Although he was completely inexperienced, he knew exactly what to do. After all, he'd imagined this moment for quite a while—more so since meeting Kallen.

Kallen continuously ran his hands through Tiago's thick shiny hair, encouraging him to consume him. And devour he did. He had anticipated this moment as much as Tiago had, and in just seconds he, too, was gritting his teeth as a startling orgasm shuddered his body. Although no one could possibly hear him, he didn't allow himself to moan too loudly. Nonetheless, several loud gasps escaped his mouth.

When he was done Kallen went down on wobbly knees. He took Tiago in his arms, placed his ear in the hollow of his neck, and hugged him tightly. His eyes teared up. This was what had been hidden from him. Holding a naked boy in his arms. Tasting him in his mouth. Feeling his body against his own. A wet penis against his. Experiencing an orgasm with him.

He reached down to Tiago's still-hard penis and touched it again. Kallen was in ecstasy. He had stepped across the barrier of desire and felt a joy like none before.

They grinned, then smiled at each other as they kissed and groped, causing them to mis-button their shirts as they tried to get dressed. Kallen stopped Tiago and pulled his shirt off, making him bare-chested again, his pants down to his ankles once again, keeping him hard, making his breath stay shallow and difficult to catch. Tiago did the same to Kallen. Completely naked once again, they swapped underwear, socks, and finally, finally got fully dressed in their own outer clothing.

Excited beyond belief, they made their way back down the escalators, then to the hovercar. The rest of the tour of the waterdome could wait—indeed forever. They had something much more important to do. Kallen took a shortcut back home. Half an hour later they were in his bedroom. No one was home since both his father and mother were at work. They had the house to themselves for the next five hours.

Neither boy knew it was possible to have six orgasms in one day let alone in that short amount of time. They gave each other five the next day. It was two days later before they were only doing it once upon waking, once sometime during the day, and twice before going to sleep.

It was mid-morning of Tiago's fourth full day in New Meadows. Tiago had fallen asleep again after each had given the other the now-required morning orgasm. Kallen hadn't been able to fall back asleep. Instead, he watched Tiago, caressing him, kissing him while he lay there; feeling Tiago's warm body glowing under the sheet, stoking the radioactive fire Kallen felt in his body. A fire like he'd never known before. Everything he'd ever experienced with Naya was a badly-acted pantomime compared to this single moment in time.

Eventually, he quietly got up.

Kallen was in and out of the bathroom in record time and headed to the kitchen with his mother Abalyn. The espresso maker was just now starting to gurgle. Kallen was waiting with the soycorn milk cup in hand, waiting for the steam to start up. He wanted a latte this morning.

"Kal, Naya's left two vid messages for you. I talked with her yesterday and she said you're not returning them. You know she's going off to boot camp in a couple of weeks. Why haven't you called her back?"

Kallen had screened both of Naya's calls and couldn't bring himself to talk to her. How was he going to explain to her what was going on with him? There was no way he could. Luckily, neither of his parents had gotten suspicious about he and Tiago together.

Kallen had never known anyone who was gay before—not even in school. He simply didn't know what gay behavior was except for the imagined sexual scenarios he'd conjured up in his head for years. As far as he knew, his parents didn't know any other gay people either. As far as he could tell, he and Tiago were the only ones for kilometers around. Saying anything about what was going on with him was about as likely as all the oxygen disappearing from the room all of the sudden.

So he lied.

"I've been really busy, mom. I've been taking Tiago all over and staying out late, too. Not to worry, I'll talk to her eventually."

"Well, you will tonight when they come over for dinner."

His stomach tightened. "Here?"

"Of course here." She saw the look of alarm on her son's face. "What's wrong?"

"N-nothing. I just didn't know. When did you invite them?"

"The day you got back. Don't you remember? You were standing right there. Son, are you all right?"

If he hadn't been holding onto the countertop he would have nearly been bent over from pain. "Shit," he squeaked.

Abalyn approached him and placed her hand on his arm. "Honey, is there something wrong?"

"Nothing. I, *uhh*, just forgot," he told her with a forced smile while he faked his way through a maze of pain.

Abalyn gave him an exasperated look. "Go to the store for me. I forgot to get some things for tonight." She handed him a list.

After Tiago was dressed, they jumped into her hovercar. Kallen brought him up-to-date about having avoided his girlfriend. "I have to say something to her, but what?" Kallen said.

"Did you really think you could just keep avoiding her?"

"No, it's just that I don't want to bother with her right now. It's...well, it's just that you're only going to be here for another week and I wanted to have this time only for you."

"You are *so* sweet, Deshara. I could eat you up."

Kallen grinned. "Should we pull over?"

Tiago issued one of his huge ear-to-ear smiles, then held his lower lip between his teeth. The look on his face made Kallen want to devour him.

Tiago placed his hand on Kallen's thigh then pressed his crotch with a couple of fingers, albeit briefly. Kallen was hard as a rock.

"I can wait. But tonight you're going to do something with me that you've never done before."

"Like what?"

"What is it your girlfriend won't let you do?"

"That?"

Tiago nodded as he raised his eyebrows. "That."

Once they parked, they had to sit for a few minutes while Kallen coaxed his erection to subside enough for him to not be embarrassed in the store.

Trying to be calm during dinner that evening was tough. Kallen wanted it to be over right now so he could be with Tiago. He couldn't believe how horny he felt. *God, I can't wait to fuck him.*

He had been standoffish to Naya all evening. He felt like a traitor. Tiago seemed to be tugging him although it was just Kallen's imagination. All he had to do was pretend he was still interested in her. At least for the time being.

Naya's parents left in their car. Naya had deliberately driven her own car so she could spend some time with Kallen. Tiago offered to help his parents clean up so Kallen could spend have some time alone with her. He knew Kallen had to tell her what was going on—at least partially.

Tannert and Abalyn were enjoying Kallen's new friend. When their son was younger, he often spent the night at his friends' houses, but rarely reciprocated. Naya stuck to him like glue long before he was off to boot camp. Having another male in the house, one that he was so obviously fond of was a nice change. Tiago cheerfully assisted them in clearing the table and cleaning up the kitchen while Kallen walked Naya outside.

The automatic wall of the partially enclosed outer porch could be moved with a touch of a button when it was cooler out. It had been moved.

Warm breezes, as usual, caressed the couple as Kallen sat next to her on the wide swing looking out into the night. It was downright balmy at only thirty degrees.

"Will you please talk to me?" she asked.

"About what?"

"About what's going on with you. You didn't return my vids, your mother said you're sleeping 'til like nine every morning, and tonight during dinner you acted like you didn't even know me."

Kallen sighed. "I'm sorry. I'm really sorry. I'm feeling sort of, I don't know, squashed. I guess I'm nervous about going off to school and not knowing anyone."

She thought she understood what he was saying. "Well, after boot camp I can come visit you. I know how to cheer you up." She gave him those eyes, placed her hand on his cheek, and made him turn his head. She leaned into him and expected him to kiss her. He didn't. She looked at him, squinted, then kissed him on the lips. He barely responded. She pulled back, looking at him with questioning eyes.

"I'm tired," he told her.

She knew different. "What's up with you? You've always told me everything."

It was true. He'd told her everything about himself in the last year. Everything except for this one thing. It wasn't an issue he ever thought he'd broach with her. Already, her simply inquiry was making him feel claustrophobic. She had always been his security blanket. Like she was being now. She always made him feel right just by talking to her. Her feminine touch, mannerisms, and demeanor allowed him to completely forgo anything as difficult as this. But he had pulled off the blinders he had worn for so long. He couldn't put them back on even for a second. Still, he didn't know how to tell her. Outing himself to her out of the blue just wasn't on the menu. It seemed inconceivable to him how he had been able to ignore being gay. He had held these feelings at bay for so long that he felt like a stranger to himself. A stranger he was just now getting to know really, really well. Even with her soothing voice, the softness of her hand touching his cheek, her concerned look begging him to divulge his 'secret', he still couldn't tell her. He was sure she wouldn't understand. But he had to tell her something. Staying mute like this was going to attract too much attention.

"I think-I think I don't love you anymore," he told her.

At least he wasn't lying anymore. To himself or to her. He thought he had been in love with her. But he realized it was her proximity, the amount of time they'd spent together that made him feel that way. They had been exclusively each other's. After having been surrounded with nothing but other young men his age, being naked with them in the showers, working with them, developing comradeships more close than he'd ever developed with any other guys in school—and now sleeping with one of them—the bubble had burst. His relationship with her had been a lie the entire time. He couldn't play that game anymore.

He felt her instantaneous reaction.

Naya's look of concern disappeared. "Why did you make me think it was something I said?"

"I didn't *make* you think anything."

"Or something I did."

"It wasn't anything you said, or did...or didn't do." *It's because of something you can't be. It's because of something I can't be either.*

"When?" she asked.

"How long have I...felt like this?"

She nodded.

"A week, maybe two." He couldn't bring himself to tell her the full extent of the truth. The truth that it had been months.

"So, like, when you got back?"

He nodded.

She stood. "I'll...just go home now."

Kallen debated what to do. "I'll walk you to your car."

"I know where it is." Anger. And there were tears in her eyes. She went toward the alcove where it was parked.

"Naya. It's not that I don't love you."

She stopped and turned around. "You just said you didn't."

"I mean, I *love* you. But I...I don't want us to do it anymore. You know...it." He still had feelings for her, but he certainly didn't want to have sex with her anymore.

"That's a laugh. What'd you do, just switch off your sex drive? You're not a-a photronic circuit, you know."

"I'm not telling you this to be mean."

"Really? You could have said something before we came over. You could have told me a week and a half ago! But no, you had to wait all night." A tear started down one of her cheeks.

Kallen felt nothing but displeasure right now. He bit his lip. "I'm sorry." He started forward, wanting to comfort her, wanting this awful moment to end. They'd never had angry words with each other before.

She held up her hand, albeit briefly. "Just don't."

Maybe I shouldn't have told her that. Maybe I should have just lied after all. Maybe…. The alternatives were moot. The damage to the relationship was done the moment he acknowledged who he really was all those many weeks ago. He knew he shouldn't say anything more to her.

She pressed a button on the keystick and the driver's side door slid open. She sat behind the wheel, then pressed the on switch. The graviton generator energized. She didn't look at him again as she pressed the button on the dash and the door slid shut. A moment later the hovercar silently rose up and exited the alcove.

Kallen stood in the middle of what passed as their yard. She was his first real relationship and he didn't foresee it ending like this. He watched her taillights disappear down the hoverlane. He thought he should feel devastated, but that wasn't the case.

He walked out to the middle of the hoverlane. Not a single person was outside other than him. Not a single other vehicle was nearby. That was typical. He looked up at the sky, perhaps searching for solace in the starry sky. His mind slowly filled with images of Tiago. Of the way his heart beat so rapidly as they furtively playing footsie under the table while they were eating. Of how he felt every time he looked into his beautiful greenish-brown eyes; smiling at the memory of getting hard in seconds this afternoon when Tiago told him what was coming tonight.

Naya cried the whole way home and for a while after she went to bed. She couldn't understand what it was she did to make him turn off so suddenly.

That night, both boys lost their virginity. They did it again an hour later. The next morning, they worked on making sure it hadn't magically returned while they slept and did it once again. Kallen grinned to himself all day. How long had it taken for he and Tiago to get this far? Less than a week. How long had he gone out with Naya? Thirteen months. How many times did they do it? Never. How many times did he ask, beg, and plead with her to let him do it? Uncountable times. How he hated having to wait. How many times had he done it in the last nine hours? Three times. *Three times!* What had he been doing to himself all that time? Well, it wasn't all bad. He and Naya had had many good times together.

Abalyn was so used to seeing Kallen and Naya together that it was odd not seeing her around anymore. She was so fond of her, that she had had her over at least once a week while Kallen was away. Now it seemed as if she had simply disappeared. His mother noticed, too, that Kallen seemed to be more animated than she'd ever seen him. Happier than she'd ever seen him, too. *It must be because of his new friend*, she mused. Still, she was concerned about Naya's absence. She'd have a talk with her before she left for boot camp.

Kallen didn't tell her that he and Naya had unofficially broken up. Abalyn only asked one more time later that week why Naya hadn't come by. He managed an ambiguous reply.

Kallen was aware that the Air Defense Uniform Code closely modeled society's shunning of all things gay. In his hometown, it was traditional that everyone would marry and have a child. He knew not a single adult past their active service years that wasn't married or planning to be married and have a kid. Those who delayed marriage too long were looked upon as selfish by a disproportionate number of people. After so many decades of economic ruin—all of which ended generations before he was born—whoever didn't help add to the population was seen as anathema to the successful continuation of the NAA. Those who remained childless were encouraged to adopt. Those who were gay were worse than selfish, they were considered unpatriotic or accused of deliberately trying to undermine society. All were vilified, some were jailed, and he'd heard rumors of worse things than that happening to some of them. The media was a cruel mouthpiece in that respect.

Kallen never believed any of the prevailing nonsense about gays, even while in denial about himself. Somehow he knew that those discriminatory social traditions and laws would end up impacting his own life. Those notions were reinforced after he attended Naya's church with her. One time he even defended the right to be gay while discussing social issues with some of the elders and Naya's peers. Deacon Folmer told Kallen he wasn't versed enough in their religion to make such statements. Kallen told him he felt it was his duty to point out blatant discrimination. The deacon gave him a copy of the New Combined Bible and told him to carefully read specific passages. Kallen did and even read more of it. The more he read, the more he was sure their text, and thus their religion, was based on either illogic or ignorance, or both. Now he firmly understood why he had little interest in religion while growing up.

Kallen and Tiago's brief vacation from the military came to an end only a few days later. The day before they were to leave, Kallen secured one of his buddy's family cabins up in the mountains. The cabin was a topside structure, although most of the space was, of course, downside.

Once there, they shed their clothes and fell into each other's arms. After all, they were completely alone and isolated from everyone else. Being naked with each other was the only option. They napped continuously, waking up only to eat, to kiss, to feel each other up, and to have sex, and not necessarily in that order. It continued like that throughout the day and into the night, until they were totally exhausted. It was pushing the hell out of dawn, and they hadn't slept for more than a few hours actually, when they cleaned up, got dressed, and returned to Kallen's house. His parents drove them to the hoverport in the early afternoon.

Kallen didn't feel very emotional when Tiago left. He was too sleepy. Fortunately, his parents didn't question their yawns. Perhaps they suspected something, but chose to look the other way. Regardless, Kallen was satisfied his secret was safe.

He was sure he and Tiago could continue their relationship, even if it was clandestine. It didn't matter that Tiago was headed to Monterey and he to Vancouver. Even though they would be hundreds of kilometers away from each other, vid calls would make it seem like they were almost in the same room.

It was on the flight to Vancouver that it finally dawned on Kallen that they were really apart from each other. Gone was a sure orgasm with another human being. Another boy, to be exact. An incredibly cute boy, at that. *What would vid sex be like*, he thought? *Ugh, it would be horrible. I only want the real thing.*

Chapter 2

Monday, Sept. 20, 2477

The first thing Kallen noticed upon his arrival at the ADF Schools Division was how many people lived here. Vancouver was one of the larger cities on the west coast. The heat he was used to in his region was greatly tempered here by the ocean. Balmy breezes made it seem more like a resort town than a duty station. In that respect this part of the country was more like the Alyeskan region. Now that he'd sampled several different parts of the country, he was quickly realizing that his hometown was in one of the hotter climes. No wonder most people lived further north. Most of them here seemed to take living topside for granted, too.

Processing his entry into school had consisted of the usual routine of standing in lines, one after another. That was the first two days. He kept getting smiles and pep talks, too. He quickly realized that his very high test scores in photronics, which were part of his official record, led him to being viewed with high expectations.

With his processing being done, the next two days were spent on mindless work details until they had him properly enrolled into his class section.

On each of the last four days he had left a message in Tiago's vidbox. So far, despite telling Tiago his return vidbox address, he'd not received a single reply. It wasn't what he expected and it was beginning to worry him. He was sure that on the first day he would have received two, maybe three vids in return. With each successive day without word from him, Kallen grew more and more preoccupied. Finally, late in the afternoon of the fourth day, he located the administrative coordinator in Tiago's schools section. She could help him for sure.

"Airman Kuffdam here. How can I help you?" she asked with a smile.

Kallen cleared his throat. "I'm looking for a new student. Airman Tiago Sandoval. His ID is ADF-875JA-HD. I've left a lot of vid messages in his vidbox but he's not returning them. I'm-I'm wondering if he arrived, is okay, or what."

Airman Kuffdam spoke to her vidstation. A moment later she spoke to Kallen. "I have a message here for an Airman Deshara, K., from Airman Sandoval."

"Are there vid attachments?"

"I see one vid."

A single one? "I wonder why he didn't he send it?" he asked rhetorically.

"The delay-message subject line reads, 'Please send if Airman Deshara, Vancouver ADF Schools Division, calls.' That's you."

Kallen thought it odd that Tiago hadn't sent the message himself. He punched in the proper codes and the vid was fed into the memory of the vidstation he was calling from. Moments later, once the coordinator was offline, Kallen activated it. He noted right away that the creation date was two days ago. The screen brightened, revealing Tiago's cute round face. He was fidgeting. Right away, Kallen knew something was wrong.

"*Hey, it's me, of course. I-I got the vids you sent me,*" he said. He removed his cap and smoothed back his dark sexy hair. He looked away a great deal, but finally looked steadily at the camera. "*You're great and all, Deshara, but it's not gonna work out. We'd be apart for too long. We're already apart for too long. I'm sorry. I'm-I'm just sorry. Please don't-don't vid me any time soon, huh?*"

The pain of what he was saying was visible on his face, as well as in his halted speech. His hand reach out and the vid faded as it ended.

Kallen felt numb. How could this have happened? What about the last few minutes at the hoverport where they promised to talk even if it was the middle of the night? What about the two incredible weeks before that? All that time together. *Had it meant nothing to him? And now, it ends with no explanation? What the hell! It doesn't make any sense.*

What was worse though was he realized he'd been unceremoniously dumped. Just like he had dumped Naya. Maybe Tiago surmised that if Kallen could do it to her, it could just as easily happen to him, too. A preemptive strike, perhaps?

He fell back on the bed as a great wave of anguish fell over him. His stomach lurched painfully. He held his middle with both arms. The brilliant colors that the world had so recently been painted in started to disappear. He tried to swallow the lump in this throat but couldn't. He knew it would do no good to even bother to try to rectify the situation. It wasn't until he got back to his temporary quarters that he let his anger melt into tears at what he knew was a final ending to what he and Tiago had together. At least he'd known what it was like to finally be with a boy. At least he had memories that made him feel alive, although now they were memories stained with a certain hollowness he couldn't quite understand. A hollowness that he didn't feel when he and Naya split. He knew for sure now what it was he wanted.

Kallen remained in temporary quarters for another day before his processing was completed. They weren't all that efficient here, he decided. It had taken a full work week for them to get him into a class. But finally he was assigned residence in a building nestled high on a hillside on base. His front door opened to a beautiful view of Burrand Inlet, although it was a full two kilometers away. He could see most of the city from here as it stretched all around him outside the large training center compound. With its mixture of topside and downside buildings and facilities, the city took on the appearance of a place that couldn't quite decide what latitude it was in. This was Kallen's first experience living near the ocean and he immediately fell in love with being able to look out over the water, even if it was so far away. There was no dome to be seen anywhere. For the first time in his life he saw an expanse of water with blue sky above it. Kallen's temporary preoccupation with his new view ended abruptly as he imagined Tiago admiring his own ocean view. *Damn him.*

The air smelled so fresh that Kallen kept his door open while he unpacked. He didn't take much note of the occasional person along the walkway in front of his room. The topside walkway was a novelty. Still, the wide overhead canopy was a clear indication that even this far north the sun was considered somewhat hostile. Due to the constricted view it created, one had to walk to the railing to see both the inlet and the sky. At least he *had* a view.

Kallen had already met two other students who identified themselves as being in his class. Nothing could have prepared him for what was on the other end of the sound he heard a few moments later.

He first heard the *whoop* from someone's voice down the walkway. He came to the doorway to see who had made that kind of noise. He looked to his right. Not more than three meters away was Airman Dayler Madsen talking with two other students.

Madsen's yellow-brown hair hung down over his forehead, almost touching his eyebrows. Apparently, he was pushing the regulation as far as he could. Madsen had just come back from a run (again, topside!) and was shirtless, sweating, and still breathing hard. He had a slight cleft chin, a smooth unblemished face, and very short curly blond hair covering his forearms, legs and across most of his chest. *Nice arms*, Kallen thought. Clearly, he worked out.

Kallen had grown up with the usual smattering of blond-haired blue-eyed boys, and had had just passing interest in them, since blonds weren't his ideal type. There was something different about this guy though. He oozed total sensuality.

Madsen was the class Starter. The Starter was responsible for the students on their block. Their block consisted of twelve students along this walkway, Kallen being the newest arrival. The Starter was often the one who had the most time in grade, or was the brightest, or even the oldest. Madsen fulfilled two of those qualities, that of being the oldest and, according to test scores, was the brightest. Even more so than Kallen.

Madsen was not only sexy he was loud and full of energy. His gregarious demeanor was just the thing Kallen needed to cheer him back up. The funk he found himself immersed in after being dumped by Tiago was already beginning to stink. He felt renewed just being near the guy. But he found himself stuttering when Madsen saw him and introduced himself.

"I'm, uh, I'm…name's D-Deshara." Madsen was just too sexy for him to not be intimidated by it.

"*Duh*-Deshara?" Madsen took Kallen's chin and pulled it down. "I don't see an echo chamber. Got a problem talking, eh, Deshara?"

"It's just Deshara." No one had ever done that to him before. Oddly enough, he felt strangely enamored by Dayler's brash absence of normal social and personal protocol.

Madsen told him he was the Starter and that he needed to fill Kallen in on some things. "Come with me," he told Kallen.

They went to the end of the walkway and entered Madsen's room. Madsen pulled off his running shoes. Standing there in just his sheer shorts and socks, he picked up his vidPAD. Kallen had to immediately look away from the nice curve of Madsen's butt, lest he embarrass himself even more.

A vidPAD was an all-purpose personal access device. Somewhat teardrop shaped, they were three centimeter thick and split down the middle into a left and right half. Three titanium alloy rails fit the device's halves together, and allowed them to noiselessly telescope apart. Dayler did just that and the two sections separated a full twenty-six centimeters in width. The vidPAD could be wirelessly connected to base networks, could hold massive amounts of data, and could run other devices with the proper applications downloaded to it. Complete with a removable earpiece set that also served as a microphone, and a unique audio system, the device was the height of personal communications technology. Everyone was issued one.

With a quick touch to the pressure sensitive biometric button to activate it and logon, a holographic display awakened, creating a 26x26x10 cm rectangle that recreated real life colors and the illusion of depth. The 3D image could be adjusted from full horizontal to full vertical. The holographic user interface was so flawless one would swear they were looking at a solid mass.

Madsen accessed the base network by voice command then called up the class roster and searched it. Kallen looked on, carefully keeping his eyes off Madsen's body.

"You're number twelve; the last to be processed into our class. There, you're checked off," Madsen told him.

He gave Kallen a list of items he needed to be familiar with, then commanded the vidPAD to copy some files to Kallen's vidstation back in this room. When that was complete Madsen looked up and fixed his eyes on Kallen's. Kallen suddenly felt uncomfortable. Madsen was looking at him *that* way. Or was it his imagination? Yet Tiago had looked at him *that* way, too. Numerous times. But with Tiago, he had found out what the look signified. Over and over. But Madsen was his Starter. *How could he possibly want me*, Kallen wondered? Kallen considered himself perhaps a five or six on the standard 'good looks' scale of ten. Madsen's number was easily a nine or ten. He might even be able to squeeze out an eleven. Kallen was sure he was way out of league for someone that good looking.

Kallen swallowed. Hard. He looked away, then back. Dayler was still looking at him—seemingly searching Kallen's face. A slight grin took over his mouth. A look of amusement.

Is he toying with me, Kallen wondered now. *Yet he's not doing anything more than looking at me.* Kallen knew he better drop it right now. He could easily be wrong about this. After all, they'd just met! His experience dealing with these kinds of encounters was essentially nil—regardless of his time with Tiago. Better safe than sorry, too. Besides, they'd have to live in very close proximity for a good long time. If he were wrong the repercussions would be intolerable.

As the weeks went by and Kallen got to know Madsen, he found himself rolling his eyes at him a lot because of his comical manner, his tendency to exaggerate, and his periodic inappropriate loud vocal volume. Despite his awkward initial introduction, all of that made Madsen terribly attractive. Besides, he was a riot to be around. Kallen knew that if a good time were to be had Madsen would be the one to start it or find it.

He also found out who his main competition in class was about a week after their lessons started. Madsen had an almost single-minded approach to just about everything. Competition was his main theme in life. In contrast, Madsen disliked team sports and the competition that came along with it. To him, grades meant everything. On their first three exams he came out on top after hardly touching his homework. More than once he argued with the instructor in class about a measly one point on a pop quiz. Like he needed to worry about a single point. Kallen, on the other hand, had a vidstation screen shining on his face quite a few nights as he studied. He was pushing the envelope of his abilities with these focused advanced classes in maintenance equipment technologies. He didn't know it would be this difficult. Keeping up with Madsen had forced him to try as hard as he could, too.

Kallen also discovered that Madsen enjoyed strutting around half-naked. Just about every morning Madsen could be seen at the railing overlooking the far inlet, gazing out over the wide expanse while sipping coffee in just his skivvies or sometimes just tight gym shorts. Kallen made a habit of secretly watching him from his window, just watching him, taking in the sight of a mostly-naked Madsen against the morning sky. His body was sheer beauty.

More often than not, Kallen found Madsen that way when he visited his room and had to wait for him to get dressed. The first time it happened Kallen found himself able to keep his eyes off him. The second time, he peeked a little. He could see the outline of Madsen's penis because he had been semi-erect when he arrived that time. The third time, he let his eyes bravely dance over Madsen's body. That afternoon after class, and after they had returned to their respective rooms, Kallen couldn't keep his hands off himself. Before the next morning Kallen had beat off three times, conjuring up fantasies about him.

*   *   *   *

Four and a half months later, during the second week of February, Kallen wondered why he hadn't gotten a birthday vid from his parents yet. That's when he received an incoming vid acknowledgment request. It wasn't his parents. It was Madsen. Kallen activated the screen. "Yup," he said.

"Hey, I noticed on my calendar that there's a special event coming up for you in a couple of days. Says it's a birthday. I thought you might want to be my special guest of honor that night."

"Just *us*?"

"What? You don't like me anymore?"

"No, I just figured that the other guys would be coming along, too."

"I'm not sharing you for your birthday, Deshara. I have to share you all the freaking time, and on the," he leaned forward to look at another screen, "twelfth, it's just *you* and *me*."

Kallen didn't know what to say.

"You have three seconds to say yes."

Kallen responded immediately. "Yes!"

"See ya in class mañana." The screen faded to black.

"What the fuck was that all about?" Kallen asked himself aloud.

As much as he wanted to ignore it, he still occasionally felt the sting of having been dumped by Tiago. And, although Madsen had looked at him *that* way on and off over the last several months, he had continuously ignored it. He didn't want to feel amorous with anyone, especially if it had the potential of getting him in trouble with their higher ups or make him heartbroken again. Tonight, after Madsen's vid and the lack of his parent's call, he felt especially lonely.

The next day in class, Madsen kept looking at him *that* way all day. Kallen ignored it as usual. But toward the end of the day he could ignore it no longer. Something was definitely going on. Was Madsen really interested in him? If so, why had he waited all these months? And why now? Was it because of his birthday?

Perhaps it was a setup.

Was it possible that Madsen knew his closest kept secret? Was Madsen trying to pull him out of the closet to humiliate him? Madsen had that kind of personality.

Madsen kept grinning every time they interacted, giving Kallen surreptitious glances, but no hints as to what was really on his mind. Kallen surmised that the odd affect was a prelude to some sort of surprise birthday party instead of just the two of them getting together. He felt a lot more relieved at deciding he'd figured it all out.

Kallen got his birthday greeting vid from his family late in the afternoon on the twelfth. He even got one from Naya who told him that she was going out with someone she recently met. Kallen sent her a brief return vid to tell her that he was happy for her. Toward six-thirty there was a knock on the door. Kallen opened it.

Madsen's hair was combed and he was freshly shaved. He had a brand new civilian shirt on, nice trousers, and his boots were polished to a fine shine. He stepped in with his hands behind his back. Kallen figured he had a stun prong or some other gag device and immediately took a step back. But when Madsen produced a single bright red flower, Kallen was stunned after all.

"I, uh, I thought you'd like this," Madsen said.

Kallen had never heard him stumble over a word before. This was utterly unlike the Madsen he knew.

"I don't have a vase," Kallen told him, as he knitted his brow.

Madsen walked around the room, looking for something to put it in. Kallen stayed by the door, trying to keep out of his way. Madsen spied a tall narrow glass container that contained metal emblems for Kallen's uniform. He dumped the items out onto a tabletop and went to the sink, filled the container with water, then set it next to Kallen's vidstation. He deftly inserted the flower. He looked up at Kallen and smiled. Kallen thought he would fall over.

"Happy birthday, you cute fuck," Madsen said. He looked at him *that* way again.

"Cute fuck?"

"I can't wait to fuck you," he murmured as he adjusted the flower.

"Huh?" *He's getting bolder and bolder, isn't he?*

"Did I say that out loud? I meant *fuck* you. Let's go."

"Fuck you, too, Madsen. But thanks for the, uh, whatever that is."

"Gerbera daisy. Picked it out myself. Rare, I might add. Expensive, too."

Kallen stopped right there. "Are you sure you're all right?"

"Never felt hornier, uh, I mean better." He grinned again.

Kallen was sure something was up. It was making him nervous now. *Should I just tell him I'm gay and get it over with?* Madsen was unusual, that was for sure, but he was predictable within a certain range—similar to a chaos theory equation. This was way out of range for him.

They took a hovercab to a nightclub on the east edge of Vancouver. Although it wasn't unusual for guys to dance together at the clubs, Kallen noticed there was an abundance of guys at this one. He looked around. There were none of their classmates anywhere. Nervously excited, Kallen still felt uneasy about Madsen's behavior. He desperately wanted a gay friend, but he couldn't figure out if Madsen was honestly coming on to him or setting him up for the inevitable bad joke. After all, he'd seen it done before. With Madsen as the instigator.

They immediately dove into the crowd of young people and danced for almost an hour straight. While taking a breather over a beer, Kallen started asking the right questions. The music was loud, so he had to shout to be heard.

"I was sure I was going to a surprise birthday party. Especially since you said all those weird things in my room."

"What weird things?"

"Cute? Fucking me?"

"Well, it's true."

Kallen looked Madsen in the eye. "In what way?"

An exasperated look crossed Madsen's face. "Exactly the way you're thinking."

"Which is?" *Fuck! He is coming on to me!*

"Oh, come on, Kallen." Kallen. Madsen had never used his first name before.

"Oh, come on, Dayler," Kallen mocked. He, too, had never used Madsen's first name.

Madsen leaned forward as he spoke into Kallen's ear. "I got us a hotel room down the street." He pulled his head back to watch Kallen's reaction.

Kallen leaned into him. "Why?"

"So we could, you know…." Madsen raised his eyebrows several times in quick succession.

"Uh, are you ready to go out onto the dance floor again?"

He glanced at Kallen's bottle. "I'm not done. And neither are you."

"I think I'm done with this conversation."

"Hey, I like to dance, too. But you'll miss a really good time if we stay here all night."

Kallen took a full three seconds to stare into his eyes before he said it. "Are you saying what I think you're saying?"

Madsen had an annoyed look on his face at this point. "You are *really* trying to play hard-to-get, aren't you? Of *course*, that's what I'm saying."

"*You're gay?*"

Madsen rolled his eyes. "Like you didn't *know* that. I wanted you to feel special for your birthday. I got the room so I could make you feel even *more* special." He started laughing heartily as Kallen's mouth dropped open.

"Holy sh…!"

Madsen laughed some more, then swigged the remainder of his beer. He took Kallen's hand in his, squeezed it briefly, then let go.

"You *are* gay!" All the suspicious behavior, all the furtive glances, all the body language. All this time it was true!

Madsen shrugged. "Well?"

Kallen slammed his nearly empty bottle down on the railing. "We're outta here." He couldn't believe this was happening.

Once they got to the room, the trail of clothes that started at the locked door could have led a blind man to the bed. It was just like Kallen's first time; after only a few minutes they were both covered with each other's semen. Again and again they took each other as each came twice more in the next two hours. It was well beyond 0100 hours before they finally stopped to rest.

Kallen lay on his back with a wide grin on his face. The sheet and bedspread were in a pile on the floor. A swirl of warm dry air from the overhead fan lightly caressed them. Dayler's limp body was draped across Kallen's side as he drifted in and out of sleep. He brushed Kallen's hair with his hand, lingering his fingers along his neck. His hand came to rest on his stomach. Kallen reached up and placed his hand over Dayler's, held it, then tightened his grip. He didn't want him to move. After so long, he wanted the night to last a week. Dayler lightly snored, woke up a few moments later, and started touching him someplace else. This went on until dawn. Kallen didn't lose his erection the entire night.

When they woke the next morning, they showered together, then slowly, reluctantly started to get dressed. Kallen ventured more questions. "What were your clues about me?"

"Be serious."

"No, really. I'm that obvious?"

"Obvious? How about when you stare at me in the morning when I'm drinking my coffee. Did you think I never saw you looking out your window? Or how about all the staring at me in class, or checking me out when I'm getting dressing. I'd tease you on purpose, you know. Testing you. I was sure about you after, what, a week or two? Actually, I'm surprised no one else figured you out. But I'm the one who got you. So, their loss."

That was an odd thing to say. "There's other gay boys in our block?"

"No, just us—as far as I can tell."

"I don't get it. Why did you wait so long to…you know, come on to me?"

"Why? In case you didn't notice, this is the military. Plus, I'm your Starter. There's a certain air I have to project for you guys. Plus, I was happy being by myself. And I wasn't sure you liked me that way. But it all changed when we went out to that bar about three weeks ago. You remember that night?"

"Of course."

"You were sitting opposite me at the table. I was checking you out while you were telling that stupid joke, looking at your face, watching you laugh…. Maybe it was 'cause I had too many beers. Maybe it was just that I'd been attracted to you for so long. Something told me that I should make my move. I'd just been waiting for the right time to say something. Besides, I was getting sick of beating off alone. I told myself that I had to do it. I just had to get you."

"Are you serious? Why didn't you say anything then?"

"Hah! With the other guys there, too? No way!"

"So, ever since then you've wanted to get in my pants?"

Dayler scratched his head, trying to look innocent. He wasn't succeeding. "Since way before that," he admitted.

Kallen was quiet for a moment, taking it all in. "So, does this mean we're...going out?"

"I hoped last night woulda told you that."

Kallen pushed him onto the bed and straddled Dayler's shirtless torso. He massaged his shoulders briefly, then pulled Dayler's arms over his head, crossing them at the wrists, and held them there. He couldn't suppress his grin. He might like this. He and his Starter. Together.

After they returned to the training center Kallen managed to get in another half-hour of sleep before they went off to class. It wasn't nearly enough to keep him awake. He drank too much coffee during class and it ended up having the opposite effect than he intended. At lunchtime he fell asleep at his desk. The instructor wanted to know what his problem was. Kallen feigned being sick. Once he got back to his room he pulled off his boots and shirt and passed out from fatigue.

Toward 1900 hours there was a knock at the door. Kallen awoke out of a dead sleep and checked his watch. He was surprised he had been asleep for so long. He went to the door and pulled it open. Dayler was standing there grinning. He came in, unzipped his boots, unbuttoned his shirt, and laid down on the bed. Kallen stood there and watched.

"Nice. You kept it warm for me."

"I was asleep."

"I couldn't tell."

"I'm not in the mood. Really." He yawned.

"I'm just here to hold you in my arms."

Kallen smiled widely. This was a whole other dimension to Dayler. He was sure the flower was just an icebreaker. He had decided that Dayler's confession of having been thinking about him was mostly hot air. But maybe all of it was a sign of something that Dayler kept hidden away in his heart. Maybe he wasn't only a go-getter after all. Maybe there were things hidden inside him that he only let out occasionally. Maybe going for Kallen was one of those things.

Dayler beckoned him with a finger and Kallen fell down on top of him. Dayler's chest expanded as he drew in a long yawn. His hands were all over Kallen's back. "We need to get you to the gym."

"Why?"

"To put some more meat on your body. You have the right body type. You could really fill out with training. I could be your trainer. But that's only if you pay me back with plenty of hot sex."

"I don't have sex with guys."

"Then you have a hot freakin' twin who does. Lemme use your vidstation to call him."

Kallen placed his hand on Dayler's face and pushed. Dayler pulled his arm aside. When Kallen's armpit ended up over his nose Dayler breathed in heavily, then licked it, tickling Kallen in the process.

"Are you sure you're not ready to do it again?" Dayler asked.

"I told you I'm sleepy."

"If you're gonna be with me you're gonna have to be a little more accommodating. I don't like it when you get moody."

Kallen rose up a little, surprised at that odd statement. "Moody? Since when did being sleepy become moody? If I'm sleepy, I'm sleepy. Besides, it's only been twelve hours. What are you expecting from me anyway?"

Dayler tried to deflect his accusation. "Expecting? For you to at least listen to me."

Kallen got up and looked down at him. The sensual mood had been broken by Dayler's demands. "Just go."

Dayler swung his legs over the edge of the bed. He patted the mattress. "Sit."

Kallen sat, not sure why he did so. Dayler's demeanor was magnetic. As always.

"Look, I didn't mean you're moody. I just wanted to come by and kiss you. I really enjoyed last night and was getting lonely." The Dayler who was his new boyfriend had returned. He softly pressed his lips against Kallen's. The only sound in the room was kissing.

"See ya for breakfast. Come to my room for coffee first?" Dayler asked.

"The block's gonna know something's going on between us."

"Fuck 'em. I'm the Starter. If they talk, I'll shut 'em up."

"I can see it already. You're gonna get us kicked out of the ADF."

"What kind of trouble can we get in if we're kissing?"

"You're insatiable."

"That makes both of us." He turned to leave, then stuck his head back through the doorway before he shut it. "Don't beat off, Spunk Boy. I wanna see your next load all over *my* chest."

Kallen grunted.

Dayler grinned, then added, "Tomorrow evening we're working out together."

"Ugh. I can't even think about it. We have an exam coming up, too. I have to study."

"Fuck the exam. We'll ace it. You need some meat on those bones."

"Whatever."

Kallen shut the door, locked it, and returned to bed. He slid his trousers off, but wasn't sure if he had it in him after last night. He did. He beat off just to spite Dayler.

Over the next couple of months, Kallen gained three kilos of muscle from steady workouts with Dayler and by learning how to eat right. The workout routines were long and intense, taking up valuable study time. Because of it, he ended up further down the list in class for awhile. Kallen may have been smart when it came to photronics but he still needed to study. The rest of the students in their class needed to study a lot more than he did. Dayler rarely studied. He did most of his learning in class.

By the end of the second month, they were working out three times a week and routinely having sex. Kallen found himself fulfilled in ways he never expected. Memories of his interlude with Tiago were history, including his emotional upset at having been so casually blown off. He rarely thought about Naya anymore either.

It was next to impossible to keep their relationship a secret from the rest of the class. Surprisingly, only Deno made any snide comments. After his third one, he was shut up by a long talk with Dayler. Deno never made another malicious remark after that. Kallen never asked Dayler what he'd said to shut him up. Nonetheless, to avoid any backlash they never touched each other in anyone else's presence.

For some reason, nobody reported their controversial relationship to anyone higher up. At least their relationship was clandestine to all their superiors. Maybe the rest of the guys were afraid of them on some level? Kallen wasn't sure.

Kallen found his new relationship a bit of an enigma. He had had his suspicions about Dayler all along, but never assumed he would be intimate with him. After all, Dayler was their lead man on the block and was supposed to be somewhat removed from the rest of the class for that reason alone.

Although Dayler had an occasional angry outburst with Kallen in private, it was rare, and not ever directed at him. Dayler continued to be Mr. Harsh though with the other students during drills, at formations, and at other random times. He also stayed number one in class. He was unbeatable there.

Dayler had been Kallen's main rival for grades from day one. Once the relationship started, he told Kallen that schoolwork was the one topic they couldn't talk about together. They never studied together due to Dayler's need to beat everyone, including Kallen. Now that they were intimate he would be Kallen's ally when he made a higher grade on an exam than Kallen, then became his adversary if he were bested by even a single point. When it would happen before, Dayler would take it out on him in subtle ways, like steering clear of him in the mess hall or not calling him when the guys went out. Now it was more than that. He would stay silent when they were together (which was a stretch for him), or withhold sex (an even more difficult stretch).

Kallen began to become exasperated with his behavior.

Another thing Kallen disliked, now that he knew him better, was that Dayler was constantly trying to change him into something new and different. It had started with the workout routines, although he found that he enjoyed working out. Changes were rapidly taking place to the right places on his body. And Dayler knew what he was doing as his trainer. Regardless, he found that Dayler was addicted to excitement and wanted Kallen to be different all the time for him so he wouldn't be bored. He noticed it the first time he was told to pose (nude of course) for him so Dayler could take measurements. Every week it was a routine of posing nude, having his measurements taken, then complying with a new sexual fantasy having to do with Dayler's 'transformed hot boy'. Dayler seemed obsessed with Kallen's every millimeter of growth. The fantasies were odd, but incredibly exciting. Luckily, Kallen was complimented many times about his penis. At least Dayler was satisfied with that.

As time went on, it became increasingly more difficult to keep up with Dayler's psychological needs. Still, Kallen craved being with him. He couldn't help himself since it was easy to keep up with Dayler's physical desires.

One night, after Dayler had drifted off to sleep next to him, Kallen went to the bathroom to wipe himself up a little more. In the dim light he looked in the mirror, thinking about their relationship. He knew Dayler was only out for himself. It was obvious that their relationship was almost solely on Dayler's terms. Kallen hadn't had much say in most of their activities beyond their daily or nightly sexual liaisons. That was the odd part about their relationship. If there was something Kallen liked that turned him on Dayler was more than willing to try it or to experiment even more. He loved to give and receive pleasure. Kallen was always sated beyond his wildest imagination with Dayler's endless need for sex. And true, he'd packed on some decent musculature since working out, all because of him, so that was a good thing as well. But he was noticing something new. He wanted more.

He wanted Dayler to stop making him be something he wasn't.

He wanted Dayler's heart.

Those were two thing he didn't think were possible.

The next night they were walking back from the mess hall with soyice cones. They stopped in the corridor and, from a wide picture window, looked out over the twinkling lights that defined the edge of the inlet. Kallen licked up the trail that had dripped down his knuckle, grinning to himself at how many times he'd done that. It's just that Dayler's semen didn't taste like soyice.

They had four more weeks left of school now. Kallen greatly feared leaving Vancouver. He enjoyed the familiarity of all the buddies he'd made. And, though his relationship with Dayler was emotionally lacking in many ways, he knew he would find it difficult to be without the quite satisfying aspects of their sex life. Try as he might, he couldn't quite get completely used to Dayler's lack of emotional depth. He craved more than what Dayler could give him. The pangs of that missing element, combined with his growing trepidation of going away, were beginning to wear on him.

He turned to him, determined to plumb that depth once and for all. "Dayler, do you love me?"

"Huh?" The distinct sound of shock rang in that one word.

"You heard me."

"I like you a lot, if that's what you mean."

"That's *not* what I mean."

Dayler looked at him, then looked out the window again. "Be quiet about that."

"No. Do you love me?"

Dayler continued to lick his soyice, then proceeded down the corridor without answering him.

Kallen debated for a moment whether he should follow but, as usual, he did. "Where the fuck are you going?"

"Back to the block."

"I asked you a question."

"I gave you an answer."

"That wasn't an answer."

Dayler stopped. "What do you want me to say? That I want you to be with me forever? That I want to only do you for the rest of my life? That we're gonna get married? I knew you'd eventually ask that question. The answer's no. I don't love you."

Kallen tried to absorb the impact. Like always, his words were raw and to the point. These were especially biting. He knew he shouldn't have asked point blank like that. He knew that was coming, but had to ask anyway.

"Dick," Kallen said.

"Pretty much."

"Huh?" *He's agreeing with me?*

"You like dick."

"I was talking about *you*."

"Yeah, you know I like dick, too."

"You *are* a dick."

"Don't be a pain in the ass."

Kallen sighed, then went to the nearby waste can. He wasn't hungry anymore, even for pistachio soyice, which was his favorite.

So what about his response though. Really. Kallen had been running the numbers. Somewhere inside, he figured he might be able to get Dayler to come around. Losing him would be emotionally difficult—despite his frustrations—if they ended up at different duty stations after they graduated.

The top three students always got their pick of a list of duty stations. Dayler stayed solidly in the number one position in class. Kallen had long since risen back up to number two and stayed there. He had been wondering which station Dayler might pick. Now, he wondered if Dayler was even going to tell him where he wanted to go.

Dayler motioned for him to continue as they went back to the block. Kallen kept two paces behind him the whole way. He was angry.

Once back at Dayler's room, without saying a word, or acknowledging what he'd said, Dayler took Kallen in his arms and hugged him. He slowly eased Kallen down to the bed. There, they made out, licked the lingering taste of soyice from each other's lips, felt each other up, then consummated all the heavy petting in explosive waves. Kallen thought he would still feel angry. Instead he felt sated once again. Sated, but this time drained.

Kallen was pressing his shirt. It was the one he was going to wear for the graduation ceremony at the end of the week. Since there were only twelve of them in their class, it was going to be a small affair, with the school's commander being present only for a short commendation speech. Their instructors would be conducting the actual ceremony. Kallen still hadn't broached the topic of duty stations with Dayler but he was going to soon.

Dayler knocked on the door then pushed it open. "Hey," he said.

"Hey," Kallen said then smiled.

Dayler looked at him oddly. Kallen was sure something bad was going to be said. He was right.

"We need to talk, Deshara."

Deshara. He hadn't used his last name with him in private since they'd started seeing each other. Kallen put the iron down, then clicked it off. Steam rose from the shirt. They heard three of their fellow students talking outside his window as they passed by. Dayler waited for their voices to fade before he began. He leaned against the wall, looked at the floor briefly, then sat on Kallen's bed, looking uncharacteristically pensive.

"We've got four days left and you know I get to choose my duty station first."

"I know."

"And I know you're gonna be able to choose yours next since you're number two."

"I know that, too."

"I don't want you to choose the same one I do."

Kallen's head was already spinning. "Why?"

"'Cause it'll only hurt more if you do."

"Hurt? More? What the fuck are you talking about?"

"I really, really like you. But-but, Deshara, this isn't real life. Real life starts when we get out of this place. And I think…I think it'll be better for us if we weren't going out after we get into that real life."

"Why?"

"I didn't want to have to tell you like this."

"You're gonna tell me like this anyway, aren't you?" He knew what was coming.

"Yeah, I'm gonna."

Kallen dropped to the bed beside him.

"We need to split up." Dayler told him.

Kallen didn't know how to respond just yet.

"I know you think it would be better that way, too," Dayler added.

"No, I *don't* think that way. *You* do."

Dayler looked away briefly. "Hardly."

Kallen could think of nothing better to do than to push him. Dayler didn't respond except to brace himself. Not getting the response he was seeking, Kallen socked him as hard as he could on his upper arm. Dayler just tensed up, letting himself be hit, but still didn't try to fight back. Kallen wanted to kick him now, but didn't. Instead, he wrapped his arms around him, pushed him down on the mattress, and softly whimpered. Dayler held onto him.

Dayler was the one who steered the relationship. He always had. He controlled everything. Dayler knew he had unusual charisma and wielded it like a weapon. That's how he got into Kallen's life. That's how he manipulated their relationship. He was irresistible.

Kallen's words were muffled as he pressed his face into the pillow. Two wet spots formed on it from his tightly shut eyelids. "You're stupid, Dayler. Stupid."

"Sometimes I am."

"You're being stupid now."

"No, I'm not. You would hate me if you followed me around forever."

Kallen sat back up. "How 'bout I start hating you now?"

"Not yet. Please don't start just yet."

Dayler didn't use the word 'please' easily. There was a sad look in his eyes. Again, very unlike him. Kallen pushed back the hair that had dropped onto Dayler's forehead. He loved looking into his blue eyes, loved breathing in the scent of his skin, loved the way he looked flexing in the mirror after a workout at the gym. He desperately wanted more of him than that, but could never find it.

Dayler got up and locked the door. Both sets of their clothes ended up all over the floor. Forty minutes later, when they were both dressed again, he made Dayler leave the room. He sat in the silence, thinking. That was the last time they were ever going to do it. He knew it without him even having to say so. So, when his legs had been up on Dayler's shoulders, when Dayler's face contorted as he stopped thrusting and was lost inside his orgasm, when Kallen came a split second later, Kallen relished the feeling and the intensity like he had so many times before, even when he thought he shouldn't.

He tried to put a positive spin on it all. The last four months with Dayler helped him understand what he wanted in a relationship. Dayler's magnetism was hypnotic and Kallen knew this had led him to ignore some of what was important to him.

Now he was gone. The breakup was final.

Kallen knew this would happen at some point. Of all the boys he'd met while here in school he still felt luckily to have had his good looking Dayler, despite what the relationship ultimately lacked. And, maybe Dayler was right. Maybe this wasn't real life. As Kallen looked at it he'd barely been in the ADF for a year.

Everything was still new. Perhaps being from such a small town made him more naïve than he had thought.

The next day, the top three students were meritoriously promoted due to their grade point average. This was Kallen's second meritorious promotion. It was becoming a habit, he noticed. Kallen, Dayler, and Hans were now on a parallel technical ranking structure. That meant that instead of being Senior Airmen, they were Airman Technicians. The rest of the class would all be ATs, too, once they were promoted. All technical servicemen would eventually follow suit. Kallen had been looking forward to the new insignia and the advancement. He was even happier about the extra credits that would go into his bank account, too.

The day before they were to graduate, they all sat in class, ready to receive their new duty assignments. Kallen usually sat next to Dayler. Today he was at the opposite end of the room, not an easy task with only twelve people in the small classroom. The other nine students had already been assigned their duty stations.

Dayler was next—the first of the three students to choose his. There were four air station choices listed on the vidscreens. He chose the air base at Monterey in California. Kallen was watching his screen, too, while Dayler selected. Monterey grayed-out, making him unable to choose that one. *What the fuck*, he wondered.

Despite what he had learned about Dayler's personality, despite Dayler having definitively told them they were broken up, despite Dayler warning him to not choose the same duty station if the possibility arose, Kallen still wanted to find some way for them to stay together. He spoke up.

"Sergeant Engenock, Monterey Air Station isn't selectable anymore."

Dayler tightened his mouth and shot him a nasty look. Kallen saw his reaction from across the room, but tried to ignore it.

"Sorry, Deshara. There was only one opening there."

Not knowing a thing about the other stations, Kallen chose the next one on the list, which was Eastern Strategic Command. Dayler leaned back in his seat, satisfied that Kallen couldn't follow him. Hans chose Sandstone HQ. All three of them would soon be stationed very far apart from each other. It wasn't until after class ended that Kallen realized that Dayler would be on the same base as Tiago. *Damn it*, he thought.

After their brief graduation ceremony, and after they had dispersed back to their rooms, Kallen looked around his tiny space again for anything he might have missed. Everything he owned was packed up already, but he wanted to be extra sure. He took his bags and laid them on the baggage cart that was waiting on the walkway. There were quite a few bags already stacked up on it. He closed his door for the last time and headed down the walkway of Schools Block B. He stopped by Dayler's open door. Dayler was just coming out of the bathroom when he saw Kallen at the entryway.

Kallen stepped in. He hadn't spoken to him in four days. "I guess this is it."

"No clichés allowed."

"One last kiss?"

Dayler went up to him and stopped. "Don't think it'll amount to anything else."

"Just…kiss me."

Dayler placed his hands on Kallen's shoulders. They kissed. Kallen's thoughts briefly went to the number of nights he'd been in Dayler's room, just like now, where they kissed, then fell onto bed, continuing with their intense desire for each other. But their relationship wasn't what he thought it was after all. He had realized that he had just been an interim stop on the way to the rest of Dayler's life.

Dayler kissed him like his heart was really into it, but he could turn his heart on and off when it suited him. Kallen didn't share that skill.

That handicap.

Yet, even now, when he thought he should hate Dayler, when he thought he shouldn't even be in the same room with him, he almost melted from his soft kisses.

Without another word, Kallen left the room, not turning back to look at him again.

Chapter 3

Tuesday, August 30, 2478

It was early afternoon when Kallen arrived at Eastern Strategic Command's Central Administration sub-building in the high Rockies in Colorado. The first thing he noticed was that security was much more formalized than at school. The Vancouver Training Center seemed non-military compared to this. The number of security personnel he saw and had to see here, as he was being processed, was unbelievable. It must have something to do, he surmised, with how close the base was to the edge of the Great Central Desert. Across the fourteen hundred kilometers of hot scrubland, barren ground, and in some places, outright burning desert was the western edge of the habitable part of the United Canadian Territories.

Kallen was at his next stop. He offered the guy his security card. So far, he had seen plain MPs. This guy, on the other hand, was definitely Black Guard. He knew it from the uniform.

The guy, who only looked up at him twice, had a name badge reading Bironas. Next to his name was a metal pin with a green bar with a yellow zigzag going through it. Kallen wondered what that signified. He wondered briefly if it was for the number of kills he'd had. Of people.

Kallen inspected the rest of his uniform. His crisply pressed shirt was black. So were his t-shirt and boots. There was even shiny black piping along the outside of each black trouser leg. He was glad that in this environment he didn't have to wear black clothing. It was a lot warmer here than even in New Meadows, despite being over two and a half kilometers above sea level. It seemed odd to be dressed all in black here. Where people normally wore a vidPAD holster he instead wore a pulse stunner. It was standard issue, yet Kallen wondered why he needed it so far into the interior of this building complex. His stop with Bironas only lasted two minutes and he was silently pointed to the next stop further down a long corridor.

At the next office he was assigned quarters. On a map at the counter the airman showed him where his room was in a downside dorm complex he called 'The T', named as such because of its shape. The airman downloaded the proper protocols to his vidPAD and generated Kallen an ID using his voice print. After a successful logon he was connected to BaseNet. Using his vidPAD, he would be able to access all the wireless data ports that gave him maps, directions, local weather, a directory of superior officers, and everything else would need to know about the base and his job assignment. As Kallen sat, waiting for one of the administrators to complete his processing into Maintenance section of Operations squadron, he listened to an informational vid on his vidPAD about the base.

A female voice spoke as he watched aerial views transition to other scenes of the surrounding area. "*Eastern Strategic Command is home to over 7000 permanent National Ground Patrol, Air Defense Force, and other residents*," she said. Kallen knew right away that 'other residents' was merely code for Black Guard. "*Occupying 1200 hectares the base houses all manner of military support and has been continuously occupied since 2366.*"

Her voice stopped and several holographic icons materialized to the right of her image. The top one was labeled National Ground Patrol, the middle one Air Defense Force, and the lower one Special Security. "*Choose one*," her voice said.

This must be a generic vid, Kallen thought.

He touched the appropriate button and, at the next screen, the one labeled 'Operations Squadron—Maintenance'. Her voice resumed as all of the icons faded. "*Operations Squadron is home to several sections, of which Maintenance is just one. There are also Acquisitions, Administration, Avionics, Ground Transport, Special Operations, and Warehousing.*

"*Maintenance Section personnel are responsible for the tuning, maintenance, and general operations of all photronics-based equipment used in day-to-day base operations, as well as for special projects.*

"*All photronics technicians at Eastern Strategic Command are expected to conform to the following service agreements….*"

Kallen touched another holographic button to move to the next section of the vid. He would bother with the details later.

There was a constant stream of people coming and going in front of his seat, though he was generally ignoring them. Another airman who had been at the counter sat down two seats to his right. Kallen glanced up at him. The airman nodded, smiled slightly, sized him up, then looked away.

Kallen took a moment to do the same. The guy was the same height as him, but stocker by far. He had short thick black hair and light brown skin. He didn't appear to be concerned with the state of his boots since they were quite scuffed up. His rank insignia indicated that he was a Sergeant Technician. He looked Asian, but Kallen wasn't sure. *I'd guess he's only part Asian*, he surmised.

That's about all he was able to assess when someone appeared at his left shoulder. A very attractive female airman was looking down at him. She eyed him curiously, which made him hesitate, then he looked back down and pressed his vidPAD's off button. Pressing the halves together he slipped it into his bag and stood.

"AT Deshara?" she asked, offering him her hand.

"Yeah." He offered his and they briefly shook.

"Senior Airman Ruiz. I work in the Ops Admin office. I'm here to bring you and ST Takeda over to our area and get you oriented."

"ST Takeda?" ST was the designation used for Sergeant Technician, which would be Kallen's next rank. She stepped over to Kallen's right to introduce herself.

Kallen got a much better look at him now that he had stood. Takeda's nametag, which Kallen hadn't seen earlier, was a little crooked and his hair was definitely longer than regulation. Kallen was sure he was straight from the way he was checking out Ruiz.

After the introductions were made and Ruiz had turned briefly away from them, Takeda looked over at Kallen again. From the look he gave Kallen about her figure from the rear Kallen was certain Takeda was straight now. Kallen gawked at Ruiz as well, partly as a remnant of old habits and partly for the benefit of Takeda. *How weird it is to have to pretend like this*, he thought. *I hope I don't have to do that a lot here.*

"Um, my stuff?" Kallen asked her. He had dropped off his bags at one of the check-in stations several stops back.

"Don't worry. They've already moved your bags to your housing office. You can pick them up once you get there."

They walked through wide, well-lit corridors. Several corridor transports had passed them by. They could have taken one, but Ruiz seemed in a chatty mood and didn't bother. Kallen checked for a ring. There was none. Single. *Probably feeling us out*, he thought.

"Been stationed here long?" Kallen asked her.

"Over a year."

"Like it?"

"Love it. It's the best base of them all."

"There's over two hundred fifty bases in the NAA and this one's the best?" Kallen patted his vidPAD. "The marketing vid said the same thing. Is it really that good?"

"We get the best food and I love the mountains."

Kallen's head was instantly filled with images of the mountains surrounding New Meadows. "So do I," he said with an unconscious smile.

She turned her attention to Takeda. "What about you?"

Takeda had had one ear on their conversation, but had been eyeing everyone who went by with great interest. "There sure are a lot of Black Guard here," he replied.

"ESC is sort of split up into three commands. We have Air Defense Force and support personnel, National Ground Patrol troops and all their people, and a large contingent of Black Guard, our so-called Special Security. We have so many of them because we're at the eastern edge of the country. A lot of the BG get cycled to Fort Morgan and to the Superior pumping station way off at the lake, too. Don't worry about them though. They don't mess with us. They're just the usual lugs." She lowered her voice. "They're not all that bright."

"I wouldn't say that. I've met some pretty crafty ones," Takeda told her.

"Hmm," she responded.

"Name's Mirani," she said as she turned to Kallen.

"Kallen."

She turned to ST Takeda.

"Dwess," Takeda said as he shook first her hand then Kallen's.

It was traditional in the service to call people by their last names. Ruiz was getting their first names right up front. That seemed unusual, but he liked her lack of formality. Regardless, he barely knew them so was hesitant to just up and call them by their first names right away.

"Where're you from?" she asked Dwess.

"BC. Not far from Kamloops."

"Kam what?"

"Loops. Loops." He made rapid circles in the air with an index finger. "Up north, in BC."

Kallen couldn't help but laugh at the gesture and decided he liked this Takeda guy.

She talked their ears off while they made their way to their quarters. Kallen was getting a bit bored with the conversation. She seemed a bit too interested in him. He was ready to meet some more guys. Takeda was just average in the looks department.

When they arrived at the Ops admin office she showed him them her desk and oriented them to the actual as opposed to the official procedures of how to get things done. She was to be their first contact for anything they needed. She seemed to know a lot of people. Kallen realized that he was in a truly different environment. The way she presented it, internal politics was very important, although she didn't exactly state it that way. He was quickly finding out that it was who you knew that got you places, not what you did, or necessarily how much you knew.

For no apparent reason Kallen's stomach tightened a little. It wouldn't go well for him if they found out he was attracted to guys instead of girls. He scanned the little office area. Mirani worked with three other guys. None of them were even remotely cute.

Dwess had been transferred from a base in northern Nevada to Operations Acquisitions section. His specialty was 'components, pieces and parts' as he called it. Kallen, because he'd be fixing a variety of equipment, would interact with someone in Acquisitions a lot. He figured he should get in good with this Takeda guy right away. Politics. If Takeda ended up having any pull, Kallen might get what he needed without excess bureaucratic red tape.

Mirani next led them to the Maintenance section work area. Kallen surveyed the workbenches and little alcoves where work was being done on some larger components that looked familiar. He didn't see a single cute guy there either.

Kallen asked if he could continue on with them to Acquisitions which was next to the Warehousing section. He wanted to see where Takeda worked and get the lay of the land there as well. They spent several minutes there. While Mirani showed Dwess around, Kallen checked out all the guys. He saw two who were marginally good looking and one that was particularly stunning. *Damn, why do they have to be over here and not in my section*, he wondered.

Next, Mirani led them to The T. It was late afternoon, quitting time for most people on first shift, and lots of people were coming and going as they left their work areas. The T turned out to be a good distance from where they worked. She brought them first to the housing administrative office where they retrieved their bags. Mirani led Dwess to his room. Before he entered, they activated their vid-PADs and he beamed Kallen his vid address. "Vid me when you get unpacked." Kallen eagerly said yes, pleased to have received the invitation.

Mirani led Kallen to his room which was on the same level but about twenty meters down the corridor. He inserted his security card. The lock's LED changed from red to green and the door clicked open. He pushed the door in and Mirani said goodbye.

Kallen's room was quite nice. There was space for at least a dozen people to sit in a big circle in the middle of what amounted to a studio apartment. It was complete with a comfortable queen-sized bed, a one burner stove, a small sink, some counter space, and a separate bath. The bathroom had an ultrasonic shower, and even a real water showerhead. He dropped his bags on the bed. A sunlight fiber bundle terminated in the center of the ceiling. He adjusted the louvers to maximum and the lens illuminated. The room brightened with natural light as if there were a real skylight in the ceiling. A built-in vidstation with all the standard controls was in the corner. He pressed his thumb against the on pad. Within thirty seconds of his voice-activated logon he located some music files. *That was easy,* Kallen thought. He turned up the sound. *Hmm, they must not have any encryption protocols in place.* He was already wondering what he would end up breaking into first. This might be the place to really hone his hacking skills, especially after having been admonished all those years back at the waterdome. He immediately recalled the heavy concentration of Black Guard here. *Maybe I better wait 'til I know what's going on around here.*

After unpacking, then stowing his bags in the single, albeit partitioned closet at the back of his room, he went to the vidstation and touched the phone icon. He opened his vidPAD and accessed Dwess' vid address. Beaming it to the vidstation, it connected him.

Dwess was shirtless when he answered. "I thought you weren't gonna call. Come on over."

Kallen noticed that Dwess didn't work out. He was a little overweight. Kallen made a mental note to find the gym and get back in a workout routine as soon as possible.

When Kallen arrived Dwess opened the door. He was still shirtless. He had a pile of clothes on his bed, a couple of dresser drawers open, and two bottles of refreshments on a table. He offered one of the red bottles to Kallen. "Jolicoeur juice. Hope you like it."

"Yeah, this is good stuff. Where'd you find it?"

"Down the corridor to the right. There's several machines in a snack alcove over there."

"Good to know. Wanna get some food when you're done?"

"Yeah. That's why I had you over. I figured we could look over the place together."

"Great." Kallen was already liking it here. He'd made an instant buddy, who didn't seem like an ass at all.

"You're a newbie, huh?" Dwess asked as he finished stuffing his clothes into the drawers.

"I guess. Been in less than a year."

"And you're already an E-3?"

"I've gotten a couple of meritorious promotions."

"You must be quite the brain, huh?"

Does everyone know about my test scores? "Don't tell everyone, huh?"

"Who, me?" He pulled on a t-shirt and donned a dark brown shirt over it. "You didn't say where you're from, but I'd say Idaho or the Oregon Domain."

"Central Idaho. How'd you know?"

"I know stuff, too."

Kallen wondered what that really meant. "What kinda stuff?"

"Stuff like, oh, the fact that you're probably from a really tiny town."

"Twelve hundred." Dwess seemed to know things without being obviously intelligent. Kallen decided to test him. "What town?"

"Can't say, but you probably grew up there."

"Lived all my life in New Meadows."

"New Meadows. New Meadows. Is that near McCall?"

"Yeah, just outside of McCall. You know the place?"

Dwess just gave him a knowing smile. "By the way, you can call me Dwess."

Dwess knew about his hometown? And there it was again. Dispensing with tradition must be more common than he supposed.

"Okay, Dwess it is. You can call me Kallen."

Dwess nodded. "The vidstation says the mess hall's up on the second sub-level over in the next building."

Kallen finished his bottle of juice and they left the room. He stopped Dwess just before they got to the mess hall so he could check his bank account at a credit machine. Satisfied that everything was in order they continued on their way. Once inside the mess hall they punched up food tickets and selected their food. They sat at a table near one of the vidscreens showing the news. Kallen had an eye on it and an ear on Dwess as they talked and ate.

"So, this Mirani. You thinking about going after her?" Dwess asked.

"We just met."

"Just checking out the players. You looked at her. I looked at her. I saw that look in her eye. I'm single. You are, too."

"How do you know I'm single?"

"I know a lot about you."

"Go on," Kallen said.

Dwess leaned back and pointed his fork at him. "You've just come out of a wild and crazy relationship. You're trying to rebound. And Mirani is just your type."

"Huh. You only got one of those right."

"Good, Mirani isn't your type. I was kidding about all that anyway. That leaves her for me."

"What do you really know about me?"

"Hmm. For one, you don't do halpa root."

"'Cause it's illegal."

"And why is that?"

"'Cause it is."

"Ever wonder why?"

"No." Actually, he had never really thought about it.

"Well, that's another thing I know about you, too. You've never smoked it and don't know how good it is."

"And you have," Kallen stated.

Dwess poked at some mashed potatoes, then brought them to his mouth. He grinned as he swallowed, but didn't say anything else. He noticed Kallen had been keeping an eye on the newsvid. "You aren't really listening to that, are you?" he asked.

"Why not?"

"You're listening for entertainment, not for content, right?"

"No. Content."

"Pure entertainment. More like fiction."

"You have friends in the news industry?"

"Relatives. But you don't have to have those kind of connections to know that newsvids are ninety-nine percent propaganda."

Kallen wasn't quite sure what Dwess was getting at, but continued to listen to the newsvid anyway. Dwess grinned at him until they were done with their meal.

An hour later Kallen found out exactly how good halpa root was.

Halpa root was illegal because it was virtually impossible to detect in anyone's urine or bloodstream. The NAA liked to control what it could of its society. Root, as it was simply called, was one item that was difficult to control. Basically a weed, and nicely euphoric when smoked, it was the drug of choice for those who wanted or needed anything stronger than alcohol. It's effects, although extremely powerful when first inhaled, gradually tapered off within a few hours, and was rarely physically addictive. In addition, when it wore off it had none of the usual deleterious side effects such as headache or queasy stomach, usually associated with other harsher drugs and alcohol.

Halpa was mostly grown in Dwess' region of the country. A region mostly devoid of Black Guard presence due to it being so rural. Those from there controlled its sale to the southern regions. Dwess was one of those people.

Dwess locked his door while Kallen pulled a chair out from the table. Dwess took out a small black vial from a small box and sat down with him. Dumping out a small section of the dried spongy root, he cut a small piece off, then pulled out a wooden pipe. Stuffing it into the well-used bowl, he offered Kallen the first hit. It was so smooth Kallen didn't even find himself coughing. Within thirty seconds he found himself wondering why he had never tried it before.

"It's hard to get so far south," Dwess told him. "But I have a supplier."

Kallen heard him, but was busy holding his hands up in front of his face, looking at them from the altered state he'd found himself in. He noticed that his hearing seemed to be more acute than normal. It was as if he could almost see every note of the music playing from Dwess' vidstation speakers. He was really enjoying the feeling and was glad to be on Dwess' good side.

"You can get more of this stuff?" Kallen finally asked.

Dwess chuckled merrily.

Kallen found himself feeling very naïve.

As he asked more questions he had to concentrate to listen. Dwess wouldn't answer him directly but rather made him strain to extract information from him, especially in this state. Kallen, on the other hand, felt like an open book with everything. Everything that is except the fact that he was gay. For all of Dwess' apparent street smarts he didn't seem to detect this. *Good*, Kallen thought. *At least I have* some *secrets he can't read.*

It turned out that Dwess had been in the service for three years. This was his fourth duty station and he hoped it would be his last before his end of active service. He was a good organizer, and the Acquisitions section was in disarray. Parts weren't getting ordered fast enough, or were being ordered incorrectly and as a result things were backed up in Maintenance section where Kallen would be working. Dwess had been transferred to ESC to see if he could straighten that out. He made it clear that if Kallen treated him well, he would do so in return. Kallen found himself smiling at the pact of friendship Dwess so easily made with him. He didn't think someone as savvy as him would do so. But Dwess shook on it. *He must really like me*, Kallen thought. *Jeez, I'm lucky to have met him right away.*

The next morning, Kallen found Dwess' words about the root to ring true. He had no hangover, feeling refreshed after having slept so soundly. He wondered why he never questioned why the government thought root was so dangerous. He placed a vid to Dwess. Dwess was clearly not wearing anything, a habit Kallen was starting to notice. He also noticed that couldn't see anything below his waist. Actually, he found himself hoping he wouldn't accidentally see anything either. Dwess was perhaps a four on a ten scale in Kallen's estimation. He didn't want to see his penis.

At breakfast, Kallen again placed himself in view of one of the news vidscreens while they ate.

They'd been talking while he visited Dwess this morning, while Dwess got dressed, while they went to the mess hall, and up until a few minutes ago. It was more or less a continuation of their conversation from last night; the hours of talking they had done until midnight. Kallen was thoroughly intrigued with Dwess' conversation style. It was punching holes in his normal thought processes. Or maybe it was the altered view of reality he had obtained from smoking the root last night. Perhaps it had to do with something Dwess had told him about the group of guys he used to associate with. Whatever it was, he found himself listening to the newscaster with a different ear.

Years previous, Dwess had participated in a music group called Iconoclast. It was just three guys making music in a makeshift studio they had put together. Dwess was the keyboard player. They wrote only music, never writing lyrics, never recording any of it for profit, never publishing any of it. He told Kallen how they would smoke some root then discuss the texture of the piece that would spontaneously come out of them from their jam sessions.

"Texture?" Kallen had asked him.

"Sure," Dwess told him. "Music is way more than notes. It has color, it expresses love, it tells stories, and what's more, it's the arrangement of silence."

"The arrangement of what?"

"Silence."

Kallen had had a hard time with the concept so they discussed it for quite a while. A chill had gone up his back as he thought about it. He'd never thought about music that way before. It was like thinking backward. *What an odd way of thinking about things*, he thought.

Then they had talked about optical illusions. "What if, when you look at a mirror, you aren't really looking at your reflection, but your reflection is looking at you," Dwess had asked him.

After Kallen's laughter subsided, and Dwess hadn't joined in, Kallen thought seriously about it.

The more they discussed common ordinary things from Dwess' perspective, the more Kallen realized something very important. He discovered that he hadn't really questioned things like Dwess obviously had. Dwess seemed to have questioned the very nature of reality and come up with highly unusual answers, explanations, and viewpoints.

The range of topics they discussed was so curious yet so baffling to him that Kallen finally had to tell him to stop talking. He felt like he was being overloaded by this completely different way to think about things. Everything Dwess had told him he thought about instead of dismissing it. But all the new data, compounded by the euphoric effects of the root, had been too much to assimilate in one sitting. Dwess is one highly unusual guy Kallen had told himself before falling asleep last night.

Now at breakfast, instead of just listening and absorbing everything the newscaster was saying, Kallen found himself wondering what she *really* meant. He found himself trying to extract a greater meaning behind the words. It was as if a light had gone on inside his head. He found it curious that he never questioned the content of the news before. But it was disturbing to think this way. It wasn't right.

Or was it?

Being gay made him see things differently in the first place. He didn't view women the same anymore. With Naya, he had been lying to himself to conform to a social convention that wasn't his. He had been with Tiago and Dayler. That was surely different. But there was more. Dwess was *completely* different. He certainly *thought* differently. He didn't seem to be part of the carefully controlled society Kallen had grown up in. Somehow he lived at the edge of it.

Like himself.

Kallen suddenly realized that perhaps nothing was the way he had thought it was. In that instant his perception shifted. It was an unsettling feeling. All of it was terribly disquieting, too. But, he was terribly intrigued by it all. Fascinated even. It was as if he'd just woken up. Every moment of his life up to this one had been viewed from a half-asleep state.

While they ate, Dwess had his vidPAD open and was reading his orientation material. Kallen continued to listen to the newsvid. Intrigued. Mesmerized. Wondering.

The NAA commander-in-chief, President Brin, was angry about the Water Treaty of 2264. A newscaster was interviewing him.

"*General Lecuyer can moan all he wants about the water treaty,*" the President said. "*We have significant rights to draw the amount of water we want by way of the Lake Superior pumping station.*"

Kallen knew about the water treaty. It had led to the construction of the waterdomes and the containment of all major rivers within pipelines. The United Canadian Territories owned all the Great Lakes and had imposed the two-hundred fourteen year old treaty on the NAA after a fierce war over water rights. But the war was over much more than just drawing water from the lake. The NAA had been vying to own it outright. The NAA had lost the war, but the treaty had been signed as an act of good faith. Regardless, every twenty years or so, the treaty's legitimacy was questioned by NAA politicians. After all, the vast majority of UCT lands existed well east of all the lakes.

Only the easternmost edge of the Great Central Desert touched the pumping station in Duluth. While it was still a terrible place to live, it was habitable—but only by the military. It was an isolated outpost, far away from the rest of NAA territory. The military had been guarding their most important asset across the desperate burning expanse for centuries now. The Duluth pumping station was more important than gold, more important than platinum. It was life.

Kallen always harbored a fear that he'd one day hear that the NAA would be denied access to the vast, deep, uncovered lake. The fear only came from hearing things from waterdome personnel, from his parents, and from overhearing casual conversations between other adults. It was something most teenagers never discussed or heard about. But he had. It seemed he was always drawn to such talk. His fear was mostly irrational and always hovered just below his conscious thoughts.

Of all that water, Kallen thought, the NAA could only fill their allotment from one lake. The UCT drew all the water they wanted from them all. Why couldn't they just cede Lake Superior to the NAA? He had wondered about that for years. The Duluth pumping station was more than a precious water rights issue. It was a symbol of the NAA's authority and autonomy.

Kallen continued listening intently to the newsvid interview. Background information was being given in the form of a voiceover by the President. Aerial shots of the pumping station, the water intake crib, and the military facility that guarded it were being shown.

"*The Superior pipeline provides our single largest steady source of water. The NAA spends millions of credits a year to maintain its infrastructure and guard the pumping station. Despite the limits the treaty outlines, we've had to exceed our allotted quantity for some time now due to the destruction of the desalination plants. Those plants take time to rebuild. The entire region is still undergoing a cleanup. The Alliance Water Projects Department is still a year from completing the new pipeline from the north. The UCT knows water can't flow from it yet. We must be allowed to overdraw.*"

The President had referred to a disaster that occurred five weeks before. Two back-to-back tremors along the San Juan de Fuca plate on the NAA's west coast had struck in the span of four hours. Six desalination plants had been reduced to rubble. Six of seven! It was a monumental disaster without precedent—at least in recent history. The entire region's water supply nearly vanished. It would take months before the plants came back online. The BC pipeline—which ran along the Pacific, north of the Queen Charlotte Islands—wouldn't be completed for at least eleven months. Diversion from waterdomes further inland could help, but not for long. On the other hand, the Superior pipeline could easily handle the differential.

At the end of the northern dispersion line of the Superior pipeline at Fort Morgan were several more re-pumping stations. A network of smaller pipelines fed aquifers and reservoirs further west. It was those aquifers that were being re-supplied by the extra water from Lake Superior. How it was being done was very complicated, involving surface transports and downside pipelines, but Kallen understood partly how it was being accomplished.

The newscaster switched back to the President. "General Lecuyer isn't sympathetic to the plight of our people. He certainly isn't the proper spokesman for our issues."

The newscaster went on to quote the general without actually airing him. '*The pumping station exists only by our graces,*' the newscaster said. '*If the NAA continues to ignore our request to reduce pumping levels, we'll be forced to act.*'

Kallen thought about it. *How could the UCT possibly ignore our current problem? It wasn't our fault that the desalination plants had been disabled. What were they going to do, just let everyone die? How could they so casually deny us water?*

"Damned UCT," Kallen said between bites of bread.

"What's that?" Dwess asked, looking up.

Kallen pointed at the vidscreen. "Fucking UCT's at it again about the water treaty."

"You're not listening to that newsvid for content again, are you?"

"I sure am. They have no right to limit our water."

"You know President Brin is lying."

"About what?"

"About what's really going on."

"How do you know?"

"You can tell by just listening to him."

Kallen's pulse quickened. Dwess was dead wrong about *this* issue. "The treaty is really important. Hell, part of the reason ESC even exists is to supply troops to defend the Superior pumping station. *And* the one at Fort Morgan. You know that. Don't you care about water?"

Dwess chuckled, "Why do you care so much about that treaty?"

After they deposited their trays Dwess walked with him back to the dorm corridor. Kallen explained himself. Dwess listened carefully.

"Old Water, huh?" His new buddy was from a water family! It was one thing he didn't realize. "Deshara, I can see why you would be so attentive to that issue, but you really have to learn to read between the lines."

"About *that*?"

"About *everything*."

"What the fuck do you mean by that?"

"You need a lesson in listening."

"I can hear just fine, thank you."

"See?"

"See what?"

"Did I use the word hear? Or did I use the word listen?"

Kallen bit his lip. "Uh, listen."

"Between the lines."

Dwess had broken through. Kallen was all ears now.

"Lesson number one," Dwess said. "Ever notice that newsvids never show actual people from the UCT? Ever?"

"No."

"They don't. They only quote them. That is if they even bother to do that."

"So. The UCT isn't the friendliest country in the world. It's hard to get their people on vids."

"And you think we *are* friendly?"

"Well…I don't know."

Dwess was a little surprised that Kallen hadn't thought this one out. "What about the Black Guard?" He was clearly shifting the focus of their discussion.

"What about them?"

"Why does this country need so many Black Guard? Most of them sit around on their ass and act like they own the place."

"They're our protection."

"Against whom or what, my friend?"

"Them."

"Who them?"

"Them…the UCT…the bad guys."

Dwess shook his head. "They must have gotten hold of you *real* early." He could tell he was broaching topics Kallen was completely unfamiliar and uncomfortable with. It was stretching Kallen's comfort limit again. He could tell that Kallen had many assumptions about his world that he held as truth. But he could also tell that Kallen was thinking. That was a good sign. Kallen wanted to hear more, but that was enough for now. "Lesson one is over. I don't want to overwhelm you."

"Huh! Like last night wasn't overwhelming enough?"

The lesson might have been over, but in the days that followed Kallen kept thinking about Dwess' unorthodox approach to just about everything. In the light of the perception shift that had occurred that morning he realized there were things going on around him that he'd never paid attention to before. *Perhaps a lot of things aren't like I thought they are*, he thought. *Maybe more than I ever supposed.*

That aside, Kallen quickly became aware that his reputation preceded him. Despite consciously making an effort not to flaunt his expertise, word traveled quickly. Within a week and a half, everyone in his section knew that the newbie named AT Deshara was the guy to go to if something needed to be fixed really fast. In addition, if anyone had a technical question, Kallen had the answer in his head. He only looked up things if they were of a particularly complex nature.

Kallen found that operational military codebases were somewhat different from what he'd been taught in school. The software in the vast majority of the equipment he had been assigned to repair seemed like it had been written by amateurs. There was a procedure for upgrades, rewrites, and the reorganization of codebases. Things were supposed to be documented thoroughly. Those protocols weren't followed by most of the other techs.

Eventually he was rewriting code, swapping bad photronic modules in record time, and making sure that protocol was followed. After all, it was the only way to track his changes and make sure he didn't see a failed part twice in the same week. 'Do it right the first time' was the motto his father had taught him a long time ago. It was a good motto to stick to.

His OIC was relieved to have a truly competent recent graduate for a change. Kallen was aware he was getting special attention because of it. He was pleased his talents were recognized by his superiors.

It took a full two weeks before Kallen finally visited the gym. It was conveniently located between his work area and The T. He preferred to work out after a full day at work. He attempted to get Dwess to come with him, but he said no each time. He eventually stopped asking. Dwess told Kallen that he thought he'd never stop.

The gym was three times the size of the one back at school. It was equipped with state of the art machines as well as free weights. There were so many stations that it took a full three days before he was able to develop a good routine to utilize most of them. Finally, by the end of the week he found his rhythm, assisted by the three vidstation kiosks that provided personalized workout programs.

Dwess continued to have conversations with Kallen about seeing past the obvious. A week later he managed to get Kallen to forego one of his workouts to partake in some root with him. Just them both.

"So, Deshara, have you done any more thinking about what we were discussing a while back?"

"About the newsvids?"

"Of course."

"I noticed something kind of weird. Who decides what's *on* the news?"

"Whoa. I didn't think you'd ask that question so soon. That's exactly what you're supposed to ask! You're coming along faster than I thought."

Kallen grinned, more from the root than from Dwess' comment.

"So, anything specific?" Dwess asked.

"Sure. How about the President. He condescends, speaks in platitudes, and moralizes, but he doesn't actually say anything of value or substance. And he keeps harping on the treaty. A lot."

"You never really questioned that treaty before, did you?"

"Never. I've lived my entire life thinking that that treaty is the most sacred thing. Any time there's any discussion about it, I've always had my opinion. But-but I'm not so sure about my opinion anymore."

Dwess stood up and circled him. Even though he did it in slow motion, it still made Kallen dizzy. "You're supposed to question your very life, Deshara. Even reality. If you're not doing that you're not living, you're just existing. You see, the

UCT is actually just fine with the treaty and with how much water we're drawing from the lake. They know we've sustained an unprecedented disaster. The President's creating a non-existent issue."

"Why would he do that?" *He'd deliberately mess with our precious water treaty?*

"He's a politician, that's why."

"You'll have to explain that."

"It's a sham. Have you actually read the treaty?"

Kallen wondered when he had. He couldn't recall ever having done so.

Dwess waited a moment before answering for Kallen. "Just as I thought. That's exactly what the politicians are hoping."

"I bet my dad's read it."

"Wanna vid him and find out?"

"Fuck no, I'm high."

"You might want to consider that your father may be towing the party line. People believe what they *want* to believe—what they're *told* to believe. Distortions and outright lies repeated frequently enough eventually become 'the truth'. That's what our President is counting on. By you never questioning 'the truth'— by never reading the actual source—your sacred treaty, in this case—'the truth' becomes what the politicians *want* it to be."

Kallen felt terribly confused now. He worshipped his father. To consider that his dad had worked his entire adult life in waterdome operations and might not have ever read the treaty was outlandish. *Or is it? And what was that about 'the truth'? That lies repeated often enough become the truth? God, he's right. I just know it. How does he* know *all this stuff?* Dwess had a way of making him pry into his core thought processes to find out things he never questioned before.

"How do I get a copy of it?" Kallen asked him.

"Not from BaseNet," Dwess told him.

"It's not there?" Kallen replied, quite surprised.

"It's not in any of the databases I have access to."

"Are you sure?"

"It might be someplace on the I-net but I don't have access to it. One thing's for sure, though. *You* and *I* can't read it to find out what it says. I might be able to get a copy from my brother, but he's hard to get hold of nowadays."

"Shit."

"Yeah shit. We never get a direct feed from any UCT newsvids. We rarely hear anything they really say. So, I'm sure that the President bitching about the water treaty is another government cover to deflect our attention from what they don't want us to see."

"How do you *know* all this?"

"I have a naturally suspicious nature."

"What if you're looking for conspiracies where none exist."

"Hmm." Dwess thought about that for a moment. "I don't think so. *You're* not plugged in to what's going on in your very own country."

"I've never been into politics."

"Then you get to be run by it or run over by it."

"I do *not*."

Dwess pulled a chair up turned it around less than a meter in front of Kallen and rested his arms across the back.

"Let's see. You're in the ADF. That means you're run by the government. Or should I say its governmental policy of conscription. So am I. So is every able-bodied man and woman in this country that's our age. We're all run by the government. They tell us where to live, where to work, what to wear, what to eat. You and I both know that they control what information we get. Need I go on?"

Kallen was annoyed that Dwess was interfering with his buzz. But he was absolutely correct. It was Kallen who had never connected the dots. Before this moment, the whole conscription thing was simply another phase of life. A phase everyone older than him, including his parents and grandparents, had had to participate in. And it was true. The government controlled everything, although they pretended they didn't. They even funded the waterdome authorities. Before that, they funded the piping of the rivers and the domes. They billeted tens of thousands of Black Guard. They were in every sizeable town in the country, including McCall near his hometown. Occasionally, Black Guard would even come by to 'inspect' waterdome operations. Kallen remembered how tense everyone felt whenever they made their inspections, but never really understood the implication until now. The Guard were simply intimidating.

Kallen realized only at that moment that he had been immersed in government control of everyone's lives for so long that it didn't occur to him that there might be a different way to do things.

"How the fuck did you get so smart?" he asked.

Dwess grinned then reached for the pipe. "Let's just say that root makes one see things differently…. Look Deshara, the government wants everyone to think we live wonderfully fulfilled lives, full of individuality, full of joy, full of happiness. What's really going on is that our daily lives are manipulated in subtle ways. It's rarely overt. It seems innocuous. It isn't. Not at all."

Kallen was shaking his head now. "Shit," he said again.

Dwess grinned and nodded his head. It was sinking in. He stuffed the pipe, lit it, drew a hit, then passed it to him. Kallen took a long hit and let the euphoria to take him higher.

Dwess continued to steer the conversation. "Recent history lesson, Deshara. Remember that UCT transport that came into our airspace a few years back?"

"The spy transport that was shot down?"

"Wrong."

"It was, too. I remember the newsvids...."

"Exactly my point."

"It *didn't* happen?"

"Oh, it happened. But they weren't spies. They had a malfunction. Just like our aircraft have so many malfunctions."

"The photronic code here sucks. That's why I'm so 'valuable'." He raised his fingers in quotations when he said that.

"You know they use the same type of code."

"You mean...?"

"They were shot down by NAA gunners. The UCT transport used their emergency frequency to disclose their unintended encroachment. Did our troops care? You know those early-warning perimeter personnel shoot first and ask questions after everyone is dead. Remember the furor afterward?"

"No. I was like fifteen. I didn't follow much of it."

"I did. That's when I first started realizing our government's not telling us everything."

"You're not shittin' me, are you?"

Dwess glared at him, then snapped the root's vial top shut. It was the only sound in the room when he did it. Kallen knew he wasn't lying.

"How about that attempted coup. You know, last year?" Dwess asked.

"That one I followed. It was all over the vids. My parents talked about it for weeks."

"What do you know about it?"

"Some of the legislators were trying to overthrow President Brin and his cabinet."

"BS again."

Kallen stretched his legs out, then cocked his head. "Go on."

"Brin's the biggest liar ever. He and his cronies simply fed the newscasters whatever they wanted to hear. They wanted to report about an attempted coup. He helped deliver that report. But what really happened was that those legislators were merely trying to correct a disastrous development in the Department of Military Readiness. What was the last you heard regarding those guys?"

"I don't remember. Hmm, they weren't mentioned in the newsvids much after that."

Dwess made a funny sound with his mouth. "Ever wonder why?"

"No."

"You wanna know what really happened?"

"You're gonna tell me, of course."

"Of course."

No longer annoyed with the conversation, but rather terribly intrigued, Kallen leaned forward.

"Brin was installed, not voted in. We've been led to believe otherwise. Remember the fiasco over the voting count?"

"Who could forget?"

"He wasn't elected by a majority. Ultimately, he was installed by the Supreme Council. Once installed, his military buddies decided that the nation was hot for his national mandate. Do you know what his mandate is?"

"Not a clue."

"'Let's take Lake Superior away from the UCT'."

Kallen's eyes widened. "Against the treaty?"

"Against the treaty. That much I know."

"*Fuck.*"

"All of the legislators were told to pass his emergency spending bill to build up more reserves for the invasion and capture of the UCT outposts on the northern and southern shores of Lake Superior.

"Those twelve men knew it was a dangerous move. We lost once. We could lose again. They knew that. They tried everything they could to stop him. When he wouldn't listen and they refused to pass the bill Brin had a closed-door meeting with them. It apparently didn't do any good. A couple of them later tried to warn the UCT of Brin's plan. I'm sure you know how hard that is since our government doesn't allow much communication with them, nor do we even have an ambassador to their country—treaty or no treaty.

"Brin found out about that and 'exposed' them as seditious. They weren't seditious at all. They were probably the most patriotic people we had. Now they're gone. Desaparecido—after their so-called trial. Most likely they're rotting in those prisons in western Nevada. My previous duty station was only one hundred twenty-five kilometers from a military prison. We heard things. That's how I know all this."

Kallen's mouth had dropped open. It was so unbelievable, so incredible, and in utter contradiction to what he'd been taught about his government. But Dwess hadn't ever lied to him. Not once. Kallen was sure he wasn't lying now.

"They're rotting in prison for no reason other than trying to fix a problem that's systemic in our government. Brin and his gang of military cronies can't allow that. Their power base would be eroded and they'd lose control. Remember the riots that happened afterward?"

"Yeah, Black Guard were everywhere. Scared the fuck out of me."

"Scared the fuck out of me, too."

"So, what happened?" Kallen pressed.

"The protestors were pissed off about the false imprisonment of those guys. Quite a few of them were picked up, hauled off, and never heard from again. Ever heard the phrase 'unlawful protestor'?"

"No."

"Well, you should."

"Why?"

"'Cause it's a meaningless phrase, conjured up for expediency, just to get rid of or silence opposition. Some of the BG platoons that carried out the roundups are directly controlled by Brin's office."

Kallen was feeling a little frightened now. "Were you involved?"

"Only by remote communication."

"With who?"

"My brother."

"Is *he* in jail?"

"No. He was smart enough to keep his mouth shut, his face covered, and his trail cold. You have to know when and where to pick your fights.... There's more, Deshara. Lots more. But let's just say that I hope you don't look at the newsvids again and *don't* wonder what's *really* going on."

Kallen spent many nights the next several weeks talking to Dwess about all sorts of new things. Dwess had more common sense than anyone he'd ever come in contact with. Because of the discussions, Kallen slowly but surely learned to be wary when it came to listening to the official word of authority. He'd spent months training in boot camp to carry out all orders without so much as a thought of not doing so. Now this.

They talked about the interactions he'd had with the higher-ups in his section, with the officials at the waterdome, with his older friends, with his relatives, and even with his parents. *His parents?* The more he thought about it, the more he was sure that everyone, including himself, had been ingeniously brainwashed. It was a traumatic transformation to be sure, but Kallen came to realize that all indeed wasn't as he'd been lead to believe.

Knowing Dwess was a like winning the lottery.

Now, if he could just get him to go to the gym.

One month into his workouts Kallen noticed that someone named A. Racelis had been logging in recently to the kiosk he used most frequently. Racelis' workout routine was very similar to his. There were no cross-references; so he was unable to discern what section he or she was in.

They met a day later. Kallen was working on his third set of military presses when he observed a guy he'd not seen before, perhaps four or five centimeters taller than himself, with dark hair, dark features, and especially hairy legs standing there waiting for him to finish.

Yummy, Kallen thought, *and distracting*. He peeled his eyes from the nice legs and saw piercing hazel eyes and an angular face with nice full lips. As Kallen was finishing the set and was starting to struggle the guy stepped up to spot him. When he completed the last rep, Kallen thanked him. The guy extended his hand.

"Racelis," he said.

"Deshara," Kallen replied. "So, you're the A. Racelis in the database." He pointed to the nearest kiosk. "Looks like we have similar workout schedules."

"You must be K. Deshara."

Kallen took a stab and dispensed once again with tradition. "The K's for Kallen, by the way."

"Acton," he told Kallen with a grin.

"I never saw your name on the display until recently. You new here?" Kallen asked.

"Nope. I just shifted my schedule, so it'll be here about this time every other day for a while."

He observed Acton in a little more detail, glancing at him furtively. Acton was a little older than himself, perhaps four or five years older. He took another stab, mostly because he liked what he saw. "Well, I *am* new and don't have a workout partner. I, uh, wouldn't mind a spotter."

"Depends on your schedule. But don't think I'm gonna go easy on you."

"Don't even try."

The ended up spotting each other. A half-hour later they were ready to hit the shower.

Since first coming to the gym, Kallen had kept his eyes to himself. He didn't want anyone to be suspicious of him. The ultrasonic showers were in separate stalls so Kallen didn't get to see him naked when they stepped in. Back in the locker room Kallen dropped his towel then slipped on his skivvies. As he turned around he caught Acton squarely checking him out. In Kallen's experience it wasn't uncommon for guys to look at each other in the locker room. But he knew it was either out of jealousy or secretive admiration for a particular build, not something sexual. Acton had a studied and steady gaze, seemingly with a little something extra behind the look. It made Kallen wonder for a moment. He immediately dismissed the thought as he slipped into his street clothes. Acton was doing the same, too, lastly pulling on a tight-fitting t-shirt.

"Hey, I'm gonna go to the juice bar over near the BX. Wanna go with me?" Acton asked.

"Sure. I need a recharge."

Acton insisted on paying for their fruit smoothies. They sat at a small round table away from the rest of the crowd.

"So, Deshara. ADF or NGP?"

"ADF."

"Which squadron?"

"Operations."

"Really. Same here. What section?"

"Maintenance. I'm the guy they come to when stuff breaks."

"They've needed some good techs there. Our equipment repair cycle has gotten a lot longer recently and we need some of our things back real soon."

"What section are you in?"

"Avionics."

"Hmm. I've been to Avionics a couple of times. I've not seen you before."

Acton was stirring his smoothie with a straw, staring at the swirls. He glanced up at Kallen briefly. "Officers get the quiet offices."

"Oh. I didn't realize you were an officer."

"And you?" Acton asked.

"AT."

"1st Lieutenant," Acton told him, then sucked on his straw.

Kallen completely shifted his thinking now. He had had minimal contact with officers on personal speaking terms. And the fact that Acton was a Lieutenant meant he had re-enlisted. It also meant he was definitely older.

"Are you good?" Acton asked.

"Whadda ya mean?"

"Good techs are hard to come by."

"I'm the best. That's why I'm here." He knew he was boasting.

"I'll let you prove it."

Shit, he thought. "How?"

"There are two pallets of equipment that have been sitting in your section for months. We need the items back and no one has scheduled them for repair. Maybe we can work something out. Like, oh, I don't know." Acton looked first at Kallen's face, then his arms, then lingered on his chest. "Maybe I'll buy you dinner in Estes Park if you can get both pallets back to my section in a week."

Estes Park was the small town northeast of the base. Situated outside the valley a couple dozen kilometers from the base, it was the first major town, albeit small, in the area.

Kallen listened carefully. "Both of them? In a week? What kind of equipment are we talking about?"

Acton rattled off a list of avionics modules used not only in the HeavyAir transports, but also in some of the short-range desert reconnaissance jets. "Some of the pilots have been forced to use backup systems, but that's completely outside regulations. If you can get those non-functioning modules repaired, you'll not only get your dinner but you'll help get my section back into regulation. Deal?"

Kallen thought about it. He was familiar with every single component Acton had just spoken of. "Why not? Everyone wins, huh?"

"That's thinking like an officer. I like you even more now."

Kallen noted the 'even more now' comment. It seemed clear that Acton's invitation to the BX was inspired by more than wanting to have a smoothie. Acton seemed to genuinely like him, Kallen thought. It felt good to have the attention.

The next day, all the necessary documentation had been forwarded to his vidstation. Kallen found the pallets. They had been cordoned off, almost abandoned from their position off the queue. Kallen made a special request to his superior to work on only the equipment on those pallets for the rest of the week. He was at the gym three days later.

"Made any headway with that equipment?" Acton asked as they changed into their gym clothes.

"It's hard going. Some of those modules have some pretty old components and outdated code base objects. I've had to rewrite a lot of it and we had very few of the parts I needed for the repairs."

They spent the next hour and a half working out. Acton didn't ask for any more detail or even raise the issue again. Kallen deliberately didn't mention that he had only two modules to complete before both pallets were not only repaired, but upgraded. By ten hundred hours tomorrow morning he'd be finished with the last item, ahead of schedule. He wanted to keep it a surprise to gain whatever political advantage he could.

Luckily, Dwess was able to procure all the parts he needed. Without him it would have been impossible to do what Kallen had done in less than a week. The Jerozny ion coil, which he figured would be readily available, wasn't. Despite it being a common component, they were in short supply. Dwess had two shipped from another base. Kallen had him order two more as spares. His friendship with Dwess had provided him with more clout than he ever suspected it would.

The next morning, shortly before lunch, Kallen walked over to Avionics section to see Acton. He ushered Kallen into his office.

"Your vidstation's not working?"

"No, it works just fine. I wanted to personally tell you that I'm done with both pallets. I sent the completed work order to your section a few minutes ago."

"Are you serious?" Acton was wide-eyed.

Kallen nodded.

Acton waved his hand over his vidstation's screen, activating it. He spoke to it and moments later the work order appeared onscreen. He studied the repaired item list.

"The pallets should be on your dock by this time, too. I saw them leave my section."

"I'll be damned. I owe you a dinner. You're better than I thought. Way better." He developed an infectious smile which made Kallen return one, too.

Acton was looking at him the same way Dayler used to. Just before they'd kiss.

Chapter 4

Tuesday, October 5, 2478

Kallen noted that despite the rules against fraternization, Acton was willing to bend that one and take him out for his promised dinner.

Kallen met him at a hoverbus stop just outside the east entrance to base. When Acton pulled up, Kallen jumped in the car and they sped along the mountainous hoverlane toward Estes Park about twenty-five kilometers away. There were only a couple of decent restaurants there, according to Acton. He was taking Kallen to the nicest one.

"So, you live off base, huh?" Kallen asked, as he took in the car's nice interior.

"Yep. Officer's Housing Complex D. It's just a couple of kilometers up the road."

"How long have you been at ESC?"

"Two and a half years. I re-upped here."

"Going out with anyone?"

Kallen couldn't help asking that one. Several clues about Acton's sexuality had been stacking up. He could almost Dwess whispering in his ear: *All is not as it appears*. Kallen was starting to have his suspicions that Acton might be gay. There was something sensual about the way they interacted. It was something he hadn't felt from anyone else except Tiago and Dayler. Several times he had caught Acton checking him out in the gym locker room. The last time it happened Acton smiled broadly at him. When Acton spoke to him, he was usually a little 'too close'. Then he visited him in his office the other day it was as if the air-conditioning had ceased functioning. Their interaction could only be described as 'hot'. He'd already established that Acton wasn't married. As far as he could tell, too, since Acton never mentioned any women in his life, he might not be going out with one either. He wanted to make sure about that last item, thus the reason he was so bold.

"No. I don't have time."

"Oh," Kallen said. *Put another checkmark in the 'yes' column,* he thought.

Acton glanced his way, grinned, watched the hoverlane, then glanced over at him again. Kallen had been watching the hoverlane, too, and noticed that Acton looked his way again after responding. His suspicion was growing.

Dinner was spectacular. Acton, of course, made a lot more money than Kallen did. More than just returning a favor, Acton had treated him to a lavish meal. It was complete with the finest bottled water and a huge piece of chocolate-lemon mousse cake which Kallen only mentioned in passing when he saw it on the dessert section of the menu earlier.

Kallen slid the last bite of cake in his mouth and placed the fork on the empty plate. "You know, all I did was repair that equipment. Why the nice meal? We could have had a soy burger."

"I like you way too much for a soy burger, Kal."

Kallen immediately noted that Acton used his nickname. He'd never done that before. Acton's tone of voice indicated he felt an intimacy he'd not expressed before, too.

"Kal?" Kallen asked.

Acton nodded as his eyebrows went up.

The restaurant was darkly lit. There were no other officers nearby, at least ones that Kallen might have recognized. Acton had already mentioned that he didn't recognize a single person he knew or worked with. Apparently, that made him feel bold.

Kallen's heart started to pound. *Is this what I think it is?* "Uh, do you have a nickname you want me to use?"

"When we get back to my place you can call me anything you want."

"Your place?" Kallen's pulse started racing. *It is! He* is *coming on to me!* "Are you sure you want me there?"

"Positive. Ever since I met you that day in the gym I've been waiting for this night. Dinner with you. Taking you back to my place. Kissing you. More."

Kallen whispered. "Holy shit, you *are* gay."

Acton touched Kallen's foot with his under the table. "So, you knew. Took you long enough to say it."

"Duh. I can tell my own." Immediately, he felt his penis spring to action. Acton's overt moves were just what he needed. "Uh, let's 'see' your place. I'm pretty much a loaded weapon right now."

Acton's face lit right up. "I was hoping you'd say that." He immediately called for the check.

Acton's quarters was a spacious downside loft, with a covered surface deck that faced the mountains to the east. Kallen never got to the deck after his short tour of the space.

They slowly undressed each other by the bed. Kallen wasn't kidding about being a loaded weapon. He was hard as a rock well before his skivvies hit the floor.

Acton was deliberately slow in his actions. He was being thoroughly romantic. He had even lit a couple of candles for the occasion. Kallen had never had sex with lit candles before.

They sat on their knees in his bed and felt up each other's naked bodies. Acton made growling sounds as Kallen ran his hands over Acton's skin. Kallen drew in deep sharp breaths each time Acton touched him below the waist. His balls had drawn up tight against his groin. His penis was pulsing noticeably, erect and firm, as Acton touched it with just his fingertips. Kallen could barely stand the delay. He wanted to discharge his weapon in a big way. Acton was keeping the inevitable at bay.

Acton fell backward and Kallen collapsed on top of him. With their arms wrapped around each other, Kallen humped against Acton's abdomen, using their sweat as lubrication. They both came at the same time, making quite a sticky mess between their bodies, and breathing heavily and loudly in each other's ears as they continued to hump each other, all while holding the other tightly. Kallen wouldn't let him go, even as their semen began to liquefy. Exhausted from what seemed like a deliberately extended workout, Kallen finally unwrapped himself and sat with his legs underneath himself.

Acton reached his hand out and fiddled with Kallen's still-hard penis for a moment. "Now, that's a workout. We'll have to do this often. You don't mind, do you?"

"An officer and an AT having sex? Isn't that going to be a problem?"

Acton reached over and pulled a towel from a side table drawer. He wiped his belly up then pressed his hand against Kallen's chest. Kallen sank backward into the pillows.

"Not unless you tell someone."

He wiped Kallen up. Kallen had gotten limp, but at Acton's touch, he quickly stirred to full attention once again. "Looks like you need another set." He moistened Kallen's penis with his tongue and began to bob up and down on it.

Acton's tongue was so warm and skillful that it wasn't more than four minutes later before he was unloading a second round, this time into his mouth. Kallen's hairless chest was heaving up and down while Acton relentlessly continued. Kallen thought he would pass out from one of the most intense orgasms he'd ever had.

Acton pulled open the drawer of the nightstand again and took out a small tube of lube. He applied it to his rear end, then to Kallen's penis, which was still erect. He straddled Kallen's middle and slowly sank down on it. It wasn't long before he was working himself up and down in a steady rhythm. Kallen grasped Acton's penis and pumped as Acton flexed his thighs. In another moment he unloaded several volleys, some of it splashing Kallen's neck. Kallen thought he might actually come again but Acton had stopped his piston action. Slowly, he pulled himself upward. Kallen's penis, still glistening with lube, flopped out onto his belly.

Acton' rolled over onto his side. "God, I haven't felt like this in a long time." He pulled Kallen's head toward him and started kissing him.

Having been pushed almost to the edge of a third orgasm but not having it, Kallen felt incredibly horny. He kissed back with equal passion. *Wow*. He'd been on base hardly six weeks and already he'd met someone. This was becoming a very interesting duty station.

Before he left the next morning Acton told him that he wanted to see him again—and not just in the gym. Kallen was thrilled.

Kallen's reaction was short-lived. Acton's time-off schedule was very difficult to sync up with. And, although they continued to work out together Kallen found him to be increasingly aloof. Kallen kept making comments as they worked out about how much he enjoyed their first time together and how much he wanted to be with him. Acton kept ignoring them. It was beginning to bother Kallen.

Finally, at the end of the second week and after having had no contact except at the gym, Acton had Kallen come back to his quarters with him. He made a Japanese-style dinner which Kallen relished. He figured Dwess would be jealous. Dwess probably hadn't had an authentic home-cooked meal in a long time.

Then, from sundown to one in the morning they made love. Over and over Kallen found himself in ecstasy. He was so sated that by the time they fell asleep he wondered why Acton made him wait all this time.

They didn't get naked again for another two weeks. Again, Kallen found himself getting more and more frustrated at the length of time between their encounters. Kallen wanted more time with him.

That first night they had decided to forgo any electronic communications. It wouldn't do well if anyone found out that Kallen was spending time having casual conversations with an officer while in uniform, or vice versa. That made it doubly worse for him since he craved contact with Acton even if it were in a short vid.

Eventually, they began to see each other semi-regularly. After their infrequent liaisons Kallen found himself making comparisons between Dayler and Acton. Dayler had been loud. Acton was reserved. Dayler had wanted to be number one in everything. Acton didn't have a thing to prove. Dayler was enlisted. Acton was an officer. Dayler had told Kallen he was naïve. Acton hadn't mentioned it. In hindsight, Dayler seemed immature. Acton seemed more mature than most people he knew. Whereas Dayler and he had what amounted to a publicly announced relationship, his and Acton's was strictly a secret.

They continued with their workouts and kept their eyes off each other in the locker room. Kallen called him Lieutenant Racelis when he saw him in Avionics or when Acton came to Maintenance section, which was rarely. Eventually, although neither acknowledged it, they were officially in a relationship. And although their passion for each other burned at a steady pace Kallen found himself simmering with frustration. Perhaps it was because of the secret they had to keep. Perhaps it was the need for them to do other things besides go for short drives in the mountains, or the occasional dinner in Estes Park, or the steady diet of workouts where they pretended they only knew each other professionally. But Kallen knew he couldn't push the issue. If anyone had the slightest notion that Acton was in a relationship with a man, and an enlisted one at that, the punishment would be swift and harsh.

Despite the drawbacks, Kallen clung to the thought that things might turn around for them. Perhaps he'd be able to get quarters off-base and thus have his own place. Plenty of enlisteds lived off-base. All of them were married though, so the prospect seemed slim. Kallen also clung to the thought that he'd be able to see Acton a lot more often. Unfortunately, more time with him wasn't materializing.

The New Year's Eve party in the huge fighter jet hangar included most of the personnel in the squadron. It was in this environment that Kallen first saw Acton totally letting loose. He drank a lot, was animated beyond what Kallen thought was in him, and he danced with every girl he could find. Kallen had to wait over two months to see the party side of him? It seemed sad in a way.

That got Kallen to thinking. He hadn't asked Acton why he had re-upped. Why would anyone do that if they knew they were gay? It wasn't like a gay person could have any semblance of a normal life with a military career. He wondered if he should bother asking. But Kallen was sure of one thing. He had no intention of re-upping if he had to stay closeted about what he liked and who he was. What a bizarre time to have discovered his true nature, he thought, right when he had been drafted. It sucked. And slowly but surely he was noticing that the way he was conducting this relationship with Acton wasn't the healthiest way to live at all. Too many secrets all the time.

It was still forty-five minutes before the New Year. Acton met up with Kallen at the punchbowl.

"Hi Kal," he said with a big smile. No one heard him use his nickname as he refilled his cup.

"Hi! Having a good time?"

"Never better. I've, uh, been thinking about you."

Kallen looked around. "Who? Me?"

"Say, I, uh, need to take a leak. You know the heads over in the east wing?" Acton glanced in that direction.

"Yeah," Kallen replied with a grin.

"Meet me in two minutes."

"Are you serious?"

"Of course I'm serious." He glanced down at Kallen's crotch and licked his lips seductively.

Fuck, this is awesome, Kallen thought.

Kallen arrived less than a minute after Acton did. No one had seen him slip away. He arrived at the head completely undetected.

Acton pushed him into a stall where he proceeded to smother his face with kisses. It was thrilling as well as awkward in the confined space. Acton slid his hand down the front of Kallen's pants, felt his swelling hardness, then reached further down. Now he had Kallen's balls in his hand, cupped them, then slid his middle finger back and forth against his perineum. He tried to get it even further back but wasn't successful. Acton pulled his hand out and unbuttoned Kallen's pants. He slowly pulled the zipper down while staring into Kallen's eyes. After pulling Kallen's pants and skivvies down to his knees, he turned him around, bent him over, spread his cheeks apart, and proceeded to flick his tongue all over his hole. Kallen was sure someone would discover them, but they were well away from the revelers. Within five seconds he didn't care anyway. Acton's tongue, now poking into him too, had become his entire focus.

Acton's tongue from behind, his hand kneading Kallen's balls and stroking his rock hard penis, and the sheer excitement of this forbidden moment, made Kallen come much more quickly than he would have liked. It was all he could do to stifle his moans. Regardless, several slipped out. After he caught his breath, he listened. No one had entered. He turned around, fished Acton's penis out through his zipper, slathered it with saliva, and started sucking him.

Although he stayed hard, Acton didn't come. He had had too much alcohol. After a good five minutes of sucking, then realizing Acton wasn't going to come, Kallen stopped and just stroked his well-moistened penis. Kallen was a little disappointed, but Acton didn't seem to mind.

Despite still being hard, Acton stuffed his penis back into his pants. "God, that felt great," he told Kallen. Acton raised his watch to his face. "Shit. Look." It was just a few minutes before midnight. "We gotta get back."

With that, they zipped up and buttoned everything, then checked themselves in the mirror. They hugged with much passion and Acton left. Kallen waited a full minute before he left the head and rejoined the crowd, too.

Although separated by peer groups, Acton looked Kallen's way several times, each time winking at him. Kallen winked back and they rang in 2479 amidst much noisemaking.

Their exciting, albeit covert, rendezvous in the hangar receded into the past. The warm embrace Kallen had gotten from Acton before they rejoined the New Years revelers became a distant memory as the days went by. The first couple of weeks of January became the same old routine of work and too many days between their liaisons. Kallen longed for something adventurous like their hot New Years Eve meeting, but realized it was a fluke that had even happened at all.

Everyone in the military was offered higher education. That way if they decided to stay in and had received their degree at the end of their initial five-year stint they could opt for officer training. That's how Acton had gotten his commission. Shortly after arriving on base Kallen had enrolled in one of the local on-line universities and signed up for a degree in Photronics. It was completely self-paced. With the virtual professors giving the lessons it was easy to recreate an environment similar to a classroom. Kallen staved off boredom by diving into his studies. So far he had only been taking preliminary classes. If he kept at a steady pace from now on he was sure he'd be able to complete his degree just about the time he reached his end of active service date. He didn't let Acton know he had no intention of re-upping.

Three weeks and a day after the New Year, Acton told Kallen that he had more time and that he wanted to see him at least twice a week. His free time was

Kallen's. Kallen jumped at the chance for them to be together more often. He couldn't wait to feel his comfortable bed again, experience the romantic way he acted when they were alone, and the dinners. Ah, the dinners at his place. Acton was an extraordinary cook.

In February, even though Kallen's birthday was only two days before Valentine's Day, Acton made a special effort to celebrate both days with equal gusto. Kallen turned twenty. Two weeks later Acton turned twenty-five. Shortly thereafter, their relationship reached the six month mark, although Kallen could barely add up thirty days of actually being together. Time at the gym didn't count since none of it was personal.

During this time Acton threw his weight around and pressured Maintenance section to promote Kallen. He ensured Kallen got most of the Avionics work. Kallen made sure Avionics equipment was the first thing off his workbench, or out of the Maintenance bay immediately after it was repaired. In working order, of course. Acton made an equally concerted effort to let everyone of importance know how valuable Kallen was.

The second week in April Kallen was granted a meritorious promotion to Sergeant Technician, well in advance of normal time-in-grade. It was an excuse for Acton to slather Kallen with attention once again. Kallen loved every moment of it. Even though he didn't get a lot of time with his boyfriend, at least Acton made up for it with his attention to details. Still, Kallen wondered how long they could keep up a relationship like this. The restrictions on their time, their rank, and the sheer fact that they couldn't be seen together in public were burdensome. Regardless, Kallen resolved to ignore it and continue to enjoy what was there for him. What little he felt he had.

Chapter 5

Monday, May 29, 2479

An ancient dented bronze plaque attached to a cairn of rocks at one of the entrances to ESC stated that the valley was once called the Rocky Mountain National Park. It was dated 1977. Over five hundred years ago. Kallen had seen it once and was sure it had been salvaged from some other place. The plaque had a short description of the area and why it had been set aside as a park. It described nothing like the environs he knew here. Regardless, Eastern Strategic Command was the best duty station, mostly because of the interesting geography of the region and its choice location so high in the mountains; the surface temperatures being reasonable most of the year.

Not so for the Lake Superior pipeline re-pumping station located several kilometers below them and a hundred to the east in the dusty town of Fort Morgan. The re-pumping station had been active for over two hundred twenty years.

The town had been abandoned by the civilian population centuries ago. For nine months out of the year the surface temperature hovered between forty-nine and fifty-six degrees. The rest of the time it was a balmy thirty-nine or so. Now, the limited inhabited space was below the surface—like most of the world Kallen knew.

Four days ago a mysterious explosion had rocked Fort Morgan. Kallen heard about it during a breakfast newsvid. If the station quit pumping water it would mean several million deaths in as little as two months.

Later that morning, after his arrival at work, special orders were given to select personnel in Operations Squadron. Kallen discovered quite abruptly that he would be involved in a rescue and recovery mission at Fort Morgan. It was highly unusual since his duties so far had been to repair only ESC equipment. He was nonetheless selected because of his unique knowledge. His specific duty was to assist some of the other technicians in any way he could to get the photronics equipment at the facility back on-line as quickly as possible.

Ninety-eight hours later they sat inside the air transport on the flight line just outside of Fort Morgan waiting for clearance to return to ESC. Kallen had barely slept in the last four days. He had fallen asleep in the comfortable padded seat within five minutes of buckling his seatbelt. As they climbed upward on their way back to Eastern Strategic Command he was dreaming about water. This wasn't the first time he had dreamed about it. Cool, crystal clear water splashing over his head, lying in a field of tall green grass, under a cloudy gray sky, cool rain running down his face, his neck, his chest, soaking his dusty clothes….

The transport hit an air pocket within minutes of liftoff and woke him. He stretched out his legs, lifted his cap, and took a brief look around. To his left out the ovoid window was clear blue sky and the Front Range in the distance. When he pressed his nose up to the window he could see two HeavyAir Y-78 equipment transports up ahead. To his right sat Dwess. He was out cold. He hadn't slept much either. They all had been on non-stop go, sorting, salvaging, and crating up what they could of the equipment that hadn't been damaged in the blast. He had discovered he didn't need to get anything online at all. The pumping station had only sustained minor damage and everything was still functioning. On the other hand, a nearby facility had sustained heavy damage. It was impossible to bring anything there back online. In fact, he had been told that his doing so was out of the question.

Kallen reached down to his hip and unsnapped the holster that held his vidPAD, pulled the halves apart, and activated the holoscreen. He poked the tiny removable earpiece into his ear and whispered so he wouldn't disturb Dwess. Something didn't add up about what they'd been doing this last four days. He was bothered by the air of secrecy that had dampened his enthusiasm for this special ops mission. He intended to go over some of the records they'd generated.

"System. Access database. Text mode response."

The vidPAD displayed text that appeared to be floating in space several centimeters above the flat plane of the device. "Ready," it stated.

"Fort Morgan disaster."

Immediately the display returned clusters of icons: about two-dozen shortcuts to video and text that had been recorded on-site by the recovery crew.

Dwess stirred then opened his eyes. He craned his neck to look at Kallen's display. "Four days of this wasn't good enough for you, huh?"

"It's still bothering me."

"It's just equipment and a bunch of dead bodies. Be glad no one you knew was burned up." Kallen had previously discussed his concern with him about the secrecy involved with this 'rescue' mission—which turned out to be a recovery mission only—after the second day there. He expected to see water flowing all over the open desert or to see a shambles of the pumping station. He saw nothing like that. In fact, what they saw was a series of downside buildings well away from the station. The turbines were perfectly intact. The pipelines were all still secure in their concrete casements. And the weirdest part was that the disaster had taken place in facilities that weren't documented in any official database.

Most of the facilities they had been involved with were totally destroyed. Many of the floors had collapsed in on themselves, spilling hot dry topside earth inward, covering over a lot of what had happened. Kallen noticed that no one from their squadron was allowed to view the bodies pulled from the accessible sub-levels. Black Guard had been stationed in perimeters as security. By the dozens. That was very odd. They were in the desert and still well within the NAA's eastern border. The need for this much security wasn't at all clear to Kallen.

But there was more.

Although they had come in low on the HeavyAirs, and later, had been on the surface only after dusk, there was clear evidence that the explosions hadn't originated from downside. Kallen was sure that what he saw were bomb blasts. Craters. Concave craters. He could swear a strike of some sort had come from above. He had direct evidence that what they were told about the facility wasn't reality. Dwess' lesson of being suspicious of the 'official' word had given him a new eye. Dwess had taken note of the evidence, too, but had had little comment about it so far.

"Something's just not right about this," Kallen told him.

Dwess leaned in to him so he could whisper. "Deshara, there are times when you should be suspicious about things, but this isn't one of them. Put that away before someone realizes you're trying to fit this puzzle together."

Kallen glanced over at him, not believing he'd so easily give up on a mystery like this.

"Really, give it a rest until we get back. You can do all your checking then. I can't believe you're not tired."

"I was asleep until we hit that turbulence." He pushed the two halves of his vidPAD together, thumbed it off, and shoved it back into its holster.

It took two hours after they landed back on base before Kallen and the rest of the recovery crew were processed out of the hangar. The landing crew had already taken charge of the recovered equipment that he had helped packed in crates. The hangar he was in, which looked like a huge sloped berm, had few windows from the downside corridor. Kallen stood at one of them and eyed the hospital plane still out on the tarmac beyond the huge maw-like hangar entrance. Finally, it pulled into the hangar. It had the last of the charred bodies in it. There seemed to be quite a few of them, too.

The odd nature of the operation was still nagging at him. What had really happened out there? Why did the newsvids report that the pumping station had suffered an explosion when clearly that wasn't the case? Where were the news crews while they were there? He had not seen a single reporter. Why did the Black Guard insist that the entire recovery crew stay in that confined area when they had completed each day's recovery efforts? No communication had been allowed back to base either. Network access to BaseNet had been completely disabled. That meant that even when he had some downtime in the evening he couldn't even catch up on his lessons. He'd forgotten to download them to his vidPAD before they left.

Dwess tapped him on the shoulder, breaking Kallen's reverie. Kallen turned around. Standing there with him were the bleary-eyed faces of ST Jost from Warehousing, and ATs Gailsben and Gressler, both from his section. Dwess' voice was a whisper. "We're gonna fire up some you-know-what after we get some sleep. Wanna come by, say, 1900 hours?"

Nowadays, Kallen was never one to pass up a bowl of root. He grunted. "Of course."

"See ya then." As they turned to go, Kallen looked at his watch. That gave him four and a half hours. He turned back to the window. The wide low doors to the hot outside air were shutting. The hospital HeavyAir with its charred remains of the dead was being wheeled to a little-used section of the huge hangar. Partitions were being closed around it even now. They were high enough to completely obscure his view.

Kallen took the shuttle to their housing section with the rest of them. Once in his room he shed his clothes, put them in the ultrasonic cleaner, took a quick lukewarm shower, then lay on his bed. It had been four days and he was ready to explode. In seconds he was hard. He did explode. All over his belly and chest. After wiping himself up, he set his alarm and almost immediately nodded off on top of the sheet in the cool of his room.

Later, Kallen gave the usual two knocks, a pause, then another knock on Dwess' door. It opened and he stepped in. There were three others there besides him.

"Where's Jost?" Kallen asked after he pulled a bottle out of the little refrigerator. As if on cue there was the obligatory knock. Dwess pulled open the door again. As Jost closed it, Dwess motioned for him to lock it.

Jost pulled up a chair while Dwess retrieved his pipe and little tube of halpa root and brought it to the table. He dumped the root onto a thin metal plate that Gressler produced from his pants pocket. A moment later he was cutting pieces off with a little pocketknife. He lit the first bowl and passed the pipe around.

Kallen took a good long toke and passed it. Gressler handed Kallen a slice of pizza. He devoured it since he had missed dinner hours in the mess hall, then pulled another slice from the box.

As the evening progressed, the music got louder and Dwess fired up his selection of 3-D vid games.

Gailsben was a dark-skinned lanky guy of African descent, and a year older than Kallen. He was the friendliest guy in Maintenance section and Kallen enjoyed hanging out with him. They decided to play a traditional game of Dice-Mac.

The topic of conversation came back around to Senior Airman Ruiz as it sometimes did. "I'm not kidding. Takeda says he's boinking her," Gailsben whispered as he picked up the dice cup. Kallen watched the dice as he dumped them out onto the game board.

"He's busting your balls," Kallen told him.

"I saw a vid she sent him. She was, uh, you know, telling him how much she enjoyed their last 'date'."

Kallen looked up at him. "You're shittin' me." He tallied up the numbers then looked back at the board where his game piece was. "Dice-Mac. That round's mine."

Gailsben shook his head while Kallen slid the scrips to his side of the table. Kallen took up the cup and shook the dice after anteing up.

"Ask him yourself," Gailsben said as he slid his ante up scrip to the middle of the board.

Dwess had his virtual gaming glasses on. He and Jost were engaged in a wicked sword fight in the center of the room. Kallen had adopted Dwess's game persona once before, playing against the computer that time. Paladin Wolfram was a persona that Kallen knew Dwess really was. The persona who protested, the one who stood up for truth and justice, the one who questioned everything and everyone.

"He's busy fending off Jost The Slayer," Kallen said.

"It's more than boinking though. They're going out."

Kallen had wanted to pursue the mess about Fort Morgan with Dwess. But now he didn't know if he should with the other guys around. Dwess would probably not want to tell him about Mirani either. He'd been involved with both her and Dwess so sporadically for the last several months that it might seem a little odd if he just up and asked him about her.

Could it be true though? They were in a relationship now? And right under his nose?

Chapter 6

Friday, June 2, 2479

It was almost a week after his return from the Fort Morgan recovery mission. Kallen and Acton were eating a light dinner at the kitchen counter. Both were in just their skivvies, though Kallen had his socks on, too. It was after sundown and the sconces on the wall behind them were casting a soft, warm glow in the room. Several candles were lit as well. Kallen had discovered that Acton loved them.

"I think some of the guys are starting to suspect something's going on," Kallen told him.

A fleeting look of fear flashed across Acton's face. "I hope you're not being followed."

Kallen shook his head. "No way. It's just that a couple of my buddies know I leave the base on Friday nights. I never tell them where, of course. Maybe it's because they see me with a smile on my face on Mondays. I'm sure they suspect I've got some poon on the side or something."

The soy drink Acton was swallowing nearly jettisoned out of his nose as he laughed explosively. "I haven't heard that word in a while. Are you calling my ass poon?"

"I'm calling *you* poon."

"Careful. I outrank you."

"Not when I'm inside you." Acton would have Kallen make love to him as slowly as possible every time they got back together after their long hiatuses.

"You're right." He blew his nose, then took another bite, grinning the whole time.

Kallen looked down at Acton's lap. The slit in the front of his skivvies was opened in a diamond shape, exposing part of his penis. It mesmerized him. Just a half hour before, its full hard length was in his mouth and he was reveling in the heady taste of Acton's semen. He couldn't wait to have another helping and decided it would be a great dessert. *It's almost as good as chocolate-lemon mousse cake*, he thought.

"What've they been saying?" Acton asked.

"They're just razzing me about this unknown lady I'm seeing. I've been avoiding it though. I don't need them getting any clues."

"Hmm. Maybe we should, uh, tone it down a little, huh?"

"Tone it down? We hardly see each other as it is." Kallen tried to reassure him that he had never come in contact with anyone near Acton's off-base building complex. In fact, he found it a bit odd that he had never even seen Acton's next door neighbor. "Mirani's the one I'm worried about though. I hate having to avoid her."

"Mirani?"

"Senior Airman Ruiz."

"Oh, her."

"She's my friend but I've been avoiding her a lot. We used to do stuff together. She probably thinks I hate her or something."

"Well, if we cooled things down everyone would be happy."

Kallen stopped chewing. "What are you saying?"

"Less chance of people finding out about us."

"I *like* coming here." Kallen didn't like this kind of talk at all. If there was more time apart from each other would mean even fewer tasty meals, or sleeping over, or the really great sex—as sparse as it was anyway. He had had no idea he liked to cuddle before, but Acton did, and that's how Kallen discovered he liked it, too. He used to just stay up for hours with Tiago and Dayler and do it over and over again. They never bothered to cuddle.

"Remember when we first met and you got all that equipment fixed for me?" Acton asked.

"Sure."

"Remember how you said 'everyone wins' or something like that?"

"Yeah."

"This may be one of those situations."

What the hell is he getting at? "Do you want me to leave?"

Acton touched Kallen's shoulder then squeezed his arm. "Of course not." He dropped his hand, then picked up Kallen's empty plate, stacked it on his, and moved them to the counter by the sink.

Relieved at that, yet still disturbed by Acton's statements, Kallen told him another story. "Mirani has this female friend of hers she's been hanging out with a lot nowadays. I was in the BX tonight just before I took the shuttle. That's when I saw them. I made sure they left before I did. I avoided her. I actually avoided her. I hate doing that. I work with her. I used to eat lunch with her all the time. I was so paranoid seeing her there that I didn't want her to see me."

"Why were you avoiding her?"

"I don't know. Maybe it's because I'm afraid she'd ask me where I was going or what I was up to, or something."

Acton leaned on the counter and knitted his brow. His legs were crossed. The diamond-shaped opening had completely disappeared. "You just added another reason why we should cool it down."

Kallen could have kicked himself. He never should have said that. He was only telling Acton how bad he felt, but it had only added fuel to the odd way Acton was handling the discussion.

"Shit," Kallen said aloud.

"Shit what?"

"Nothing."

Kallen watched him put the dishes in the dishwasher. He was still feeling bad about having divulged that. But when Acton dried his hands off and took Kallen's hand leading him to the soft carpeted floor in front of his couch, Kallen forgot all about what he'd said. He felt hornier tonight than he had in weeks. It was the proximity of the hard, masculine Acton, the way they didn't bother to properly dress for dinner, the knowledge that there would be more of what had come earlier, waiting until they'd filled their bellies with food first.

After they were done on the floor, and rested, they finally got up, fell into bed, and slept until Acton woke several hours later. With a great big smile Kallen yielded to his touch, turned over, and took him inside himself, feeling happy that he would be satisfied again before morning light. Acton was like a slow burning torch, always lit, always needing more sex to fuel his fire.

It was almost nightfall on Sunday before Kallen left, bleary-eyed, on the last shuttle of the day. Acton told him he wanted to see him again soon but didn't plan a date.

Kallen only saw him once at the gym during the week on Wednesday. He had hoped Acton's odd affect the Friday before had just been talk. But it wasn't.

Acton had somehow shifted from being carefree to his original aloof self. Regardless, he got an invitation to come over the next Friday. Kallen wasn't sure what was going on. Their conversation at the gym had been furtive, stilted, halting. Maybe Acton was losing interesting in him? Maybe there was someone else he had his eye on now? Kallen wasn't sure. But their relationship had taken a new turn. It was with a certain melancholy that he realized their time together was back to the way it had been originally: days between get-togethers, long silences, and little communication.

* * * *

Ever since his initial discussions with Dwess, Kallen had been interested in breaking through the security protocols that were configured on BaseNet. Now that he and Acton were no longer seeing each other with the same regularity as before he used that time to develop his hacking skills. Whenever he took a break from his online school lessons he switched screens and worked on breaking through the switches and routers that protected BaseNet from unauthorized access. Up until now he'd been accessing the standard data objects he had permissions to from his room vidstation. Now that he had more time he dove right in. It was a good way to divert his attention from how he was feeling. Just as Kallen decided to take a break, there was a knock at his door. It was Dwess.

Kallen went to unlock it, then ushered him in.

"I thought you were still here. Aren't you supposed to be off banging your girl?"

Kallen's eyebrows went up as he closed and re-locked the door. It was the first time Dwess had ever mentioned that. "I can't fuck all the time."

"I never thought I'd say this, Deshara, but I'm jealous of you. You weren't here like, what, two month, and you were already up to your eyeballs in pussy."

"Yeah, *you* jealous."

"Decent girls are hard to come by."

"What are you talking about? I thought you were going out with Mirani." He was fishing, since he already knew about it from his conversation with Gailsben.

"You'd know more about all that if you hung out with us—like you used to. So, what's her name?"

"I'm not gonna talk about that."

"I figured as much. You haven't talked about her at all."

Kallen sat back down at his vidstation. "Some things are best left unspoken and unknown."

Dwess realized he wasn't going to get Kallen to talk.

Kallen didn't know that and quickly changed the subject. "So, have you investigated our little mystery?"

"What mystery?"

"The Fort Morgan disaster."

"Of course. I've done some preliminary investigating, but haven't turned up anything yet. I've got a couple of leads though. If I turn up anything good I might let you know." He pulled up a chair and scooted it over a little more so he could check out the vidscreen. He feigned a look of surprise. "My, my. Looks like you're doing some investigating of your own."

Kallen waved his hand over the screen and it went black.

Dwess feigned being offended. "Hey, just 'cause I see stuff on your screen you shouldn't be looking at, doesn't mean that I can't help you."

"Help me?"

"You think I haven't tried to get around those security protocols?"

"I should have known you'd at least try." He waved his hand again and the screen faded back in.

"I'm not very good at hacking," Dwess added. "I just mess around." He pointed to the screen. "What's that object there?"

A vidstation could be set up to view local and remote objects either in text, representational, or virtual reality formats. Kallen was using a local enhanced virtual shell to view the data objects.

"Stealth Around," he replied.

"That's seriously illegal. Where'd you get it?"

"I have a friend who sends me encrypted software on occasion." Kallen received this one on a data crystal a few weeks ago from one of his high school buddies. This was only his second attempt at using it.

Dwess looked at the other stealth access tools Kallen was using and spent the next half hour observing as Kallen repeatedly tried to get past through a router. He failed every time.

Finally, Dwess had had enough. "This stuff is way over my head. You have fun, huh?" He slid his hand into his pocket, then up a bit. Out peeked the mouth end of a pipe. "You wanna take a hit with me back in my room? That's why I came by."

"Nah. You go ahead."

"You used to beg to have a hit."

"I can't think when I'm high."

"No one's supposed to think when they're high. You know where to find me if you change your mind." With that, he slipped out of the room pulling the door shut behind him. Kallen rose up and quickly locked it again.

The sudden silence was an odd companion after the last half hour of talking. He went back to his chair and looked at the seven colored icons on the screen. The problem he was facing was that although the software he was using had stripped his vidstation of logon identification packets, the routers were totally locked down with protocols he'd never seen before. If he could figure out a way to bypass them or get through them, he was sure he'd be able to get past any router on BaseNet. The stealth software he was using didn't have that capability. It wasn't designed to handle layer after layer of added security found on military networks. He shut the vidstation down.

He looked at the clock. It was just past 2100 hours. Dwess had just left. *I guess I'll join him.*

Chapter 7

Saturday, June 10, 2479

Kallen was sitting with Acton at the counter adjacent to his small, nicely tiled kitchen. The morning sunlight was brightening the mushroom-shaped lens on his rooftop deck, which in turn was bathing them in ever brighter light from the diffuser overhead.

Kallen swallowed a mouthful of juice and put the glass down. Something had been bothering Acton after he checked his vidmails before breakfast this morning. Something in Acton's voice told him that he was holding something back.

"You heard about what happened yesterday, didn't you?" Acton finally asked.

"Yeah, what about it," Kallen asked haltingly. Kallen knew exactly what he was referring to. During lunch the day before he had watched the short base newsvid about the incident.

Acton stood up and tied his robe even tighter. "It's getting dangerous on base. Especially now, with the UCT…with what's going on at the lake."

Kallen was well aware of what was happening there, too. He had the official word and the unofficial speculation running through his head simultaneously. Supposedly, the UCT was becoming increasingly miffed about the amount of water being drawn from the lake. In typical NAA fashion, diplomacy was non-existent. Under the pretext of renovations, one thousand extra National Ground Patrol troops, all from ESC, had recently been sent to the base in Duluth. The base was adjacent to the pumping station. More troops were scheduled to ship out in the next week or so. The UCT protested, questioning why so many troops were needed for so-called routine maintenance of the station. Kallen was sure that the official word about renovations was a convenient cover so that the arrival of extra troops and supplies wouldn't appear so threatening.

Kallen's frequent talks with Dwess had turned him into a skeptic. He was questioning things much more frequently nowadays—even if only to himself most of the time. *It's almost as if Dwess is a UCT operative from the way he talks sometimes*, Kallen thought. He constantly used words like 'caution' and phrases like 'what's the real story' and 'why don't you dig deeper'. So, Kallen questioned each article or newsvid. Dwess was infinitely more nonconformist in his thinking than Kallen. It was still a struggle for Kallen not to trust the establishment that had always made him feel secure. But now he was thinking differently about a lot of things. He and Dwess had even discussed at length why the base was on Alert Status Two, one step away from war alert. Massing troops in Duluth was like stirring an anthill—a UCT anthill.

He only broached those topics with Dwess. Certainly not with Acton. But Acton wasn't concerned as much about the water treaty issue as with the specifically more significant base news vid.

"Dangerous?" Kallen asked him. He couldn't help but get angry right away. "What are you talking about? We weren't the ones caught."

"We could be next, Kal," he lowered his voice. "You know that."

Two enlisted Avionics Airmen, named Lang and Dolan, had been caught by a surveillance camchip in one the sublevel stairways of the hangar where most of the Avionics personnel worked—including Acton. Lang and Dolan had been kissing there. Homosexual activity of any kind was forbidden by the ADF and resulted in immediate brig time, then an eventual court-martial. All of their associates would be investigated, too. Maybe not right away, but it would eventually happen. Lang and Dolan got caught because they were stupid. Kallen knew a camchip could be put just about anywhere. If they'd been smart they'd have known to scan the stairwell with a camchip detector. Although microscopic in size, camchips emitted a very weak signal, anywhere from 118.644 to 118.737 GHz. They were impossible to identify without a detector. Yet, those two guys were foolish not to know one was on every level of the stairwell.

Kallen took a deep breath and felt a familiar lurch in his belly. That hadn't happened in a while. Here was the man he felt so comfortable with, and it was happening again. His stomach then started pounding nails into his middle. He couldn't eat another bite. "Fuck, Acton. They got caught 'cause they were careless."

"The slightest evidence makes a case." Acton started for the kitchen.

"D-did you know about them. That-that they're gay?" Kallen asked, trying to get him to talk it out.

"They don't report directly to me. But they do, or rather did, report to my NCOIC."

Kallen was intently watching him. Acton was clearly nervous. He started to do little things like wiping the counter where there was no mess and straightening things that were already in order.

"Acton…" Kallen said as the pain in his stomach eased up. He was going to tell him that since Acton didn't have direct contact with the two men that he was under no threat of investigation. It just wasn't going to happen. He didn't get to finish. Acton cut him off.

"I think we should break it off. Now."

There. Just like that. Like their relationship meant nothing.

Kallen should have realized it would end up like this. All these months, stretched out like eternity, and now it ended just like that.

"But, Acton…" He sounded pitiful.

"Sergeant Deshara, I think you should get dressed."

Kallen felt hollow inside when he heard that. Acton had never pulled rank on him in private, but right there Kallen knew he meant it.

Kallen got up and went to the bedroom. Everything was in slow motion. He dropped the shorts he was wearing onto the floor and kicked them into the corner. They were Acton's anyway.

Acton stayed in the kitchen as Kallen gathered his things from the bathroom. After Kallen finished dressing he went back to the dining room with his bag and set it on one of the chairs. He could tell Acton wasn't happy about what he had done. He had a look on his face like he didn't want to give away his real feelings.

Kallen looked at his plate. He hadn't finished his toast. His glass of juice was still half full. He wanted to touch Acton, to hold him, to tell him that everything would be okay. But he didn't. He wanted to so badly, but knew he didn't dare try to tell him he was wrong. Perhaps he'd be able to reconcile with him later on.

Kallen left without saying a word.

The topside shuttle ran back to base every forty-five minutes. He got to it just seconds before it pulled up to the stop near Acton's quarters. It usually took only fifteen minutes to get to his stop by the gate on base. That morning it seemed like it took fifteen hours. When he got back to his room, he inserted his keycard and the door quietly opened.

He dropped his bag near the door, slowly pushed the door shut, then sat on the bed in total silence, wondering if life was going to be this way forever. He craved being in a relationship, yet was scared to death that they would all end in the blink of an eye. Just like it had now for the third time. *The third fucking time!*

He began to wonder if society was right after all. Maybe being gay was just going to make him unhappy. But how could he change what he was? He had no choice in the matter. Being gay was a part of him, not something he could choose or un-choose. Why did his country despise gays? Why was their society designed to keep gay people hidden away? Why was the military so terrified about something they were incapable of screening out? Why did Acton feel threatened by disclosure—he was perfectly safe.

Kallen wondered why his life had to be punctuated with periodic despair. As he thought about all of it, he followed the ebb and flow of the waves of pain that squeezed his stomach with an invisible grip.

Damn him. Damn Acton Racelis.

No. Lieutenant Racelis. No more would it be Acton. Ever. He fell back on the bed and hugged one of his pillows, letting tears spill from the corners of his eyes. He cried because of the sense of inequality he felt. He cried because it wasn't fair. He was relationship material. He was sure of it. But he kept choosing incorrectly. How was he ever going to find the love he was searching for? The sadness that filled his soul overflowed just as the tears did.

He felt so sick the next day that he spent most of it lying in bed. It took all day for his stomach to feel better. When he showed up for work the day after, Mirani immediately knew something was wrong with him. She gave him a questioning look, but their friendship had been cool these last months so she didn't ask for an explanation.

Kallen noticed her eyeing him several times. He knew she suspected something. Something emotional. He wanted to tell her he still liked her, he really did. But he knew if he started that way he'd end up telling her much more than he intended. This wasn't something he could share with just anyone. Mirani had her illusions about him just as everyone else did.

A few minutes before lunchtime, Mirani strolled over to his workbench. She observed the many pieces and parts that were scattered all over it. She noted that his usually organized work area was in complete disarray. It was obvious from the forms he had been filling out all morning, too. She had to redo most of them before she could forward his work to the completed queue.

"You're going to lunch with me," she said.

He looked up at her. "I'm not hungry."

"Today you are. Look." She pointed to the clock on his vidstation screen. "Lunchtime."

She wasn't angry at all. She was trying to cheer him up.

"Alright," he told her. He put down the laser solder, pulled the speaker-mic from his ear, then pressed a key to lock his workstation.

They found a table away from the rest of the usual lunch crowd in the mess hall.

"Okay, Deshara. Don't BS me. You were in love and she dumped you. I know I'm right. Now tell me about it."

"How did you know?" he answered with downcast eyes.

"Be serious. Do you think I didn't know why you've been going off base all these months?"

He must have been more obvious than he suspected. Maybe Acton was right after all. If they had been carrying on for any longer maybe they would've been next in line for a court-martial. Perhaps the goodly amount of time away from each other helped keep at bay any suspicions about them being together after all. He slumped down in the chair. He smelled her faint perfume and saw her crinkle her face in that familiar way. She was still his friend. *Thank God*, he thought.

"Spill it," she said.

Kallen modified everything as he spoke. Acton was Isha. Off-base housing was the south side of Estes Park—a dumpy part of town. Everything had been going along just fine. For no apparent reason Isha was just no longer interested in him. He didn't elaborate in any detail. He told her he would never understand women. When he was done he felt an excruciating mixture of happiness and sadness. He managed to get part of it off his chest but he had to lie to do it. He hated himself for doing it but couldn't tell her the truth. His freedom depended on it.

There has to be a better life than this, he thought. *There has to be a better way than keeping secrets from friends or having to lie to them. There has to be a way to get what I need without having to feel like a criminal. And the worst part? I wasn't even in love with him. He was nice, good looking, was more insatiable than even I am about sex, but the spark wasn't there. I guess he knew it.*

"What you need is a good night at the club," she said as they returned to work.

After work, she took Kallen out with Dwess and a couple of others from Maintenance section. It was just like old times—as if Kallen hadn't been aloof at all these past several of months. He was sure she told the rest of the group his story, but for some reason no one asked him a thing about 'Isha'. Not even Dwess.

Kallen got as wasted as he could on cheap beer. He managed to avoid too much ruminating about Acton until he got back to his room. The last thing he remembered was whimpering a little when he thought about his dog back in New Meadows. Wáshaki was fifteen when she died. They had literally grown up together. He remembered how empty he felt for months after she died. Owning a dog was rare, since it took a lot of resources. He had insisted. After all what little boy wouldn't want a puppy? He really loved Wáshaki. More than anything.

Kallen hoped he was finished feeling sad about Acton, but as the week went by he couldn't help but think about him. Several times he thought about going over to the Avionics sub-building to see him. But that was out of the question. Acton would freak due the investigation now underway about those guys from his section.

A quiet inquiry was being conducted about Lang and Dolan. Kallen wondered why there hadn't there been a follow-up story in the base news about them. In fact, when he did a query in the newsvid archives their names didn't even turn up. There wasn't even a record of the newsvid he had personally watched. It was as if it had never existed.

Kallen wondered where other camchips might be hidden. He even wondered if his room was bugged. He finally took a deep breath and decided that it wasn't so.

While the NAA wasn't known for being the most open of societies, he also knew there wasn't a spy network on base, despite the high presence of Black Guard. But, to be sure about the camchip issue he secured a detector from the equipment room. The first place he used it was in his quarters. It only detected the comm link chips in his vidstation and the ones in his vidPAD. That's all it was supposed to detect. He was glad for that. Otherwise, someone might have been watching him beating off an awful lot.

Saturday morning rolled around. Kallen couldn't help but think about going to Acton's place. Maybe Acton had mellowed out and would see things differently if he talked with him. Kallen briefly considered just talking to him from his vidstation or sending him an encrypted message over BaseNet. But he knew he couldn't. No photon trail, less chance of being nabbed. Especially while the Strong and Lang investigation was going on. After all, communications were routinely logged. After he got dressed he eyed the detector sitting on the table next to his bed. He debated with himself about it for exactly two seconds. He took it with him to the hoverbus stop.

As he approached Acton's back entrance Kallen realized that his voice authorization had probably been inactivated. He was right. It didn't acknowledge his presence at all. He used the buzzer. He had only used it twice in the past—and that was months ago. Kallen was surprised when Acton's face showed up on the screen, since he could easily have used a voice-only channel. He said three words, "Come on down." His voice had an uncomfortable tone to it.

When he got to Acton's door it slid open and he motioned Kallen in. Kallen immediately felt his remoteness.

"What the fuck are you doing here, Sergeant Deshara?" he said after the door shut. He wasn't angry really, more like annoyed.

"What do you think, *Lieutenant Racelis*?"

"You made the trip for nothing. We can't see each other anymore."

"Maybe you don't have anything to say to me, but I have something for you." He pulled out the detector and energized it.

Acton didn't know what it was.

"Camchip detector," was all Kallen said as he set it for maximum scan.

It only found the comm link chips in the vidstation next to the kitchen and the ones in Acton's vidPAD in the bedroom. Just like Kallen's room back on base. Kallen was satisfied, but knew that if Acton's quarters had been bugged they'd have found out about it months ago and they wouldn't be having this conversation.

He placed the detector on the counter and pointed to its little screen. "No hidden camchips. Are you satisfied?"

Acton found the off button, pressed it, then picked it up and handed it back to Kallen. He still hadn't even offered to have him sit down. Kallen was getting annoyed since he'd just proclaimed the place bug free but wasn't being shown any further hospitality.

"Deshara, you shouldn't be here. I already told you things aren't going they way they should be just now."

"You'd find that things are fine if *you'd* stop being paranoid."

"Look, you don't know what I have to face every day."

"I don't? You don't think I have to face my friends? You don't think I have to lie to everyone to see you?"

"You're not seeing me anymore, remember? And, no, you don't know what I have to face. I'm in those guys' chain of command. You're not," he said, pointing at him. "The Lake Superior issue is really heating up, too. Security is going to be doubling on base very shortly."

Kallen ignored most of what Acton said, mostly because he didn't like him pointing like that. "Fine! I'm not in their chain of command. But they weren't sleeping with you."

"And I keep reminding you that you aren't *either*. Now will you just leave it at that?"

"Damn it, Acton." He was holding back the hurt so he could continue talking. "You can't do this to me. They won't catch us. It'll work out. Trust me."

Acton didn't make a move to comfort him, despite knowing that Kallen was hurting.

It wasn't until that moment that Kallen knew he'd made a mistake coming back. To prove what? He took a deep breath and forced the air out between his teeth. He knew he had overstayed his welcome and figured he better leave. "I'll keep in contact," he said, taking a step backward toward the door.

"It's best you didn't, sergeant," Acton told him as he pressed the button next to the doorframe. The door slid open.

Pulling rank on him again. Kallen wanted to haul off and punch him. With great willpower he held his clenched fist to his side. He was so angry he almost crushed the detector.

"Lieutenant *Asshole*, I mean, Racelis. You'll be sorry you did this." He shouldn't have said a thing, but it came out before he knew it. What he meant was that Acton would be sorry he had broken it off; that he'd want Kallen back for sure.

He realized on the shuttle as he came back to base that Acton probably took his parting shot as a threat. His stomach jumped around the rest of the day.

Chapter 8

Monday, June 19, 2479

The following Monday Kallen saw Mirani mulling over something at her vid-station. It wasn't like her to look concerned, so he decided to check up on her. The other guys in the office were busy attending to their business, stacking vid tablets, doing whatever it was that office personnel did—stuff he found terribly boring.

"What's so interesting?" he asked as he came up from behind her.

Startled, she jumped, almost hitting the bottle of Jolicoeur juice he was holding. He turned quickly. *Whew, just missed it.*

She passed her hand over the screen-off sensor. "Deshara, don't do that!" she whispered loudly.

He couldn't see a thing, as was her intention. "What's the big secret?"

She hesitated, then decided to tell him. "It's the weirdest thing."

He pulled up a chair and sat down, placing the bottle next to the screen. "Weird?"

"Either I've just been given some kind of data clearance I didn't know I had or there's been a big mix-up." She took a quick look around the room. Airmen Brey and Fillgere had left the office and were in the corridor now. She crinkled up her face. "Don't tell a soul. Promise?"

This sounded good, so he did. "Promise. What's the deal?"

"This morning I went to Central Admin to pick up the data access crystals like I always do on Mondays."

"Yeah," he said. *That's her normal routine, so what?*

"I think this one belongs to someone else." She popped it out and showed him.

Data access crystals were about ten centimeters long, two wide, and half a centimeter thick, and were clear except for one end which was color coded. Issued by Central Admin, they were manually coded for departmental users. The crystals allowed time-limited access to databases, vidmail, and other files. Most of them were useable for a week, at which time they automatically expired. She normally kept them for a month then gave the accumulated expired batch back to them. The crystals were just another layer of security used on BaseNet. The one she showed him looked perfectly ordinary.

She inserted it again. "Look here." She waved her hand over the screen and it illuminated again. She touched an icon and the screen faded in to more icons and data paths to a variety of departments unrelated to Operations Squadron.

Holy fuck, he thought with surprise. He'd hacked all over BaseNet and had never seen these data paths before. Those icons were for other squadrons. Authorization to other squadron databases wasn't normally granted unless one had a much higher clearance—something Mirani didn't have.

Until now.

At that moment Kallen felt a twinge of jealousy. With access like this he'd be able to dig into databases so deeply it would take months to wade through it all. He knew that vidstations transmitted the user's logon ID and the station's node name. He was well aware of the repercussions *she'd* receive if she started snooping around. If she attempted to access data objects she wasn't normally allowed access to, the audit trail would be impossible to deny.

"I think you better return it as soon as you can," he offered.

"Not now. I've already used it. Can you imagine the investigation that would result if I just 'gave it back to them'? It's bad enough that security all over base is tight right now."

Kallen was alarmed. She could be in big trouble already. "Why didn't you wipe it when you realized what you had?" He looked over to the data crystal erase module sitting next to her desk.

She pulled the crystal out of the reader and the screen faded to black. "I couldn't. So I had the reader display the owner stripe. It has *no* owner code *and* it has Gamma 3 clearance."

What, Kallen wondered. *She couldn't erase it?* The look on his face must have been worth a million credits. Gamma 3 was highest clearance level he was aware of. And this one had no owner stripe? How was that possible? He wanted to just touch the crystal again. It was a gold mine. Someone in Central Admin had made a serious error. But more importantly, Mirani had the mother lode. A Gamma 3 clearance meant that private emails would be transparent. BaseNet would be an open book. The NAA I-net would be accessible. It didn't make sense. How the hell could someone goof like this?

"It only has the standard five day life cycle, so I only have the rest of the week to use it," she told him.

His heart was racing. She didn't realize the full extent of what she had here. "How did you know it had that extra clearance coding in the first place? You don't ever go into those databases."

"I was accessing routine files this morning using the crystal—you know, for parts and such for Acquisitions section. I had to do an index search and saw all these data objects that I'd never seen before on the screen along with my search form. I know enough about the databases I usually have access to, to know that I *don't* have access to data objects like that."

Kallen's plan seemed to come out of nowhere. "Give it to me. I was just on my way to Central Admin and can make up a good story about how you got it."

"You're crazy! You could get into serious trouble if they knew *you* had this crystal."

"Ain't gonna happen. Here's how it works. Access to squadron databases comes with a standard audit trail. Everyone's vidstation transmits a data object that contains your logon and station ID. There's an entry for every transaction that takes place. Even read access to any file or database will add an item to the security audit trail. If you happened to get into anything you don't normally have access to they'd know about it already. If you've not done anything wrong, you're safe. So, let me take it in. Unless, of course, you've been looking around where you shouldn't have been."

She quickly popped the crystal out and handed it to him.

Good, she's safe. Kallen continued. "Don't say another word about this to anyone, not even to the idiots in Central Admin next Monday. I'll do all the talking. Deal?

She nodded her head, not saying a word. She looked more than a little scared.

"Oh, wait. What'll you do in the meantime?"

"I'll, uh, use Brey's crystal. He won't mind." She swallowed the lump of fear lodged in her throat.

Kallen knew that titanium-pressed platinum wires, diamond vapor coatings, nano-Fullerene tubing, and a variety of other materials were extremely valuable. But in his estimation this crystal was the most valuable thing he'd ever touched.

He skipped lunch. He couldn't think about doing anything else except to find out if the crystal would do what he needed it to do. If it didn't, he'd go to Central Admin after all. He went straight to his room, fired up his vidstation, activated the Stealth Around software, which stripped his vidstation of all ID objects, then inserted the crystal. Immediately, the screen filled with unfamiliar data paths.

He activated the virtual glasses, slipped them on, and started surfing. It was incredible. He could see through every router he'd been trying to get through earlier as if they were glass. Transparent. He could see all of the ESC's vast interconnected databases, including archived and top level ones. He had access to the NAA I-net, since the firewall was as good as gone.

Kallen nearly wet his pants with excitement.

He pulled the glasses off his face, not believing this had happened. What a stroke of luck!

He touched a few icons on the vidstation screen, logged off, and it went black. He stood with the data access crystal in his shaking hand, staring at it. In four and a half days the crystal would expire. He had to put it to good use.

Shortly after lunch, back at this workstation, he found himself feeling anxious to get the day over with. He couldn't keep his eyes off the clock.

Mirani came back to see him. His area had finally returned to its normal tidy condition, a sign, she surmised, he was no longer pining away about what's-her-name.

"Well, what'd Central Admin say?" she asked. She was a bit upset that he hadn't come to talk to her as soon as he had returned.

He was in a reverie when she arrived, thinking about what he might be able to dig up now that he had unrestricted access to BaseNet. He didn't even notice that she was only a few steps away.

"Whoa! Sorry, you startled me. Uh, there were some raised eyebrows, but they didn't say anything else except that your court-martial will be next Tuesday."

He chuckled when she angrily stamped her foot.

"You're safe," he told her. "But don't press the issue. You don't want to draw attention to *their* screw-up. It could backfire." He told her that so she wouldn't ask any questions or make any comments about it later.

"They really didn't say anything?"

"Nothing. I swear." In a way it was the truth since he never went there.

"As far as I'm concerned it never happened either," she told him.

Later that evening, Kallen was so hungry since he'd skipped lunch, that despite wanting to immediately start hunting around BaseNet he had to first visit the mess hall.

When he passed by Dwess' open door in The T, he was so absorbed in thought he didn't notice the three people inside the room.

"Hey!" he heard as he passed by.

He stopped in his tracks. *Who said that?*

"Numb nuts!" Dwess called out.

Kallen backtracked a few steps, then pushed the door in. Dwess was standing with Gailsben and Jost. They were in civilian clothes and looked like they were ready to take off somewhere.

"Where are you going in such a hurry?" Dwess asked, almost as if conducting an interrogation.

"Mess hall. I'm starved."

"Why are you still in work clothes?"

Kallen shrugged.

"It's after five. You should be changed."

"I'm in a hurry."

"Deshara, you're way too busy. You need to lighten up. When your life catches up with you, you're gonna be sorry you never slowed down to have some fun. Now, go back to your room, change, and go out with *us*."

Kallen stopped himself. He desperately wanted to use the crystal. He had even counted off the remaining hours before it expired. But his hunger was overpowering him now. And Dwess was right about what he said.

Dwess saw his hesitation. He snapped his fingers a couple of times. "Change. You're going with us," he ordered.

Kallen put the lure of the crystal aside, went back to his room to change, then went with Dwess and the gang. It was like old times. Times he sorely missed.

It was a little past nine when they returned to The T. He tactfully declined their invitation to get high and returned to his room. It was a little warm, so he pulled off his shirt, shed his shoes, and activated the vidstation.

Now that the beer had sufficiently worn off, he was ready to do the searching he wanted. He put the glasses on top of his head as he wended his way through onscreen data paths. Then, once he got past the third security router, he slid the glasses down and leaned back in the chair. Now it was just voice commands as he told his cursor where to go. He had just passed the sixth router and was at the nexus of dozens of data path junctions. There so many he didn't know where to go next.

Then it came to him. *Torvadred. Commander-General Darka Torvadred.* He only knew the commander from pictures in the Base newsvids and the photos of him in various offices. The commander knew the entire base chain-of-command. *I have access to every file on BaseNet. Why not start at the very top?*

Using the Stealth Around software to hack passwords, it took less time than he expected to break the one that guarded Torvadred's vidfile database. He was certain the database would have been under dozens of layers of encryption, too, not just the single one he so skillfully breezed through. There, he broke the password in less than three milliseconds. No wonder. It consisted of a woman's first name (he wondered if it was the man's wife's name), part of their last name, and a couple of digits tacked on to the end. *What an idiot*, Kallen thought. *He probably thinks security is so tight at his level that good logon encryption isn't necessary. He never thought someone might actually hack into his vidfile database.*

Confirming again that there was no way he could be detected, he immediately launched into the General's latest vidmails. So far, so good. This was becoming great fun already.

One of them was from his wife. Sure enough, the woman's name in the password was hers. Several of the vids were from other base commanders and twelve were from those that reported to him. Some had attachments. All were boring. After failing to find anything of interest there, he decided to change tactics and head to another part of the general's database. He immediately hit a wall of security protocols. That was odd. Wasn't the crystal's Gamma 3 clearance supposed to get him anywhere? After all, he'd already broken his password.

Irritated that he'd been thwarted after only a few minutes, and getting nowhere despite having full, albeit stealth clearance, he decided to download the entire database to his vidstation. Despite the huge datastream and the amount of bandwidth used to do so, he could do it in random data bursts, stripping the sequence numbers off the stream or randomly changing the data path of the packets so that the stream wouldn't be traced. *Thank you Stealth Around*, he said to himself. After the entire database finished downloading he would simply apply a decryption algorithm to the folders tomorrow before he left for work. The Stealth Around application was a beauty for that purpose, too.

While he waited for the files to copy, his face lit up. Why not download information pertaining to the recent Fort Morgan disaster? The secrecy of it had been killing him. Dwess might have his leads, but this would outdo anything he could possibly come up with. Kallen was still surprised that they'd not been properly debriefed about the mission, and that they'd been kept from what he considered important data regarding what had actually happened there.

After fifteen minutes of searching in the highest stealth mode he could tune he found exactly nothing. Not a single word in reference to the Fort Morgan disaster? The incident had only happened a couple of weeks ago. How could there be no mention of it anywhere? *Maybe it's being referred to by a code name.* He tried several different names. Some obvious, some not so obvious. Even after query after query he turned up not a single data object referencing it. Just in time, too, since the commander's vidfiles had just finished downloading.

Reaching an impasse, and assured that no automated security system had tracked his movements, he logged off the vidstation, then looked at the clock. It was nearly eleven-thirty. It was well past time to beat off.

He unzipped his pants, slid them off, and fell into bed. He slowly slid his skivvies off and closed his eyes. Funny how Tiago's face—not Acton's—came to mind. All his anger about Tiago's sudden exit out of his life was gone, he noticed. Thoughts of his assignments piling up at his workstation briefly disrupted the focus he had gathered onto his penis. Finally, he was able to smother all the intruding thoughts and concentrate on his building pleasure.

When he was done, he licked one of his wet fingers, toweled himself off, then wadded the towel up, and tossed it into the hamper at the far end of his room. Part of it draped over the lip briefly before it slid down and disappeared.

Five minutes later he was fast asleep.

Chapter 9

Tuesday, June 20, 2479

Mirani quietly stepped into Kallen's workspace. He had a magnifier visor over one eye and was working on a component she couldn't identify in its current state of disassembly. On the screen was a full page of code. Several lines of it were highlighted in red. He was giving the computer instructions on sections to correct. Kallen often likened his code fixing to snipping out offending strands of DNA and repairing them. He was just about to clip out this exceptionally badly written snippet inserted by someone else, months previous.

She stopped, crossed her arms, then cleared her throat.

He pulled up the visor and rubbed his eyes. He had stayed up a little too late last night and was feeling rather fatigued, despite the cappuccino he'd recently finished off.

She handed him a messagePAD. He activated the tiny screen, wondering about the worried look on her face. She hadn't said a word so far.

He looked at the PAD. '*ST Deshara, Kallen J., report to Central Security, Sublevel 12 Immediately.*' It was marked with Major Vaulkner's signature block and office codes. Major Vaulkner was Chief of Intelligence. Vaulkner had more than enough contact with the Commander-General. Kallen felt immediately nauseous.

He looked up at her. He could tell now that she was really pissed off.

"You didn't give the crystal back, did you?"

"I did, too." He barely squeaked it out since his stomach was starting to tighten.

"You did *not*."

He was whispering now, mainly because he was finding it hard to speak. "Okay, I didn't."

"You stupid, *stupid* fuck!" she replied.

"Mirani!" She never talked to him like that.

"Vaulkner? You know who he is?"

"Sorta. He knows General Torvadred, right?"

"No *kidding* he knows the general. The only time anyone sees Vaulkner is before they go to the brig. By default, *I'll* be next." There were tears in her eyes.

He glanced down at the messagePAD again. "We don't know what this is about." But he was just about sure he knew. He was still feeling nauseous and beginning to feel scared but didn't dare show it.

He had left his vidstation on back in his room. It was still decrypting the files he'd downloaded last night. When he checked on them before he left this morning his program had gotten more than a third of the way through the general's encryption algorithm. At least his decryption software was working as designed. He figured it would be just about done by the time he broke for lunch. *How the hell did anyone detect me? I checked everything. Everything!*

But something else was not right about this. If he had been detected downloading those files, why would Security generate a messagePAD to call him there? Shouldn't there just be a Black Guard hauling his ass straight to the brig right now?

"Yeah, wait a minute," he said. He inspected the message in detail. There was a routine message header and nothing else. "This is a standard message, Mirani. Look." He gave her the PAD and she touched the bottom icon. Sure enough, there was no unusual coding to be found anywhere. It was indeed a standard message.

She set it back down on his workbench. "Still, why do you have the crystal? And why did you *lie* about not returning it?"

His shoulders slumped down. "I'm sorry I lied. I'll tell you why later." If there *were* a later.

After shutting down his workstation he raced back to The T. He was completely out of breath as he inserted his keycard into the door, noting it was still securely locked. That meant no one had entered since he left this morning. *Whew!*

Still breathing hard, he sat down at the vidstation. He activated the screen and looked at the flashing icon. 'Job Complete', it said. *Thank God,* he thought.

He yanked the crystal out of the reader. In his haste he stuck it in his pants pocket. He beamed the decrypted database files to his vidPAD and secured them under six layers of encryption. Once done, he wiped the files from the station and deleted the transaction logs. Next, he ramped the presentation layer processor down to text mode. Doing so would remove all traces of his most recent activities, as well as scramble all the local files. He hated doing that since it would erase all of the customizing he'd done to the screens. It would take hours to reinstall the operating system and reorganize all the screens back into 3D mode again. It was better that than having his vidstation looked at if he were, for some reason, 'detained' at Security and someone just 'happened' to be assigned to check it out.

He stashed the vidPAD in the closet, burying it under a pile of clothing. What good that would do he didn't know. Places to hide things in his room were non-existent.

He took the downside shuttle to the Central Security building. Since it was on the other end of base, it took twenty minutes to get there. He had never been in that sub-building before and was unfamiliar with the corridors. The kiosks were quite informative. He stood at a vidscreen that wrapped around a meter-wide column and traced the route he needed to take. He shoved his other hand into his pocket and fiddled with the objects in it. Suddenly, he felt something familiar.

Fucking shit, he said to himself. *I stuck the fucking crystal in my pocket?*

He quickly glanced around. There was no place to hide it. The corridors were completely sterile, without even a single architectural detail in which to dispose of it. He had no choice but to leave it where it was. *I'm walking into my own fucking funeral!* But even as he was chastising himself about it, he realized another thing. Those two guys in Avionics who were caught kissing. They had been processed through Central Security. It didn't even dawn on him until now. Vaulkner's name had been mentioned in the newsvid. Had someone clandestinely told the security people about him and Acton?

He peered around the kiosk. Someone had just approached the low semi-circular black console in front of two sets of closed double doors. Behind the console were two Black Guard. Although the man who had just arrived was not facing him, Kallen instantly knew who it was. It was Acton. *Oh fuck! My worst fear is confirmed!*

Acton handed the larger of the two Black Guard his security card. The guard inserted it into the reader, brought something up on his vidscreen, then handed it back to him. He pointed and Acton walked past the console. One of the doors slid open for him and he went through. The door slid shut behind him. Kallen continued to stand behind the kiosk. There was no one else in this part of the corridor except for himself and the two Black Guard.

Kallen started to sweat profusely. He *was* nailed. And it appeared to have nothing to do with the secure data he'd downloaded. He was about to explode with fright when his stomach lurched a good one. Perhaps the investigation into Dolan and Lang had spread wider than he thought? Perhaps Acton had been implicated after all? *But how?*

At first, he thought maybe Acton had been called in ahead of him. Then he wondered if it was Acton who had registered an accusation against him. *Maybe my little tantrum after I brought over the camchip detector more than just pissed him off.* Or maybe he'd simply been called to Vaulkner's office with regard to those two guys. It was impossible to determine what was going on here. There were just too many unknowns. Kallen tried to keep his racing thoughts from spinning him out of control.

This sub-building had more security guards on every level than any other building except the brig. Kallen was a single troop going in unarmed and defenseless, with an unauthorized Gamma 3 data access crystal in his possession. He began to tremble with fright.

He continued to stand behind the kiosk, attempting to muster up something to use in his defense. Trying to keep his thoughts clear was becoming difficult. He knew he couldn't pretend to hide here all day, too. Camchips were all over the place. The image of his arrival had already been captured and archived someplace in holographic storage. Just getting this far had twice required his ID card, plus the certainty of retinal scans without his knowledge. Ducking out of here would be impossible.

Slowly, while he silently talked his nervous stomach into calming down, he walked from behind the kiosk to the console. Uh oh, it was happening again. That slow motion feeling that happened just like when Acton had dumped him. This time he felt like he was high, too. *God damn it*, he thought. *Not now.* He tried to pretend everything was okay as he stood before the two Guard.

The same Black Guard sergeant who had passed Acton through eyed Kallen as he stopped in front of their station. "Sergeant?" he asked.

Kallen could barely speak. "I'm, uh, supposed to, uh, report here?" He held out the messagePAD, then handed him his security card.

The Guard squinted at him, as if there were some detail he was trying to discern. Kallen wiped his temple with his shirt sleeve. He was sweating profusely.

"It's nineteen degrees on this level, sergeant. Why are you sweating?"

"I, uh, was, uh, topside."

The Guard pointed at him. No, he was pointing further beyond. Kallen's turned his head to look. "The water cooler's over there. Drink. I don't do resuscitations."

Suddenly, the Guard's concern was comical. Kallen managed a forced laugh. Is this what it's like to have one's last drink before they're thrown in the brig? *Fuck it.* He drank. When he returned, the Guard handed him the PAD and his security card. "You're the last victim, uh, I mean, person," he said with a slight grin.

Kallen wanted to say 'fuck you', in a big way, but didn't. He was sure anything he said from here on in was being recorded. No use adding fuel to the pyre he was sure he was going to be tossed on to.

The Guard pressed a button. The corridor door slid open. The same one Acton had gone through. Kallen felt his knees growing weak. At least the slow motion feeling was dissipating.

The corridor was as cool as the central hub area he'd just left. It seemed like it went on for a kilometer. The floor was carpeted, muffling the sound of his footfalls. Solar fiber bundles lit the ceiling light diffusers every three meters. It was as if he were walking along an enclosed, suspended catwalk between tall buildings in the middle of the day. Indeed, lit up this way it was easy to forget he was forty meters below the surface. But inside himself, he felt he was headed toward a dark dank dungeon.

Kallen looked into doorways that were opened along the corridor. He didn't see him anywhere. *Where is Acton? Waiting like a coiled rattler in Vaulkner's office? The asshole!*

He looked down at the PAD. The Guard had replaced the message with one that read, 'Vaulkner, E., Colonel. Room 54.' He'd just passed a door marked 23. He had a way to go.

A bench outside room 35 looked inviting. He sat, wondering if there was another water fountain someplace along the way. He hadn't seen one so far. He badly needed another drink. At least his knees hadn't given out on him.

It was at that moment that everything shifted. Despite not knowing exactly what he was walking into, he resolved to be on the offensive. *Fuck Acton*, he thought. *How the hell is he going to be able to accuse me of being gay when he's gay himself? A check of his housing unit would turn up my DNA in a second. God knows I left plenty of it there. He can go to hell with me.*

Room 54 had a large lobby in front of the door. As the corridor opened on to it, he saw other servicemen sitting along one of the walls. Two were Black Guard. That much he could tell from their uniforms alone. It wasn't just him. There were others! Kallen's fear was worse than he supposed. This was really, really bad. He avoided looking any of them in the eye as he went toward a station where a female National Ground Patrol sergeant was sitting. She seemed nonchalant as she quietly talked with someone at her vidstation screen. After Kallen approached, he presented his security card and the PAD. She looked at both of them only briefly. "You're the last one. Take a seat over there. Colonel Vaulkner will be right with all of you."

Kallen turned and decided to at least look at each man sitting in the two rows of chairs. All were enlisteds except for a major. Acton was nowhere to be seen. *Where the fuck is he?*

Kallen's breath lurched when his eyes reached the man at the end of the second row of chairs. Long suppressed—and he had hoped forgotten—feelings rushed to the fore. His heart started beating like mad. This wasn't possible. He hadn't seen him in nine months. After all that time, why would he be here?

In the last chair sat Dayler Madsen.

Chapter 10

Tuesday, June 20, 2479

Kallen was in shock. Dayler fixed his attention on him, then stood up. At first Kallen thought it was because he was going to point at him, perhaps sneer at him. But he didn't do that at all.

"Deshara! Is it you?" He came forward and stood right in front of Kallen.

"Yes, it's fucking me," Kallen whispered back.

Kallen was obviously upset and Dayler noticed it right away. "Hey, why the attitude?"

"What are *you* doing here?"

"I received orders to report here. I was on a late flight. Just arrived, like, an hour and a half ago."

"But why?" He noticed that Dayler seemed not the least bit agitated. He wasn't sweating like Kallen still was.

Dayler shrugged his shoulders. He glanced back, indicating the others. "No one else knows either. I guess we'll find out in a few minutes. It's about time, too. I'm getting seriously pissed off about all the secrecy."

Some of the enlisteds in the chairs stood up, their attention focused behind Kallen. Dayler looked past Kallen. Kallen turned to see that a previously shut door was open. The sergeant behind the counter announced that Colonel Vaulkner would see them now. Everyone started for the door. Dayler grasped Kallen's hand and held it tightly for a brief second in what appeared to be a handshake but was definitely more. With that gesture, Kallen's anxiety level eased just a bit. Whatever they were all walking into it wasn't anything like what he had thought.

Kallen was completely confused now. Certainly, Dayler wouldn't have taken his hand like that if he was involved in what Kallen thought was an accusation of being involved in a gay relationship. If he wasn't here to be court-martialed for being gay, what was this all about? Could it be, after all, about his use of the data crystal, still perilously tucked away in his pocket? If so, what was these other people's involvement? He hoped there wouldn't be a shakedown once they got through the doors. They'd find the crystal on him for sure.

The men were escorted through the door, then down a private hallway where they were ushered into a large conference room. A long, red, real wood oval table sat in the middle of the room. It was surrounded by eighteen chairs. There were pitchers of water scattered on the table top and upside-down glasses at every chair position. The floor was as shiny and black as obsidian, perhaps made of it, Kallen thought. The high ceiling had tiny white LED lights brightly illuminating the table in front of each seating position. The chairs were large, comfortable, and made of real leather, Kallen noted. The room appeared to be an important meeting place, clearly for high level personnel. A wide vidscreen was at one end of the room. He sat at the table and was silently comforted when Dayler sat next to him. The rest of the men followed suit, selecting seats around the table. Kallen flipped over the glass in front of him, poured some water, downed it in one long gulp, then poured again and drank it almost empty. Dayler watched with an amused smile on his face.

The door they had come through shut. Another door on a slightly elevated level over to their left opened and they watched as three people made their way down a short staircase. As their faces came into view Kallen recognized Colonel Vaulkner only because of a vid he'd seen him in months ago. He was leading two other men he'd never seen before. One was Caucasian but perhaps half-Indian as well. He couldn't tell what his racial background was exactly. The other was very definitely Asian. Based on their attire they appeared to be civilians.

Vaulkner surveyed the men. Kallen studied Vaulkner. He was wearing the crisp uniform of a National Ground Patrol officer. It was tailored to look similar to a Black Guard uniform, but it was brown and didn't have the black piping along the outer seam of his pant legs. He was bald, with a ruddy complexion. The deep crags in his face made him appear to be perpetually mad. Not a very pleasant man to look at.

The two other men with him pulled chairs out and sat near the head of the table. The taller one had dark but graying hair, was thin, and sported a goatee. He looked scholarly in that he was wearing a white shirt and a tie, which immediately identified him as an academician. The Asian man with him was short, easily the shortest man in the room. He had jet-black hair, quick eyes, and dark brown skin. He seemed alert as well as intelligent. He was also wearing similar attire. Another academician. Neither was smiling. The mystery of this gathering only deepened. Kallen was relieved he wasn't sweating anymore and his heart had returned to a more comfortable pace.

The lights above them dimmed and others shone directly on the center of the table. Vaulkner, who had been slowly working his way around the table, spoke. His voice boomed, sounding authoritative. "Men, you've all been gathered here for a special project mission. This mission is unlike anything you've ever been involved with before."

Kallen's thoughts immediately strayed to the Fort Morgan disaster. *Does it have anything to do with that?*

"Each of you was selected because you possess specialized skills that are vital for its success. Your service records have all been combed and each is spotless. Starting immediately, those of you whose security clearances are not already at secret have been upgraded to that."

Kallen realized he had been holding his breath since Vaulkner began speaking. Relaxing slightly, he took a deep breath. Whatever this was about it clearly had nothing to do with anyone accusing him of being in a gay relationship at all! He'd just been informed that his record was clean. No hidden surveillance had been involved in any of his activities with Acton either. That also meant that his use of the data access crystal had gone undetected. He felt greatly relieved and was now terribly intrigued.

Vaulkner continued. "Now, the two gentlemen here with us." Vaulkner had still been circling, but stopped as he came to the two civilians. "Dr. Shon Katterjay and Dr. Iwasenji Hatsu…Hatsuwa…."

"Hatsuwakan," the Asian man said, nodding to the group. Dr. Katterjay nodded, too.

"The matter these men have brought to our attention is of the gravest nature. What they've uncovered could potentially unravel our past and our present unless we act decisively."

While the colonel was introducing the two men, Kallen was at full throttle trying to discern what was going on. *Were they at Fort Morgan after our team was there*, he wondered. *Do they know something about the bomb blasts?* Kallen wondered about the last remark by the colonel, bringing his speculation to a screeching halt. *What did he just say? Something about the 'unraveling of our past'? What the hell does that mean?* Kallen studied the faces of the others at the table, looking for clues. He found none there.

Dr. Katterjay rose up and looked out over the men. He took a remote control off the table and pressed a button. The vidscreen at the front of the room illuminated, showing a lush deciduous forest. Kallen had observed scenes such as that before and wondered if it was being used for some sort of calming effect.

Katterjay assumed a classic scholarly pose, clasping his hands behind his back. "What I'm going to tell you must never leave this room."

"Dr. Hatsuwakan and I work for Bedrosian Sciences, Limited, just south of here. I'm sure none of you have ever heard of it before. It's a small agricultural research firm. My specialty is theoretical physics. His specialty is agriculture.

"Several years ago, we teamed up to find a way to accelerate the growth rate of crops that are used in the production of the majority of our foods, as well as the fibers used in the making of clothing, and the oils and plastics we use in everyday products.

"Our experiment involved the use of a bio-regenerative circuit, commonly known as a Veles Ring, but greatly modified from standard design. Controlling our experiment is a specialized neural-core processor that I programmed specifically for our project. This specialized processor was engineered to control the regenerative field but on a much larger scale."

Kallen was familiar with the regenerative field created by a Veles Ring. Using a little understood physical principle, a Veles Ring circuit created a time-displacement field at the quantum level. The unusual field effect had been known for about a century but its practical application had only been in use for about half that time. It was used exclusively to heal human tissue. In fact, Kallen had personal experience with one. When he was six years old he broke his wrist when he fell using an older friend's skates. At the local hospital the doctor placed his painfully swollen forearm into a metal cylinder. While he was being entertained with a stuffed animal, the regenerative field healed his wrist within thirty minutes. Not only had the swelling completely disappeared in that half hour, but afterward he was out the door without so much as a sling. Its affect on healing larger bones was equally well-known. No one seemed to understand exactly how it worked, but many theories had been put forth.

Dr. Katterjay continued. "Our experiment was designed to accelerate the maturation rate of quinoa, amaranth, kamut, and soycorn, which, as you know, are our staple grains. Our experiment required us to build a large ring which we call a photonogrid. Unfortunately, our results were not what we expected." He stopped to clear his throat. "A large version of a Veles Ring had never been built before. In addition, no one had previously done any serious research using one on plant tissue."

Dr. Hatsuwakan stood and rested a hand on the back of his chair. "I'm afraid our results couldn't be predicted. You see, instead of shortening the maturation rate of those grains—displacing a great deal of the growth time—the photonogrid opened a fracture or portal, for lack of a better word, in space-time."

Kallen and Dayler glanced at each other with shocked looks on their faces. Several of the other men looked equally taken aback. Dr. Hatsuwakan cleared his throat to get everyone's attention. All eyes went back to him.

"We're not expecting you to understand how that happened exactly. What you do need to know is that you all will be assisting us in repairing some…uh…damage we caused."

Dayler spoke up. "Damage, sir?"

Dr. Hatsuwakan looked at him with his bright eyes. "An unexpected side effect of the massive amount of energy that was used to keep the portal open. Specifically, the damage caused by uncontrolled ionizing radiation that threatens them and us."

Dayler spoke up again. "Them?"

"Those who're living in 1820."

There was some snickering from several of the men. Vaulkner called for quiet. The snickering immediately stopped.

Dr. Katterjay touched Dr. Hatsuwakan's shoulder, then spoke. "We're quite serious, gentlemen. The photonogrid focuses a tremendous amount of energy at the quantum level. It was designed specifically for our research experiment. Once this…portal was detected, we kept it open so we could determine what it was we were observing.

"You see, instead of simply displacing time within a circular area, we noticed an unusual pattern emerging inside the ring. After some adjustments, we were able to discern an image of something other than what was within the ring. Much later we determined that what we were observing was a portal to a time in our distant past, in 1820, and a place on our continent, at the northern edge of the Disputed Quarter."

They were all familiar with the Disputed Quarter. It encompassed a large portion of the southeastern part of North America. It was an alternately hot and dry or hot and humid area, and devoid of normal interacting ecosystems due to the erratic, and often devastating, weather patterns that regularly swept through there. The rivers that had once flowed into or through the Disputed Quarter had all been piped long ago; potable surface water was very difficult to come by. The water left behind during storms certainly wasn't drinkable.

The Disputed Quarter's shoreline to the south and east was crawling with bandits and outlaws of both the NAA and the UCT, along with those from the South American Confederation. Few dared to live there permanently for fear of the yearly monster hurricanes, of which several might hit in a single season. Moreover, no government claimed the region due to the fierce lawlessness, limited infrastructure, and the nearly impossible habitable conditions.

The Black Guard sergeant directly opposite Kallen spoke. Kallen looked at his nametag. Craistok. He had an angular face with a sharp upturned nose. Kallen could even see his nostril holes head on. He was wide and beefy, sported a short crew cut, and had a dangerous looking expression on his face. Kallen knew nothing about him, but hoped to stay out of his way. He was surprised to find Craistok quite well-spoken and intelligent—not something he expected from a Black Guard.

"Sir, with all due respect, why would we want to put ourselves in harm's way in the Disputed Quarter? No one claims that territory and there's nothing particularly valuable there. So what if ionizing radiation threatens the area."

"Good question, mister…?"

"Sergeant Raddo Craistok, 3rd Justice Guard."

The other Black Guard issued a brief guttural 'oo-rah' sound when Craistok mentioned their unit. Kallen focused on his nametag. It read Biggert. He was a sergeant, too. Kallen sized him up. He had blond, almost white, hair with a very light complexion and dark red lips. He was at least five if not seven centimeters taller than Kallen, and was thinner than the beefy Craistok. It seemed to Kallen that most Black Guard were larger guys. At least all of the ones he'd had contact with were bigger than he was.

"Sergeant Craistok, we're concerned with the present, but we're much more concerned with the past in this particular instance. You see, in 1820, the area that the portal has opened to was called Kentucky. More specifically the opening is on a bluff overlooking a major tributary to what used to be called the Cumberland River." He pointed to the vidscreen at the front of the room. Dr. Katterjay cycled through some old photos of an un-piped river. Completely nondescript-looking, the scenes could have been of anywhere in the far distant past for all Kallen knew.

"A small town called Williamsburg is approximately six kilometers downriver from the opening. Our data indicate that there are about one hundred people whose lives could be lost if the storms that our ionizing radiation caused, continue unabated. If something isn't done and done soon, the devastation to that area will be enormous.

"But there's more. We have reason to believe, although we can't prove it directly due to so many lost records from the past, that the first President of the NAA had ancestors from that general area in Kentucky. If those people lose their lives due to our mistake, he might not ever exist. By default, we might not exist as a nation."

The men looked at each other.

"I know this sounds incredibly far-fetched. Yet gentlemen, even if it's not true that President Nordmark's ancestors were from Kentucky, we still can't risk the past being changed by anyone's death that we may have caused. We can reverse the effects of the radiation, dissipate the potentially deadly storms—and it will take less than a week. Once you're done, you'll return the same way we got there. When the processor is powered down hopefully nothing will have changed."

Dayler spoke up as he pointed to himself. "We're going there?" He already knew the answer, but had to voice it anyway.

"Correct." Dr. Katterjay looked at Dayler's rank stripes, then his nametag. "Sergeant Madsen. You're going to be taking a short trip to 1820." He raised his eyes and surveyed the rest of the men. "All of you."

Chapter 11

Tuesday, June 20, 2479

After the looks of astonishment faded, Dr. Katterjay continued. "The entire time we were making our observations we used ninety-two percent of maximum power to charge the photonogrid. That kept the portal's image fully viewable. Ever since we understood that the ionic storms, that eventually started occurring, were caused by us and our device, we've kept the grid's power at a bare two percent. At that low power level no detectable ionizing energy has crossed the portal to add to the existing disturbance. But the radiation is still present and continuing to coalesce, powered by none other than solar energy. There will be more storms soon, so we have to act fast. Our plan calls for grounding the energy before any serious damage is done. It's as simple as that.

"We'll be setting up a temporary camp here." He pressed a button on the remote and the forested image changed to another one. Kallen was unable to discern much difference from other one.

"We're very lucky that the portal opened in this location," Dr. Katterjay went on to say, "It's at the top of a bluff well above the tributary. The forest is quite thick there, but fortunately it's a perfect place for us to accomplish our mission undisturbed. The immediate area is uninhabited. We won't see anything but trees and animals.

"Your commander has assigned Colonel Vaulkner as our liaison. He's the one who gathered you all together and is providing us with the equipment we need.

"It's unfortunate that one of the problems facing our country right now is Lake Superior pipeline debate. Security on your base was heightened recently. As such, it was difficult for us as civilians to gain good communication with authorities here. We would have been having this conversation earlier if not for that issue. I want to thank your superiors for their swiftly directing all of you here despite that." He looked over at Colonel Vaulkner as he said that, then back to the men around the table. "Can I answer any questions?"

Kallen definitely had some. "Sir, how is this even possible? I mean time travel? Portals into the past? When was this technology invented?"

"As I explained, a Veles Ring works because it generates a quantum-level temporal displacement field. Our photonogrid operates using a similar principle, but on a much larger scale. As far as we can determine, the portal effect resulted solely because of our unique neural-core processor. It caused the displacement field to behave entirely differently than we predicted or could plan for. I'm-I'm afraid this discovery was completely accidental and entirely unique."

Kallen immediately placed his follow up question. "But holes in space-time have nothing to do with plants. Accident or not, this seems...highly unusual, to say the least."

The doctor grinned. "You are correct. Experiments test a hypothesis, of course. More often than not a hypothesis is proven invalid with the test results. This is one of those times. Unfortunately, our results were completely unpredictable and unexpected.

"If I may add, the universe is what you might liken to a hologram. Because holographic storage and retrieval is such an efficient use of space, all of our modern computing devices use it.

"Some of you might know that a neural-core processor is designed to mimic some of our brain functions, one of which is holographic memory storage and retrieval. The past and present are concepts the neural-core processor has awareness of on a rudimentary level. Perhaps awareness isn't the right word, since neural-cores are only partially organic. Using algorithms and heuristics very similar to the ones used to control a Veles Ring, I programmed our particular processor to access specific holographic memory regions. The program was written to tap into 'future memories' of when the plants had matured, greatly enhancing the effect that a Veles Ring produces. The process was supposed to generate a field whereby, from our perspective, an immense portion of the plant's growth stages would be bypassed. Obviously, the program caused our processor to tap into a past time instead, as well as to function in a manner we didn't intentionally design the photonogrid for. If you're interested later, I can explain the conservation of energy principles we're not circumventing.

"We initially tested our theory on a very small scale, using a much smaller photonogrid. Since that was successful, we felt confident that the process was scalable. But, the results, using a larger photonogrid were, again, nothing like we expected. Part of the program had to be rewritten to accommodate the new components. Obviously, it didn't operate in the same manner as before. As we quickly learned, we had little control over the displacement field once the photonogrid was energized again.

"Our intention was, on that larger scale, to have the time displacement field confined to a test plot of amaranth and simply observe rapid growth. Instead of a ring of energy focusing on the plants, an image appeared in the center of the ring—an image of this leafy forest." He pointed to the vidscreen. "We were on a platform above the plot, making observations. The image appeared almost immediately. I must say that we were both taken aback when we saw it. It was much later before we moved the ring to a vertical position and started determining what it was we were viewing."

Kallen was greatly intrigued with this explanation. He wanted more. "Sir, why did you wait so long to determine what was going on?"

"As you're probably aware, anytime you troubleshoot a problem you think you caused, you take away changes you've made until you're left with initial conditions. Since we saw an image, we searched the databases we were using to see if we were somehow displaying something from within them. That wasn't the case. We went over the code base that was running the processor's functions, from beginning to end, to see if there was something we might have inadvertently added to cause this to happen. We weren't using anything remotely like holo-projection code objects, yet an image persisted. It wasn't until we observed the image lightening and darkening that we suspected we might be observing a diurnal cycle—that is—day and night. Working out of pure intuition, hunches if you will, we suspected something much more unconventional than problems with our code. After we raised the ring to the vertical, we conducted a geographical analysis to gather initial longitude and latitude measurements. That was after using the rock method."

"The rock method?"

"I threw a rock through the ring. It didn't land on the other side in our lab."

Katterjay's humorous delivery was just the thing to break the tension that had built up in the room. Kallen wanted to burst out laughing, but held it at a snicker. Vaulkner, on the other hand, didn't look amused. He seemed to be annoyed at Katterjay's extended explanation.

"It took another two and a half weeks of steady observations to determine that we were viewing a window into the past—more than six hundred and fifty years ago."

The colonel was slowly but surely making his way closer to the doctor. Kallen had been focusing his attention on Katterjay, but since the colonel had gotten into his line of sight he couldn't help but glance at him on and off. Kallen noted that Vaulkner seemed visibly struggling to restrain himself from cutting Katterjay off. Something was going on but he didn't take much more note of it.

Dr. Katterjay seemed to have gotten the silent message to discontinue his discussion. "Any more questions?" he asked.

No one responded. At this point everyone was too stunned to know what else to ask.

"Thank you, gentlemen. I-I want you to know that you're doing the NAA a great service with your assistance in this most unprecedented matter."

The two scientists were ushered out. Once they left, Colonel Vaulkner took charge of the meeting.

"Each of you has been selected for very specific reasons. Major Montarco will be in charge of the operation. He's handled other special operations missions flawlessly. For the duration of the mission he will be your superior officer. Those of you in the ADF will defer authority to him as outlined in Section 18 of the NAA Uniform Code.

"Sergeants Craistok and Biggert will serve as security. The STs here, Lander, Madsen, and Deshara, will rotate around the clock and be in charge of the Zelinski Energy Converter that will be taken with you."

Kallen raised his hand. He was very familiar with Zelinski energy converters. He'd already repaired two while at ESC. About the size of a two-meter cube, it was used as a power plant to supply large amounts of electricity: two phase, three phase, DC or AC—in the megajoule range. Why would they need to man one? And in shifts? Okay, so they were a bit touchy in operation. Maybe that explained the shift work. But if there was already too much energy that had gone through the portal, why would they need such a powerful energy source?

"Sir, can you be more specific about the converter?" Kallen asked.

"I'm not technically versed on the subject as you men are, but Dr. Katterjay has determined that the converter, used with a...," he looked down at his PAD, "...reverse control accelerator circuit, along with what amounts to a lightening rod, can be used to attract, then ground, the ionizing radiation. Your sole purpose there will be to support the five days of its continuous operation to do just that, then return to our time. To make our little adventure as quick as possible, it will be essential that the equipment be operational around the clock.

"STs Lander and Madsen are also familiar with the operation of the converter, and I've been informed that you ST Deshara, are the best maintenance technician this side of the Rockies. Am I accurate that you're familiar with the device?"

A compliment, Kallen wondered. He mentally went over the schematics of the converter. He'd never thought to use a reverse accelerator circuit with a Zelinski energy converter since it would normally make no sense to do so. "I, uh, I guess, sir."

"You guess?"

"I mean, yes. I know the converter. Very well, in fact." That part he was sure of.

"Deshara, you'll primarily be in charge of the rest of the photronics-based equipment. A supply crate of the most used and repairable modules for the converter and other equipment will be sent along with you. I've authorized some test equipment to be provided as well. Hopefully, none of it will be needed, but it's coming with you anyway."

Kallen nodded.

Vaulkner continued. "From the National Ground Patrol are Sergeants Lackson and Guyez. You two men will oversee the setup and breakdown of the bivouac and will handle food and water issues.

"Those of you stationed here will need to secure personal belongings and clothing to last you a week. Major Montarco you, along with Deshara, Craistok, and Biggert won't be reporting for duty tomorrow. The rest of you, since you are from other bases, will be in temporary quarters already assigned to you. See that you get some rest this evening.

"I don't have to remind you not to talk to anyone else about this mission. If I hear that one word has leaked out, you can be sure that the repercussions to you and your rank will be swift.

"We leave base from Hangar 4A tomorrow.

"Another thing before I dismiss you all." He leaned forward with his hands flat on the tabletop. He made sure everyone's attention was focused on him before he continued. "Those two scientists might be brilliant men, but they're no longer military. They know nothing of the real gravity of the issues facing the NAA with the 'Superior pipeline debate', as Dr. Katterjay incorrectly put it. Water rights is more than a mere debate. It may have to be resolved with all out war. That's the reason our base is on Alert Status Two. In addition, those two men are no longer combat trained, like you all are. They may have specialized scientific training of their own, but their theories and ideas can and will be considered subversive if they counter our intentions with regard to the pipeline or the pumping station.

"Dr. Hatsuwa-, uh, Dr. H. will be the only one of the two to accompany you. Dr. Katterjay will remain at their lab facility to monitor his equipment from our side. I recommend that you keep your conversations with Dr. H. to a minimum while you're there. We don't need him putting ideas in your heads that could be construed as seditious. Am I understood?"

There were nods all around. Kallen noted that Craistok and Biggert were grinning at each other. He didn't like any of this at all. The warning that the scientists might be seditious was odd. The colonel had been holding back something, that much Kallen could tell. And why were Black Guard going to accompany them to the ancient past. To keep an eye on Dr. Hatsuwakan? It didn't make any sense. Why would Vaulkner trust the scientists at all if he considered them potentially seditious?

In a way, all of this was going to be a much-needed education. Beyond the obvious, due to the time travel aspect of this mission, Kallen was going to watch very carefully how Dr. Hatsuwakan conducted himself. And, he knew not a single Black Guard personally. Maybe it was time to get to know who they really were. *Hmm, this is more than a* little *interesting*, Kallen thought.

The colonel looked at his watch. "All of you will be visiting the infirmary next. There are lots of nasty little bugs you'll be inoculated against before you go." The colonel motioned for them to rise and they were ushered out.

Kallen glanced at Dayler, who was ahead of him. He had all sorts of questions for him but they would have to wait.

Chapter 12

Tuesday, June 20, 2479

The men were led by Colonel Vaulkner down the hallway to two corridor transports. They headed directly to the infirmary. Kallen was desperate to talk to Dayler privately. There were all sorts of things he needed to ask him. Like, why hadn't he kept in contact? He had an extra stripe now, too. Had he regretted his decision all those months ago? Hell, what had been going on with him in the last nine months? Unfortunately, Dayler had been led to the other transport, so their conversation would have to wait.

Once they reached the infirmary and were off the transports, Kallen found himself standing next to him. "ST now, huh?"

Dayler nodded. "You, too."

"Promotions aren't that difficult to find around here—if you know the right people."

Kallen studied Dayler's face. Surprisingly, he found himself uncomfortable with the mixed feelings he had for him. Despite being dumped by him, he still had affection for him even after all this time. He thought he wouldn't feel this way, but couldn't help himself.

They were led to a waiting room where a nurse checked their name off a list on a PAD. She led them into a sterile room and instructed them to remove their outer garments in preparation for a gauntlet of shots. Kallen wasn't expecting that. It was nice to see Dayler mostly naked again. He was still the same nicely built guy he'd gone out with not all that long ago.

They were each given a series of six shots—the pneumatic hypo administered them two at a time—then they were handed a small bottle of purple pills and instructed to take one a day. Supposedly, they would ward off mosquitoes. Kallen could count on a single hand the number of times he had been bitten by a mosquito. The waterdome harbored them, but he only saw them on occasion and they avoided him for some reason.

They passed from the sterile room into a second one where they were scanned first by a machine, then by a real doctor. Each man was given an okay by the doctor and they were on to their next stop.

At the supply department they were handed a pack that had been filled with items they would need for their deployment. They were instructed to pull the items out on top of a long counter and inspect everything. Kallen checked off two lightwands and an umbrella. He found a rain poncho, a small tarp, a digital compass, a microcell-cushioned sleeping pad, a couple of blankets, a manually-operated water filtration pump, several boxes of ready-to-eat meals with heat capsules, and a few other items. Nothing unusual here. All of this was standard issue, except for the rain gear.

After inspecting their gear and making sure everything was in working order, they re-stuffed the bags, and shouldered them. They were to keep them so they could pack their clothing and personal effects, too.

Guyez and Lackson inspected an a-grav stroller in a nearby equipment bay. They made sure that the tents, portable shower, air conditioning units, heat stoves, cots, and the rest of the equipment they'd need were there and in working order. Kallen and the other two technicians checked through the three containers that contained the replacement equipment modules and test instruments. They were also already on the stroller.

Next, they proceeded to the armory where they were issued pulse stunners. On only three previous occasions had Kallen been authorized a weapon. All three times were to qualify on the range. He'd been such a good shot that he'd received three expert badges which were part of his permanent record. He signed for the weapon and checked it for a working safety. The stunners were put into a locked container and whisked away. Ostensibly that container would also be awaiting them tomorrow as well.

They were given orders as to where and when to meet in Hangar 4A, since it was a large hangar and had multiple staging areas. Finally, they were told they could return to their quarters or get a meal in the mess hall. Kallen was free to return to his quarters so he could pack his personal belongings.

Once the crowd of men began to disperse Kallen tugged on Dayler's sleeve. He'd been thinking about it the last several minutes with mixed feelings. Should he bother to talk with him after all? Did he really want to know anything about the second boy who dumped him? Part of him did and part of him didn't. The part that did, won. Besides, they were going to be spending almost a week in very close proximity. He might as well get started now. "Come back to my quarters," he said.

"Why?"

"Because I haven't seen or heard from you in a long time. Because I wanna know how things are going."

"Things were going just fine until I got orders to report here. I barely had time to pack my toothbrush. I had forty-five minutes before I had to get on the transport. The next thing I knew I was in that waiting room…looking at you."

"I thought *I* was getting nailed for some snooping around."

"What kind of snooping around?"

"On BaseNet. I, uh, have some tools to pry into some rather secret files."

"You?"

"I hack."

"You're gonna get caught."

"Don't count on it."

Dayler walked with him, avoiding significant eye contact. Their conversation died for a moment.

"So, going out with anyone?" Kallen asked.

"Just like that? Asking me that kind of question?"

"I'm sure you get around—still."

"There's been no one recently." He continued to avoid Kallen's gaze.

"Have you dated anyone?"

"Here and there."

Dayler was obviously being evasive. Kallen sensed there was something different about him, too. The cheerful carefree Dayler he remembered wasn't there. Maybe it was the unusual situation they'd found themselves in. Maybe it was something else. He regretted being inquisitive so quickly and changed the topic.

"That briefing. It's like something out of science fiction, huh?" Kallen asked him.

"It's seriously hard to believe."

Dayler was having a harder time believing he was having this conversation. He didn't know Kallen would be in the briefing, let alone ever want to talk to him again.

"Time travel," Kallen stated with wide eyes.

"And they pulled me in on this, too. I guess it's a compliment, huh?"

"Whadda ya think about those two scientists? Think they might be seditious like the colonel says?"

"Impossible to say."

"Hey, the mess hall's near my quarters. Let's get something to eat, okay? I can take you back to your quarters later."

"That's the most normal thing I've heard all day. I'm starved."

They reached The T about ten minutes later. Just as Kallen inserted his keycard he saw Mirani coming towards them in the corridor. She was off duty and no longer in uniform. Something was wrong. She looked like she'd been crying. Perhaps she was distraught about his apparent security breach and was coming to look for him?

"Deshara," she said.

"Come on in," he told her as he pushed the door open. Dayler gave him a questioning look. Kallen motioned him in with a jerk of his head.

Once she stepped in she looked at Dayler, who she didn't realize was going to follow them both into the room.

"Oh, this is a…buddy of mine from tech school. He's okay. Dayler, Mirani Ruiz."

It was an awkward introduction. She was terribly upset. She shook his hand anyway.

Dayler dropped his pack to the floor.

"Were you crying?" Kallen asked as he dropped his pack, too. "I can explain everything. It's not what you thought. I'm not in trouble. *You're* not in trouble."

"Deshara. Kallen. It's not that. It's Dwess. He's in the brig. They took him away this afternoon. They said he was selling halpa root. Here on base. Can you believe that? Halpa root?" She looked up at Dayler, searching his face, perhaps for some measure of support.

Kallen was immediately alarmed. Dayler had already shut the door and was leaning against it now, making sure it was tightly closed. He knew halpa root was illegal.

Kallen made sure his voice was low. "When did *that* happen?"

"Just after you left for Security."

"I can't believe it. He was so careful."

"You *knew* he was selling it?"

"You *didn't?*"

"Why didn't you ever say something about it?"

"Why would I? *You* were dating him. I thought you'd already know."

There was a second of silence as she considered what to say next. "I don't know why I came to you."

"Hey, I'm sorry. W-why are you so upset about this?"

"He didn't tell you?" she pressed.

"Uh, no. Tell me *what*?" She wasn't going to talk about them just dating. He could tell that.

"I'm pregnant."

"Oh, shit."

"Please don't pretend be surprised."

Why didn't Dwess ever tell me he was actually boinking her? "H-how far along are you?"

"Seven weeks. This can't be happening. I love him."

"Uh, say again?"

"Oh, don't tell me you didn't know. Guys tell each other everything."

"I swear I didn't. I swear." He wanted to pummel Dwess for not talking to him about this.

"What am I going to do? There'll be an investigation. I'll be called in for questioning."

"Were you planning to keep it or get married or something?"

"We were going to decide everything this week. This is just awful. Why is this happening? I've never been in trouble like this before."

"Look, at least they don't know about the data access crystal. Be thankful about that. I certainly wouldn't be back here if they did." He remembered again that he still had it in his pocket. It felt like it was heating up. He could swear it was starting to burn his thigh, but it was purely his imagination. "And no one's gonna know you knew Dwess—that way—unless you tell someone."

"The infirmary has it all on record, including the DNA match. They know whose it is. My friend Janda knows it's his. *You* know."

Kallen shook his head. It was already common knowledge. "This totally sucks. And I'm, uh, going away for a few days. That's why I was called in to see Vaulkner. I won't be able to do anything at all to help."

She glanced at their packs. "Where are you going?"

"It's a special ops project. That's all I can say. I'm assigned to the NGP for the duration." He pointed to Dayler who was glued to his spot at the door. "We're both going. But we'll be back on Sunday. In the meantime, don't worry. Do they have any evidence?"

"Evidence? How's half a kilo?"

"*Half a kilo*? He had that much? What happened? Was there a security sweep of the dorm wing?"

"No, I heard he was trying to sell it to a Black Guard."

Kallen bit his thumb as he thought. "Something's not right here. I know he's not that stupid. He must have been set up."

Kallen knew that Dwess stayed as far away from Black Guard as possible. Just because there were a lot of them on base wasn't any reason to risk that kind of exposure. Profit or no profit, he wouldn't have taken that chance. Had one of their buddies squealed? Suddenly, he wondered which one of them might have.

Dayler had been listening to all this without a sound. *What a way to be introduced to ESC*, he thought. *Kallen must have really changed, too. I never thought he'd ever be so bold as to have friends who sold drugs.* At least he never thought Kallen had such friends. *A lot seems to have changed about him. He's not as naïve as I thought!*

Mirani sat on Kallen's bed, still looking distressed.

Kallen spoke up, sounding concerned. "The base is on Alert Status Two, Black Guard are on more-than-normal corridor and surface patrols, and we're being shipped out. Now this. What else could possibly happen?"

Dayler spoke for the first time since entering the room. "We might not come back."

Kallen glanced at Mirani. She was still looking upset. Her face didn't register the remark. While she was looking at the floor Kallen drew his fingers across his throat. Dayler mouthed 'sorry'.

Kallen sat down next to her and put his arm around her shoulder, not sure how he was going to be able to console her. He wouldn't be able to offer any support in the coming days either.

"Mirani, if I'd known you were pregnant I swear I would have said congratulations or something."

She managed to eek out a smile and Kallen felt a little better now. "Look, I gotta go," she told him. "Janda's waiting for me in her room. I'm sorry you saw me like this."

He took her shoulders, then properly hugged her. Her perfume was nice. It reminded him of Naya.

Dayler opened the door for her then shut it and turned the lock. He waited a full fifteen seconds before he said anything, wanting to make sure she wasn't listening.

"I know I'm in a freakin' nightmare now. The country is one step from going to war. You and I are going back in time. She's pregnant. Her boyfriend is in the brig. And what's with this data access crystal."

"Her boyfriend is in one of the sections I work with. He's a buddy of mine. Once they start their investigation—and you know how it works—I'll be on the list. So will she. Then the whole thing's gonna unravel."

"What's gonna unravel?"

"My nice little quiet world's gonna get real noisy. So I've smoked some root with him. So I've smoked it with a bunch of his customers, too. So I've been in his room when he's sold it. Everyone who came by knew I would never say a word. That would be suicide. The deal about the data access crystal is a long story. But that's the way I was able to download unauthorized encrypted files. Which, by the way, I haven't even seen yet." Kallen sighed.

Dayler's stomach rumbled loudly in the ensuing silence. "I'm hungry."

Kallen stuck his hand in his pocket and fingered the crystal. He had to get rid of it. He went to the closet and pretended he was rummaging through his things. He shoved it up to the toe of one of his dress shoes, then stuffed in a rolled up pair of black socks after it. He realized he was lucky to have downloaded the data when he had the chance. The crystal had only a couple of days left before it automatically expired. He'd be gone in about twelve hours. His BaseNet search was effectively over already. Keeping the crystal was irrelevant already, but he didn't want it on his person right now. He pulled his vidPAD from the closet and stuffed it into his pack. He expected his stomach to be gripping him tightly at this point. It wasn't. Thank God. He was starved, too.

At dinner, with Dayler still being oddly quiet, Kallen kept an eye on the vidscreen. As usual, the news was on. Commander-General Darka Torvadred was being interviewed in his office. The commander was a large man with a shiny bald head and a round face with deep set eyes. His uniform was impeccably tailored to hide the extra eight kilos that hung about his waist. The expression on his face made him look like he'd had a very long day, or perhaps too long a life in his position. Kallen felt the man needed to get some sleep.

An aerial view of the Duluth pumping station, the nearby NAA base, and a portion of Lake Superior was behind the general. "*The NAA has full authority to defend our base adjacent to the pumping station,*" he was saying. Kallen had missed the first part of the interview. He'd never heard this kind of aggressive rhetoric before. "*The President has authorized the use of force,*" Torvadred continued. The news commentator made a few other remarks, whereupon several pundits discussed the issue at length, which immediately bored Kallen.

Political events were taking the forefront of the news. Kallen realized that a military conflict was nearing inevitability much more quickly than he thought.

After dinner, Kallen and Dayler returned to their respective quarters. Despite being conflicted about wanting to talk to him more, Kallen was exhausted and needed to get some sleep. He had been in bed for no more than five minutes when an image of the crystal came crashing into his head. *Damn it*, he thought. He hadn't even had a chance to peek at the data he'd downloaded at such great risk. He was sure he had private high level information at his disposal. He also thought he might have some really juicy conversations between Torvadred and his wife, too. Could he even imagine them talking sexy to each other? The thought of it grossed him out. Hell, maybe he'd even find a vid between he and his mistress. *That'd be a scandal worth knowing about!*

Eventually, even while speculating about all the sordid details, he fell asleep.

Chapter 13

Wednesday, June 21, 2479

Kallen awoke when sensors opened the louvers on the ceiling to let in the dawn light. It was 0415. Way too early for him. Not since boot camp had he gotten up this early. He had to be at the designated area in Hanger 4A to catch the transport with the rest of the men by 0600, and he was usually slow to get ready in the morning. His stomach rumbled while he shaved. He tried to hurry so he could get a meal in the mess hall before leaving.

Although almost too anxious to eat, he wolfed down his usual breakfast by himself while listening to BaseNet news. This morning it was mostly local interest stories. He wondered if this was an attempt to divert everyone's attention from more significant issues. Odd that they would do that. Maybe the rest of the more interesting stuff would be presented in detail later.

Movement at the corner of his eye caught his attention. A group of Black Guard troops, dressed in full desert camos with the telltale black strip up the pant legs, had just come in, slid their trays along the railings, and one by one sat at the opposite end of the mess hall. No doubt they were being shipped out to Duluth. Kallen's transport off-base wouldn't appear to be anything unusual, he realized. HeavyAir transports taking off and troop movements on the ground were routine activities these last several days. Everything would appear to be 'normal'.

He stood, pulled his bag to his shoulder, then took his tray to the conveyor belt. He took the moving sidewalk toward Hangar 4A, found the correct staging area door off the corridor, and entered the huge space. He saw the armored personnel hover transport waiting nearby.

From their staging area inside the cavernous hangar, Dayler had been watching the exit doors from the corridor every once in a while. He was talking with two of the other men next to the transport. When the doors slid opened and he saw Kallen coming their way, he took immediate notice.

"Nervous?" Dayler asked as Kallen joined them. Kallen was looking jumpy.

"Fuck yeah."

"These guys tell me that although the base is on alert, nothing's happening around here at all. It's just a bunch of hype if you ask me."

"Let's hope that's the case. Don't forget though, the front is over a thousand kilometers from here."

The last to arrive was Major Montarco. They all climbed aboard the transport and got comfortable. It was nicely air-conditioned inside. The transport could fit twenty-five men. Today, it only held their detachment of eight men, their packs, and Colonel Vaulkner.

Kallen was quite nervous about all this. Unable to nap, he nonetheless fell into a reverie, staring out the window as the kilometers melted underneath them. When they finally pulled to a stop and he looked at his watch he was surprised that a full fifty minutes had passed. He looked up at Dayler who seemed wide awake.

A sign several kilometers back indicated that this town was called Barrett. Kallen had never been here before. When they exited, they were in the back parking lot of a one story building nestled against the side of a high rocky wall. Above and all around them were short evergreens and the usual scrub plants. Indications were that the majority of the facility was downside. Several hovercars were parked deep within a hollowed out area in the hillside. A large awning hung over its entrance. The employee garage, Kallen knew.

The double doors of the back entrance were open. Just beyond them was a well-lit corridor. They proceeded single file into the building and, in two groups, went down several floors in an elevator. Its doors opened to a vestibule. To the left, another corridor led to double doors. They looked well-secured. Two regular National Ground Patrol MPs were standing guard. Kallen was surprised to see them. He didn't expect anyone else to be there except their party.

Past the doors, they descended another staircase and Kallen smelled water and dirt. That's when he saw grow lights, sunlight fiber bundle pods hanging from the ceiling, and rows of plants in various stages of growth. Hydroponics. This lab was a fraction of the size of a standard commercial plot.

The far end of the large room drew his attention. Beyond the rows of plants was a hastily erected vertical partition. A large opening, with a curtain drawn back, exposed what looked like metric tons of very high-tech equipment.

Just past the partition, metal beams formed a cube-like structure. Inside the cube was a torus affixed to the cube for support. Kallen recognized it as the photonogrid spoken of in the meeting. The torus was three and a half meters high at its apex. What looked like light tubes, each a meter in length, were well-secured all along the inside circumference of the torus. Each one had a circuit box attached to it with leads running to a dais several meters off to the left. Standard superconducting power cables snaked from each tube and were attached to a power supply box off to the left. Kallen attempted to discern the configuration in more detail but was unable to.

On top of the wide dais to their left was a series of touchscreen control consoles. Dr. Katterjay was standing at the dais, his attention focused on the leftmost screen. Like yesterday, Katterjay was dressed in normal civilian clothing. Dr. Hatsuwakan was standing next to him. He had on forest camos.

The men filed down between two rows of hydroponics and were directed to come to a stop near the photonogrid. Now that Kallen was closer, he noted that Dr. Katterjay looked worried. Dr. Hatsuwakan was scratching his head through his thick dark hair. He looked worried, too.

Dr. Hatsuwakan came down from the dais to greet them. "Gentlemen, we've got a bit of a problem, so there'll be a slight delay."

Kallen's ears perked up. He noticed that Colonel Vaulkner didn't look happy either. *What the hell is up?*

"What kind of problem?" the colonel asked.

"A power fluctuation. It's occurred before, but it's not nearly as severe as the previous times. I think we've just about got it under control."

Kallen didn't like the sound of that, but what could he do? He took a moment to observe his surroundings in more detail. He scanned the standard control panels the two scientists were pouring over, observed normal superconducting power cables attached to everything, and noticed that the circuit junction boxes were run-of-the-mill.

The photonogrid was nothing of the sort. Kallen recognized none of the components. Looking at the torus and the tubes arranged around its circumference, he could tell that the array had originally been horizontal, like they had been told. It looked like the beams holding it upright had been recently welded. Telltale carbon smudges at the seams gave that away. Actually, it looked like the entire cubic array had been hastily constructed.

Kallen wondered what they'd been drafted into. He was expecting something a little more professional-appearing instead of something that looked like it had been assembled in a spare room.

The a-grav stroller that had been in the supply building from the day before was here, too. The largest object on it was a tarp-covered Zelinski Energy Converter. A set of hollow, carbon-fiber poles were strapped down next to it. Kallen recognized them as the antenna array. He did the math in his head and estimated they'd extend about seventy meters high once they were joined together. The rest of the items from yesterday were still on the stroller. While they waited, the men were instructed to place their packs on it, too.

Vaulkner told the men to take ten while the two scientists ran through their calibrations. Dayler stood next to Kallen. Sergeant Lander came up to them and introduced himself. He had been quiet during yesterday's conference, had been non-committal while going over the equipment yesterday, and had been asleep in the shuttle just minutes earlier.

"Lander," he said. Extending his hand, he added, "Broyles Air Station, northwest Wyoming." Both Dayler and Kallen shook hands with him and formally introduced themselves.

"You ready for this?" Kallen asked as he lifted an edge of the tarp covering the converter.

"I know those things pretty well. We use them a lot. Touchy, I'd say. They're not the best." He bent over to look at the metal plate affixed to the side of the unit. "This model sure isn't."

"Don't I know," Dayler told him as he observed it, too. He had long since memorized the functions, protocols, and operations of all of the first and second tier equipment used in ops back in Monterey. Zelinski Energy Converters were second tier.

Lander lowered his head a little closer to theirs and whispered. "This is freakin' fishy if you ask me. Time travel my ass. I don't like it at all. They're testing us for something."

Just from his demeanor Kallen suspected that Lander was a whiner, but he did have a point. Perhaps it was a test. Time travel was hardly within the realm of normalcy. Regardless, Kallen kept his concerns to himself. He didn't want to fuel Lander's grousing.

Kallen glanced across the room and noticed that Katterjay and Hatsuwakan were carrying on an intense dialogue. He was far enough away from the control console that he couldn't hear exactly what they were saying, but he could hear snatches of the conversation.

"…two more millivolts. There…check the graph…. Higher resolution…read off those numbers…. Calibration error?"

Their conversation was difficult to follow. Kallen had no real knowledge about how their device worked anyway. Finally, they appeared satisfied and both heads nodded.

"We're ready," Katterjay told Vaulkner.

"Guyez. Lackson. Fire up the stroller," Vaulkner told them.

Guyez fingered a control on the side of the stroller. There was a low frequency hum, followed by a faint blue glow underneath it. The stroller slowly lifted off the ground.

Using many of the same components as a hovercar, the stroller was able to carry tons of equipment and was designed to be used as a cart. That meant that the right amount of force, in this case pushing or pulling, would be able to create enough momentum to put it in motion. Its forward momentum could be adjusted for finer control by using an operating panel touch-screen. An a-grav stroller wasn't the safest way to transport heavy items, but they certainly made it a lot easier.

Guyez and Lackson grasped handles on the stroller's sides. Dayler, Kallen, and Lander got into position and took hold as well. The rest took their places and they all pulled the floating stroller in front of the photonogrid.

Katterjay energized the energy confinement tubes surrounding the circular framework. They brightened until a diffused rose color filled the area. Dr. Hatsuwakan nodded again, looked up at Katterjay, then took his place with the men at the stroller. Kallen's attention was solidly focused on the center of the ring. As if coming out of a deep mist, a hazy scene opened up in the circle. He saw ground, rocks off to the right, and trees all around. As the misty image became more focused, he saw that everything was a lush green. He saw sunlight, as if he were looking through a dusty window. As the scene came into focus the mist-like haze disappeared. The trees were swaying. Leaves were fluttering on branches. It was like a scene from a holovid.

Katterjay touched an icon and they heard a female voice. "*Countdown commencing. Thirty seconds, twenty nine….*"

Katterjay reduced the volume and spoke. "At the end of the countdown you'll have up to sixty seconds to go through. It shouldn't take even that long. Pretend you're looking through a doorway. Just walk normally. You won't feel a thing." Katterjay raised the volume again.

Lander briefly glanced back at Kallen. "Yeah, right. Not a thing."

Vaulkner looked his way, not sure what he had said. But he had a scowl on his face which Lander saw. He shut up right away.

Dr. Katterjay spoke again. "Once you're all through, I'll reduce the power like before and the portal will appear to be gone. Don't be alarmed. It will only be opaque to our time in the visible wavelengths. It won't actually be completely closed down."

The countdown continued. "*Twenty seconds.*"

Kallen noticed that the scene in the circle becoming a lot more focused and more real-looking.

"Wait until the computer says zero," Katterjay said.

"*Ten seconds…five seconds…zero. You may proceed*"

Lackson and Guyez pulled on the stroller's handles and it started to move forward. The stroller touched the plane of the portal and started to go through. Kallen and Dayler were directly behind them on opposite sides of the stroller, pulling as well.

Lackson and Guyez were completely across the vertical plane of the portal barrier now.

Another two steps.

Kallen saw an odd shimmering at the plane of the barrier, like rapid heat waves or a thin sheet of water falling downward. He held his breath and stepped through.

Kallen was standing on a hilltop in Kentucky in 1820.

PART II:
Chance Encounter

*"I'm living for the only thing I know
I'm running and I question where to go.
And I don't know what I'm tapping in to
Just hanging by a moment here with you.
There's nothing else to lose
There's nothing else to find.
There's nothing in the world
That can change my mind."*

—Lifehouse
Lifehouse
Hanging by a Moment
© 2000

Chapter 14

Wednesday, June 21, 1820

The early morning sun found its way through the patchy fog covering the Laurel river valley and warmed the soft buckskin that covered Aaric Utzman's thighs. The two buttons of his soft linen shirt were undone so he could catch the breezes that wafted by every so often. His loose sleeves were rolled up to mid-bicep. The evenly tanned skin on his upper body seemed to glow as he raised the oar again and dipped it back into the dark river. It quietly glided past their canoe. His deliberate strokes bore the mark of an expert canoeist. Nash Crane, almost twice as big as Aaric due to his burly body, sat at the head of the canoe and provided a good portion of the power they needed to push them up this tributary. Aaric steered from the rear.

A rock overhang came up to the left. Aaric wondered what kind of view it would afford if they could stop, climb up, and observe the river and the canyon.

If an observer had been standing on the overhang with a good pair of binoculars they would be smiling at what they saw in the back of the canoe. Aaric was 5'9" tall, two inches taller than average. He was broader of shoulder than of waist, but not overly masculine-looking. His eyes were an unusual gradation of light gray at the pupil to dark blue at the edge of the iris. His thick wavy hair was dark brown, almost black, and just touched his shoulders. He had it tied off in back by two twisted strands from his temples and fastened with a tooled rectangular piece of leather. It was secured in such a way to make it easy to slide down and remove. A fashionable English-style tricorn felt hat adorned his head. Dimples formed at the crease of each cheek whenever he smiled or grinned. It wasn't hard to get them to show. He was a sucker for a pun, unlike most everyone else he knew. His face was smooth and tanned, which made him look younger, although he was actually at the far end of nineteen-years old. In the last several weeks he had been asked twice which of the three men he had been traveling with was his father. The fact that he needed to shave a mere once a week added to that illusion. His hands, rough from hard work, proved his exceptional strength, as did his well-built lean physique. His hard body easily made up for his somewhat short stature.

Nash was seven years Aaric's elder. Although only twenty-six, he could easily be mistaken for someone older by half a decade or more. He sported a full dark beard, had long medium brown hair, which he had tied in a simple ponytail, and wore a similar tricorn hat. He tended toward being overweight; his belly hung a good three inches over his well-cinched trousers. His deep booming voice and hulking body drew attention to himself. It immediately told others he was a leader. Nash could have a swift temper, but he only used it when he was truly riled up. Otherwise, he was quick to find a chuckle in most every situation. Nash had laughed heartily when a man back at the general store in Zanesville had referred to Aaric as his eldest son. Aaric didn't think it was funny at all. Nash reminded him of it every once in a while just to get his goat. It was all in good fun.

This excursion by both Aaric and Nash hadn't been planned until last evening. Both had reached Williamsburg, Kentucky, a couple of miles downriver from their present location, after crossing the Cumberland Gap four days ago. Their other traveling companions Buck, William, and their families, had split off north to Pineville to visit Buck's sister for a couple of days. Buck's sister and her family had moved there three years earlier. Only Nash, his wife, young son, and Aaric had continued on south toward the Williamsburg settlement. The two groups were to rendezvous there before continuing their journey south to Nashville, then Memphis, down to the Arkansas Post, then eventually to Fort Smith.

Much further west were the unsettled lands. Once they all made it out there, the three family men, surveyors each, anticipated being hired to survey plots for new settlers migrating to the newly opened lands due to the government's Land Act.

Their delayed companions should have made it to Williamsburg already. It was possible that the unusual storms, one of which Aaric and Nash had witnessed, had held them up. At least the storms appeared to have left the area now.

Aaric was not a surveyor, but rather a cartographer. He planned to spend up to a year making maps to be sent back to the Cartographic Institute in Washington. He'd be returning there to personally deliver them unless he was able to send them by way of courier. He had no intention of settling out west. He only planned to visit, make the maps, and create as many memories of the experience as he could. What was the benefit to himself for all this time and trouble? The opportunity to add to the nation's knowledge, make detailed maps of places unexplored by Whites, and fill that longing for adventure that preoccupied his thoughts.

Aaric hailed from Wofford Ridge, a small Pennsylvania Deutsch community, nestled in the western part of the state. The majority of his family lived a very comfortable life since the Utzmans were one of the three majority landowner families in town. He absorbed the educational benefits wealth provided, but something still felt missing from his life. Never actually turning his back on his family, he nonetheless felt himself an outsider. His siblings, all older than he, enjoyed their good life. He did, too, but he felt that he needed to get out of his element every once in a while. He felt that a life of luxury would eventually make him soft all the way around. That wasn't for him. His unusual outlook on life made him somewhat odd in the eyes of his parents. As he grew older, this restlessness developed into a determined need to seek increasing levels of adventure. Naturally curious, he had quickly outgrown the town of Wofford Ridge, despite it being the county seat, and thus the center of community life in the area.

Just after his seventeenth birthday Aaric was sent by his parents to Baltimore to not only help his aunt and uncle settle into the new country, but to later attend Washington College. They were aware of his tendency toward restlessness and felt that higher education might help him settle down.

Up until eight months ago, Aaric had been enrolled in school. He could have lived on campus like most of the well-to-do students, but he opted instead to live with his aunt and uncle above the green grocer on Stockholm Street. Since they were childless, Aaric was their substitute son and enjoyed the attention it afforded him.

After they emigrated from Bavaria, his Uncle Gilhard had found employment at a chemist shop and quickly became the local expert on many remedies. Chemistry wasn't exactly Aaric's forte, but he developed an interest in it while watching his uncle work. After all, Uncle Gilhard was his favorite uncle. He was from the same region in Bavaria where his paternal grandfather was born. And Uncle Gilhard was, by far, the most intelligent man he'd ever known. He had become fluent in English within a year of his arrival in Baltimore. He knew not a single word when he first arrived. His aunt was having a hard time adapting to the new language and still only spoke German at home. Consequently, Aaric was forced to practice the German he'd learned as a child, which he enjoyed.

Having been gone from Baltimore now since early spring, he'd come to miss discussions with his uncle. He also missed his uncle's wild speculations about technology and medicine, the amazing laboratory he owned; and the powders, vials, and smelly liquids he kept for experiments. He also missed some of the comforts he'd left to come out this way.

Aaric's father had insisted he study law while in college. Aaric had taken a couple of pre-law courses, but couldn't keep his mind on them. His real love was the natural sciences, and it was reinforced by living with his uncle. Apparently, that proclivity ran in the family.

Some of the subjects that most strongly held Aaric's attention were geology, geography, and cartography. Aaric had long ago pieced together many mental images of what the continent looked like. With relish, he had read the accounts of Lewis and Clark's incredible overland and river journey through what had originally been the Louisiana Purchase. But even with the rich rewards of those stories there were huge gaping holes in his knowledge and imagination. The continent was so wide and so much of it was still unexplored. The Lewis and Clark party had mapped barely half of one percent of what had been bought from the French. There was so much land to still inhabit, so much adventure that awaited. If he stayed in school, all that adventure would come to others, not him.

When the Washington Cartographic Institute advertised in a local gazette that they were hiring cartographers to map out the lands near the Arkansas territory, north of Missouri, Aaric realized it was an opportunity to do something he really loved. He jumped at the chance by immediately quitting college.

Being a quick study—especially since the subject was one of his favorites—he worked under the tutelage of Mr. Willoughby, the owner of a mapmaking shop just two blocks from where he lived. He studied as if his life depended on it. If he passed the government's exam, he'd be hired on to be a mapmaker!

And it worked. After signing the contract, being outfitted with the latest gear needed for his endeavor; supplied with thick paper, bound in neat rectangular booklets, inks and pens, all manner of reference guides, and a fine telescope, he was ready to go.

Aaric happened to be in Mr. Willoughby's shop the day Nash came in to purchase maps for their westward journey. After a much-animated conversation, Aaric was invited to travel with them. Nash took to him right away and found, to his delight, that Aaric was already prepared to go.

The rest of the men, being expert surveyors, had not only their personal possessions, but their own surveying equipment, too. The three families planned to stay out west.

On the first nice spring day, they had taken off along the well-traveled highway from Baltimore, through Zanesville, down through Louisville, and had just recently arrived in the tiny town of Williamsburg, Kentucky. At least the Crane family and Aaric had made it there.

After arriving, Nash paid for a room for the four of them at the inn near the town center. These inns had been springing up a lot lately. There was one in most of the sizeable towns they'd passed through so far. Clean inns would become sparse the further west they traveled. Once they got to southern Illinois they would be lucky to find one again. Their tents would have to be used a lot more often than they had been so far.

When they arrived in Williamsburg, they quickly learned the town had been in a tumult about the odd storms that had been occurring for the last week and a half. There was lightening coming from a clear blue sky, high winds, and very peculiar noises emanating from odd roiling clouds that didn't move across the sky but rather coalesced and dissipated in the most bizarre fashion. Some of the more superstitious town folk claimed the noises were from Satan. Aaric dismissed any attempt to use Satan as an explanation for anything. He had long since discovered that it was a favored excuse by superstitious and irrational people.

The one storm he'd seen so far was mighty weird though. He witnessed the unusual cloudless lightening, strange high winds that came and went with a fierce rapidity, and odd screeching sounds over Williamsburg alright. The high winds had felled some of the trees, but Aaric detected no evil deities anywhere. It was definitely something he'd tell his uncle back in Baltimore about once he made it back that way.

Aaric had come to realize that ignorance knew no boundary. A good education was something that was mainly found in the city. It wasn't as important in these parts, he'd noticed. He wouldn't mind finally getting to Nashville and mingling with people who were a little more civilized. In addition, although slavery was a part of life, he found it particularly loathsome here. People didn't treat slaves decently in this state. American culture was definitely different this far from the coast.

In the weeks since they had been on the road, chilly mornings had given way to foggy ones, then to muggy dawns, as spring progressed and they rode southward. Although the Wilderness Road—or just simply the highway as it was mostly called—was well traversed, comforts were few and far between. Out here, it was mostly farms and small rural hamlets, some with only a handful of families, clustered in clearings or in un-felled forest. It wasn't at all like Wofford Ridge, or his adopted home of Baltimore—which had decades of history, a bustling seaport with lots of commerce, a healthy economy, and a well-known name.

Whenever they stopped and he had time, Aaric sketched topographical maps, even drawing odd insects or trees he'd seen, for later identification. He also utilized the time to brush up on astronomy, to observe the passage of Mars, Jupiter, and even Saturn in the sky. His telescope, although for terrestrial use, nonetheless had enough power to even resolve the four brightest moons of Jupiter. Astronomy was something no one else in his party had any interest in. It was Aaric's private little joy to mark the progress of the heavenly bodies across the bold arc of the dark night sky.

In anticipating the greater adventure that awaited him several hundred miles further west, Aaric found himself increasingly restless. He was young, full of energy, constantly yearning, although not always knowing for what.

But there was something he was always on the lookout for.

Always there was the wish to meet a man. Not one who might look upon him as a woman, but a man who he could consider an equal. Not someone who might treat him roughly as he saw many men treat their wives, but a man who also wished to have a man as his one companion. Like it was with he and Trevor—although they were both teenagers at the time.

But as Aaric had grown, so had his concept of the ideal companion. He no longer wished for the boyhood relationship he had experienced with Trevor. He wanted someone grown up like himself. He yearned to find someone who might whisper in his ear, kiss it—perhaps run their fingers through his hair. It was something Trevor often did to him when they made love. Their relationship had ended more than two years ago. The two years since that fateful day seemed like a lifetime ago.

Dreams, fantasies, and contemplation. Too much of Aaric's time was spent inside his head lately. He realized he was doing it again and deliberately broke himself from his reverie.

He surveyed the rugged bank to his right. Once they were done here, it would be good to get back on the road after the unusual goings-on in the tiny community where they were staying.

The latest unusual storm had been over for two days now. At least there hadn't been any rain associated with it. That would have swollen the river and made the current journey hazardous. Although money wasn't going to be an issue for months, he and Nash knew that anything they could earn would make things easier down the road. Plus, the whole process of snaring plump turkeys would be a mixture of entertainment, good practice of their hunting skills, and an opportunity to just get away from everyone.

A bend in the river and a swifter current made Aaric dip even deeper. Eventually they found backwashes to keep to. First to the left, then to the right bank, as they maneuvered further and further upriver. The walls of this canyon were quite steep here, too steep to find a place to stop.

A deerfly circled Aaric's head. He pulled the oar up and deftly smacked it into the water to his right. Almost immediately it was picked off by an awaiting trout. He dipped his oar back into the water and continued. He cocked his head to listen. There it was. The familiar call of a turkey in the distance.

"Hear it?" Aaric asked.

"Sure did," Nash responded. He glanced back at the bag that held their snares. Another dip of the oar by Nash while Aaric steered.

A trickle of water fell back into the river, then became drops as Aaric momentarily raised the oar completely out of the water. The patchy fog was clearing now. He wiped his face of sweat with the crook of his arm. Up ahead, high in the sky, buzzards wheeled in slow arcs. The high steep sides were making it difficult to see much else except a narrow strip of sky and the trees that grew atop the bluffs and hung over the river. From this vantage he couldn't possibly see what the buzzards might have found.

It was so quiet out here. Not a soul was within miles of them. That was to their advantage, and would make the turkeys plentiful. Aaric had been told that few townspeople ventured up this way. Today, it was just he and Buck, the river, and the woods. *Paradise*, he thought.

Further up, the river was a little wider than he anticipated. The current wasn't nearly as swift either. Surely, just a little further on they might find an area to pull over and set up a camp for the day and perhaps this evening.

Aaric cocked his head. No, it wasn't a noise this time. It was something else. A shiver went up his back. It was as if they were being watched. But that was impossible. There couldn't be anyone up here. The steep walls behind him were a formidable barrier to anyone stupid enough to try to hike their way from town. The river was the only route through the thick forest. He shook his head. Perhaps he saw a raccoon out of the corner of his eye and his brain was playing tricks on him. That had happened to him a few weeks before. He had actually scared himself then. How silly he had thought he was.

Just past the curve to the right, the forest came down to the water due to the gentler slope of the bank. Up ahead was a short expanse of sandy beach perhaps fifty feet long and twenty feet wide. At the far end was a tumble of limestone boulders that spilled out into the river. There were many pieces of well-rounded chunks of coal scattered here and there along the sand, like black diamonds in a sea of beige. It was well known in town that these hills yielded coal from seams that crisscrossed the land. The river had split many of those seams, washing coal up along the banks here and there. At this end downstream, the beach tapered until it disappeared against a high limestone wall.

Nash propelled their craft toward the bank. Just in time, too. Aaric's stomach rumbled loudly. He had been thinking about the trout he'd seen earlier, too. With one last forceful stroke the canoe slid onto the beach with the quick sound of wood scraping wet sand. Nash quickly jumped out and stepped heavily onto the sand. He pulled on the canoe to bring it out of the water a little more, then tethered it to a sapling. Aaric jumped out, pulling a leather out pack along with him. Tossing it away, it landed on the sand with a dull thud.

He inspected a trickle of water that spilled out into the river next to where they stood. It started well above him through a crack in the rocks. It wound its way down from a thicket, traversed the sandy beach, and disappeared into the tributary. He went to it, washed his hands, then cupped them and drank. The water was refreshing. Birds chirped loudly in the trees all around them. Two chipmunks scurried across the dead leaves over the underbrush to Aaric's left. A bald eagle, only a few feet above the surface of the water, flew silently upriver, turning its head briefly to observe them. This was the perfect location for a camp. Aaric immediately noticed that short stretch of flat rocks at the other end of the beach would be a perfect place to fish.

The two men hefted their packs and made their way up the bank. Their moccasins left prints in the sand as they approached the huge boulders ahead. With one hand on his hip, the other stroking his smooth chin, Aaric briefly surveyed the space.

"This looks good here, huh Nash?"

"Yup."

They dropped the knapsacks next to a large boulder projecting from the rocky wall. Aaric returned to the canoe and removed the remainder of their items, including the snares, which were kept in an oiled bag within a deerskin pouch, the fishing line, and their canteens. In just a few hours they'd have the snares strategically placed up on the hill. But for now, they needed to build a fire and catch some lunch.

Wood was plentiful, so Nash stacked a goodly amount into a pile. He picked up several chunks of coal as well. They'd come in handy after the wood got started. Using conveniently located stones, he made a fire circle with Aaric's help.

With several strikes of his flint, Aaric was nursing a fire. After the wood caught, he placed several lumps of the coal into it. He drank his canteen empty, then refilled it from the creek. He turned over some rocks, found some grubs, pierced one with a hook, and tossed a line out from the flat rocks while Nash looked on.

The sun was up high in the sky now. Barely a leaf quaked in the still air. It was getting even warmer, too. Aaric wished Nash wasn't here with him. If he weren't, he'd pull the cord that fastened his buckskin trousers up and pull them off. He'd stand there naked in the morning sunlight and feel a lot more comfortable. Not just with the two buttons of his shirt unbuttoned, like now. He'd not felt the freedom of running naked in the woods, or skinny-dipping in quite a while.

Within minutes Aaric pulled out a fat trout. He put another grub on his hook and let Nash try this time. Later, after gutting and scaling their catch, they placed them on sticks over the fire. It was just a matter of waiting for them be flaky and done. While he was waiting, Aaric watched a hawk across the river from him. It seemed to be eyeing their catch.

"Not today," he called out to it. His voice, having pierced the quiet, echoed back to him. The branch the hawk was on shook as it sprung up and away.

Nash looked up, pulled off his hat, scratched his head, and chuckled while he watched the hawk fly away. Aaric looked back at the fish. He couldn't help but nurse his ongoing fantasy. If Nash weren't there, he'd lay on his back on the blanket. The warm morning air would feel so good as it caressed his skin. He'd reach down between his legs and conjure up a scene in his head to help relieve the desire he constantly felt. He would grasp and begin. He knew if he did it would be a fleeting two minutes before he was done. He'd lay there, reveling in the feeling, letting the cadence of his breath return to normal. Finally, he'd sit up and inspect his chest. He knew he'd be a mess. But that wasn't going to happen anytime soon.

Growing semi-hard, but not being at all noticeable since Nash was at the canoe just now, Aaric picked up the two skewers with the perfectly done fish on them. Ahh, nice and flaky now. He placed them on a flat rock and pulled out the sticks. He took a knife and fork from his pack.

"Hey Nash. Fish's done."

"Be right there. Don't you even think about eatin' mine, you rascal."

Chapter 15

Wednesday, June 21, 1820

Leaves. Green leaves were all around Kallen, fluttering on branches, mesmerizing him almost immediately. The wind was swaying the treetops, with just the barest of breezes reaching the bushes down below. Trees were literally everywhere; they were inside an enveloping forest.

The second thing Kallen noticed was how utterly calm he felt. It wasn't just inside either. The forest they had stepped out onto was serene, quiet, tranquil. He wasn't the only one looking around either. Lackson and Guyez ahead of him had pulled back on the a-grav stroller and it came to a stop now that all of them were through. They looked up and shaded their eyes. It was a marvel to behold. Their forests, the tiny tracts they called forests anyway, consisted mostly of evergreens, not tall arching deciduous trees like here.

Way up ahead, the relatively flat area they were on rose up even higher. To their right was a long narrow outcrop of rocks with an overhang. The area beneath the overhang would fit every one of the men perfectly, along with most of their gear, if it were to rain. The air almost felt wet. Like being inside a waterdome. It smelled sweet, too. Kallen had never breathed air like this. He looked up at the sky. The sunlight coming in low from the east was dappling his face as it filtered through the branches. Puffy early morning clouds were making their way across the sky. He pulled out his compass and briefly checked his orientation. The clouds were moving west to east.

Behind them, Major Vaulkner seemed to be standing in a circular vid box. Then just at that moment, he and the downside control room started to fade.

Major Montarco, who had also been surveying the immediate area, turned his attention to the team. "Okay men, let's start unpacking. Guyez, find the stakes. They should be in that storage box," He pointed to a box on the stroller as he stood next to the rapidly fading image at the portal. He marked the ground with his heel, then went to the other side of the image and marked it again. "Stake them in here. We'll avoid this spot until they ramp up the power again."

Guyez retrieved two orange stakes and a sledgehammer, then quickly drove them into the ground on the major's heel marks. Now only the barest shimmer remained from where they had crossed over. It was eerie watching the portal fade away, then disappear like that. Until the power was ramped back up, they were here to stay.

Guyez and Lackson untied the tarps and pulled them off the stroller. Everyone lifted out their packs. Lackson found the larger marked cases containing the tents. Twenty minutes later, with everyone assisting, they were set up under the rocky overhang. The small portable air-conditioning units were placed next to the tents, attached to flexible tubes, then activated. They were completely silent in operation since they used piezoelectric circuitry. They were small, but produced a steady stream of cool dehumidified air for their living spaces.

Kallen was assigned to the same tent with Dayler and Lander and immediately felt the reduction of temperature inside it. Craistok and Biggert ended up together in another one. Lackson and Guyez were in the third tent, and the major was with Senji in the last one. The arrangement was just fine with Kallen.

The major discovered a hornet's nest several meters from their camp and told the men to be careful if wandering in that direction. In the meantime, he delineated the perimeter of camp. Craistok and Biggert started setting up the laser posts. Once configured, they delineated a hexagon-shaped area. At night, they would activate an invisible barrier. Anything that broke it would set off an alarm.

The unpacking continued until the long early morning shadows gave way to the new day.

Kallen wanted to rejoice. Everything was so alive here. He found himself just watching the gentle warm breezes sway the verdant trees. Insects and birds of all description flew back and forth amongst them. Somewhere he heard what sounded like hammering on a hollow log, unaware that woodpeckers existed in abundance here. There was a vibrant feel of life enjoying itself. Everything seemed to be following a natural rhythm. Kallen found himself feeling even calmer now, like the forest was soothing him, telling him that all was okay, despite the fact that this mission remained filled with mystery.

The major surveyed the well-wooded top of the nearby rise. They were in a dip at the top of a hill in an undulating forested piedmont range. Where he was standing overlooked a sheer drop off to the river valley below.

Kallen pulled a set of small binoculars from his pack. He had a moment after he stowed his gear to look over the drop off. The major had gone back to his tent. Kallen stood where he had been. He slowly swept his gaze through the trees. It was difficult to see much of the river due to the mist below and the foliage in front of him, but he saw bits and pieces of it anyway. He felt a little dizzy at the thought of it all. They had traveled thousands of kilometers and centuries back in time in an instant. Now they were standing in the midst of towering oaks, sweetgums, sycamores, elms, alders, and only the occasional evergreen. Some of the trees behind him were massive. A couple of them were nearly two meters across. Below him an entire river was actually un-piped. He halted his scan.

There.

That speck on the river.

Whoa! That looks like a boat.

He pressed a button and the binoculars switched to 10X mode.

It's a canoe!

He pressed the magnification mode again. Now it was at 50X. He could see two occupants. It looked like two men. Both appeared to be wearing hats, obscuring a good look at them. The motion-stabilizing circuit was working perfectly, but that was all he could discern of them, even at this magnification. "Holy shit," he whispered to himself. They had been told they weren't going to see anyone.

His binoculars suddenly became useless as the mist far below completely obscured his view. He pulled them from his eyes and looked for the terahertz mode button. There it was. He pressed it. Instantly, the green of the forest changed to a yellowish-white through his view piece. This mode allowed him to see through the mist and would easily gain him a view through the smaller tree trunks, but there were so many of them it was difficult to see through a bunch of white vertical lines. He lost a lot of resolution in this mode, too. Regardless, it afforded him a second look before the canoe disappeared behind a rock outcropping below.

Damn it, he thought. He wanted a better look. *Oh well, they're gone now.* Kallen pulled the binoculars from his face and let gravity make quick work of his descent back to camp some thirty meters away. The sheer excitement of being here made him immediately forget what he'd just seen.

"Deshara," the major said as he saw Kallen approach. "Assist Lander and Madsen in the placement of the converter. Dr. Hatsuwakan said he's found the right place for the antenna."

"No problem, sir."

Kallen joined the three other men. Lander activated the stroller. The antenna and the energy converter were the only things left on it now. They moved the stroller away from their bivouac area toward the rise of the hill. The doctor pointed out the location about forty meters from camp. They needed the converter to be a good distance from camp due to the massive amount of energy it was handling.

"This is mighty convenient," Lander said. "We can place the converter inside this cluster of rocks."

It was the perfect place to conceal their most conspicuous piece of equipment. The rock cluster consisted of five massive roughly vertical ones, jutting upward from the ground in a loose circle. Nothing but grasses, leaf litter and several small rocks—which Madsen moved—were in the open area among them. There was an opening between two of the stones that looked wide enough to pass the converter through. The rest of the openings were much narrower. Only one other was wide enough to allow a man through.

Lander activated the a-grav struts that were built into grooves along the four sides of the converter. The struts created a small-scale graviton-repulsor field so that they could easily move the converter from the stroller and place it where they wanted. While not nearly as efficient as a stroller's a-grav circuitry, they nonetheless made an otherwise impossible task much more manageable.

Using much patience, the three men maneuvered the converter to within centimeters of their intended touchdown point. Lander switched off the struts. They heard an audible tone as the hypersonic frequency created by the repulsor field wound down and disappeared completely.

The nearby trees were useful, too. They tied lengths of nylex cord through the corner grommets of a tarp and tied the other ends to tree trunks. They had to stand on the top of the surrounding rocks to make its shelter. Shortly, the converter's top would be protected from leaf litter and rain.

The doctor surveyed the top of a nearby rise. He pointed to an area right at the edge of where it sloped downward to the river valley. "This looks like an ideal spot for the antenna. Full extension of the sections will put it above the trees."

Madsen and Lander moved the stroller to a position against the rock outcropping near the converter, then deactivated it. The next hour was spent assembling the antenna's sections and pounding the hardened ceramic yttrium-doped copper grounding stakes into the ground. Although everyone had their turn, Lander complained the entire time about having to do manual labor. Why didn't they bring a repulsor-beam piston to drive them in? Why did they not even bring an auger to make this part easier? Why did he have to be part of this operation at all? Was he the only one concerned that something was going to go terribly wrong?

Kallen kept glancing at him, trying to shut him up with a look, but was only partially successful. Finally, they attached guy wires to keep the antenna rigidly upright.

Lander took charge of attaching the long, coiled superconducting cables from the antenna to the stakes. They would act as the grounding wires to discharge ionic energy attracted to the antenna. Madsen connected a control cable from the antenna's photronics junction box to the converter. While Dr. Hatsuwakan looked on, Madsen activated a vidpanel that was attached to the side of the converter.

"Do you mind if I call you Dr. H?" Dayler asked as he worked.

"I usually go by my nickname Senji."

Dayler looked up at him briefly. "Senji?"

"It's short for my first name, Iwasenji."

"Thank God for nicknames. That's way easier to remember."

Senji grinned. It wasn't the first time he'd heard that. He watched while Dayler activated the converter. Once the operating system came up, he ran an internal diagnostic. When the okay was signaled, Senji handed him a data crystal.

"This contains code that will override the built-in converter application. Once it's read, launch the icon that says 'Override Converter'."

"Will do."

Kallen and Lander looked on while Dayler inserted the crystal.

Lander looked all sorts of skeptical. "I don't see how you can override an energy converter's internal code. These things aren't built for that purpose. You could blow every circuit in it."

Senji looked at him. "I'm quite familiar with how delicate these converters are Mr. Lander."

"ST Lander."

"ST Lander, then. I assure you this code base will work."

"Why didn't you just use your own converter? Why did you have to involve us? After all, it's your mistake, not ours."

He was starting to really irritate Kallen.

"ESC was the closest place that had a Zelinski Energy Converter, which, by the way, is the only device we know of that could possibly be used to ground ionic energy. In addition, your commanding officers told us they could immediately pull together the right personnel who knew how to run one. That part is true, isn't it?"

"Well, yeah."

"So, what's the problem?"

Lander shook his head. He shut up for now, but Kallen could tell he had much more to say.

After Dayler activated the code base from the crystal and the converter was operating in reverse, he let Lander bring up the applications they would use to monitor their progress. Lander sat and placed the vidpanel in his lap. It was connected to the converter via a short-range high frequency digital signal.

"Lander, you get first watch on the converter 'til noon, since you're on the panel," Kallen told him. "Dayler gets the noon to eight. I get the next one."

"Who said you're making the schedule?" Lander asked.

"Nobody else made one. And don't complain. You get off early. Madsen gets a decent watch, too. I get the 2000 to 0400 watch. That's nighttime, of course—while *you're* sleeping."

Lander didn't say anything else. *At least that shut him up,* Kallen thought.

Kallen's attention shifted back to his surroundings. He deliberately took in a deep breath again. It was just incredible. Was it actually possible that forest air could smell sweet? And, it almost seemed as if the air were breathing him instead of the other way around. He laughed out loud at the thought. Senji and Dayler looked at him. Kallen just shook his head, not wanting to get ridiculed if they knew what he was thinking about.

"I'll bring you a meal box, huh, Lander?" Kallen told him before they started back toward camp.

"Yeah, you do that." He still had his attention on the control panel and was frowning now.

What a pain in the ass, Kallen thought. He wondered why he was bothering to be nice to him. He returned a few minutes later after Lackson pulled a meal box from the storage container for him. He checked the control panel which Lander had reaffixed back onto the converter.

"These graphs are all in reverse. The numbers don't make any sense," Kallen said.

"No kidding. How the fuck am I supposed to know if it's working properly?"

Kallen touched a few icons. The panel changed to the index screen. He found an icon that said 'Convert to Positive'. He ran that code base. Immediately all the graph's scales reversed themselves.

"There. Now they make sense." He pointed, but Lander was digging into his food.

"I'll look at it later," he told Kallen.

As Kallen returned to camp a fat green flying insect came out of nowhere, hovered, and with huge eyes pointed at him, hung in the air directly in front of his face. It wasn't a dragonfly. This one didn't have a long thin body. Plus, dragonflies weren't *this* speedy. He swatted at it a couple of times, but the insect seemed to be anticipating his movements. He finally quit swatting and continued on his way. The insect took off as fast as it had arrived; almost supersonic, it seemed. The tent felt extraordinarily inviting as he entered and lay down on his cot. He needed to rest. All this excitement was exhausting.

Guyez had finished digging out a latrine several meters downhill from them when Kallen woke up from his nap an hour later. He had only been partially successful in getting any rest. He was more wound up than he thought. After extracting himself from the tent, he wondered about Craistok and Biggert. He still wasn't sure why there needed to be any Black Guard on this mission. Wouldn't a single regular MP have been sufficient? Or none at all? And why *two* Black Guard? It's not like they were even near a populated area. That's when he remembered seeing the canoeists. His imagination went into overdrive. *Wouldn't it be the coolest thing to meet someone from this time?* He was sure the English spoken now would be unintelligible. Maybe he'd ask Senji. They probably researched all sorts of things about this era. In fact, if he could get Senji aside he had all sorts of questions for him, warning or no warning about him being subversive.

The morning wore on. The sun was quickly reaching zenith. Kallen looked at his wristcomm, the device which would provide local two-way communications; be their alert monitor and time piece. Dayler came out of the tent and to the circle where they had put the heatstove for the evening.

"Your watch is coming up," Kallen told him. "It's almost local noon."

Guyez came up to them at that moment. He had an open canteen with him.

"Hey, check this out."

They both looked his way. Kallen yawned. "What?"

"Have a swig."

"What is it?"

"Water."

"Water?" Dayler asked.

"Water that's never been processed. Water that's older than your greatgreat-great grandmother. This is *vintage*." He took a big gulp. "Ahh!"

Kallen took the proffered canteen and downed a swallow. "Man, it *is* good. Where did you get it?"

Guyez pointed to his right. "Down that slope a ways. Just outside the camp perimeter. I was strapping our shower bag to one of those trees over by those rocks and saw a wet line in the leaves. I followed it to the source and found a spring. It's coming right out of a crack in that outcropping. I was just gonna fill the shower bag from it, and decided to give it a taste first. I'm glad I did. It's freakin' great."

"You used a filtration pump, right?" Kallen asked.

"No."

"Shit, and I drank this?" Kallen was alarmed as he suspiciously eyed the canteen.

"So?"

"Where's the medkit?" He set the canteen down.

"The major put it on that table he set up outside his tent."

All three of them walked toward the major's tent.

Upon hearing their voices, the major emerged. "What's going on out here?"

"Guyez found some drinking water and didn't bother to filter it. We both drank it. I'm checking the medkit," Kallen told him.

The major grinned. "Serves you both right if you get the runs, but not on my time. Get what you need." He left, seeking out Lackson for a noon meal.

Kallen opened the silver case and looked inside. Attached to the inside lid was a messagePAD. On it, the words 'MedKits, Inc. Database Manual' were embossed into its surface. It was a standard reference database PAD that contained a complete medical reference in both text and video formats. He inspected the contents of the kit, but was bewildered. Apparently the database PAD was all they needed, Kallen surmised. No medtech for this trip at all. Two Black Guard, yes. A medtech, no. *Odd*, he thought. Kallen activated the PAD. The virtual nurse instantly appeared onscreen.

"*Query?*" it asked.

"Diarrhea, tainted water," he said.

The nurse read off a short description of what diarrhea was and how to treat it. While she spoke, Kallen searched for the coded bottle that was listed at the top of the screen. He found it, opened it, and spilled a couple of gray tablets onto his palm. "Here," he said as he offered one to Guyez.

"If I get the runs, I'll take one."

"Suit yourself." Kallen put one of the pills back in, pocketed the other one, then replaced the bottle cap. He'd probably be up long enough to know if he needed to take it or not.

He unrolled an LCD display screen that was packed into one of the compartments and read through the list of contents. It contained much more than the standard array of items found in a first aid kit. It seemed someone had anticipated exactly what they'd need for this odd mission. He wondered who else knew where they were, which made him recall that he still hadn't looked at the vidfiles he'd decrypted from the commander's database. Tonight. Tonight there would be plenty of time to read through them. He would be essentially isolated from prying eyes. Who here would bother him in the middle of the night?

Dayler had left camp for his watch about five minutes ago. Kallen waited a good fifteen minutes so he could get settled, waited for Lander to return, then went to see him.

Dayler watched Kallen as he came toward them. Guyez was there, too, looking quite animated as he talked with Dayler. Kallen stopped and listened in.

"I'm thinking of starting my own business when we get back," Guyez said. "I'm callin' it 'Sweet as Wine Kentucky Bottling.' All we have to do is keep the photonogrid on, minimum power only, of course; and run a pipe from here to our time. Add a pump, some holding tanks, some nice clean bottles, and presto, bottled water that's better than anything we have."

"Just water?" Dayler asked.

"We might add some juices."

"You didn't even *mention* beer."

There was an alarmed look on his face. "Shit, I must be losing my mind." He smiled briefly at them both, then headed toward camp.

"I think he's got a good idea there," Kallen said as Guyez strode away. He took a seat on the a-grav stroller.

Dayler sat next to him. He had a full canteen in his hand which Guyez had given him. "Here. It's nice and cold."

"I don't know." Kallen opened it, thought for a moment, took a whiff, then guzzled a quarter of its contents." He felt for the tablet in his pocket with his other hand.

"Jeez, someone was thirsty. At least leave me a swallow."

"Sorry." Kallen gave the canteen back to him. They locked eyes as Dayler drank. He wiped his mouth and twisted the cap back on. Kallen looked away for a moment.

Dayler broke the awkward silence. "You're still working out, huh?"

"Three days a week. Thanks to you, I can't stop. You're still working out too, I see."

Dayler was wearing a tight green t-shirt. His upper chest was very nicely outlined through the thin fabric. Neither of them were anywhere near bulging with muscles, both of them were just nicely defined. Dayler, on the other hand, had a good four centimeters of diameter on Kallen in the upper arm department. He raised one and flexed his bicep. "Twice a week most weeks."

"We need to talk. Just you and me, huh?" Kallen said.

Dayler set the canteen aside. "Sorry I've been, I don't know, aloof. It was just a...surprise to see you. Imagine that, Deshara and Madsen together again."

"It's not like before."

"Yeah, my bad."

"Huh?"

"Entirely my bad."

"I'm listening."

Dayler appeared to be at a loss for words. He wasn't sure how to explain it. "I-I was just trying to insulate myself. From the inevitable. We were going to be apart and there was no way it was gonna work. Maybe you were right, though. You thought we should 've stayed together."

"No, you *were* right. It wouldn't have worked. Long distance isn't the same as being together. Besides, you kept trying to make me into something I wasn't. Except for the working out thing.... So, *have* you been seeing people?"

"Here and there, but no one as decent as you."

Kallen was eating up the compliment. "Decent?"

"About everything." He looked down momentarily, then back at Kallen. "Nice, intelligent, good looking, great butt. Did I ever mention that you have a great ass?"

Kallen grinned. "No less than a dozen times."

"How about you? Have you gone out with anyone?"

"I was in a relationship for a while, but it turned into a disaster." At Dayler's behest, Kallen told him about Acton, about how they got together, and why it failed in the end. Dayler listened, just taking it all in.

"At least you were *in* a relationship. I've barely been with two guys. A sergeant in Warehousing and an imagery guy in Intelligence."

"Intelligence?"

"A real cutie, too."

"What was his name?"

"Tiago."

Kallen nearly fell over. "Tiago *Sandoval?*"

Dayler furrowed his brow. "How could you possibly know him?"

Kallen spent the next twenty minutes telling him all about it.

"You and I were going out for how long and you never even *mentioned* him?" Dayler asked.

"He obviously never mentioned *me* either. Besides, he *dumped* me. I didn't like him after that. There were times I hoped I would just forget he existed."

"Did you not like me either? After I-after I called it off."

Kallen scrutinized his face. "You were hard not to like. Even after we split up. You and I went out for a lot longer that I was with him. I actually got to know you."

Another awkward silence. Dayler could tell that Kallen was thinking about Tiago. "He's a heartbreaker, Kallen. You're better off not thinking about him."

"You say that after bringing his name up?"

"Well, if it makes it any easier, he has some…personal problems. He landed in the brig."

"*What*? He's in the brig?"

"Just like those two guys you said Acton was freaked out about."

Kallen stood up, still not believing it. "Tiago's in the fucking brig?"

Dayler's eyes grew wide as he looked around. Kallen had said that pretty loudly. "Shhh! There was a sting. He got court-martialed."

"No way," Kallen said weakly.

"Luckily, he and I only did it like, I don't know, three times. I didn't know him well enough to get close to him. It was just sex. He's not the relationship type. I hadn't seen him in months when I heard about him. The group of guys I found—at least the ones who're out—is a pretty small one. The consolation prize is that he didn't squeal on me or anyone else we know."

Kallen wasn't sure what to think, but his heart was doing some of it. Tiago was the first boy he'd ever been with. Despite having been dumped by him, it hurt to hear that he'd been court-martialed just for being gay. Perhaps Acton had been more right than wrong after all. Perhaps if they'd continued seeing each other they would have been next.

"When did that happen? When was he put in the brig?"

"Three months ago. No, two and a half. That's the last I heard about him."

In the brig because of being who he is, Kallen thought. *It's awful. Why is life like that?*

Kallen studied Dayler's face again. Gone was the carefree boy who was his Starter, his boyfriend, his study-sparring partner. In his place was someone who had grown way too old, too quickly. Dayler was only twenty-one. He acted like he was thirty.

"Why are you so serious now? You were never like that before. Except for grades."

"I'm just practical. Before, I was all over the place. I didn't have any responsibility, nothing. Well, just you, and those other guys in school. I have an entire section I'm *really* responsible for now. It's way more than just being a Starter."

"You're a section head?"

"I gotta think about fifteen men and women, and report to a Lieutenant. I'm up for Staff Sergeant in a few months. I could do with a pay raise."

Kallen was justifiably surprised at Dayler's status. "All that time. Trying to change *me*—and look at you. You've *completely* changed."

Dayler looked pensive for a moment. "We didn't know when we were drafted that we'd be put in jail just because we suck dick, huh? I just got wise to what was going on. What did you think I would do, just announce that I'm gay to my superiors?"

"Well, I'm sure not gonna re-up like Acton did. He was stupid, if you ask me. I'm outta here at the end of my active service."

"Exactly my point. The way I figure it, the shortest distance between now and the end of *my* active service is a straight line. As it were."

"You *are* too serious." This wasn't the Dayler he knew at all.

"You think so? Look, I have three years left. I dumped you, and I shouldn't have. Someone I could have fallen for is in the brig. Things haven't gone exactly like I thought they would. I've, uh, I've wondered now and then what it would have been like if we were still together."

Kallen snorted. "It'll never happen. We're way too different. Besides, we live on opposite sides of the country. I'm not coming up for a transfer anytime soon. I'm guessing you aren't either. This is just an awful twist of fate that we're here together again."

"Awful?"

Kallen scooted closer to him. They were almost touching as they sat side-by-side. "I didn't mean it like that."

Dayler reached up, touched Kallen's cheek, and smiled. It was a broader smile than Kallen had seen this whole time. But within the smile was a remnant of past sorrow.

Kallen could tell Dayler wanted to speak. "Don't say anything. It'll just hurt," Kallen told him. He vaguely remembered Dayler having said something like that to him a long time ago.

Yet it was Kallen that was hurting.

A lot.

Chapter 16

Wednesday, June 21, 1820

Kallen knew it was time to leave. Dayler needed to decompress from their discussion and Kallen needed to nurse the wounds Dayler had inadvertently opened about them, and about he and Tiago. He didn't return to the stroller until just before his watch.

The top of the stroller's platform was a dozen centimeters above ground level. Kallen unfolded a blanket on one end of it, then doubled it up. Once Dayler left, Kallen pulled the vidpanel off the converter and sat it next to him. He unbuttoned his camo shirt and pulled it off, then wadded it up and put it behind his back while he leaned against the stroller's railings. He checked all the settings on the vidpanel, then set it aside. He noticed he had no gastric upset, nor were his bowels acting weird. *Hmm, the water must be clean after all.* Assured that all was fine with the converter and with himself, he pulled out his vidPAD and activated it. He craned his neck back toward camp, making sure that Dayler was indeed gone. He had been waiting for this moment so he could look through all the files he'd downloaded from Commander Torvadred's personal database. He removed the security protocols he had applied to them and started digging in right away.

He slid to the edge of the stroller, his booted feet firmly on the ground now so he could watch for anyone who might sneak up on him. It was getting dark now and Kallen wanted to be absolutely sure he'd see someone approaching. With the wireless earpiece securely fastened for complete privacy, Kallen hadn't watched two of the vids before his jaw dropped open from surprise.

The first vid started as a typical vidmail from the commander to an officer Kallen hadn't heard of before. It dealt with the off-limits section of the base in the southeast corner. Kallen knew that that section of base had no topside shuttle and that lower level shuttles required special clearance. There were checkpoints all along the way. Foot traffic was always thoroughly checked out, too.

The southwest gate topside wasn't used by regular base personnel. He knew that. He also knew that there were two checkpoints along that route leading off-base. In other words, double security existed to and from that section topside and downside. After his initial week at ESC and, after discovering it was off-limits, he just forgot it was there. He thought it might be a special munitions dump or something. Apparently, the secrecy worked on Dwess, too. Once, Kallen had asked him what he thought was over there. Dwess had asked him what he was talking about.

Now he knew why there was so much special security over there.

That entire section was a nursery. But it wasn't for plants. It was for people called 'The Children'.

Fort Morgan didn't just have a water pumping station. It also had an extensive downside housing facility nearby. A secret one.

There was no mysterious explosion. The UCT had bombed it, just as he'd suspected.

More vids and text files told him everything. There were authorizations dated back almost two years for the movement of personnel and equipment off-base—all to Fort Morgan. There was a receipt for the purchase of all sorts of items, mostly rations. There was a vid of a roundtable discussion about the date of an 'attack'. Endurance testing had been performed on the Children, who were labeled with numbers, not names. There were vidmails between Torvadred and someone named Dr. Ditmala about the bombing. The commander was telling him that someone in the upper echelon of the UCT military had found out about the secret proving ground facility at Fort Morgan. It was a proving ground?

Kallen came across the manifest of the damaged equipment that had been crated up and shipped back during the recovery mission. No wonder he couldn't find anything out about the disaster. All mention of it had been kept securely in the commander's own database! Right away, Kallen recognized that some of the equipment on the list was used only for genetic engineering research. He knew because of the manufacturers names. He had read about some of the models of the listed items before. At least some of them. Most of it was rare and very expensive equipment. He had no idea anyone actually used those type of devices in real life.

Kallen had been randomly playing the vids. He was going completely out of chronological order, so none of the story he was piecing together was making any sense. But as he read further, bit by bit, it started to fall into place.

The nursery at ESC was being used to engineer the Children to tolerate extreme heat. Why? To create an elite fighting force capable of withstanding a hot dry climate—their climate. Engineered to withstand being exposed. Out in the open. For extended lengths of time. For an impending battle. A battle that was being orchestrated by the ESC commander to take Lake Superior. And it was to start with the securing of the Duluth pumping station against a sustained attack.

Kallen pieced together more of the story as he watched more vidmails. Fort Morgan had a downside facility that served as a biomedical hospital and a military training center. The new Children had been grown using a modified regeneration biocircuit, much like a Veles Ring, and vaguely similar to Katterjay's photonogrid, and were eventually shipped off to Fort Morgan to be 'proven'.

Kallen didn't know that was possible. *How could an entire human being be grown using a Veles Ring, however modified?* He did another search and found a partial schematic. Most of it made no sense. It involved bioengineering, which he was completely unfamiliar with. Regardless, there was enough explanation and text to suggest that they had radically altered some of the time-displacement circuitry and were able to contain the effect to culture an entire human from a single stem cell. Since it was technology used in the medical field, Kallen really didn't understand how they had come up with this idea in the first place.

How odd. Perhaps this sort of technology was beginning to emerge everywhere. He'd heard of that before. There were several incidents even in his lifetime where simultaneous inventions from different parts of the country came to market as finished products at the same time, but under different names.

Kallen watched more of the vids. These 'Children'—who looked like adults—were taught specific skills, strict obedience and allegiance to the NAA, and were put through all sorts of combat training and situations to ready them for being part of a front line defense in President Brin's vision to take Lake Superior.

This is Brin's plan, Kallen realized. Dwess had told him about it. He just didn't know how it was going to be accomplished.

This Dr. Ditmala had been working with Commander-General Torvadred to accept millions of credits of taxpayer money to fund the project. The commander authorized the purchase of the equipment and had it shipped to Fort Morgan. He acted as the overall coordinator for the entire project. Ditmala spent the money and reported directly to the commander on their progress with the 'new troops'.

One vid showed the commander speaking directly to President Brin's Strategy Aide, with Ditmala conferenced in. *The freakin' Strategy Aide,* Kallen thought. The Strategy Aide was appointed by Brin. Although Kallen hadn't seen the commander speaking directly with the President just yet, he was sure he would find one shortly.

The implication of what Kallen was listening to and reading about was horrible. Somehow, despite the fact that perhaps up to a hundred people were involved with engineering all these new 'troops', no one had talked to the NAA media. And no one was locally in charge of it except Commander Torvadred.

Kallen's mind was revving. *What would happen if anyone found out I know this? Could I be silenced?* As scared as he was that he even had this information, he didn't dare delete it. He hadn't gone through more than a quarter of it yet. Regardless of his fear he had to know the rest of the story.

As he watched more of the vidmails he kept hearing about a timeline. It seemed to be quite important to those involved. What the timeline referred to wasn't evident so far. Maybe he'd find out more if he stopped using just key search words. If he wanted to find out when an attack was planned for and who had authorized it he needed to go in chronological order. As much as he wanted to find out everything at once, he calmed himself down and went in order after all.

As he watched, he realized that Brin had been regularly funneling information to Torvadred through his Strategy Aide, and vice versa to Torvadred (he had to infer that last part, since he couldn't quite figure it out). Torvadred was authorizing the purchase and transport of the equipment using complex accounting and shipping procedures. That way, none of the lower-level accounting people on base would become suspicious. There weren't enough vidmails to figure out the whole process, but there was enough information to implicate a lot of top-level people. And one thing was obvious. Torvadred and this Dr. Ditmala had had a lot of contact, personally, over BaseNet, and through vidmails. They were in constant communication, it seemed, to make sure that they stay on schedule. *The timeline. What's the freakin' timeline?*

Kallen stopped and did some serious thinking about the issue now. He had gained a whole new perspective on the water treaty in the last several months. Whereas, before he would have spoken up in favor of getting as much water as the NAA wanted or needed, he realized now that the impending battle might end up limiting their right to water instead. Maybe even eliminate it! If the NAA lost, which was entirely possible since the UCT seemed to have better firepower, the NAA might be told that they could draw no more water from the lake. Was Brin really willing to risk having the pipeline completely shut down? The bombing at Fort Morgan seemed to be just a taste of the UCT's power.

Kallen wondered about a more immediate point. How were they going to keep Torvadred's Children a secret once they were in combat? The situation seemed completely preposterous. And how had this all been going on at ESC, for almost two years, and no one had leaked a word? But then, there were hundreds of Black Guard acting as security. *There must be a special detachment involved in the security of the nursery section on base,* he thought. *They keep their mouths shut, and they're intimidating enough for people to keep clear of them. Perhaps they* did *silence people if they found out things they weren't supposed to know about. Maybe that's what happened to Dwess?*

Oh shit!

What if he did some investigating that I never heard about? He never told me about Mirani being pregnant. What else *did he not tell me?*

Kallen found his mouth dropping open time and time again as he scanned through more vids and messages. He wondered which officers he knew, also knew about this, too. The only ones he could think of at the moment were Acton and Majors Vaulkner and Montarco. He did a search of those names. Acton's never came up. Neither did Montarco's.

Vaulkner's did.

Major Vaulkner was in direct control of two platoons of Black Guard that regularly shuttled equipment and Children back and forth to Fort Morgan. They kept the new troops under total cover and isolation from the rest of the base and away from the pumping facility.

Anyone who shouldn't know about them didn't.

Until now.

Kallen put the vidPAD down and stood up. He felt his hands trembling. He leaned up against one of the trees that the tarp was tied to, biting his thumbnail. This complicated things terribly. His peripheral contact with Vaulkner put him dangerously close to the source of the campaign. *What about the two BG on this mission? Are they directly under Vaulkner? Or are they just two lackeys?* It was impossible to tell. He had minimal contact with them so far. If he even hinted that he knew anything about this he would be in serious trouble—or his very life might be in danger. *Fuck, fuck, fuck!* He had no idea he would find out something like this. His little game of looking at the commander's vidmails had led him to data he wished he'd never seen. *Should I tell Dayler? Fuck no. The fewer that know the better.*

Kallen's head was boiling over with the details. What was going to happen when he got back? He figured it might take a couple of weeks before they came after him due to Dwess' arrest. After all, they would discover who all of Dwess' buddies were. Kallen hoped that when the investigators came after him they wouldn't use any undue interrogation methods on him. He didn't want to entertain any thought of what might happen to him if they discovered he knew any of *this.*

Kallen deactivated the vidPAD. He needed to stretch, to get his body back in motion. He'd been sitting for three straight hours with his eyes glued to the display. He looked over at the monitor panel to make sure everything was okay then picked up his lightwand.

About the same thickness as a broomstick, a lightwand was about one-third of a meter in length. It consisted of a row of one-dozen high-intensity white-light LEDs with a sheath drawn over it. He pulled the sheath back all the way. The q-cell energized the LEDs and it produced immediate light. A touchpad at the end varied the intensity. He touched it a couple of times so that it glowed at a dim setting. He took it with him so he could see where he was going. Moments later he arrived near the top of the rise. The antenna, higher up the rise and some twenty meters from him wasn't visible this far away. Besides, he was much more interested in seeing if he could view any of the river. The moon had crested the far hills and had drawn a silvery glow over the valley below. He pushed the sheath over the light tube. Darkness enveloped him. The crickets and other night creatures were all around. That's when he smelled it.

Smoke.

He was instantly alarmed. Smoke meant a fire, which they didn't need to build since they had brought heat stoves. If there were one below, and moving its way up the rise, they might not be able to outrun it. He scanned the dark for any sign of flame. Nothing. He craned his neck over what he could of the treetops below him downslope, but it was too dark. He decided it would be a lot easier to retrieve his binoculars, switch to infrared mode, and look for a flame that way. He dashed back to the stroller, searched his bag, and pulled them out. Breathless, he returned to the rise. He scanned the whole area below. As he scanned, he noted that he could no longer smell anything except damp earth and foliage. There were no telltale crackling sounds either, and all the insects were still singing away. He continued to scan with the binoculars. *There!* Just at the edge of the river, with only a sliver of a view available to him through a crack in the rocks below, was a flame!

It wasn't moving uphill like he expected. Had the canoeists he saw this morning stopped to make camp?

A loud crackling noise came from his right. Kallen pulled the binoculars from his face and turned. The sky nearby seemed to sizzle and spit. He felt an odd sensation, like static electricity was dancing all over his hair. There was a faint blue light, like a mist illuminating the antenna. A bright flash appeared at the top of the antenna. Instantly, a thunderclap reverberated throughout the woods and echoed all around him. Kallen tumbled to the ground, losing the binoculars as he rolled. Both of his ears rang. He opened his eyes. Everything was a pure featureless white. It was if a completely obscuring snowstorm had suddenly descended upon him.

Kallen panicked. *Oh my God, I'm blind*, he thought.

Chapter 17

Thursday, June 22, 1820

Aaric awoke with a start and was immediately at the ready. Nash flung off his blanket, rose up, and looked around. The sound was deafening. The echo of the blast had already reverberated several times.

Breathing heavily from being startled so, and looking disoriented, Aaric grabbed for his smooth bore and was standing a second later. A large piece of wood within the fire circle snapped and fell in on itself, flinging up a few bright sparks from the black and gray ash. A gust of wind fanned the orange coals, starting a new flame. It illuminated his bare heaving chest with a dull glow. His shadow flickered and danced on the rock wall behind his head. He gulped as he tried to calm himself. He put the weapon down.

"Thunder. It was just thunder," he said aloud.

He looked up, saw a ribbon of bright stars overhead, and wrinkled his brow. It was just like before. Some of the townsfolk said that the first storm had started with odd-colored lightening from a perfectly clear sky, accompanied by bizarre-sounding thunder. He walked down the beach a short way. Somewhere in the darkness a raccoon chattered briefly. Already the crickets, which had become silent, were beginning to chirrup again. Satisfied there wasn't going to be fireworks all night he returned and lay back on his bed in the soft sand.

"We're leavin' as soon as we can after we pull the turkeys from the snares tomorrow," Nash told him. "I don't want to be caught out here in any of them storms." He turned over and pulled the blanket up to this neck. He was asleep a few minutes later.

Aaric couldn't get back to sleep right away. The same feeling of being watched annoyed his normally composed self. He placed his .57 caliber weapon to his side and pulled the top blanket back over himself. He was fast asleep shortly after Nash began lightly snoring.

The next thing Kallen heard was muffled sounds, then shouting, orders being yelled. Someone called out to him, then pulled him to his feet. His vision was returning. The featureless white had already transmuted to a dull green with a large purple spot in the middle of his vision. As he blinked, it started to fade, as did the ringing in his ears. Finally, he was able to see Senji's face at the periphery of his still-impaired vision. With him were Dayler, Major Montarco, and both of the Black Guard. Everyone had pulse stunners drawn.

Senji picked up the binoculars and lightwand Kallen had dropped, then helped him back to the stroller, where he sat. Kallen felt a little disoriented, but he had his wits. He felt around and found his vidPAD, which he'd left there. He quickly holstered it.

"What the hell happened, sergeant?" Major Montarco asked.

"I-I don't know. I was standing over there," he pointed, "when all the sudden the sky blew up."

Craistok and Biggert were illuminating the antenna with their lightwands. It was still perfectly intact. Dayler had his nose in the converter's control vidpanel. Senji was looking over his shoulder.

"Hey, look here," Dayler told Senji. He pointed to one of the graphs. "This spike in the ionic energy. A clear indication of a lightening strike." He checked a few of the other graphs now: voltage, the ionic disturbance pattern, amperage, and amplitude of the spike. "Look at this resistance value. It doesn't make any sense. The antenna is completely grounded. So is the converter. That shouldn't have happened. We should be having a slow, continuous drain."

Senji shook his head, also wondering how it had happened. They continued to cycle through the graphs. Lander showed up now. He was wearing just camo trousers and hastily zipped up boots. His arms were across his naked chest, as if warding off cold. He looked at the panel, then joined the two Guard who were still inspecting the antenna.

"Hmm. Look at this," Dayler told Senji. "This graph tells me that one of the gounding wires is loose or disconnected. The resistance is way too high to be a good earth ground."

Senji nodded. "I think you're right. Let's check."

They went to the antenna. By now, Kallen's ears had quit ringing and the purple spot had turned bright yellow. He followed them to the antenna.

"Here's the problem," Dayler said. He was playing his lightwand on one of the grounding stakes. "Who didn't connect this cable?"

Lander looked at him and made a face.

Craistok came up to him. "You didn't connect that cable, did you?"

"Wh-who me?"

"You're Lander, aren't you?"

"Hey, I was tired after staking those things in. How was I supposed to know it wouldn't stay connected?"

"Your incompetence might have jeopardized this entire mission."

Lander stood his ground. "The converter's still working, isn't it? The antenna isn't damaged, is it? Is it?"

Craistok played his beam all over the antenna. "It looks okay to me, but we'll know in the morning."

"Huh! We'll know right now."

Craistok gave him a nasty look but didn't escalate the issue. Dayler retrieved a tool bag and re-connected the grounding cable. Back at the control panel the techs decided that that was all they needed to do to rectify the situation since all systems appeared normal. The backsurge circuits were still operating, no fuses had been blown, and all systems appeared normal.

Ten minutes later, after the major and the Guard had decided that all was indeed okay, they turned in. It was pushing midnight. Everyone was yawning. Everyone except Kallen and Senji. Kallen was wide awake now, still shaking his head periodically, trying to dislodge the residual ringing in his ears. The bright yellow spot had faded considerably now. Senji decided to stay with him for a few minutes.

Dayler returned a few moments later with a pulse stunner and a holster. "The major wants us to carry these at all times."

"Why?"

"Don't know. But they were issued to us."

Kallen strapped it around his waist, opposite his vidPAD, while Dayler turned to go.

Senji continued to monitor the control panel.

"Hey, it's still my watch. I can do all that. Why don't you turn in," Kallen told him.

"I can't sleep."

"I don't blame you. It's unnerving hearing something like that out of the blue. Literally."

"It's not that. This place gives me the creeps."

"The creeps? That's not a word I would have expected to hear from a scientist."

"Why not?"

"I don't know. I thought you guys were in love with this whole mess."

"We did our research, but it's creepy here anyway."

"I think it's kinda cool."

"The ancient past as 'cool'. That's definitely not a word I would use to describe this time."

"Why not?"

"This is an *awful* time to be alive."

Kallen listened to the soft sounds that had finally returned to the forest. An owl hooting someplace far off, the wind that occasionally rustled the trees overhead, the creaking sound of branch against branch behind the rock outcrop. He still had a clear mental image of the sheen from the silvery moonrise that had spread over the river valley below. *An awful time to be alive? With an entire river un-piped below us?* "You gotta be kidding," he countered.

"That was no joke, sergeant."

"Then why is it so awful?"

"For starters there's no electricity. At least none that's in use. The phenomenon is known, but is purely academic. Batteries have just been invented but are amusing diversions. Electromagnetic induction won't be discovered for another year and even then it won't be used for anything practical for another dozen years."

Kallen snickered. "What do you mean?" He was sure electricity had been around forever.

"Just that. Electricity is known to some in this time, but only as an amusing academic phenomenon."

Kallen frowned. "Go on."

"And diseases. In this time smallpox, yellow fever, polio, and other completely curable or preventable infectious diseases killed millions each year. Vaccines don't exist yet. There isn't even aspirin. No anesthesia, no organ regeneration, no auto bone mending, nothing. The average life expectancy, from diseases that mostly struck in early childhood, was about forty. Plenty died before they reached ten years of age."

"Are you sure?"

"Of course I'm sure," Senji stated emphatically.

"Slavery is a big issue in this time, too. Some races were bought and sold like cattle. Colonial powers butchered people because they were from the 'wrong' continent or were the 'wrong' race, or the 'wrong' religion, or had the 'wrong' skin color. Imagine what might happen if *I* showed up in this time out of the blue. *I* could be sold into slavery."

"What? Here?"

"Perhaps not on this continent. Most of the slave trade in this part of the world was with African nationals. In this time, my ancestors are from Indonesia. The Dutch, you know, from Europe, control much of the trade in their lands now. Just decades ago—from this time period—they had control of most of the world's sea trade. They practically owned most of the shipping. That includes to and from Indonesia. Their culture was quite powerful. Sometimes they killed my people for the sport of it."

Kallen was beginning to wonder how much of what Senji was telling him was true. "What about our time? Most of our country is too hot to live in, food isn't exactly abundant, we fight over something as basic as water. The military runs practically everything. We barely know anything that happened after the Third Wave."

"What do you know about 'after the Third Wave?'"

"Nothing. Hardly anyone knows what happened then."

"Who told you that?"

"One of my teachers in grade school."

"You don't actually believe *that* nonsense, do you?"

"What nonsense?"

"First wave, second wave. All that."

"What do you mean?"

"What if I told you that it's a pack of lies."

"What are you saying?" Kallen asked him, greatly intrigued.

"Lies. All of it. There was no First, Second, or Third wave. There were no Waves at all. Economic ruin caused the huge gap in our history. We don't know what happened 'after the Third Wave' because it never occurred."

For some reason Senji's tone of voice conjured up a mental image of Dwess in Kallen's mind. Kallen was warned about the possibility of Senji being subversive. Dwess wasn't subversive in the military sense of the word. And maybe, just maybe, it *wasn't* true what he'd been told about Senji.

Hmm.

After all, Dwess had taught him some of the most important lessons of his life. How to question. How to peel back the layers of propaganda.

Hmm.

Maybe Senji's assertion was something to consider, however odd.

Senji stood. He could tell Kallen's silence was because he was debating his contention. "I wouldn't want you to believe me. How about I show you instead. But you have to promise me something."

Kallen hoped everyone was back in their tents, out of earshot. He hoped no one was secretly listening. He gulped. "What?"

"I have some very interesting data in my vidPAD. If I upload some of it to yours you have to promise me that you won't tell any of your buddies here. Look through it, then delete it. I'll ask you about it later."

Kallen didn't answer right away. He was still nursing his tiny spark of a thought about Senji. *He might not be subversive.* Dwess *isn't. He's not! He's my friend. He talked all the time exactly like Senji just did. During the briefing Vaulkner was the one who said to not listen to him. Vaulkner's involved in Brin's conspiracy. Everything the* colonel *says has to be taken with caution. Not what* Senji *says.*

Hmm.

"Deal," Kallen whispered back.

"What encryption key do you want to use?"

Kallen nervously pulled his vidPAD from the holster and energized it. He activated a security screen and picked a wireless encryption code at random. "Use Alpha 2 Iota 6. A2I6." He activated the code.

"A2I6. I'm turning in. I'll beam the data to you. I'll set it to beep when it's done."

"Okay."

"Remember, delete everything when you're through reviewing it."

"Promise."

Kallen set his vidPAD on the stroller and went to inspect the antenna again. Moments later he heard the beep. He returned to the stroller and started looking through the material.

Less than an hour later Kallen was terribly confused. Apparently, *nothing* was like he'd been led to believe.

According to Senji's data the Great Climate Change had started well before the end of the 21st century! In fact, something referred to as the Greenhouse Effect had been known about and described since the late 20th century. At that time, the world's economy was dependent on petroleum. Some sort of consortium controlled most of its production. It was bought and sold in a marketplace that spanned the entire globe. *A world market economy?* He'd only heard of such a thing before, not believing it could have actually existed. But what was worse was that it was well known that the burning of petroleum products and other fossil fuels was heating up the planet. Atmospheric CO_2 was constantly rising due to it and other greenhouse gases emitted by other industries. It was even emitted from the hundreds of millions of animals that were raised for food. *Hundreds of millions? Of animals? For food? My God,* thought Kallen. *The planet must have been overrun by people and overwhelmed by the food resources needed to sustain them.*

He sped through reference after reference. Right here on this continent, the United States had been one of the major users of fossil fuels—and only one of the minor producers. At one point in the country's history it generated over seventy percent of the world's energy output from the burning of coal, natural gas, and gasoline. Apparently, just like in the NAA, well-moneyed and entrenched politicians ran the government and had total control over their energy policy. Although alternate and less harmful sources of fuels were available, known, and somewhat utilized, too many people were getting extremely rich in the buying and selling of this world commodity to even consider weaning themselves from it. Funding for alternative sources was always kept at a minimum. Research into conservation was ignored or ridiculed. In the early 21st century heavy energy consumption was greatly encouraged by Western powers who had the most to gain by it.

Even as the world started heating up, powerful politicians never seriously considered finding a way to cut back on the use of fossil fuels. Gasses from burning such fuels continued to fill the atmosphere, seriously disrupting normal seasonal temperature cycles. It was reported that glaciers began to melt at a record pace, as did polar ice. Still, no one did a thing to curtail their use, even though the cause had been well-identified.

Kallen had seen pictures of polar ice in ancient digital still photos but knew that neither pole had any in his time. There weren't even any glaciers on Mounts Foraker or McKinley in the far north adjacent to the recruit training center when he was in boot camp. In fact, he'd heard that the last one had disappeared well over a century and a half ago. He also knew it snowed up there but always melted within weeks.

Finally, as he continued to watch and read, it started to sound familiar. As the world heated up, shorelines changed, populations became displaced, ecosystems were disrupted, and hundreds of plant and animal species disappeared in an ever faster death spiral. Weather patterns became increasingly erratic with entire regions experiencing extended droughts and famine. Water was on everyone's priority list. In fact, that had been so for decades.

Then he read the story about the Sahara. As the 21st century wore on, it expanded southward, mostly due to the continued industrialization of North America and Europe. Somehow aerosols cast into the atmosphere by large-scale power-producing stations kept the rains from coming further south. India and China seemed to be trying to outdo each other in their quest to industrialize, and using the most polluting energy sources available. Their populations grew well past one billion and a half each. *One billion? And a half?* Kallen knew that there were barely a billion people alive on the entire planet in his time. It didn't seem possible that that many people could occupy a single country, much less two.

The continued use of fossil fuels as the planet's primary energy source disrupted the monsoon rains that India was dependent on to feed their huge populations; their deserts expanded as well. It was about that time that the productivity of most of the world's oceans crashed, producing a famine the likes of which had never been experienced before.

Kallen was horrified to learn that several of the large oilfields north of the Arabian Peninsula had been nuked by multiple tipped warheads in 2086. It was a well-planned targeted attack against several of them at once. The resulting firestorms weren't extinguished for over a year. It was the last straw. The global cooling that followed lasted only a year and a half, after which there was a return to steadily rising heat. By that time, a worldwide economic collapse had developed, devastating the entire planet for over two and a half centuries.

The world had plunged into chaos.

Kallen felt tears coming to his eyes. Everything he'd ever learned in school about his world was false? No neatly delineated time periods where the Great Climate Change had occurred? No First Wave? No Second Wave? No Third?

It was just like Senji said.

But it was worse. He had been taught that it was a *natural* occurrence. That the Earth had *naturally* heating up. According to these records it happened purely because of politics. Based on greed. It could have been delayed. It could have been stopped. It could have been avoided.

But it wasn't.

Virtually the whole world had developed a desert-like climate because of it. A huge portion of the world was searing hot and, in some places, still growing hotter, due to climatic feedback. The equatorial regions of the earth were virtually devoid of life. At least in his time. According to one of these reports, the equatorial belt had once been home to jungles and most of the world's genetic diversity.

What a concept! To think that the equator could have held biological diversity instead of being a virtual no-man's land.

Kallen found himself realizing that he had inherited a world that was whimpering its way into oblivion. How many decades did the earth have left? Was it years instead? Even if he were to have kids would they be born into a doomed world?

Maybe that's why President Brin was desperate to obtain Lake Superior. Despite what Kallen had discovered about Brin's plot and Commander Torvadred's involvement, somewhere inside Kallen was still convinced that the NAA was right to obtain that water resource.

Quickly, he changed files on the vidPAD and dug as deeply as he could into the commander's vidmails. He spent the next several hours trying to determine what the real reason was for their need to take control of the lake. He found nothing except a desperate desire for power. That's all there was to it. He could literally find no reason other than the President and Torvadred wanted more power. Perhaps obtaining water for their country had been their original reason for wanting the lake, but their intentions had clearly changed. It wasn't about supplying more of it to a thirsty population, or satisfying a need, or protecting national interests. It wasn't about any of that.

It was only about power.

Owning water was power.

Supplying it wasn't.

Finally, in a short communiqué from the President's Strategy Aide to the commander he caught a single line that said it all. '*The success of this mission will propel you to command a genetically enhanced defense force to next take Lake Michigan and regain the old Michigan, Wisconsin, and Illinois shorelines that are unlawfully claimed by the UCT.*'

That did it. Here was direct evidence that the coming campaign was nothing less than a power shuffling measure to give more control to President Brin and to delegate some of it to Torvadred.

Kallen couldn't absorb any more of this. Not only did he feel intellectually raped, he was emotionally drained. He rubbed his eyes before checking the clock on the control panel. His watch was nearly over. He re-encrypted the commander's files and buried them under as many layers of security encryption protocols as he could. He did the same to the ones Senji uploaded to him, too.

He saw a lightwand coming in his direction. It was Lander. Kallen quickly de-energized the vidPAD.

"Morning," Lander said with a very sleepy look on his face.

"Didn't sleep well?" Kallen asked. He didn't know why he bothered to ask.

"No. I've crossed too many time zones in too short a time. Plus, my little accident woke me up out of a perfectly good sleep."

Kallen didn't want to harp on the incident. "Everything's pretty much on autopilot. I just checked things every once in a while."

Lander took the control panel and examined the graphs. One of them was showing a dip in the amount of discharge energy. He adjusted a control to zoom in on its value.

Kallen noisily yawned several times. "I'm turning in."

"You didn't fall asleep?"

"Are you kidding? I was wound up like a spring." Lander had no idea how wound up he'd been!

The sun had risen, obscured only by a line of morning clouds on the horizon that Kallen could just barely see through the tree line. The crickets and other night creatures were slowly losing interest in their nocturnal serenade. Kallen was dead tired, his head swimming with facts. His heart was full of fear, and his stomach was rumbling from hunger. *Food. I need food before I get some sleep.*

In more ways than one, this was the weirdest night he'd ever experienced.

Chapter 18

Thursday, June 22, 1820

The perimeter security poles had been encoded with their thumbprints. Kallen touched the biometric pad on one of them and the lasers deactivated between the two poles he was standing at. He stepped across, touched the pad on the other side, and the security field turned back on. He realized he was holding his breath, imagining that his vidPAD would somehow take on a life of its own and beam all his files to everyone. Of course, that was impossible.

No one was awake except Biggert when Kallen returned to the tents. Biggert nodded at him as he approached. He had his pulse stunner drawn and was walking the camp perimeter, attempting to peer into the remaining shadows in the distance. *What's he doing up so early*, Kallen wondered.

Kallen ate quickly, then exhausted from lack of sleep, sat on his cot. Dayler was still asleep. Kallen's entry into the tent hadn't woken him. Kallen unbuckled his vidPAD holster and stuffed everything into his pack. He hesitated, then pushed it as far down as he could beneath his personal effects. Ten minutes later, he was dead asleep.

Kallen was disturbed only twice in the next several hours, once by Dayler standing at the entrance of the tent saying something to one of the men outside, and a second time by an odd dream fragment that woke him briefly.

It was eleven-thirty before he woke. When he exited the tent it was so humid it seemed as if he had been slapped in the face by a wet rag. That brought on a flood of memories of his youth working in the waterdome. For a moment, the memories were pleasant, then he remembered bringing Tiago there, and he felt suddenly sad. Tiago The Handsome. Tiago The Missing. Tiago in the brig. *Shit*.

Their shower was a large black bag strategically placed half a meter above head level. Like Guyez had described, creek water ran into it by way of a flexible hose. Surrounded by a waist-high circular girdle attached to a massive oak tree, all he had to do was stand under the spout and pull the chain. Gravity did all the work. The water was only tepid, even though it was sitting under the warm partly sunny sky. Regardless, it did the trick and Kallen felt refreshed in a few short minutes. He stood on a nearby flat rock and dried off.

Craistok was sitting near the un-energized heatstove some distance away, reading something from his vidPAD. He glanced up a few times. Kallen saw him out of the corner of his eye and wondered what he was looking at. *Probably my ass*, he thought, laughing to himself. He decided to bend over and give him a much better look. He deliberately pointed his butt in Craistok's direction as he dried his feet. Craistok only glanced up one more time, then quickly looked away. *Got him*, Kallen said to himself. *He won't look over here again.*

After a quick breakfast, which wasn't all that bad even though it was once again canned, he sought out Senji. He saw him as he came back from the downslope latrine. Looking around first, Senji came up to him. Neither Craistok nor Biggert were in view.

"Did you look through that data?"

"Some of it." Kallen was lying, of course. He had looked through nearly all of it.

"Did you note that all of it is well-documented and cross-referenced? In other words, they're not fake vids. They're all real."

"Everything looked legitimate to me."

"And?"

"I don't know what to think. I still have to look through more of it to draw any conclusions."

"Can I talk with you candidly?"

"I guess."

Kallen found Senji intriguing. He barely knew the guy and he wanted to 'talk candidly'? What was this all about?

"Have you ever wondered why our military-minded government leaders expect us to believe whatever they tell us?"

Kallen's eyes grew wide. Senji hadn't whispered when he said that. He hoped the major wasn't within earshot. Kallen put a finger to his lips. "Let's, uh, go over there, okay?"

Senji clasped his hands behind his back and they slowly turned away from camp toward the ridge. Craistok had turned off the security field at dawn and they crossed the perimeter poles unimpeded. They eventually reached the top of the ridge and looked out over the verdant river valley. A flock of birds dived out of sight several dozen meters away, chattering madly about something.

"You realize I'm *in* the military, don't you?" Kallen asked.

"But you don't believe everything you're told, do you? You seem different."

Kallen was suddenly struck with an odd thought. Could Senji be working with Vaulkner? He couldn't quite tell yet. That made him think about Dwess. Which also made him pissed off again that he was in the brig. "Uh, most of it. Why?"

A big smile crossed Senji's face. He could tell Kallen wasn't so sure about that. "The official view, taught in classrooms around the country, is that a natural series of events took place centuries ago which caused our world to start heating up. It didn't happen that way. I know it. Dr. Katterjay knows it. Thousands of others know it. You know it now.

"My colleague and I have been very interested in why we're taught an 'official' version when a completely different set of circumstances brought it about."

"All of that happened a long ago. We can't do anything about it."

"That is indeed so. But we might be able to do something about bringing forth the *truth* of how it occurred."

"Who would believe you? You'd be discredited. Actually, I wouldn't be surprised if it'd be worse than that." That was all he dared throw out. *Did Vaulkner plant him on this mission to test my allegiance?* It was really confusing.

Senji paused for a moment, taking in what Kallen had said. Kallen noted that Senji was actually mulling his statement over. Was he wrong about him after all?

"Maybe you're right," Senji offered. "But maybe a single individual can make all the difference when it comes to what's the truth and what's fiction. You think about that while you look through the rest of those vids."

"I'll do that."

Kallen had no interest in getting himself under suspicion any more than he figured he would be when they returned. After all, once the investigation with Dwess heated up Kallen was sure he'd be questioned about his friendship with Dwess. Getting through what he was sure would turn into an interrogation was going to be difficult, too, he figured. He had more than enough things to worry about now that he knew what Torvadred was up to.

"Hey, I have a question for *you*," Kallen asked.

"Shoot."

"I'm familiar with the photronic software that runs a lot of equipment, but I can't figure out how you guys did this. I mean, what kind of device could possibly open a hole in time? I know Dr. Katterjay gave us an explanation. But that can't be the whole of it. And aren't you afraid this technology is going to cause all sorts of problems? I mean, look, we've got two BG on this mission. They're in the same government-funded military you just ragged on."

"I knew you were more intelligent than you look."

Kallen smiled briefly, then realized it wasn't quite the compliment it sounded like at first.

"You've asked some good questions. You deserve some good answers. As for the device, I don't think we really have to worry too much about that. The heart of this entire operation is the Type C-704 neural processor. It's unique. There's nothing like it in the world."

"Huh? Type C-704s have been around for over two years," Kallen knew them quite well actually.

"This is an enhanced one, one that can't be duplicated since Dr. Katterjay coaxed it to learn in a completely different way than the standard type."

Kallen thought they were all taught the same algorithms in the same strictly controlled environment so that they would all function exactly the same way. As the neural processors grew they created hundreds of millions of cross-connections to reduce instruction lag time and to enhance the execution of photronic code. Combined with photronic fiber bundle circuits, tens of billions of sets of instructions could be executed at one time. Type C-704s were the fastest and most complex in its class. It was neural in operation, very closely mimicking human neural firing patterns, even to the point of being independently intelligent if properly applied instructions were programmed into it. Apparently, this one was even more intricate.

"It's unique?"

"It's the only one in existence. You are correct in reasoning that technology such as this could be used for, let's say, unsavory purposes."

"To say the *least*."

"Regardless, the situation is completely under our control," Senji told him.

"You think so?"

"For the sake of security—our security—once this mission is completed, no one will ever use the processor again. Not even us. We plan to destroy it. If we want to continue with our experiment, we'll have to start over with a different one. Our funding hasn't been pulled so we should be able to complete our research later."

Craistok was in view again and Kallen didn't want to be seen having a private conversation with the supposedly 'seditious' scientist.

"Uh, let's talk about this later, huh? I need to get some exercise. I'm gonna take a hike," Kallen told him.

Senji gave him a quick two-fingered salute and walked back to camp. Kallen paused briefly, listening to the wind in the trees. There was no gym within several centuries of here, so a hike would have to do to get his blood flowing. He returned to the tent, attached a canteen to his utility belt, and took off toward the converter. He stopped only briefly to say hello to Dayler and Lander, both of who were eating.

"Going somewhere?" Dayler asked.

"I'm just gonna take a circuit around the area to stretch my legs."

"You're not gonna get very far," Dayler told him as he observed the dense undergrowth.

"Or you're gonna get lost," Lander offered.

"Yeah, yeah. I'm not going too far away and I'm not going to be gone for very long."

Dayler and Lander both continued eating. Kallen started south, parallel with the ridge. Leaf litter completely covered the ground where he walked. Not really caring what direction he pursued, Kallen followed an animal path through the brush before it disappeared into a thicket of low bushes. He stopped, looked around, and turned left to follow a narrow path that was mostly devoid of underbrush. As he walked, he touched tree trunks, crushed a leaf here and there, examined a termite nest between two branches of a tree, fended off an occasional flying insect, and avoided a huge spider web. In the dead center was a zigzag-shaped patch of white web. Sitting on the patch was a large black and yellow spider. It was almost the diameter of his outstretched hand.

Kallen suddenly realized that he'd unconsciously drifted on a downward path that took him near the river. He stopped, cocked his head, then wondered. *If I 'accidentally' found those canoeists, while I'm hidden from view, of course, who would be the wiser? No one has to know a thing. Hmm. That is, if they're still there.* After his return to camp, no one would ever have to know he'd deliberately done that. His heart pounded with excitement. As if he hadn't had enough in the last twenty-four hours!

He deliberately continued toward the river, stopping every once in a while to get his bearings. It wasn't all that difficult since there was a half-meter thick outcropping of weathered limestone right at shoulder level to his left. He followed its curve and the slope of the land. *Damn*, he thought. *I didn't even think about bringing binoculars. Oh well.*

He continued along the weathered outcropping. As he went downhill, the outcropping plunged downward, too. It eventually was only chest high, then at waist level. Finally it disappearing into the ground. He found a couple of fallen branches, made an arrow with several sections of it, placed it on the trail as a directional indicator for himself, checked the compass again, then listened for the river. Off to the left he heard what sounded like rushing water.

A few minutes later Kallen reached a very steep, nearly vertical bank. He was at least five meters, if not six, above the river. The river was obscured by a dense growth of short bushes that drooped over the edge. He crouched down and carefully looked out through them. In front of him was the wide un-piped river! Below was a long narrow sandy bank that stretched to his left and right. It extended about four meters out through most of its length. Upstream was a tall tumble of rocks that jutted out into the water. Off to the left was a little creek that spilled out onto the sand, then disappeared into the water. It was just at that moment when he caught a glimpse of two canoeists paddling away, dozens of meters in the distance. If he'd reached this spot just a few seconds later he would have completely missed seeing them. They quickly disappeared through a stretch where the sides of the canyon narrowed. They were gone so fast he didn't even get a look at their faces. *Damn it*, he thought, *I was so close!*

Kallen watched until he was absolutely sure the canoeists had gone, backed out of the bushes, then proceeded toward his right. He found a way down to the stretch of sand and looked around. Footprints were everywhere. Blood was everywhere along the water's edge. Feathers were, too. The canoeists had apparently butchered an animal.

Unknown to Kallen, Aaric and Nash had had the best of luck. All three of their snares had captured plump turkeys. They'd just spent the last several hours plucking, gutting, then wrapping them in game sacks. With their bounty ready, they were quickly paddling back to Williamsburg. They'd fetch at least five cents for them at the meat market.

Kallen looked back toward the bank. What was that over by the rock wall? Two blankets left behind, eating utensils, a bag with a shirt in it (he opened it to see). A pile of firewood, and a smoldering fire within a stone circle.

That was all he needed to see. He found a branch with plenty of twigs and leaves on it and broke it off. He carefully wiped his footprints away as he traced his way back up the tumble of rocks. He needed to get back to camp. His chance to see the canoeists was gone. But he had a wide grin on his face. Judging from what remained behind, they were going to return.

So was Kallen.

It was, of course, much more arduous heading back up the slope than coming down. As Kallen trudged, his concentration meandered between making sure he was going in the right direction, to thoughts of the men in the canoe, and to all the information he'd taken in over the past couple of days. He felt so full of secrets now he thought he would explode. He wished Dwess was here to help him process and interpret what he'd learned. Not having anyone to talk to was difficult. He stopped to catch his breath, hoping Dwess was alright. Kallen wished he knew what they were doing to him. He wondered what would happen to himself, too, once they discovered that he'd been in contact with Dwess fairly recently. That issue seemed to be haunting him.

Soon, he saw the opposing cone-shaped top of the antenna over the rise. A few hundred meters more and he'd be at the converter. He looked at his wristcomm and checked the time. Dayler would still be on watch.

"So, what's going on over here?" Kallen asked innocently as he approached Dayler.

"It's boring as hell. The diagnostics are showing fine and the energy discharge has leveled off already. The converter's doing its job. It's completely automated. We don't need to be here."

Kallen nodded absentmindedly. "I'm hungry. Any food left or did you guys eat it all?"

"Be serious. There's plenty."

Kallen was sweating quite a bit. Dayler handed him a canteen. "Where were you?"

It took a moment for him to answer as he downed quite a bit of the water. "Down by the river." He wiped his mouth on his sleeve.

"The river? The big one down there?" He was pointing.

"There's only one big river nearby."

"It's, like, a kilometer away. I thought you were just gonna take a circuit around the camp."

"It's more than a kilometer. And my legs know it."

"Why did you go that far?"

Should I tell him I was spying? Fuck no. "Exercise."

Kallen was midway through his shift. It was just past 2400 hours. They'd been in this forest for barely a day and a half, but Kallen thought it had been at least a day longer. Volunteering for the graveyard shift might have afforded him daylight hours to explore, but it was throwing off his sense of time. After his shift was over in four more hours, it would have only been their second day here.

Several times after his shift began, Craistok came by with Biggert in tow. Both of them had pulse stunners in hand and seemed to be listening to the woods. Kallen asked Biggert what they expected to hear. Biggert told him to mind his own business. Kallen had the control panel glowing in his face when Craistok approached him before they left the area for good.

"By the way, Deshara, next time you take off like you did this afternoon, you come talk to me first."

Kallen wondered if Craistok was just trying to be a dick.

"Orders from the major?"

"Biggert and I are in charge of security on this mission. No one is gonna mess it up. Not you, not no one."

Who the hell says I can't get some exercise? "Not anyone," he countered.

The grammatical correction didn't register with Craistok. He thought Kallen had been asking.

"Yeah, not anyone."

Finally, Craistok and Biggert retreated into the darkness.

A half hour later, Senji came by. Kallen was beginning to find the early morning foot traffic amusing. He had figured that once he was on his shift no one would have come by at all. That certainly isn't how it had been turning out so far.

"Did you finish reviewing those vids?" Senji asked.

"The BG are back at camp, right?"

"Biggert's on watch. He's not going anywhere."

"You uploaded a ton of vids to me. It's gonna take a couple more days to plow through 'em. I reviewed the CO_2 graph and checked out those early 21st century newsvids, though. Where did you get them? I've never seen a vid that old before. I-I didn't even know vids existed back then."

"Vids have existed since about the mid-twentieth century, sergeant."

Kallen felt condescended to. "Hey, I don't know everything. As you pointed out already."

"I'm afraid the NAA school system has conducted a well-orchestrated plan to assure we remain unaware of large portions of our past." Senji paused and looked around. "This country is poised on the threshold of the Industrial Revolution. Mass production has yet to commence, the universal burning of fossil fuels to drive their mechanical and technical revolution hasn't yet been ingrained into the national consciousness yet. Energy barons…"

"Uh, what's a baron?"

"A baron is a businessman who thinks big, countrywide, even worldwide."

"Oh."

"These barons have yet to create their cabals or their empires. They haven't yet discovered that they can burn oil and coal on a massive scale to drive these new industries. But they will. And that's why we live in the world we live in."

That last part Kallen had already surmised, but Senji seemed single-mindedly focused on it.

"I don't think they knew that was going to happen," Kallen told him.

"They knew. They knew all too well. But they didn't try to change things. They let the madness of their greed—the trillions of credits that were generated by interlocking industries—to prevail over reason. Yes, the weather pattern and climatic changes were subtle, and easily dismissed. At first. But in time, the relationship of unchecked industrialization and planetary warming became impossible to ignore. The vids prove that. But they ignored it anyway. All of them did. The greed of living for nothing but profit was too powerful."

"Still, I can't imagine how anyone in this time period could possibly have predicted all that."

"Not in this time. Later. Much later."

"Would you want your business empire to crumble if you were making trillions of credits?"

Senji shook his head. "Perhaps not. Greed has a way of making you blind."

"No wonder they let it go on." He studied Senji's face. Did he dare tell Senji any of what he'd discovered about Torvadred?

"They knew exactly what would happen," Senji said. "Maybe not about the formation of our Great Central Desert, nor about the rest of the global changes that were to occur, but they knew about the horrible detrimental effects of unlimited industrialization. It wouldn't matter to them after they had made their trillions and were dead." Senji shook his head again.

"Politics," he said as he continued. "It's been the downfall of nation after nation. That's why that country in Central Asia was attacked with nuclear weapons centuries ago. Citizens got fed up with multinational corporations forcing the world to consume oil. Those huge corporations already owned all the water, they had control over the lines of communication, they even told people where to work. People hated it. It took nuclear weapons to finally pull the foundation out from under them. Once the oil stopped flowing, their stranglehold evaporated."

"Taking out the entire world's economy, too, from what those vids said."

Senji nodded. He stood, yawned, stretched, then looked at his watch. "I'm turning in. Keep looking through the data. I trust you're not discussing it with anyone else here."

Kallen tried to lighten the heavy mood that had descended on them. "Craistok and I had a nice conversation about it just thirty minutes ago." He couldn't help himself and cracked a smile. Senji could tell Kallen was kidding but didn't smile in return. Kallen immediately wiped it from his face.

Kallen was so agitated about the conversation that it was several hours before he bothered to look at more of the vids. He really should have been studying, too. He needed to catch up on his schoolwork. Before they left he downloaded a full month's worth of classes from his continuing education courses. He figured he might be spending time doing a lot of nothing. He kept trying to get to the lessons, but couldn't keep his mind on English, history (which he was sure was a sham now), or the rest of his classes.

So instead, he listened to some tunes from the music crystal Dwess had lent him, letting them soothe his feelings. He loved Dwess' mixes. They always had a wide range of beats and melodies that Kallen had never thought to put together in a single playlist. He figured he'd never be able to give the crystal back to him. He tried to keep his emotions in check about that but had a difficult time of it. Feelings rose to the surface about him, about Mirani and her pregnancy, about what Kallen had learned about Tiago, about seeing Dayler again, about being here in this beautiful but so foreign place.

It was frightening knowing what he knew now. Things would never be the same. In less than three days, everything he knew about the past and even the present—his innocuous little world—had been irrevocably altered.

Dwess had been completely right. Not just partially right. Completely right. Things just weren't how they were depicted on the newsvids. Maybe that's the real reason he'd been thrown in the brig. It surely couldn't have been because he had been caught selling root to Black Guard. That was simply impossible. Maybe it was because Dwess knew too much. Kallen was sure that someone on base had figured that out.

Not long ago Dwess had used the word desaparecido to describe those legislators who had 'disappeared' somewhere in the Nevada prison system. What was scariest about everything he was feeling was that it was entirely likely that Dwess was desaparecido, too.

Chapter 19

Friday, June 23, 1820

Kallen slept fitfully until ten the next morning. He was considerably groggy when he awoke. Despite Biggert's warning last night, he figured that his time was his own. He was already becoming excited thinking he might get a glimpse of one of the canoeists down by the river today. He had over eight hours to make another foray and would be able to make a quick trip of it since he knew a relatively easy way down there now. After a quick breakfast and a shower he returned to the tent.

He took his pack up from next to his cot, and pulled out the holster and vid-PAD. He briefly inspected the pulse stunner then attached it to his utility belt. He exited the tent, unscrewed the top to his canteen, and refilled it with water from the water source Guyez had found. All the men had been doing the same now that they had determined it was pure.

With everything affixed to his utility belt he headed toward the converter. No one noticed that he had all that gear with him.

Lander had ear buds in both ears. His eyes were closed and he was tapping out a beat against the stroller with two sticks when Kallen approached. Kallen tapped on one of the stroller railings to get his attention. Lander opened his eyes, then pulled one of the buds out.

"Oh, it's you."

Kallen yawned again, sipped more of the coffee he had with him, then inspected the control panel. "Things are still going okay?"

"Have you seen any changes since my unfortunate incident?"

"Nope."

"Then things are still going okay." He replaced the ear bud and went back to tapping out a beat.

Kallen wasn't sure why he decided to tell Lander where he was going but had determined that he ought to at least say something. After all, Lander would see him take off into the woods in just a few moments. "I'm going to get some more exercise."

Lander pulled the ear bud out again. "What?"

"Exercise. I'm going hiking."

"And you'll be back in a half-hour, right?"

"Maybe."

"Then, I didn't see you."

"That's right. You didn't." Kallen dumped the almost empty coffee out and placed the cup out of the way in one of the corners of the stroller. He started downslope, looking back a couple of times to see if Lander was watching. Lander was looking at him the second time he checked, so Kallen waved briefly then resumed his course. He retraced the steps he took yesterday, taking in some of the landmarks he hadn't noted the day before.

Fifteen minutes later something swooped by him out of the sky. He ducked and pulled his stunner out in reaction. He phased it off when he realized that what was furiously scolding him was a blue, white and black bird with a feathery crest on his head.

"Fuck you, bird," Kallen said; much relieved that no one saw how a tiny bird had so startled him. He returned his weapon to the holster and continued on his hike.

By following the same limestone outcropping as yesterday, he soon heard the rapids and slowed his course. Like yesterday it was difficult to find an opening in the foliage to see the sandy river bank. Now on all fours, he quietly crawled forward through the brush and looked down. There! The canoe was back, tied up to a sapling almost directly in front of him.

Fresh footprints in the sand led over to his right. He looked that way but the foliage was too thick to see much of the upstream portion of the sandy bank. He'd have to make his way to his right, to the other end of the bank where the tall rocks spilled out onto the beach.

He slowly extracted himself from the bushes and carefully headed in that direction. Once he made it to a tall boulder that looked like it had been thrown hard against the canyon wall, he recalled that directly below were the two blankets.

Out of the silence Kallen heard someone humming. He froze. His heart started to race. He slowly dropped to all fours and crawled out of earshot. He had an idea. He wanted no technology on his person, or the belt around his waist, since it had made a slightly audible squeaking noise when he was walking earlier. He unbuckled it, pulled off his wristcomm, stuffed it into a side compartment, and quietly placed the belt behind some nearby rocks.

He wanted just a look. To do so he'd have to get a little closer than he'd been moments before. Kallen crawled on his hands and knees again as he slowly made his way back. There. It looked like that opening through those large rocks might afford him a well-concealed view. Try as he might, he could only barely see a portion of the beach below.

Aaric had returned to try to snare more birds. He was alone today. Nash had stayed in Williamsburg to see if the Spatton and Daniels families would be arriving this morning. They should all be there by today. Being out here sure beat waiting and doing nothing back in town. At least here Aaric could be by himself and enjoy some solitude, something he rarely got nowadays.

He sat shirtless on a log with his back to Kallen not more than four meters away. The log was laying parallel with the shore, washed up here perhaps months ago. It seemed to be the reason why this sandbar had been created.

Aaric was humming a tune. He alternated with something lively, then something slow, then something lively again. As he hummed he thought about the one thing that kept gnawing at him. When he first began this journey, he had no idea it would be so trying keeping up pretenses all the time. It took a lot of effort to keep his real self at bay. The constant pretending meant he needed time alone, to 'recharge' himself. This was one of those rare times.

Despite the affection he had for each and every one of his traveling companions, he felt constantly on edge, hiding the fact that he preferred the company of men. He had to feign that he liked women the same way others did, pretending he had no more than the usual interest in men. He was well aware of the stigma attached to men if they were known to have 'unnatural' affections. It was worse though if a man were proven to engage in sexual acts with another man. Religious outcries about what he found to be a completely natural part of himself were known to be used to stigmatize those with his inclination. It stung knowing that. Indeed, after Aaric arrived in Baltimore, he discovered that his natural affection was considered by others to be not only vile but immoral. Regardless, it wasn't something he could just turn off and ignore. His affection was a part of his innermost being. He couldn't pretend or lie about it. It just wasn't in him to do so. After all, he'd been with Trevor for five years. It was five years of happiness. Five years of developing a view of himself that he couldn't ignore. There were far worse things than having to keep his true self concealed from his companions. At least there were no laws governing or covering such affections—much less the acts he and Trevor engaged in as often as time would allow them. In Britain he knew there were such laws.

Kallen cocked his head as he listened. There appeared to only be one canoeist today. He hadn't seen a hint of the other person who had been here yesterday.

Kallen moved to the far edge of the opening in the rocks. The canoeist was in view now, directly in front of him, but he still couldn't see the guy's face. Kallen absorbed every minute detail of his body nonetheless. The canoeist appeared to be not much older than himself. His wavy hair was shoulder length and quite dark, almost jet black. A strand from each side of his head near the temples was pulled back and tied with a piece of leather. Kallen noticed his triceps, too. It looked like he'd been working out for years. No, he decided, they were probably natural, the result of merely using his body in normal daily tasks in this much more physically demanding time. Plus, he obviously had good genetics to start with. His back was deeply tanned with a couple of lighter-colored patches along his shoulders. He was barefoot and wearing buckskin trousers that were so low on his waist Kallen could see the top of his un-tanned buttocks. They were hard, beautifully shaped, and milky white. Blood rushed in Kallen's head and he felt a stirring in his pants as his eyes lingered. If only he could get a meter closer!

Aaric looked to his right and gently rested his weapon against the log. It was loaded. An hour before he had set the snares. He had noticed that there was fox spoor near one of them. If he caught another turkey in that snare and the fox found it, he'd be ready. From a distance he'd be able to scare it away before it got to his game, or perhaps he'd shoot it. He had returned to the beach to keep his scent clear. In another hour or two he'd return to a secluded location near the snares and wait.

Kallen's foot was starting to fall asleep. He was squatting in an awkward position and badly needed to stretch his leg out. He moved it to the side. As he did so, some of the loose rocks he was on clanked together. He instinctively ducked, fearing he'd given away his position. He realized that the canoeist had heard him—just as he ducked the kid turned to look behind himself. *Damn it!* Kallen still didn't get a good look at his face. This was becoming very frustrating. All he wanted was a look and then he'd go.

Aaric was momentarily distracted from his solitude as he heard a clinking sound behind him. He looked back. Nothing. He saw just the fire circle, which was set in the sand directly behind him about a foot from the vertical bank, and his blankets nearby. His eyes traveled up the little column of smoke that was rising in the still air. He saw nothing out of the ordinary along the rocky wall or at the top. *Must have been another ground squirrel*, he thought. He turned back around and started humming again.

Kallen slowly rose his head back up when the humming started again. Still, he couldn't see the canoeist's face. *This isn't going to do at all*, he thought. He slowly made his way further along, taking care this time to not step on any of the loose rocks at his feet. No matter where he maneuvered himself he still couldn't see the canoeist's face. *Damn it, why doesn't he turn his head even a little when I'm looking?* A large boulder to his right might afford him some cover. But to get to it he'd have to crawl across an open area that wouldn't give him much cover at all. *Hmm. Maybe if I stayed crouched down really low I could make it over there.*

Two flat rocks, several centimeters thick, and each about a quarter of a meter wide were on top of a low area to his right. He made his way over to the boulder, crouching down on the balls of his feet right on top of them, unaware that the flat rocks had recently spalled and were slippery underneath.

The humming stopped again. Kallen froze. He was resting most of his weight on one leg now, tensing his thigh so much it was starting to quiver. He looked up ever so slowly. The canoeist had disappeared. So had the weapon. Where had he gone? Kallen's eyes shifted left and right. He saw no one. He rose up even higher, placing more of his weight on the spalled flat rocks, not knowing how precarious his perch was on them. *Is he right below me?* That would mean he was literally only two or three meters away. Kallen rose up higher, higher. The top flat rock he was resting most of his weight on slid out from under him, causing him to lose his balance. His foot went flying backward, shifting all of his weight forward. Before he could catch himself he was tumbling, falling head first. He was high enough and slid just far enough forward that when he landed he ended up flat on his back.

"*Unnnh*," he emitted as he hit the sand with a loud thump. A small shower of rock debris fell all around him, with Kallen sputtering as some of it hit him on his mouth and his ear.

"N-now you just lay right there, mister!"

Oh fuck, Kallen thought. *I'm screwed*. He opened his eyes to see a muzzle not more than five centimeters from the center of his forehead.

At the other end of it was the most handsome face he'd ever seen in his entire life.

Chapter 20

Friday, June 23, 1820

Kallen was sure he was seconds away from being dead. But he noted hesitation, an awkward stance, a nervous look. The canoeist wasn't going to pull the trigger. He could tell.

Kallen had lost his breath for a moment and was unable to speak. He'd fallen a good two meters. He was resting right on the canoeist's bedding; underneath was soft sand. It explained how he'd survived the fall without sustaining major injuries. A small black pot his foot had hit flipped away and was just now coming to a rest several meters ahead of him.

Aaric planted his bare feet in the sand again, renewing his resolve to not be terrified of his sudden visitor. "Where did you come from?" he said as calmly as he could, but his calm wasn't holding.

Kallen was sure he wouldn't be able to understand a word from anyone of this time. But that was perfectly understandable English!

He was suddenly overwhelmed with elation. He was sure this was the first time anyone from the future had ever met anyone from the past. But there was more to his reaction than that. This canoeist was hauntingly handsome, with unusual-looking gray-blue eyes, a smooth face, a cute sloped nose, tanned cheeks with a touch of red, and that shiny dark hair. Kallen guardedly glanced down, noticing his flawless bare chest and muscular forearms terminating with big hands. Kallen's mouth dropped open slightly.

Looking at the muzzle still pointed at his head, Kallen struggled to spit out the words. "P-please d-don't shoot. I fell! It was an accident."

Briefly, he considered putting a finger on the muzzle and pushing it away. Clearly the weapon was loaded, but Kallen was unfamiliar with the workings of the ancient weapon and didn't dare touch it.

Aaric released the hammer and put the weapon down to his side, still close enough to bring it to the ready in a second. There was a surprised look on his face. "Trevor?" he asked quizzically.

"Trevor?" Kallen responded, seeing the surprised look on his host's face. There couldn't be anyone behind him since he was right up against the vertical embankment.

Aaric was sure he was looking at a ghost. "You sound like someone I used to…know."

"Name's Kallen," he offered. He rose to his knees, his hands out in front of him, as he tried to look innocuous. "See, no weapons." He laughed nervously a couple of times, tried to dust himself off, and saw that one of his palms was bleeding.

Aaric was mesmerized. His mysterious guest was unbelievably handsome. He inspected Kallen's camo trousers. *What kind of material is that?* His guest's boots had some sort of odd-looking metal stitching on the sides. No, it wasn't metal. It was made of something else altogether. It appeared to be holding the leather together. *I've never seen such a thing.* His guest's tight-fitting white shirt was perfectly molded to his nicely proportioned upper body. It looked like cotton, but was the most finely threaded cotton he'd ever seen. He knew cotton was expensive. *Upper-class for sure.* But he was clearly a hard worker since his muscles showed that. And he was young. Perhaps his age. He had no beard. It was rare to see anyone in these parts over the age of seventeen clean-shaven, like himself. His guest's hair was really short, too. It was sandy-brown and looked so soft. He hadn't seen such a close haircut for a while.

Aaric eyes rapidly shifted back and forth between Kallen's. There was something in his guest's eyes he'd seen only a few times before in other men: in the mirror, when he and Trevor had been together, and that time he met Zebulon last month back in Virginia.

This Kallen fellow had the same look in his eye.

Aaric and Zebulon had met while on a stop just over the state line in Atkinson. Their eyes locked for a few seconds in the back of the general store. Aaric instantly knew what was happening when the man gestured for him to follow. Their five minutes of groping and kissing like starved men in the shed had been his first contact with another man in two years.

As desperate as Aaric was for a man's touch he had been equally repulsed by the furtive nature of the encounter. Both of them had gotten their frenzied release, and both clearly enjoyed it. But he had never done anything like that before and hoped it wouldn't have to come to that again. Regardless, he was well-aware how rare such a meeting was. In the course of their moments of ecstasy Aaric asked how Zebulon knew he would do it—that he'd follow, that he'd willingly let his trousers down for a perfect stranger.

"It's easy to know," Zebulon had told him. "If a man looks upon you as you do him, you'll know for sure. You looked upon me that way." Aaric never realized that mere eye contact could tell so much.

Until then.

It was happening again. Right this moment. He was sure of it.

Hmm, Aaric thought. "I'm Aaric. Aaric Utzman." He held his hand out to help Kallen up. "Come over to the water. You're bleeding."

Kallen let Aaric pull him to a standing position. Aaric was shorter than him by several centimeters. He was quite strong, judging from how easily he pulled him up, although he was certainly not formidable-looking. Kallen didn't expect the quick eyes, the assured demeanor, and his intelligent face. His speech wasn't clipped or abbreviated. Perhaps he had an educated upbringing?

Together they went to the water's edge. Kallen thought his breath would leave his body at how he felt just now. He was enraptured by this handsome boy. As they squatted he let his eyes linger on Aaric's endearing face. There was an innocence, a playfulness, even a sadness there. Kallen was intrigued. He'd never met anyone that had those qualities all at once. Clearly, he'd never met anyone who had been born over half a millennium ago. The thought made him chuckle.

"What are you laughing at, Kallen?"

"You."

"I didn't do anything."

Aaric was indeed doing something. He was dipping Kallen's hand into the water, washing it carefully, inspecting his palm for sand. He was surprisingly gentle and caring.

Kallen was getting aroused.

He certainly couldn't let Aaric see that he was getting hard. Luckily, his baggy pants were able to hide his growing tumescence.

"What's your last name, Kallen?"

"Deshara."

"I've never heard your accent before. Where are you from?"

"Idaho," he responded before he realized what he'd said. *Uh oh, I probably shouldn't have told him that.*

"Is that near Williamsburg?"

Kallen furrowed his brow. "You're not from around here?"

"Nope. Just passing through. Been there a couple of days. We haven't left on account of the storms."

"What are you doing out here in the middle of nowhere?"

"I'm traveling with some families. We're on our way out west, but the rest of our party's been delayed, so I decided to come out here to trap some turkeys."

"So, you saw storms?" Kallen asked.

"We didn't actually see 'em. Just heard about 'em. I hear tell they were mighty odd ones, too. You didn't see 'em?"

"I, uh, heard about them."

Aaric continued to wash the blood off his hand. Still being careful. Gentle. "What did you call it where you're from?" Aaric asked again.

I've already said it, so it can't hurt to repeat myself. "Idaho. It's a state, you know, out west."

Aaric furrowed his brow and studied Kallen's face momentarily. "There aren't any states that I know of west of here, 'cept Missouri. Do you mean the Arkansas Territory?"

"What's the Arkansas Territory?"

"South of Missouri, of course. You said you're from out west."

"I am. Idaho. You know, the state." Kallen said, thinking if he said it again Aaric would understand him this time. *Oh shit. Maybe it's not a state yet! I better keep my mouth shut.* "Uh, I'll explain later."

Aaric looked into Kallen's eyes. He knew there was no state named Idaho. Why would Kallen make up something as outlandish as that?

"You're okay. It's just these two scrapes. See?" He held up Kallen's wet hand.

The blood on Kallen's palm was completely washed away. Aaric looked back at the boulder from which Kallen had slipped and fallen. His lips were parted. Kallen decided that it was one of the cutest looks he'd ever seen. As Kallen studied his face in more detail he noted that Aaric's teeth were pure white and perfectly intact. He was sure that here in this ancient past people would have been missing whole groups of them.

It was amazing really. They'd been given odds of meeting anyone while on this mission. They hovered somewhere around zero point zero. He'd not only beaten those odds, he'd met someone cute. Overwhelmingly handsome even.

But it was more than Aaric's looks that intrigued Kallen. *He so easily took my hand. His voice is so gentle, soothing, his smile so playful.* Kallen felt breathless as he thought of those cute full parted lips. The dimples that dug into his cheeks when he smiled were drawing him in. He wished he could kiss Aaric.

Aaric felt a little lightheaded. *What a smile this Kallen has.* He dared not rise up right now, for fear of revealing his own growing tumescence. He dared not let this mysterious stranger see that he was growing hard just touching his hands. *And his voice. My God, he sounds exactly like Trevor!* He was wondering whether Kallen hadn't fallen from the rock above his bedding after all, but rather had fallen from heaven. After all, Trevor *was* an angel now, even though Aaric didn't actually believe it. *Perhaps he came back to life in a new body.* What a thought. To imagine Trevor in another body. One even more handsome than the original!

Kallen rested most of his weight on his knees in the sand. Aaric was squatting on his haunches. Kallen found it difficult to think clearly as he took in every detail of Aaric's body.

Out of the corner of his eye, Aaric was intensely aware that Kallen was looking him over. He looked up. Kallen immediately averted his eyes.

Aaric grinned. He had honed that particular skill himself. *There's only one reason for a man to do that,* he thought. His eyes slowly traveled across Kallen's triceps, lingered on his chest, then he slowly looked down at Kallen's crotch. He was sure he saw a hardness straining his odd-patterned trousers.

Kallen was aware that Aaric was checking him out now, drinking in the sight of him. He realized there was only one reason for Aaric to be doing that so intently. Only one reason he was aware of.

The same reason he was doing it.

Somehow, almost as if it were out of his control, Kallen reached up and touched Aaric's face. He brushed back a stray hair that had fallen into his eyes. Aaric didn't make a move to stop him. Kallen felt a pounding in his head as he slowly leaned forward and, with the slightest pressure, placed a kiss on the tip of Aaric's nose.

He was so bold for two reasons he could think of just now. None of this seemed real in the first place. Perhaps Aaric was just a hologram or a figment of his imagination. Perhaps he was still flat on his back in some sort of stupor. But no, it was because Kallen was so completely mesmerized with him. And it was so forbidden.

Aaric didn't know what to think. But he was almost positive now that Trevor had come back to life somehow, in someone else's body even, to be reunited with him. Any other man would not have even considered doing that.

Kallen came to his senses and pulled himself back in a flash, sure he'd be punched out. "I'm sorry. I don't know why I did that."

Aaric reached out and grasped his forearm. "It's okay," he said gently.

Kallen looked down between Aaric's legs. The buckskin was bunched up at his crotch. The flesh was trapped inside, pressing against it; it was obviously trying to make its way out.

Aaric wasn't flaccid, but he wasn't fully hard either. He saw Kallen looking between his legs. He looked at Kallen's crotch, too.

"Trevor?" Aaric asked again.

"Why do you keep calling me that?"

"Don't you remember me?"

"I swear we've never met before."

Aaric was mystified at Kallen's insistence that they didn't know each other. But Kallen wasn't wearing a disguise. He certainly wasn't Trevor either. No matter how much he would like that to be true, it simply wasn't.

"Kallen," Aaric stated.

"Yeah. Kallen," he said, nodding.

Aaric changed positions and rested his weight on his knees. He spread his legs a little wider. The waistline of his buckskin trousers was so low that Kallen's eyes followed the narrow trail of sparse dark hair that started from his navel and traveled downward, only to disappear. Kallen realized he being teased. *Clearly he enjoyed the kiss.*

Aaric saw Kallen staring at his navel. Or was it further down? Aaric glanced at Kallen's baggy pants. They couldn't conceal what was happening anymore. Clearly, Kallen wanted more than to kiss his nose. *He is guarding the same secret you guard.* Aaric was sure now. *He* is *like me!* The more he studied Kallen's face, the more he was sure. He saw an unmistakable look of longing, an unmistakable look of fearful desire. *For me?* His guest certainly wasn't attempting to leave. He seemed desperate to talk to someone.

"Just say it," Aaric told him.

"Say what?"

"You didn't kiss me just because I'm being nice."

"Wow, you're not dumb at all."

"I'm not *dumb!*"

"I didn't mean it that way. So, you're-you're gay?"

"Of course I'm happy. You can't believe how happy." A wide smile stretched across his face, ending again in dimples on each cheek.

Kallen thought he would melt from how cute the smile was. It was exactly like Tiago's. It brimmed from ear to ear, complete with those endearing dimples.

"I don't mean happy. I mean you like men."

Aaric put his hand over Kallen's mouth, fearing he'd say more.

Kallen gently pulled it away. "Don't do that. Look, there's no one else near here except at our camp a kilometer up…" *Oops, I never should have said that.*

"Our camp?"

"It's, uh, it's a mining camp. We're mining up on that ridge." He pointed up to the canyon wall.

"Out here?"

"Uh, we just got here." *This is not good. I'm in deep now. How the hell am I going to explain that?*

I know he's making that up. But why? Maybe he's running from someone? It sure seems like that. Aaric leaned forward just a bit. "I can keep a secret," he asserted.

If he's never spoken about being gay, then he's definitely able to keep a secret. "A secret?"

"If you're hiding from someone, I won't tell."

Something hard and cold inside Kallen sloughed off, as if a layer of armor had peeled from his entire body. He slumped down onto his butt. Something in the pit of his stomach released its grip. He'd never felt this relieved before. He looked over at the undulating waves as they pulled the river from one eternity to another, then looked up at Aaric again.

Secrets.

He had way too many of them stuffed inside himself. With Aaric's insistence that he knew about at least one of them, it was as if a bubble had burst.

"They don't know I'm here. My, uh, my buddies," Kallen told him.

"Buddies?"

"The rest of my team. Up there."

"You're hiding from your messmates?"

"Messmates?" Kallen had never heard that word before.

Aaric looked at him funny. "Your squad."

"Not exactly."

Aaric took Kallen's scraped hand in his and briefly inspected it. He grinned. "I don't bite *this* hard."

Nice. He's incredibly cute and *humorous?* He got back on his knees and held Aaric's hand in his now. "This Trevor. Is he…?"

Aaric's smile disappeared almost instantly. He pulled his hand away. "Trevor was my friend from back home in Pennsylvania. He got The Pock and died."

"The Pock?"

"You know, smallpox."

"Recently?" *Smallpox?* That was one of the inoculations they had gotten. For Kallen, it was a booster. Everyone was inoculated for smallpox when they were kids. He had heard that it had once been the worst disease known to man, had been eradicated from the general population, then had been reintroduced centuries ago by terrorists, killing millions all over again. Ever since the 21st century everyone had been inoculated against it since it hadn't been re-eradicated again. Regardless, it was rare to hear of a death from it.

"Two years ago," Aaric told him. "When we were seventeen." He slid a little closer to Kallen. "We were betrothed. You can't ever tell anyone that. We never told anyone."

"Then...why did you tell me?"

"Because...somehow I feel I can trust you. You're like me. You *won't* tell anyone, will you?"

"Who would I tell?"

"Your...team. Your buddies?"

"Are you kidding? If I told them I was here I'd be court-martialed." Kallen couldn't believe it. He meets this guy. He kisses him. He suspects him to be gay. He turns out to definitely be gay. And he's the only guy around? And this cute, too? *I'm freakin' dreaming*, he decided. He laughed.

"It's not funny!" Aaric told him.

"I'm not laughing at that. What's *funny* is that I fell into your camp. What's *funny* is that you're so cute I can hardly believe it. What's funny is that I can't wake up from this dream." He stuck his hand briefly into his pocket to adjust himself.

"I'm not asleep." He reached out and pinched Kallen's cheek.

"Ow!"

"And neither are you."

Kallen held his cheek. "Why did you do that?"

"To show you."

"Fuck," Kallen said, rubbing the spot.

"You have an *awful* mouth."

"Are you scolding me?"

"If you keep talking like that."

Kallen's eyes lingered on Aaric's nipples. They were a beautiful chocolate brown, flat against his chest, and barely a centimeter in diameter. They rose and fell as he breathed. Kallen wanted to kiss them, lick them to tiny points, nip them with his teeth. Aaric started to blush. He could tell Kallen was looking at him *that way*. Kallen sniffed the air.

"Licorice?" Kallen asked him.

"What?"

"Licorice."

"What's licorice?"

"That smell." He sniffed again, this time closer to Aaric's face. It was on Aaric's breath. How he missed it moments before, when he kissed his nose, he wasn't sure. He must have been holding his breath. "You're chewing something."

"The meetin' seed."

"What's it called?"

"Meetin' seed."

Kallen shook his head.

Aaric got to his feet and tugged on Kallen's arm. They went back to his bedding and he retrieved a little pouch. He opened it and showed it to Kallen. Kallen put one of the small black seeds in his mouth and bit down.

"This tastes exactly like licorice to me. I didn't know it came from a seed. What kind of 'meetin' are you talking about?"

"Church, of course." *How could he not know about that?*

That's when it struck Kallen. This went much further than just not wanting to hold in another secret. He had breached protocol and not only spied on this guy, but had met him. It wouldn't matter what he did or said now. The contamination of the timeline was already there. It was too late to take the last twenty minutes back. *Fuck it*, he thought. His unwavering attraction to Aaric was doing all the thinking now.

Aaric was intensely studying Kallen's expressions, how he held himself, his demeanor, his odd speech patterns, his unusual accent.

Kallen went ahead and asked his questions. "What year is this?"

"You don't know?"

"I'm testing your knowledge."

"It's June. 1820."

"Fuck!" Kallen slapped his forehead. "I don't know why Dr. Katterjay didn't just ask someone. I just confirmed it's true!"

"What a filthy mouth!"

"I'm, uh, sorry." It was clearly evident that he was here. After all, no river this wide in 2479 would be free flowing. Certainly not in North America. There was this endless forest all around him which didn't exist in his time either. Aaric was wearing buckskin trousers. Buckskins (*and nothing else*)! Those facts were proof enough.

Even though Kallen's boots were webbed on the sides, they were still confining. He sat down and unzipped them. He pulled them off and stuffed his socks into them.

Aaric took one of the boots and inspected it. It was green, with the same camouflage design of Kallen's trousers, and had thick soles of material he'd never seen before. The mesh on the sides was made of some other material he was also unfamiliar with. The unusual stitching was quite inventive, too. It certainly beat having to lace them up. As he pulled the zipper slider up and down, he decided it was one of the most ingenious things he'd ever seen. He thought that having lived in Baltimore would have been enough to introduce him to whatever he missed in Wofford Ridge. Apparently, there were many things he was completely unaware of.

"Did you go to school out east?" Aaric asked.

"My school is way west of here. This is the farthest east I've ever been."

"There aren't any universities out west. Missouri's barely a state. What are you really doing here?"

Kallen sat down on the log right next to Aaric. "You *do* seem pretty smart."

"Humph. Maybe not. I should be back in school myself."

"Huh?"

"I left the university months ago. I couldn't stand the thought of all this land opening up out here and never seeing any of it. I wanted some adventure, so got hired on with The Cartographic Institute. That's why I'm here."

"Wow, you gave up college to come out to the woods?"

"No, to find adventure. To draw maps. I'll eventually go back to school. I think. Unless I'm killed out in the Missouri Territory. It's still unsettled. Heck, we don't even know what most of it looks like."

Kallen had no idea what he was talking about. There was an awkward silence as Aaric, still perplexed at Kallen's arrival out of thin air, looked him up and down. "Your friends don't know you're here, right?"

"They have no idea." *And if they did, I'd be dead.*

"I'm ready for some belly timber. You, too?"

"Belly timber?" Kallen asked.

"Do you want to eat with me?"

Kallen saw the eager look on Aaric's face, the mischievous look in his eyes, and no longer wanted to leave. "Sure."

"You'll have to help me fix it."

"What do you want me to do?"

"You can build up the fire."

They went to Aaric's fire circle. Kallen could feel residual heat coming from beneath the white ashes. Aaric handed him a stick, charred on one end. Kallen had rarely stoked an open fire. He had either turned on a heatstove or he had been taught long ago to put out any open flames. He quickly got into it though and placed some sticks in it from Aaric's woodpile. Once it was blazing, Aaric found a thin flat piece of limestone and laid it across the fire, its ends held up by the circle of stones. He splashed a few drops of water on it. Soon its porous surface sang and spewed steam.

Kallen felt hypnotized by the flames. He looked up at Aaric, studying his face. "How did you get that scar?" He touched Aaric's chin.

Aaric put his thumb there and rubbed, not knowing what he was talking about. "Oh that. I burned it on the toe toaster when I was young."

"What's a toe toaster?"

"You never had one?"

"I've never even heard of one."

"You know, the thing you use to toast bread?"

Kallen shook his head and shrugged. "A toaster?"

Hmm. How was it possible that someone with Kallen's obviously well-to-do background didn't know about a toe toaster? Maybe he was lying? About that? No, he wasn't. Something was really odd about him, but Aaric couldn't place it. "What did you have in Idaho?"

Kallen wondered how he could tell Aaric about q-cells, air-conditioning, photronic software, or inoculations. Let alone about time-travel! He opted for the simplest explanation he could come up with. "I was deprived as a child."

Aaric didn't understand him again. That was clearly not true.

Aaric turned over a couple of rocks now, looking for grubs. Finally, he found a couple which he placed onto a big piece of bark. He went back to his pack, with Kallen following him like a puppy, and retrieved his fishing line. They went up to the huge flat rocks that reached out into the river. Aaric knelt on his knees, hooked one of the grubs, and cast it into the shallower side of the clear pool. Kallen looked at the soles of Aaric's feet. They were calloused and leathery. His own were soft and pink. It seemed a rough life Aaric was leading, one he deliberately sought, too. He wondered why anyone would do that. Was adventure the real reason?

In only moments, Aaric was yanking on the line. A fat trout was on the hook.

"Wow, that took all of two minutes," Kallen exclaimed.

"It only took that long yesterday, too. The river is full of 'em."

Aaric attached another grub to his hook and took even less time to catch another slightly smaller fish.

The waterdome back home had special filters to keep out most of the larger water creatures. Regardless, it was impossible to keep them all out, especially fish. The waterdome superintendent would allow groups of people to fish the waters on occasion. Twice in ten years Kallen had gotten to eat a real fish, cooked right in the waterdome by one of the lucky fisherman. Fishing in the dome was a matter of luck and lots of patience. Here, within minutes, Aaric had dipped his line in a couple of times and caught two!

After gutting and scaling the trout, Aaric rubbed the flat rock with a cake of lard he'd had in an oiled bag and placed the fish on the stone. They sat side by side as they watched them cook. In a few minutes the rich smell of cooked fish was wafting through the air. After a time, Aaric reached into his pack and pulled out a faintly orange-colored crystal about the size of his fist. He dragged it across a rough stone hollow and gathered together what looked like some sort of residue. He sprinkled it over both strips.

"What's that?"

"Salt, of course."

"Salt?"

"You've had salt before," he stated. He looked at Kallen like he was crazy.

"Uh, not from a rock." He picked it up and inspected it. "I've only had it processed. You know, in little granules?"

Aaric wasn't sure what that meant, but he had a lot of questions for him. This was just one more to add to the list.

Aaric found some large leaves and placed them on two pieces of wide concave-shaped bark. They would serve as plates. Placing the flayed-open fish on each, he handed one to Kallen, along with a fork. Aaric watched Kallen stab the flaky meat. He took a bite and, pleased with the taste, immediately took another one. They had finished most of their meal when Aaric picked up a piece of meat from his plate. He leaned over and offered it to Kallen.

Kallen couldn't resist Aaric's gaze. His simple gesture was so sensual. Kallen felt himself growing hard again. He opened his mouth and Aaric slowly placed the steaming meat on his outstretched tongue. Kallen could barely chew or swallow.

Kallen picked up a chunk of his fish. Aaric produced one of his ear-to-ear smiles, clamped his lower lip between his teeth from emotion, then opened his mouth. He sucked the fish in and gently took Kallen's wrist. He held on so

Kallen couldn't withdraw it. He brought Kallen's fingers to his lips and licked them. He did it slowly and deliberately while staring into Kallen's eyes.

Kallen thought his erection would burst through his trousers. He glanced down. The front of Aaric's trousers was pushed firmly outward. His penis was hidden only because of the drawstring.

Aaric picked the remainder of the fleshy chunks from his fish and offered it to him. After Kallen swallowed the tender flakes he put his hand around the back of Aaric's neck, drawing him close.

He knew he should never have met Aaric.

But he was about to kiss him.

Again.

A proper kiss this time.

Aaric felt dizzy. He was so hard it felt as if all the blood had rushed from his brain. They slowly pressed their lips together, making sure they connected perfectly, completely.

It was all so elemental. The water to their left. The fire crackling to their right. The sun beating down on them from the open sky above. Knees firmly planted on the sand below. Surrounded by rocks and endless forest.

Kallen fell into a whirlpool of emotion. He felt as if his heart was beating a thousand times a second. The feelings rushing through his body were unlike anything he had ever experienced before. And now he knew why he felt such utter calm when he arrived. He knew why it had enveloped him, had seeped inside, fused with him. Somehow, it was because of Aaric—even before they had met. Aaric was the nexus of it all, and Kallen knew it. *This is completely impossible*, he thought.

Aaric let go of Kallen's lips and whispered in his ear. "I was waiting for you."

"You were *what*?" Kallen whispered back, breathlessly, almost inaudibly.

Aaric continued to whisper, afraid to speak too loudly, terrified he would break the spell he felt he was under. His voice trembled with emotion. "After Trevor died I was sure I would never find someone else."

Kallen forced himself to say it, even though he didn't want to. "It can't be me, Aaric."

Then, almost to himself, Aaric spoke. "This is what magic is."

Kallen was afraid to say anything more. *It can't be me. I'm going to be gone soon.* "Aaric…." He wanted to tell him to stop speaking nonsense. He pulled back a little and reached up to caress Aaric's cheek. Aaric's eyes were filling with tears.

Tears, Kallen wondered. One fell to the sand, another lingered on his lower lid, then slowly rolled down his cheek. "Why are you crying?"

"Because my heart is bursting," Aaric said with a sad smile.

Kallen gave way to the flame that was engulfing him. He passionately kissed Aaric again, taking his tongue, giving him his, holding him in his arms, hugging him with all his strength, pressing his hardness between them.

Aaric yielded to Kallen's sturdy arms. He thought of Trevor again, but only for an instant. It was as if a ball of bright white light had descended onto Kallen's head. Aaric knew he was imagining it, but let himself think it was really happening anyway. Trevor's soul was gently enveloping Kallen. All the beautiful moments he and Trevor had had together, all the stolen kisses, the squeezed hands; the young innocent love they had made in the pond, in the shed, in the barn, in the woods, in their beds, all poured into Kallen. It poured with an intensity of emotion that Aaric was unable to stop.

"You heard my prayer, didn't you?" Aaric whispered.

Kallen felt an ache deep inside himself. He wished Aaric would stop it, that he would stop making this moment be something more than it was. But even as Kallen thought that he realized the moment was much more than he was willing to admit.

Aaric stood and pulled the cord that held his trousers up. They fell to his feet. Kallen felt as if he were in a dream. Aaric stood there fully hard, incredibly beautiful. He pulled Kallen to standing, then tugged on his belt, trying to undo it. Kallen took over while Aaric pulled his t-shirt up. There was an awkward fumbling moment when they crossed purposes, laughed, then resumed. Finally, with his clothes scattered around the sand Kallen stood there completely naked and fully aroused, too.

Aaric pulled them together, held his arms around Kallen's shoulders, slid them down his back, then rested them on the meaty flesh of Kallen's buttocks. He leaned back, still touching Kallen's waist with his own, looked down, and observed their penises aiming skyward. He could see only the heads. Aaric pulled Kallen's hand and led him to the river's edge.

They walked a few meters up to the flat rocks where only an hour before Aaric had caught the trout. The clear pool, made by an arc of large stones, was perhaps neck deep. Aaric stood with Kallen's hand still in his. He looked over at him; touched the sensitive underside of Kallen's penis with a light caress. Aaric's touch made him shiver.

Aaric stepped off feet first, making quite a splash. Kallen was surprised that he just jumped in like that. Yet, he abandoned all but fun, too, as he jumped in after him. The cold shock made him lose his erection almost instantly.

Aaric's hair was dripping with water when he surfaced. It dripped from his face as his smile threatened to touch each ear. Kallen was sure that the dimples in each of Aaric's cheeks would be etched there forever. Kallen dipped his head underwater then shook it after he surfaced. Both of them laughed. Kallen reached out and held Aaric's hard, muscled shoulders, even while he felt afraid of the feelings that were erupting from him like a volcano. He seemed to be tumbling headlong into the unknown. Although he had the experience he needed to know what to do with another man, this was completely different. He was already in serious trouble even being here. Now this!

Aaric held him in an invisible net. Kallen was losing control, unable to tear himself away from this moment. He felt fear and joy simultaneously. They embraced yet again. Aaric was growing hard once more. He reached under the water and felt Kallen's genitals. He grasped, pulled, tugged, kneaded, all gently. That made Kallen rock hard. Taking Kallen by the waist, he set him on a narrow underwater ledge and looked down. In his sitting position on the projection, the water just barely covered his lap. He observed Kallen's rigid penis sticking up, his balls tight and firm underneath. Aaric felt he would explode with excitement while Kallen placed his legs around Aaric's middle, crossing them at the ankles while they kissed, drew their hands across each other's wet hair, and squeezed each other's arms and shoulders.

Kallen was disappearing, merging into him as his senses overloaded. Aaric grasped Kallen's shaft and started pumping it. He rapidly became relentless. Aaric spread his legs apart and placed his feet onto two underwater rocks. He maneuvered himself until he was thigh deep in the water. He continued working on Kallen's penis. Kallen had hold of Aaric's now and was doing the same to him.

They came within seconds of each other, far sooner than either would have liked. They moaned with deep resonant sounds. Kallen's semen washed away in the current that swirled around them. Aaric shot six, seven, eight times into the air. Arcs of the thick white goo landed on the wet surface of the rocks behind Kallen, on his neck, past his neck, into the water, finally disappearing into the current, too, as Aaric's orgasm finally came to an end. His moans faded. Time slowly returned to normal. A wide smile crossed his face, reawakening the dimples again.

They spent long minutes caressing each other's bodies, playing with each other's penises, and staying hard because of it. They planted kisses on each other's faces, lips, chest, and neck. Kallen didn't ever want it to end. But he could sustain his full erection no longer. Aaric's finally gave way, too. Kallen pulled himself up and sat on the warm dry rocks. He pulled Aaric up with him and they sat side-by-side, leaning back on their hands while the air dried their skin. Aaric's face continued to be one huge smile, his eyes filled with satisfaction, his heart filling with waves of joy. This was nothing like the furtive groping he'd experienced with Zebulon. This was completely different. There was some sort of connection he felt he had with Kallen. And Kallen was far more handsome than anyone he'd ever come in contact with before.

Even more handsome than Trevor.

Kallen looked up at the sky, watched a slowly passing cloud, and grew concerned that he had come down here after all. He knew that too soon he would have to leave this daring cartographer and eventually this ancient past. He would have to forget Aaric ever existed. But not yet. *Not yet!*

Aaric maneuvered himself to Kallen's side and crossed his legs Indian style. He tugged on Kallen to lie back. Kallen rested the back of his head on Aaric's thigh. He felt Aaric's hard abdomen against the back of his head while he looked up into his upside down smiling face. It was crazy! Completely crazy.

Dayler would never believe this when he told him. That is if Kallen dared tell him. *What would he say? That I'm totally stupid? That I'm crazy? That's what the new and 'improved' Dayler might say.* The old one, the one he used to know—the one he had been in a relationship with—would have probably just smiled and said, 'Tell me more', perhaps even listening eagerly to every sentence. So, no. Kallen knew he couldn't say a word. Not to anyone. Not ever. This would have to be his secret. One he'd have to keep for the rest of his life.

He watched a cloud of gnats dance a chaotic ballet in a confined ball of space just above the water where they had been. He glanced over at the drying trails of semen that Aaric had launched onto the rocks. He looked up at Aaric's hair, matted crazily. He looked goofy, but it only added to the appeal of his cartographer friend. If he could call Aaric a friend.

Kallen felt a sudden pang of despair. He felt so close, so painfully close, to Aaric right now. It was utterly unlike anything he'd ever felt before. But once he left this place, this time, there would be no vids, no correspondence.

They'd never hear from each other again.

In a couple of days there would be just silence. He'd be back on base trying to console Mirani, wondering when or if Dwess would be out of the brig, knowing that his country would soon be embroiled in a war. And he would also have a hole in his heart from the memory of meeting this beautiful boy from the past, never able to speak to him again.

Aaric discovered the half-thimbleful of water inside Kallen's navel. He dabbed a finger into it, then drew it across Kallen's lips. "Sit up so I can kiss you again."

Kallen didn't need to be asked twice. In fact, he decided that a different venue was in order and led him back to the bedding. Aaric picked up the blankets and shook them out. He spread them both back out and lay on his back. Kallen straddled him, then leaned down to kiss him. They both grew to full hardness again as they kissed and felt each other up. Aaric eventually ended up on top again, kissed him, finally just touched him, all the while smiling from ear to ear. Kallen was sure he was just dreaming that this was happening.

Aaric's roaming hands finally settled down and he lay by his side, sighing a few times. Eventually, Kallen no longer heard the sighing or heard his breath at all. The next thing he knew Aaric was touching him as he rolled over.

Kallen immediately opened his eyes, sucked in a startled breath, then sat up. They were still naked. He was flaccid, Aaric was mostly hard. Aaric's leg was over his thigh. The shadows against the far rocky bank were longer than when he fell asleep. His sudden movement made Aaric open his eyes. He smiled again upon seeing Kallen awake.

"What time is it?" Kallen almost demanded. He shouldn't have removed his wristcomm, but it certainly was a good thing he had or else he would have had to try to explain what it was.

Aaric yawned, stretched, then stood up to stretch some more. He looked up at the trees, the far bank, the water, surveying all the shadows. "A little after five."

"Oh, no!" Kallen jumped up, shook out his clothing, and started putting everything on.

"What's wrong?"

"I've been gone for, like, five hours."

"So?"

"Five hours? I must 've been asleep a long time."

"Just a little over an hour."

"Shit!"

"Where did you learn to talk like that?"

"Never mind that. I gotta go. They're gonna kill me."

"I might kill me a deer before I go." Aaric picked up his smooth bore and aimed it into the distance. "They'll come back out at dusk."

"No! You can't."

Aaric lowered the weapon. He looked so odd standing there completely naked with a partial erection and the long heavy smooth bore in his hands. If Kallen hadn't been so nervous about having been asleep for so long, he'd find the scene comical.

"Why not?"

Kallen nearly ripped his t-shirt pulling it down over his head. "Because, if they hear a weapon fire down here, they'll come to investigate. You don't know the Black Guard. If they see you and realize I was down here they'll want to know if I contaminated…uh, talked to you."

"You're talking crazy."

Kallen clasped Aaric's shoulders with both hands. Aaric's penis swelled even more. "Please, you have to trust me. I don't want anything to happen to you. Don't fire your weapon until we leave."

"When's that?"

"In three days. You can shoot all you want to then." He laughed as he looked down at Aaric's tumescent penis. "Boy, can you shoot."

"You don't want me to hunt for three whole days? That's ridiculous."

"Please trust me."

"I do have some snares to check on. I should 've checked them hours ago." Aaric touched Kallen's chin and tilted his head up slightly. He rested his weapon against the rocky wall as Kallen devoured Aaric's mouth with his own; Kallen fully clothed, Aaric now with a full erection.

"You're quite the bold one, aren't you?" Kallen asked the kiss was done.

"I feel shy most of the time. But inside I've never been. With you, I don't feel that way at all."

Kallen felt fear seizing him. He had to leave. The clock was ticking. He had no way to know the actual time until he retrieved his wristcomm. He found a toehold and started climbing the rock face he'd fallen down hours ago. "Will you be here tomorrow?" he asked as he climbed.

"Can't I just follow you up?"

"No! I wish you could. I swear I do. But the only way I can see you is if I come down here. Please don't try to follow me. You *have* to trust me. You can't come with me."

"They don't have to know about us."

Kallen climbed back down. "It's not what you think. I'll-I'll show you tomorrow. I'll show you something that'll explain everything, okay?"

"When?"

Kallen started climbing back up again. "I can be down here shortly after noon." He stood at the top of the rocky wall with a full view of the entire flat sandy bank. "Tomorrow's okay?"

"I'm gonna go back into Williamsburg, but I can come back," Aaric replied, looking up.

"I'll-I'll come back down here to see you. I promise."

That was the last Aaric saw of Kallen as he quickly reached the apex of the boulder. Kallen retrieved his utility belt and, while dashing uphill, unzipped the little compartment. Out came the wristcomm. It was only five-fifteen. Aaric was right about the time. Kallen had no idea how he knew that. Still sprinting up the hill, he was quickly out of breath and, needed to catch it, he stopped.

Even though it was just the blood racing in his veins, he felt something changing, moving like a live entity inside him, as if new life was pumping into him. He was transforming. He felt as if he had no thoughts and every thought at once. Everything inside him was focused on Aaric. He saw their afternoon together as if a slow running vid were in front of him. His mind's eye lingered on images of them touching, Aaric feeding him the trout, them naked in the pool of water, their hair dripping as they hugged, as they held on to each other, as they orgasmed together. It was as if Aaric was still with him, as if they were connected in a way he couldn't possibly explain or even understand. He wondered what Aaric was thinking this very moment and felt saddened that he couldn't ask him. He stopped, turned around, and thought briefly about going back to ask. He even took a step downslope. But he knew better. He turned, looked ahead, and continued on.

It didn't make any sense what his mind was telling him—demanding even—as he got closer to camp. *I'm going back to a dream. A dream I've been living for the last twenty years.*

Chapter 21

Friday, June 23, 1820

Kallen stopped in his tracks and squeezed his eyes tightly shut. He found them watering when he opened them. He tried to fight it, tried to quell the feeling, but couldn't. Maybe Aaric was right. Maybe magic actually existed. Maybe it was this kind of meeting. This kind of feeling. *It's something that's completely outside the realm of what you know!* Traveling through time, as improbable—as absurd as it was—could be called magic he supposed, but it was nothing compared to the intensity of the feelings that were overwhelming him now. What exactly it was that Aaric had done to him was impossible to describe. All they did was meet, eat together, and have sex. It's not like he'd never done those things before. He'd even done them in that order! Why did he feel so crazy now? No one had ever made him feel this way.

Until today.

What was most odd though was that he no longer felt like he was part of this mission, but rather a stranger who had come along for the ride.

Just so he could meet Aaric on the riverbank.

He trudged for another twenty minutes, with frequent stops to catch his breath. It was only then when he realized he hadn't activated the voice circuit on the wristcomm. He touched the button. The tiny screen lit up, indicating two missed calls. *Shit!* A familiar-looking gnarled tree off to his left told him he was only minutes away from camp.

He looked back again. What was that feeling? Aaric was tugging on him, pulling him back by way of an invisible cord. It was stretching tautly the closer he got to camp, threatening to snap him back down to the river.

Invisible, yet so real.

Dayler was the first to see Kallen upon his return. "Where the hell have you been?" he asked as Kallen came to a stop and sat on the edge of the a-grav stroller. He was completely out of breath.

"I, *puff*, went, uh, *puff*, down there," he said as he pointed. He saw Biggert coming toward them. Biggert had seen him arrive. *Why the hell did he have to show up right now?*

Biggert came to a halt in front of him. "You better have a good explanation for why you didn't answer my calls, Deshara."

Kallen had no intention of saying anything to him. Biggert could try all he wanted, but Kallen wasn't going to be intimidated by this idiot. "I'll talk to the major."

"Answer *me*, Deshara."

Dayler observed Kallen. His hair was a mess. There was dirt smeared on the side of his t-shirt. He was sweating heavily. Something was odd about this, but he was sure it was completely benign. Interrupting Biggert's visual interrogation of Kallen, Dayler interceded, "Uh, Sergeant Biggert, can I have a word with you?"

"I want an answer from Deshara."

"Now? Please?" Dayler said that last word slowly. To get his attention. "Over here?" He pointed to some trees. Away from the stroller. Away from Kallen. Biggert complied and they went just out of Kallen's earshot.

"You know there's only three of us on watch, right?" Dayler told him.

"Of course."

"You know that Deshara's one of the best techs in the entire ADF, right?"

"Who says?"

Oh, brother. "I say. And if you ask the major, you'll hear the same thing from him. Plus, I remember Colonel Vaulkner saying so, too. You were there."

"So what?"

"You don't want to piss him off."

"I don't want to *what?*"

Good, that got his attention. "I know Deshara pretty well, since we went to school together. He can get pretty riled. If he decides not to fix something because someone pissed him off, I know some Black Guards who might get a serious ass chewing when we return."

"What the fuck are you saying?"

Dayler lowered his voice even further, forcing Biggert to pay even more attention. "We all have to cover our asses. Imagine what would happen if you didn't cover yours. What would it look like on *your* record if someone you were in charge of, on this-this *dangerous* mission, screwed things up for *you*?"

"He's screwing things up by leaving camp."

"Hmm. Looks like he came back. And well within time for his shift. You don't think he's, uh, conspiring with the locals, do you?"

"What locals?"

"Oh, I don't know, the raccoons? Maybe one of those—what did the major call it? An opossum?"

Biggert sneered, then turned back to Kallen. When he got back to him he sniffed the air. He sniffed a little closer to Kallen's neck now. "What's that smell? Smoke?"

"You didn't give me a chance to tell you anything. I fell in a creek and built a fire to dry off." He had just made up his cover story. It was a good thing he had that few moments to do so.

"A fire?"

Kallen went eye to eye with Biggert. "I wasn't gonna come back to camp soaking wet. A little fire, which I *put out* when I was done, dried me off. Now where's the harm in that?"

Biggert was busy trying to be all business, but at the same time thinking about what Madsen had told him. Madsen was right, of course. He didn't need to get any of the techs pissed off. A warning was all that was needed this time. Regardless, he had to make his report. "Come with me, Deshara."

Kallen stole a glance at Dayler. Dayler motioned for him to go with Biggert then shook his head. He seemed to figure that Kallen wasn't in any real trouble. Kallen grinned, realizing that Dayler had helped cover his butt, then took a hike with Biggert back to camp.

"Wait here while I get him," Biggert said as they stood outside the major's tent. Kallen was sure this was as comical a situation as he'd seen in a while. So what that he'd been gone for so long? He *had* come back. He had no intention of *not* coming back.

Biggert was in the tent for a few minutes longer than Kallen expected. The tents were pretty insulated, their thick material being quite soundproof. He only heard muffled voices inside. When Biggert came out, the major stood outside the tall zippered flaps as Biggert walked past Kallen. Kallen watched him go. The major beckoned him with a finger.

"I got him off your ass this time," the major said. "Next time, let someone know you're leaving the camp area. And don't be gone for that long. Don't even think about not answering your wristcomm again. How far did you go anyway?"

"Sir, I'm sorry I didn't tell anyone I left, but I fell in a creek about five hundred meters from here, waited until I was dried off, then fell asleep. I was so passed out from the time change and my odd sleeping schedule, that I never heard the calls."

The major pointed a finger at him, trying to look stern, but not quite succeeding. "Don't *even* tell me you've fallen asleep during your watch."

"Never, sir."

"Did you get enough sleep to stay awake for your next watch?"

"More than enough."

"That's all I need to hear." He waved his hand for him to be gone.

Just like that.

Kallen let out a breath as the major retreated to his air-conditioned comfort. Kallen wasn't prepared for him to be so lenient, but then realized that in comparison to the antsy Black Guard the major was about as a normal person as one could get for a mission such as this. Biggert and Craistok were the ones who weren't normal.

Biggert kept a watchful eye on him while Kallen ate. He'd obviously spoken to Craistok about the issue since he too was eyeing him on occasion. *It was a simple excursion away from camp*, Kallen told himself. At least that's what everyone knew so far. No one could possibly know what really happened.

After Kallen was finished eating, he went to the medkit and retrieved a neoskin patch and the dermal regenerator unit. He applied the patch and the electrical pad to the palm of his hand. The dermal regen had a timer based on the severity of the wound. He energized the tiny screen and pressed the icon twice. He could barely feel the unit working. The timer said it would be done in nine minutes. It wasn't a bad wound anyway.

While he felt the warmth that the regen unit produced on his rapidly healing hand, Kallen tried in vain to forget his liaison with Aaric. The harder he tried, the more the image of Aaric's smile, his naked body, his eyes, his hands, all etched themselves into his mind. Later, Kallen decided to relieve Madsen a half hour early, partly because he wanted the distraction from thoughts of Aaric and partly because points would be scored. Perhaps the two Black Guard would notice and back off a bit.

"So, how'd it go with the major?" Dayler asked.

"He said to just tell someone if I leave the immediate area."

"Really? That's all he said?"

"He doesn't know where I went. I told him I fell asleep.

"Okay, where did you *really* go?"

Kallen looked around. No one else was nearby. "Down by the river."

Dayler gestured with his hand. "Again?"

"I couldn't help it. There's a whole river—completely un-piped. It's wider than you can believe. I had to just *touch* it."

"And the fire?"

"I really built one."

"I could smell the smoke, too. How did you build it? Did you rub sticks together?"

"I rubbed something else." Kallen was smiling.

One of Dayler's eyebrows went up. "You beat off down there?"

Kallen guffawed. "I was alone. Wouldn't you?"

Dayler grinned, then left for the main camp area.

Darkness slowly enveloped the forest over the next three hours. Soon, the night insects and little animals hidden by the night, rustled the leaves and bushes around him. Before it got too dark to see, Kallen had pulled a lightwand out and hung it on a nearby low hanging branch. It illuminated the area with a soothing even glow.

Kallen checked the control panel for the third time in as many hours. Their established routine was becoming repetitive. He adjusted one of the settings on a graph so he could read it a little better then set the panel aside. He opened his vidPAD and looked over some of his school lessons again. He needed something to ward off boredom. What a tug of war though. He wanted to dive right in to his lessons, to catch up, since he was already way off his target date for the next chapters of his English text. Half-heartedly eyeing several pages, he worked on some of the questions but finally just cleared the screen.

He called up some of Senji's files. He couldn't help himself as he watched some of them. It was like watching a hovercar wreck or perhaps like being locked inside a nightmare. The images were frightening and compelling. Right in his vidPAD was the real history of the world, not the fabricated one he'd learned as a child. Yet he was completely unable to even keep his attention on the vids. Images of Aaric kept intruding. His penis stirred with excitement as he recalled the image of Aaric's semen arching high into the air, splattering against the rocks, and the look on his face as his orgasm tensed his body. Now it seemed like it had happened days ago, although in reality it was just been just a few hours.

As the night wore on, Kallen's main concern was whether Aaric would be there when he returned tomorrow. He smiled to himself as he realized he'd not even debated whether or not to return to see his 19th century friend. He kept noting how he felt while he had been there. So completely at ease. So utterly calm inside, even while concerned about his duty to the team. It was completely natural to be with him despite the fact that they were from totally different worlds. Aaric's was young, vibrant, and full of potential life, only just now on the threshold of that Industrial Revolution era that Senji spoke about. One that would eventually lead the entire planet into a death spiral. The world Kallen was born in. The one Kallen lived in. The world he had inherited.

As Kallen thought of them together he alternately found himself getting angry at Aaric for having met him, then getting angry with himself for putting himself in a position to do so. Then he retreated from that stance and found himself restless with anticipation, longing to see him again, even if only for an hour tomorrow.

He found himself admiring Aaric more and more as he thought about it. What courage he must have to take off like that and sleep alone on the river. He only had that ridiculously ancient weapon for protection!

Kallen set the vidPAD aside as he stared into the dark forest. An unwavering image of some still digital photo of a forest fire from the early 21st century illuminated his hip from the vidPAD's virtual screen. Without de-energizing it, he slid the two halves together and set it back down. That would effectively put the device into suspend mode.

He stood, his mind on fire, too, and walked to the edge of the lightwand's area of illumination.

As the lightwand hanging behind him dipped and swayed in the breezes, thoughts of Tiago came to mind. But it wasn't like the last time he'd thought of him. Kallen noticed things about Aaric that were like him. The beautiful dark hair for one. The dimples that appeared in each cheek when he smiled that incredibly wide smile. The innocent yet mischievous look. The passionate way he hugged and kissed.

As suddenly as Tiago had come to mind, images of Dayler flooded in, too. But it wasn't the Dayler on this mission. It was the Dayler he first met. The Dayler that had been his boyfriend those short months back in tech school. The things he had most cherished about Dayler were embodied in Aaric, too. He was terribly intrigued at these newfound comparisons that suddenly occupied his mind.

What was it about Aaric and Dayler? The first thing that came to mind was that Dayler and Aaric had the same body type. Kallen was on the slender side. Dayler and Aaric clearly started life more muscular than him. Aaric was quite toned too due to the energetic life he led. Then there were his quick intelligent eyes. Dayler's intelligence had been evident after Kallen heard him speak his first sentence way back in school. Aaric's intelligence was more subtle, but there nonetheless. Although he was dressed like a backwoodsman, Aaric was much more than that. He seemed out of his element in that respect. Then the last, and what Kallen thought was the most important trait they shared was their playfulness. Dayler had been like that before. It was something he seemed to have lost somewhere along the way. *In less than a year?* Aaric had a wonderfully playful nature.

Kallen had never thought this way about someone before and was terribly intrigued that it was coming all so easily, too.

What about Acton, he wondered. Did Acton have any traits he could compare, too? There were. Kallen's thoughts went all over the map, searching his memory. Acton had the most sexy silken hairy legs and butt of anyone he'd ever seen naked. He'd been lucky to have him just for that alone, since he liked it so much. There were times he would just caress Acton's naked butt cheeks just to feel the furry covering. He often did that just before they'd fall asleep, caressing them, then sliding his fingers into the cleft of his cheeks, his palm resting on Acton's solid warm buttock.

Aaric had a similar furry hair pattern on his butt and legs too but not as much. Tiago had been mostly smooth. He had only four hairy areas: his head, his armpits, and his crotch, and it was sparse at that. That was it. Cute and hairless. Dayler just had light blonde down all over him. But, oddly enough, his butt was almost hairless. It was nothing like Acton's.

Then, there was the sense of calm that Acton always had about him—except at the end where he simply lost it with his paranoia. But until that time, he had always noticed that Acton had this interesting calming effect on him. When they were together he always felt 'safe'. Being with Aaric was unlike anything he'd ever experienced before. It was if Kallen was connected to Aaric on some level, one he could easily interpret as 'safe', too.

The last item for comparison was that Aaric could cook. He hadn't known Tiago long enough to know whether he could cook or not. Dayler never cooked a thing. Acton could cook better than Kallen's mother. And, although Aaric had merely cooked two trout, he was obviously skilled at it.

Kallen felt as if his thoughts were no longer under his conscious control. The essence of all three of them—Tiago, Dayler, and Acton—people that Kallen had such an affinity for, mixed, swirled, and merged.

All of them melded and became Aaric.

The focus of Kallen's attention rested solely on him. His heart pounded as he watched everything he loved about his previous relationships become embodied in this single person.

A chill went up his back.

Kallen's attention was diverted when he heard the muffled sound of footsteps behind him. He turned to see a lightwand swinging back and forth. Whoever was holding it was coming closer. Kallen touched the button on his wristcomm to check the time. It was 0113 hours. He felt wide awake.

It was Craistok. He hadn't shown up so far during his watches—at least by himself—and now he comes by? Kallen figured something was up.

"You awake, Deshara?"

Kallen snorted. "You expected me to be sound asleep, didn't you."

"I'm glad my daily report will say you weren't."

"Daily report? When did that become part of this mission?"

"This afternoon…after you returned." Craistok held onto the lightwand that hung on the branch, keeping it from swaying momentarily, then he let it go. "It probably gets pretty boring standing watch on nothing, huh?"

Kallen could tell he was probing for information. For what, he couldn't tell. He decided he'd play his game though. "What could possibly be boring about fixing a leaky ionic energy seal? I mean it's exciting knowing we're here to save the future, wouldn't you say?"

"Exciting? No, boring is definitely more like it. I'm sure you'll agree."

Kallen was certainly not going to agree to that and said nothing in return. He stepped over to the stroller and sat. Craistok sat next to him. Kallen's vidPAD was between them. Craistok picked it up. Kallen became instantly alarmed. He had slid it closed with the paused vid of the forest fire on the 3D display. If Craistok decided to open it and the image resumed on the display, it might lead to questions he'd rather not have to answer. After all, wasn't Craistok a little too interested in what he was up to already? Kallen felt his anxiety level going up past the redline.

Kallen's fear was unfounded. Craistok didn't open it at all. He casually started tossing it from hand to hand as if it were a baseball.

"Hey, that's a sensitive piece of equipment. Do you mind?"

"Think I might drop it?" He tossed it toward Kallen. Kallen was fast and snatched it out of the air. He relaxed slightly, now that he had it back in his possession.

Craistok stood up. "Montarco seems to think you're special or something. I got news for you, Deshara. No one's special. And certainly you're not." His eyes burned into Kallen's.

These guys must get lessons in intimidation, Kallen thought. He thumbed the off button, then snapped the vidPAD into the holster hanging from his belt. He wanted to rebut the nasty remark, but decided against it. Instead he picked up the control panel. Its light washed out everything, including Craistok, who seemed to be lording over him.

"What I'm saying is if you take off like that again, you'll have to answer to a much higher authority than me or the major."

Kallen put the panel down, wondering why Craistok was obsessing about the excursion. Kallen realized it probably had to do with nothing more than boredom. Hadn't Craistok used the word boring twice? At least he, Lander, and Dayler had something to do. In fact, so did the rest of the men. Everyone had tasks that occupied at least part of their day. But two so-called security guards? *Who are they defending us from? The two deer that ran along the edge of camp yesterday morning and set off the perimeter alarm? The family of squirrels that seemed that they have to run around that big tree southeast of camp every morning—making quite a racket? The hornets in that nearby paper-like hive?*

"Nothing to do except bitch and complain, huh?" Kallen told him.

"My orders are to make sure no one gets maimed or killed on this mission. That includes you."

"I've got this pulse stunner," he touched it with his right hand, "a working set of eyes, a brain, and I know how to hike. That's gonna keep me un-maimed and quite alive."

Craistok shook his head. "You just don't get it, do you?"

"Get *what*?"

"Biggert and I are security here. If we remind you to follow orders, you just say okay. Why don't you just say it?"

Kallen grinned. He'd never see the guy again after they returned. Messing with the prick wouldn't do any harm.

"I think I just lost half my brain."

"Huh?"

"I might have forgotten how to hike, too."

"Don't fuck with me, Sergeant Deshara."

Kallen stood and stepped forward. This game had gone into double overtime and Kallen was doubly bored with it. Craistok wanted him to give in to his so-called authority. It wasn't going to happen. It didn't matter whether he was Black Guard or not. Craistok didn't outrank him. Only the major did. "Don't fuck with *me*, Sergeant Craistok," Kallen echoed. "I sure don't want anything to happen to the converter."

Craistok wondered for a moment whether Kallen was threatening him or the mission, or what. Surprisingly, he backed down. Kallen noticed the slight change in his demeanor at that moment. Craistok pulled on his lightwand sheath and it lit up. Without another word he retreated toward camp.

Kallen couldn't keep his mind on anything important. Visions of Aaric kept flooding his mind periodically. He fired up some music files and put several hours worth into a play queue. He put the vidPAD on the stroller and widened the sound field to maximum dispersion so he could be enveloped by them while he stood or sat or danced around. An hour later Kallen again saw a lightwand coming toward him. He figured it was Craistok back for another round. This time he was ready. He stood and waited. But it wasn't him. It was Senji. Kallen muted the volume as Senji approached him.

"Jeez, it's the middle of the night. Doesn't anyone sleep anymore?" Kallen asked.

"I was tossing and turning. I already woke the major once. I didn't want to do it again so I came out here."

"The answer's yes, by the way."

"To what?"

"I finished looking at those vids. It's horrible. I can't believe the only thing I ever learned about the past was what I learned in school. I thought…"

Senji interrupted him. "I know what you were taught. We were all taught the same things."

Kallen's thoughts flashed briefly to the base newsvids. All of them were produced by base news personnel. None of them were civilians. Many had re-upped to continue doing that job. After all, it was a pretty cushy position to occupy. They had a seal on what kind of information was 'supposed' to be spread as well as what was supposed to pass as the 'truth'. After all, every one of the vids were cleared by Intel. He'd come to understand the implication of that due to Dwess. If it ever became known that Kallen was the index case on base for the dissemination of the real history of the past he would certainly be questioned about how he knew it.

"Senji, look. If I ever told anyone that I know any of this, at least while I'm in the ADF, it's entirely possible that I could be court-martialed. At minimum, I would certainly be silenced."

"Then don't say anything. Just realize one important thing. Things aren't always the way we're told they are."

Funny how Dwess said that exact same thing to him shortly after they met.

First Dwess, now Senji. Perhaps there were lots of others who suspected that many things weren't the way they seemed. Kallen was gearing up to tell him what he knew about the commander.

Should he?

Could he?

Senji seemed trustworthy. Didn't he upload a ton of data about what really happened in the past? Kallen could return the favor by doing the same for him.

"Where's your vidPAD?" Kallen asked.

"Back in the tent, why?"

"I, uh, I have some data you might be interested in, too. You might want to reconsider ever contacting ESC again."

"Why so?"

Kallen took Senji to the edge of the lightwand's area of illumination. He told Senji all about the commander's vids, the reports, and the timetables he had, all with Torvadred as the center of attention, and what he thought of this mission overall. He didn't exactly tell him how he got hold of the information he'd downloaded, but he told him everything, all in a whisper. Senji's normal look of peace and calm started melting away. Out came a nervous man, one who began to even look terrified.

"Who else have you told this to?" Senji nervously whispered back.

"No one."

"This is very bad. If I had had *any* idea that was going on we *never* would have considered contacting your base. But ESC was the only place we knew that had a Zelinski Energy Converter. Given the nature of our emergency, we *had* to contact your commander. Our technology—this whole endeavor—may be under a whole lot more scrutiny than I ever supposed." Senji looked extremely agitated now and started pacing. "I have to get a message to Dr. Katterjay right away. Who knows what kind of surveillance he's under. Who knows what kind of surveillance *we're* under right now."

"I doubt there are any surveillance camchips out here," Kallen asserted as he looked around.

"All this time I thought we were going to finish this mission and be done with it. But it looks like our little experiment may end up falling under the authority of the military after we're back—and be everyone's biggest detriment. Perhaps it might become a weapon. Everything becomes a weapon. And, like you, I've wondered why two Black Guard are with us. What you've told me puts a whole new spin on why they're here."

Senji looked at his wristcomm and yawned. Although he was feeling somewhat fearful now, he was even more so feeling the day's fatigue starting to catch up with him. He shook his head. "Enough of this. I'm going to try to get some sleep. We never talked, okay?"

"Never. But maybe you can leak it out to the media when we get back, huh?"
"I don't think so."
"Why? You're immune to military prosecution."
"Do you really think so after what you just told me?"
Kallen looked away for a second. "Hmm. Maybe not."
Both of them sighed. Senji shook his head, then returned to the tent.

The rest of Kallen's watch was alternately spent worrying about what he shared with Senji, robotically checking the control panel every half hour, and enjoying the hard-on he got when he remembered Aaric's naked body entwined with his.

Dawn broke, and despite being fatigued from his many hours without sleep, Kallen's pulse quickened at the thought of seeing Aaric again. Soon enough Lander showed up with a box for him. Breakfast. They ate together, engaging in small talk, but mostly eating in silence.

Kallen left the converter area and took a quick but refreshing shower before turning in. It was difficult getting to sleep, but finally his eyelids became impossibly heavy and dreams stole his consciousness.

Chapter 22

Saturday, June 24, 1820

It was just past noon. After Dayler relieved Lander, Kallen joined him for lunch at the stroller. He was dressed for a hike. That much Dayler could tell.

"So you *'fell in the river'*, huh?" Dayler asked. "Why can't you just beat off in the tent like Lander and I did last night?"

Kallen's face had a look of disgust on it. "You guys beat off together?"

"Fuck no. I heard him beating off. After he was out, I did the same."

"Oh. Look, I'm just heading out to get some exercise. I owe you if Biggert comes looking."

"He was up for over fifteen hours. He looked pretty sleepy when he turned in. I don't suspect you'll hear from him anytime soon." Dayler glanced at the control panel. "I could use some exercise, too. When you come back, show me where you went."

"I just sorta randomly explore," Kallen responded, not wanting to divulge his true course.

"To the river, you said."

"Not today. It's too far. And, I'm not gonna be gone for long." *Just enough time to be with my handsome cartographer!*

"I'm timing you." He mock-touched his wristcomm. "Keep yours on or some BGs we know will have a shit fit."

Kallen didn't bother to acknowledge that last comment as he stashed his trash into his ration box, set it aside, then pulled his daypack up to his shoulder.

Earlier, Guyez had, with great ceremony, filled several canteens. Kallen had one of them stuffed into his pack. Lackson had checked the water three times now with the microbial testing agent from the medkit. It kept coming up negative. They'd all been guzzling it down, knowing that very shortly that would be it. No more pristine water from the past.

Thinking about that great tasting water, Kallen swung the pack around, unzipped the flap, pulled out his canteen, finished off nearly a quarter of its contents, then recapped it. He then made a beeline to the river. Every thirty seconds or so for the first five minutes of his descent he stopped, looked back and held his breath, checking to make sure he wasn't being followed. Satisfied that he was alone, he picked up his pace, getting more and more excited as the meters melted beneath his boots. The thought of again being with Aaric made his adrenaline surge.

Finally, twenty minutes later, after having gone at a pace much faster than yesterday, he reached the low rock face at the bank of the river. He peeked through a clump of bushes. There! The canoe was back, tethered to the same sapling as yesterday.

Breathless now, he found the boulder where he had fallen, planted a foot at the very edge, and cautiously looked down. Aaric's smooth bore was visible, lying against the log, but where was he?

A phantom hand touched his shoulder. No, not a phantom. Aaric had silently come up from behind him. Kallen looked like he was going to lose his balance from having been startled. *Not again!* Aaric was quick. He reached out, grasped Kallen's bicep, and held on, steadying him.

"I didn't mean to gull you," Aaric told him. His face was aglow with mischief.

"English please."

"I wasn't speaking German."

"Gull me?"

"Trick you. *You* don't speak much English, do you?"

Aaric was shirtless, like yesterday. Today though, high-topped fringed leather boots covered his feet up to mid-shin. That same wide smile reached out to Kallen, tugged on him, and moved his heart. It wasn't just a smile of friendship. It was something more. That same connection he felt just yesterday rushed to the fore.

Kallen slid the pack off and let it gently drop to the ground. He took Aaric in his arms and hugged him, trying desperately to understand the feelings that were welling inside him.

Aaric must have been exerting himself recently. His aroma was earthy and masculine; not altogether unpleasant. He let go. Aaric pulled him closer again to initiate a long satisfying kiss. They slowly dropped to their knees. They ended the kiss with as much body contact as they could muster in that position. Kallen feeling Aaric's hardness grinding into his groin, Aaric feeling the same from Kallen.

Aaric took the lead again, stood, and beckoned Kallen to follow. Kallen took his pack in hand and followed him, climbing down the boulders.

As they sat on the log, delicate black-winged damselflies rose up from the wet sand and flitted off to their left. Aaric pulled the smooth bore closer to himself. That's when he noticed the wristcomm strapped around Kallen's wrist.

"What's that thing?"

Kallen had deliberately not removed it this time. The whole way down he had been fighting a tug-of-war in his mind. He was going to stick to his promise from yesterday about showing Aaric a few things, but wasn't exactly sure how much to tell him. He figured he might not have to say a thing after all, thinking Aaric might not even notice the wristcomm. But it was too late now.

"It's a watch and a communications device."

Aaric looked at him, puzzled.

"Look Aaric. I wasn't exactly truthful about everything yesterday."

"I know."

"You know?"

"Like I said, I'm not stupid. You're hiding from someone or something."

"No, you're not stupid at all. But what I'm gonna say is going to take a little, uh, imagination, to believe."

"I've got a good imagination. Maybe too good. All night I was imagining seeing you again. It was all I could do to keep from," he touched his crotch as he looked down, "you know." He blushed, then looked back up at Kallen.

"You are *so* cute," Kallen told him as he touched Aaric's taut shoulder. He shook his head a few times, not believing he was actually in Aaric's presence again. "Here." He started to unzip the pack.

Aaric watched the zipper as it opened the pack. It was like to the ones on Kallen's boots. "What is that thing?"

"What thing?"

"That stitching on your pack. It's on your boots, too."

"What, the zipper?"

"Zipper?" Aaric said, like he'd never spoken the word before.

"Have zippers not been invented yet?" He said it mostly to himself.

Aaric reached out to pull on the slider, then ran his fingertip along the chain. "I've never seen this kind of thing until I met you." Aaric took the pack from him and worked the pull tab back and forth. He noticed now that he wasn't handling canvas. It wasn't oiled, it didn't smell, and it was extremely lightweight.

"What a great invention! How does it do that?"

"I don't know. I just use them." *If he's never seen a zipper before, then I probably shouldn't show him the vidPAD, but I have to.* "Look, yesterday you said you're out here for adventure, right?"

"Yeah, but not exactly here. Out past Missouri. That's where the adventure is. Where hardly anyone's living yet. It's not like here, where it's tame."

Kallen looked around. "Tame?" he asked. "This is tame?" He couldn't believe the difference in their perception. "Well, I'm gonna give you an experience you'll never forget." He took the pack from Aaric and pulled out the vidPAD. He pulled the two halves apart and touched the on button. A black rectangular screen materialized several centimeters above the plane of its surface.

Aaric's eyes grew wide as he stood up and backed away a couple of feet. "What *is* that thing?"

Kallen was calmly sitting with it on his lap.

"It's called a vidPAD. Watch. 'System. Display music files'." A folder showing dozens of vids of some of his favorite musical groups materialized in the center of the open space. "Start vid number one." The vid immediately started. Kallen adjusted the sound field to maximum dispersion, then turned up the volume. Aaric stepped around to behind Kallen. Both of them were instantly enveloped by stereo sound.

After initially being startled from hearing music come from seemingly nowhere, Aaric leaned over Kallen's shoulder to watch more closely. He leaned over even more and stuck his hand out, then waved it behind the image, then in front of it. Of course, he'd never seen anything like this before. He was speechless.

Aaric wasn't exactly scared of what he was seeing, more like incredibly dumbfounded. Nothing that Uncle Gilhard had ever done in his lab, or what they had ever talked about compared to this. He was certain this wasn't even in the same league as what his uncle knew and understood.

"He's not going to believe me when I tell him about this!"

"Who?"

"My uncle."

Kallen reduced the volume. "Your uncle?"

"Back in Baltimore. He's a chemist. An inventor, too. But I bet he's never heard of this thing before." Still greatly excited by the device, he sat down next to Kallen again and continued to look on. "What kind of music is that? I've never seen such instruments. How do those images move? Where is that sound coming from? How does it work?"

"Okay, okay. Enough questions." Kallen was trying to lead up to this moment. He wanted to reveal who he really was. But how to do it was difficult. Then it hit him. *Just tell him the truth.* He cleared his throat, knowing that what he was about to say would be impossible to understand. "You hear that it plays music and shows these images. It can also record vids; display text, graphics, animation. You name it. It follows my commands, does auto-searches and scans, can provide multiple types of encryption, connects to any type of network, uses standard x-ray holo-crystal data retrieval, and has twenty exabytes of storage. Oh, and it's powered by a standard q-cell. Anything else you want to know?"

Aaric didn't understand a word Kallen had said. He stood up, no longer looking at the vidPAD, but rather at Kallen's face. He was suddenly quite fearful. "W-where are you really from?"

Just tell him. "I'm not from your time."

There was a moment of awkward silence as Aaric looked first at Kallen then to the vidPAD, then back to Kallen's face. "That doesn't make any sense. How can you not be from 'my time'?"

After having barraged Aaric with technological words to gain his attention, Kallen tried his best now to be a lot more coherent. "I know this is going to be impossible to believe. I hardly believe it either," He looked around himself. "…even though I'm sitting right here. I'm, uh, I'm visiting, uh, from the year 2479."

"2479." Aaric repeated, looking completely incredulous.

"That's why I'm hiding. I'm not supposed to be talking to anyone here. We're not even supposed to *be* here. There was…an accident, you might say. Senji and Dr. Katterjay made a mistake and we're here to help them out."

"Senji? Dr. Katterjay?"

"They're these two scientists who accidentally created the portal, uh, the doorway that brought us here. We're only here to stop the storms. Have you noticed that there 've been none of them lately?"

Aaric only nodded his head, then briefly looked up into the sky. Hardly a cloud was to be seen.

"That's 'cause we set up a device to keep them from coming back. We're making sure they don't coalesce again and cause permanent damage to your time. If they harm anyone here it could affect the future. We can't let it be altered."

Aaric studied Kallen's face, searching for the telltale signs of a total lie. But there were none. *He's telling the truth! A fantastic truth to be sure, but the truth nonetheless.* "You're not lying," Aaric acknowledged.

Kallen shook his head. "No, I'm not."

Aaric was alternately not sure how to ask the question and so full of them he didn't know where to begin. He furrowed his brow as he attempted one. "How is that possible? How can you…be here…uh, how can you go into the past?"

"It's because of the nature of space-time. I couldn't possibly explain it correctly, but space-time is holographic. Every place and time—past, present, and future—is accessible, although we're only aware of the present moment. Those two scientists used a device that, uh, that opened up a doorway, and we were able to step across…to here and now." Kallen looked around. It was still unbelievable. "And that's how you and I met."

Aaric completely lost him with the word space-time, but he'd been counting the centuries between now and when Kallen said he was from.

"You can't be that old," he said softly.

"Huh?"

Aaric knelt down and scratched in the sand, subtracting one of the two four digit numbers from the other. "You won't even be born for another…"

Kallen finished for him. "Six hundred and thirty-nine years."

Aaric's mouth fell open for a second as he looked away, then back to Kallen. "But-but yesterday we kissed. We-we fell asleep together. We kissed again today." He reached out and touched Kallen's knee, making sure he was real. "I'm touching you right now. How can you not be born yet?"

"Silly boy, I *was* born. In 2459. In Idaho, out in the Rockies."

"The Rockies?"

"Hmm. Maybe you don't call them the Rockies yet. It's the mountain range that runs…wait, I'll show you." Kallen halted the vid and told it to display a topographical map of Idaho. Aaric got up from the sand then sat down next to him on the log again.

"This is an outline of my home state. It's a couple of thousand kilometers from here. I live in a country called the North American Alliance. It covers territory that was once called the United States and Canada. But that was hundreds of years ago." He laughed a couple of times. "That would be *now*, of course. This whole area here," Kallen pointed to the Great Central Desert on a different map, "is a wasteland. I was stationed west of it, here, up in the mountains." He pointed to the range that delineated what was left of Colorado. He looked up and pointed out in front of them. "This river doesn't exist in my time."

Kallen didn't want to say any more since he suddenly felt bitter. Here, it was lush, green, and wet. Somehow, after being in this time, and for only a couple of days he felt cheated living in his world. "Everything's different in my time. Completely different."

Aaric's face revealed a mixture of fear, astonishment, and disbelief now. It was overwhelming what Kallen had shown and described to him. There was a country out west? There was a huge desert-like area in the middle of the continent? State names he had never heard before? Kallen had even shown him maps, the likes of which he'd never seen before.

"Those maps. How did you make them? How could anyone draw like that?" They didn't have the slightest resemblance to the pencil drawings he had labored over for so many hours.

"They aren't drawings. They're photos."

"What's a photo?"

"Are you kidding me? No photos either?"

Aaric shook his head. "I've never heard that word before."

"It's a recording of an image."

Aaric looked at the display again, then put his finger into the three-dimensional field, thinking he'd be able to touch something solid. When his finger touched nothing he quickly withdrew it, looking at his finger as if he'd touched something forbidden. "It's-it's not real!"

"It's a holographic interface."

Aaric shook his head.

"I'm sorry. This is just everyday technology to me. Here. Let me do something fun for you." Kallen blanked the virtual 3D screen. "System. Font Program. Keyboard style. Purple background. Font name: Motten Large. Display: E-r-i-c, point size one hundred, shadowed, 3D, motile." Four rotating letters appeared, projected in 3D.

"That's not how you spell my name."

Kallen furrowed his brow. "It's not?"

"It's A-a-r-i-c. The German spelling."

"Oh. System. Delete letters. Display: A-a-r-i-c. Same parameters." Aaric's name started rotating above the plane of the screen. Several times Kallen changed the font, the point size, and the format of the rotation, each time eliciting more boyish looks of awe from Aaric.

Aaric leaned toward the vidPAD. "Kallen and Aaric," he stated. Nothing happened.

Kallen smiled. "It'll only listen to my voice."

Both of Aaric's eyebrows went up. "It's alive?"

"Not like you and I are but just the same it'll only do what I want. System. Display the following three words." He spoke them, then spelled them out, 'K-a-l-l-e-n a-n-d A-a-r-i-c'."

The screen changed and displayed their names. Kallen manipulated the program. The letters started dodging, twisting, turning; changed to anagrams of their names, then reassembled in their original sequence. Finally they just hovered, slowly changing colors.

Aaric's eyes strayed to Kallen's hand. He looked closer at the one that had been scraped yesterday. He took it in his, then checked the other one, thinking he'd forgotten which one it had been. "Your hand."

"I have two of them."

"Of course you do. I mean, yesterday it was bleeding. I don't even see a scab now. You must heal really fast."

"I used a dermal regen unit on it."

"Dermal regen unit," Aaric said slowly, attempting to understand those words, too.

"We have a way to heal wounds really fast." He quickly changed the subject. "Hey, let me take a vid of you."

"A vid?"

"Those moving images? They're called vids."

"What do I do?"

"Stand out there." He pointed. "In the sunlight."

Aaric stepped away from the log, turned, and faced him.

Kallen activated the recorder. He pointed the camchips in Aaric's direction and watched the screen. He took a couple of stills. "Now do something."

"Like what?"

"Anything."

Without hesitation Aaric pulled the drawstring on his trousers. They collapsed in a heap at his ankles.

Kallen immediately started laughing. He couldn't stop and laughed so hard his sides started to hurt. Aaric's penis was starting to swell as he watched Kallen laugh. It made him grin from ear to ear. Finally, Kallen caught his breath and steadily aimed the camchips again.

Aaric scratched his balls, dusted something imaginary off his thigh, leaned against a boulder, and flexed his triceps. Even though he'd never been in front of a camera before, he seemed to know how to ham it up. Kallen panned up and down his body before he went back up to his face.

Aaric mustered up one of his mischievous grins. Kallen zoomed in to his face, snapping stills of those dimples digging deeply into his cheeks, his eyes shining with playfulness, the sun perfectly shading his brow, his hair in just the right place. It was breathtaking how photogenic he was.

"You can pull your pants up now." *That's probably the only time I'll ever say those words!*

Aaric pulled them back up and re-tied them.

"Come back here and I'll show you what I was doing."

Aaric came back, sat next to him, and placed an arm around Kallen's waist. Kallen played back the vid, then showed him the stills. Aaric was mesmerized by them. It was as if he, as a tiny living being, were suspended in midair in the vidPAD. It was alternately amazing and scary seeing himself like that naked, play-acting as he had for Kallen's device. Aaric laughed as he watched his antics, but he had enough of the device for now. He tugged on it, silently telling Kallen to put it away. Kallen thumbed the off button, snapped it together, and put it back into his pack.

Using his index finger, Aaric summoned Kallen as he walked backward toward the blankets. He pulled off his boots then started undoing the drawstring of his trousers again.

Kallen found his pulse racing and his heart ramping up. He quickly pulled his t-shirt off. He unzipped his boots, pulled them off, then stood in front of him. Aaric's trousers were being held up this time only because a stiff erection was keeping them from falling. Kallen hooked the waistline with a finger, pulled it forward, then let go. They dropped to the ground just like before. Aaric stood there with his penis arching perfectly upwards. Kallen dropped to his knees and plunged his mouth onto it. He sucked and licked while undoing his belt. It was as if yesterday never had happened. It was as if he'd waited a thousand years to feel Aaric's penis in his mouth, pressed against his tongue, touching the back of his throat.

Aaric's back arched as he held Kallen's head in his hands. His gentle moaning rapidly became louder. Kallen didn't let go even as Aaric gushed into his mouth. Kallen held Aaric's tight scrotum in one hand, his other holding onto the shaft, letting liquid-Aaric slide down the back of his throat. Aaric tried to pull Kallen's mouth off, but he wouldn't let go as he milked every drop into his mouth.

The rhythmic pulsing of Aaric's penis finally slowed, then stopped as his orgasm faded. Kallen pulled the glistening shaft from his mouth and licked the underside, then nuzzled his balls with his nose. Aaric stayed fully hard.

"My turn," Aaric told him after his breathing returned to normal.

He tugged Kallen's trousers down, then pulled them off each foot. He laid him down on his back and, on his knees, scooted in front of Kallen. He lifted Kallen's legs up and let them drape across his back. He scooted back a little and rested his palms on the blanket at Kallen's waist. Lowering his head, he took

Kallen's rigid penis in his mouth and began. Not since he'd been with Trevor had he felt so filled with desire. It seemed like a lifetime ago.

He started slowly, then sped up, then slowed down again. He stopped every once in a while and shifted his position so he could lick Kallen's nipples. Aaric hoped he would enjoy that and was pleased to find out that Kallen did.

Kallen was becoming wild with desire, squirming all over the place. Aaric went back to Kallen's slicked up penis, licked around his scrotum, then went back to sucking on the shaft, pulling it in as far back into this throat as he could.

Kallen came without warning. At first, Aaric had thought Kallen had stopped breathing. Well, he had, but it was because the orgasm was so intense. Finally, Kallen drew in a mighty breath as the last of his semen oozed down Aaric's throat. Aaric immediately pulled himself from Kallen's penis and, still on all fours, stuck his tongue into Kallen's mouth. Kallen reveled in the taste. Of himself. In Aaric's mouth. But it was more than semen that passed between them. Kallen felt his very soul exchanging places with him.

Like it was supposed to be this way.

Centuries before he would even be born.

Aaric hung over him on all fours. His slowly softening penis leaked a long, thin, glistening strand of clear semen. It slowly pooled just above Kallen's navel. Aaric licked it up with the tip of his tongue, and deposited it on Kallen's. A gift of himself. A gift from inside his beautiful body; now on Kallen's tongue, now in his throat, now in his stomach. He pulled Aaric down onto him and squeezed him, feeling his bare skin against his own, his breath in his ear, the taste of him still on his tongue.

Aaric whispered into Kallen's ear. "I want to live for another six hundred and thirty-nine years. So I can wait for you to be born. So I can be the first to hold you. So I can watch you grow up and be the first to kiss you. Then be the first to…be with you."

Kallen felt his heart swell with emotion. Tears welled up in his eyes. No one had ever said anything like that to him.

Beep! Beep!

Aaric jerked his head up and looking around.

Beep! Beep!

That sound. It was coming from the thing around Kallen's wrist.

Kallen sat up and put a finger to his lips. "Shhh," he said, looking obviously concerned. "Don't say anything. It'll pick up any sound." He touched the wrist-comm with a finger. It was Dayler's comm channel. "Deshara here."

"*Where are you?*"

"Uh, I'm about a half kilometer from camp. Why?" He was lying, of course. He brushed the tears from his eyes. He heart was still swirling from emotion at what Aaric had said to him.

"*Biggert's looking for you. You might want to get back here as fast as you can, if you know what I mean. Madsen out.*"

Kallen dropped his arm.

Aaric cocked his head as he looked at the wristcomm. "It doesn't listen to only you?

"No. It's a general communications device. Anyone can use it."

"Is Biggert one of your buddies?"

Kallen started to scramble for his clothes. "Hardly. Get dressed. You have to get out of here."

"Why?"

"'Cause there's no telling what he'll do if he sees you here. Please get dressed." He reached over and covered Aaric's face with kisses. "I can be back tomorrow. Can you be here?"

"It's gonna be difficult to fend off Nash. Buck and William and their families are sure to be here today. They're gonna want me to stay in town. We're supposed to leave day after tomorrow and I'm gonna have to help get supplies. We have wagons to load."

"Just one more day. That's all."

Aaric shook his head, not sure how he was going to comply. "I can try."

"Please try hard." Kallen was already dressed. "When I come back I have something I have to tell you. Some information that might change everything for you."

"How's that?"

"I can give you some information that could change your life. But you'll have to come back tomorrow." Kallen knew information was wealth. Almost as valuable as water. He knew it was a huge risk telling Aaric any more than he already shown him, but he had to give him something in return for the incredible hours he'd spent with him. He went to the bank. Using both hands, he broke a branch off a sapling.

"What are you doing?" Aaric asked as he pulled on his trousers.

"I'm gonna wipe out all the footprints. Can you help me?"

"Sure." He snapped a leafy branch off, too.

"If Biggert happens to come down this way, I don't want him seeing anything."

Aaric collected his things and tossed them into the canoe. They both used the branches to wipe away all their footprints. Soon, it looked like someone had done just that, but nothing resembling their myriad footprints remained.

Kallen followed Aaric to his canoe. He pulled the pack off his shoulder and pulled out a lightwand.

"Here. A gift."

"What is it?"

"It makes light."

"How?"

Kallen showed him. He activated the row of LEDs and showed him how to use the touchpad to vary the intensity. He ramped it up to maximum. The LEDs were so bright that Aaric couldn't look directly at them. He blinked a couple of times then handled the clear plastic covering, feeling for a heat source.

"It does that without a flame?"

Kallen had a puzzled look on his face. "Why would it do that?"

"The future must be amazing."

"I wish I could say that was true."

Aaric snapped the lightwand shut like Kallen had shown him then stuffed it into his knapsack.

Kallen untied the rope from the sapling but hesitated before tossing it into the canoe. He didn't want Aaric to leave, yet felt a pang of despair knowing Aaric had to get out of there now.

Aaric wrapped his arms around him again. He pulled his hat off and looked into Kallen's eyes. His own were pleading. Kallen felt as though his heart were being ripped out. But in less than twenty-four hours they'd be back together again.

For the last time.

Kallen almost had to force Aaric to get back into the canoe, after which he pushed it off the sand into the awaiting river. He struggled to fight back tears. Why, he didn't know.

Aaric adjusted his hat, picked an oar up, and pointed the canoe into the current. He stood up, balancing himself carefully as it started taking him downriver. "I'll see you tomorrow, Kallen Deshara. Tomorrow!"

That was the last Kallen saw of him as the narrow opening of the rocky bank obscured him from view. He took the branch and wiped his last footprints away as he retraced his steps back toward the rocky bank. He grabbed his pack, climbed up, then inspected the sandy area below him. It was pretty obvious that someone had been down there scratching around in the sand. But perhaps as the sun continued to beat down, drying the ground, it wouldn't be so obvious. *God, I'm being so paranoid*, he thought as he tossed the branch as far as he could into the brush.

With a satisfied, but slightly sad smile on his face he started up the hill toward camp. He checked his wristcomm. He'd been gone for about an hour and a half. If he hauled his butt he might make it back more quickly than yesterday.

Biggert didn't like being out in the woods alone, regardless of his training. He had always done recon with at least one other person. That person covered his ass, or he was covering their ass. But finding that prick Deshara was first and foremost on his mind. He didn't like it one bit that Deshara had left camp again. He'd gotten Madsen to tell him that Deshara had gone somewhere he didn't say *where* the prick was going. People didn't just up and take off like that for no reason, let alone when they'd been given orders not to do so. Perhaps he'd found something valuable? Maybe he'd found some food? That would be a good reason, he decided. Eating something other than these god-awful canned rations would make him leave, too. Regardless of the reason, something wasn't right about it. He was determined to find out what was going on. If Deshara didn't want to cooperate then he'd just have to discover the reason for his secretive behavior himself.

Biggert followed the natural contour of the slope, not at all sure where he was going. He had his stunner out and the safety off. Animals were crawling around all over the place—mostly at night, he had noticed. If he saw anything charging at him, he'd take it out in a second. He glanced at the setting. Force three. That was enough to kill the largest animal they'd seen so far. He watched the ground, the bushes, and his back. Every once in a while he glanced at his wristcomm. It would certainly have been easier to contact Deshara that way, but he was sure he wouldn't get a truthful answer out of him. The third time he checked it, he ran right into a large spider web. His immediate reaction was to flail his arms. Out of the corner of his eye he saw a huge ugly-looking spider skittering across one of the anchor strands. He held off just long enough to see it get away, then fought to remove the nasty web from his face and clothing. Clearly, Deshara hadn't come this way. *Why did I have to run into this thing? Fucking Deshara. I hate spiders!*

It took a good forty minutes, but as he progressed toward the river valley he arrived at a flatter area. That rushing sound had to be the river. Had he reached it already? He thought it was much further away. He rounded a clump of bushes and stood on one of a series of flat-topped boulders, the very ones where Kallen and Aaric had knelt to kiss and hug only two hours previous. He saw the long sandy embankment down below. Ahead of him was the river. He sniffed the air. Smoke. Looking directly below him he saw a circle of stones. Some of them were partly blackened. Sand covered most of them.

Being careful, he made his way down. He squatted by the fire circle and felt a couple of the rocks. They were only warm from the sun. Still, the circle made him suspicious. Obviously, someone had been here not long ago. Had it been Deshara? *Deshara insisted he'd been at a creek, not this river.*

He stood and observed the rest of the area. Not a single footprint was to be seen anywhere. He saw an unusual sweeping pattern in the sand. It looked like something had been dragged around to wipe out all traces of footprints. Maybe not. It was impossible to tell what had gone on here.

He walked along the river's edge, savoring the sight. In a way, he felt glad he'd made this journey. Despite himself, he'd been curious about this un-piped river. He knelt and dipped his hand into the undulating water as it flowed past. Clear, cool. He held some in his palm, letting it drain out. It was nothing short of amazing.

He had almost reached the end of the sandbar when he saw what looked like a shallow groove in the sand. From what, he couldn't tell. He looked through the water's surface. The gouge appeared to have come from the direction of the river. Had a vessel of some sort pulled up here? And what was that about a third of a meter out? It looked like the outline of a heel and a big toe. *Is that a footprint? Hmm, I can't tell.* The more he inspected it, the more he *wasn't* sure. Most of it was obscured by tiny pieces of dark flotsam that had settled into the depression.

Had Deshara build some sort of craft? Had he *found* some sort of craft? *Maybe that's what he's been doing. Maybe he's taking excursions up and down the river. But why?* He shook his head. Clearly, Deshara wasn't here. And if he'd been here, perhaps it was he who had brushed the sand. There was no way to tell.

Exasperated, he touched his wristcomm and signaled using Kallen's channel.

Kallen answered almost immediately. "*Deshara here.*"

"Where are you?" Biggert demanded.

"*At camp.*"

"Prove it."

"*How?*"

"Who else is there?" There was a short silence.

"*Madsen here.*"

"Is Deshara there?"

"*He's sitting right next to me.*"

"Where?"

"*On the stroller. Wanna talk to him?*"

"I *was* talking to him." He heard muffled laughter. "Deshara, I'm at the river down below."

"*The river?*" Kallen answered.

"Yeah, you know which one." Biggert was baiting him.

"*Why did you go down there?*"

"To look for you."

"*I'm up at camp.*"

"You weren't an hour ago, were you?"

"*No…*"

"I found your fire."

"*What fire?*"

"Where you dried off."

"*By the river?*"

"There's only one river nearby."

"*I wasn't anywhere near the river. I was by a creek.*"

This was getting nowhere. Deshara wasn't the typical type he was used to dealing with. He was just a little too smart.

"We'll talk about it when I get back."

Chapter 23

Saturday, June 24, 1820

Biggert knew that if there was one spider web, there was another. He had no intention of getting near one again. He carefully scanned his passage back to camp. Once there, he strode past Dayler without acknowledging him. He went straight to the main camp area and into Major Montarco's tent. By that time, Kallen had seen him and was standing outside the tent waiting for him to come back out. He was sure it was going to be a repeat of yesterday.

A couple of minutes later the major came out with Biggert right behind him.

"Deshara, you won't be leaving camp again," the major told him almost immediately.

"Sir, I was gone less than three hours."

"As of now, you won't be gone at all." The major had no malice in his eyes. He was simply doing his duty as the commanding officer; ordering Kallen as he should have yesterday, actually.

Biggert sneered at Kallen.

This is awful, Kallen thought. *Tomorrow, Aaric will show up and I won't be there to meet him.* He found his throat tighten up.

Kallen knew better than to argue with the order. With Biggert standing there, listening intently, anything he said in rebuttal could be construed as incriminating or subversive. But he had to make something up to deflect Biggert's attention. "I was just getting some exercise, sir."

"Exercise here." The major turned and went back into the tent. His order was final.

Biggert stood with his arms crossed and grinned. He felt immensely satisfied that he'd been able to thwart Kallen's plans, whatever they might be. He didn't care what Kallen wanted to do. It was more that something had taken place at the river bank, away from his watchful eye.

Kallen was feeling anger mixed with the need for revenge. He spoke with Lackson briefly, obtained a meal box, and returned to sit with Madsen on the stroller. He explained what he felt was a predicament.

"This is ridiculous. He doesn't outrank me," Kallen told him between bites.

"But the major does."

"Fuck him."

"Are you trying to lose your stripes?"

"No."

"Then what are you complaining about?"

"It's the principle."

"Do you really need to leave camp anyway?"

You don't have a clue, Kallen thought.

It was coming toward the end of Dayler's shift. They had long since finished their meal and had just been chatting. But Kallen was aching to tell him what he'd really been doing down by the river. He figured it would be easier if he just showed Dayler the stills he took of Aaric. He dared not show him the vid he'd taken. He reached down to his holster and retrieved the vidPAD.

"I have to show you something. Promise you won't tell anyone."

Dayler looked at him oddly.

Kallen fired it up and retrieved the photos of Aaric's face. He cycled through them as Dayler looked on.

"Cute. Who is he?" Dayler asked.

"His name's Aaric Utzman."

The name didn't register. He was busy trying to figure out how Kallen had even taken the pictures in the first place. "When did you take those?"

"This afternoon."

"Holy fuck! Biggert was right!"

"He's gay," Kallen quickly added.

"Biggert's gay?"

"No, you idiot. Aaric is."

Dayler laughed mockingly.

"I'm not kidding. He, uh, sorta told me." *Hell, he* proved *it to me!*

"You're a lying sack of shit."

"I swear." Kallen wasn't smiling, so Dayler knew he wasn't kidding.

"You're *not* lying?"

Kallen shook his head.

"He *told* you he's gay?"

"Takes one to know one."

"There isn't supposed to be anyone within five kilometers of here. How in the hell did you meet him?"

"The first day we were here I saw a canoe on the river. I got curious, so I investigated. Then I fell into his camp."

"Fell?"

"I slipped on some rocks and down I went." He pointed to the sand in the last photo. "I didn't have much choice but to talk my way out of it since he had some sort of rifle in my face."

"Serious?"

"He seems to know how to use it, too."

"How the fuck did you *really* know he was gay?"

"Like I said. I just knew."

"Wow. There were gay people in 1820," Dayler said rhetorically.

Kallen pushed him. "There've always been gay people."

"So that's why you've been heading off. To *fuck* him."

"We didn't quite get that far."

The look on Dayler's face changed. "Oh shit. This is *fucked* up. *Really* fucked up!"

"Why?"

"You were messing with the timeline!"

"Yeah, right. It's not like I got him pregnant."

"But you wanted to."

Kallen grinned. "Well, yeah."

Craistok appeared out of nowhere. Fortunately, Kallen happened to have his finger on the vidPAD power button. He instantly pressed it, blanking out the screen.

"Seems everyone's gonna be staying at camp now, eh, Deshara?" He appeared not to have heard their exchange.

"Yep," Kallen began. "Seems everyone's gonna stay here. Including you."

"I've had no desire to leave our little…resort. But you have. A little too often, I might add."

Kallen stood up now. *Is it somehow their duty to get me as pissed off as they can?* "What is your and Biggert's problem? So what if I left camp. So what if I can't stand the smell of either him or you." He overreacted, but in that moment he could tell that Craistok's intention was to rile him up.

"Kal, uh, Deshara," Dayler warned.

"You're watch starts when?" Craistok shot back.

"Guess," Kallen said angrily.

Craistok's face tightened up. He didn't like Kallen's attitude. "I'll be checking on you."

After Craistok left, it was another twenty minutes before Kallen calmed down. So far, no one except Dayler knew a thing about what Kallen had really done on his excursions. Funny thing, too, Kallen noted. Dayler didn't want to know anything more about Aaric.

Craistok only checked on him once at 2100 hours. On the other hand, Biggert came by twice afterward in two hour intervals. Why, Kallen couldn't figure. It wasn't as if he would dare take off through the woods in the middle of the night. Apparently, both of the BG thought he might do just that. Kallen was beginning to see why the BG were so hated by some. They needled. They prodded. At least these two did. And the major was deferring to them now, too.

The night wore on. Several times Kallen picked up a rock and flung it into the darkness out of anger. One hit a tree with a loud crack, echoing the ache he felt inside, as if his heart were cracking open. The others just sailed into the blackness and disappeared. He checked the panel a few times, purely out of duty, not really caring what the readouts said. As much as he tried, he couldn't get Aaric out of his mind. Fear of never seeing him again was only surpassed by realizing that, for the rest of his life, Aaric would think Kallen had broken his promise to return.

Sometime after 0200 he read the chronometer on the control panel. It was only the beginning of their fifth day here. It seemed like a month had gone by. At least they still had another day after that before enough of the ionic energy would be grounded. He'd figure something out. He had to see Aaric again. Kallen knew he should have done more than just given him the lightwand. He should have given him a wristcomm. That would have helped, but their range was limited. Only slightly more than two kilometers. Regardless, he'd get a message to him. He had to.

Dawn came more quickly than Kallen expected. The converter was working properly, as always. He felt panicky. He hadn't thought of a single way to get away from camp.

Lander found his way over, yawned, then tossed Kallen a breakfast meal box. As usual, Lander complained about every little thing, including the time it took to heat his meal. Kallen didn't say a word, something which Lander didn't even notice.

It was shortly after 0440 hours when Kallen got to his cot and fell fast asleep.

Chapter 24

Sunday, June 25, 1820

K<small>allen</small> *stood with Aaric by his side. They were on top of a towering stone wall that stretched an infinite distance to their left and right. They were higher than the clouds. They were both naked. The sky was all around them. Above, behind, below. The sun was far above them, shining down, warming them. The view was exhilarating; they could see for hundreds of kilometers. Kallen stretched his arms out. Aaric did the same. They dove into the blue as if the sky were a depthless placid lake. They flew downward, leveled out, sailed back up, dodging clouds, laughing, effortlessly following invisible air currents.*

Aaric flew upward, skimming along the side of the towering wall, just centimeters from it with breakneck speed, then halted. He gently lit down on the balls of his feet at the top where they had begun. Kallen swooped down and landed next to him. Kallen found Aaric aroused, which aroused him, too. Kallen touched him gently, then held him in his arms, hugged him, and they kissed. Aaric started to disappear from his embrace…

Kallen woke with a start and sat bolt upright. His heart was beating rapidly. The dream. It seemed so real.

Like he'd really been flying.

With Aaric.

The feelings surging through his body were like none other in his life.

Aaric was his breath, his soul, his reason for being alive.

He felt the sting of separation, the pang of not being able to hold him. He'd felt it last night, but now it was different.

Completely different.

He knew with absolute certainty the magic Aaric had only mentioned before.

It's love.

It was flowing through him this instant. His mind was filled with thoughts and images of Aaric. Aaric was the only person Kallen had ever had this feeling for. It had never been like this with Tiago, or Dayler, not even with Acton.

This is what it's like, he realized, *when you're in love!*

Why now? Why did I have to fall in love with him now? Aaric would be waiting for him down below. And he wouldn't be able to say a word to him, much less ever see him again.

Kallen had fallen asleep wearing just his camo trousers and socks. He quickly donned and zipped up his boots. Still shirtless, he exited the tent. Ignoring Guyez, Lackson, and Craistok, who were eating by the heatstove, he went to the top of the ridge with his binoculars. Once there, he energized them and scanned the river below. What he could of it, at least. He leaned out as far as he could with one hand wrapped around a skinny tree trunk. He could see nothing more than he had when they arrived.

He pulled himself back, sank to the ground, and let the binoculars drop to his lap. They slid off, then tumbled across his thigh to the ground. He felt his eyes grow watery. He pounded the ground with both fists. *This can't be happening!* This was the most intense feeling he'd ever felt for anyone and he was unable to act on it. He sat there for long minutes, lost, completely lost, yet awash in powerful feelings that surged inside him, overwhelming him.

"Deshara!" It was Guyez. He was several dozen meters directly in front of him. He looked upset.

Kallen instantly came out of his reverie. "What?"

"Get over here!" He was frantically waving at him.

Kallen grabbed for the fallen binoculars and, following closely behind Guyez, wiped his eyes of tears.

Everyone was there, including Lander, who had been on watch at the converter. All eyes were on Senji. Good. No one could tell that Kallen's were red.

"I just got a communication from Dr. Katterjay," Senji told them.

"You did? How?" Lander asked.

"With this." He produced a small two-way communications device that was designed to transmit data instead of voice. "I've been periodically beaming messages to him about our progress. But now we have an emergency situation. One of the components that keeps the photonogrid operational is acting up again.

That means we have to break camp and get back as quickly as possible. If we don't return and the component fails, we'll be stuck here."

"You want to explain that, doctor?" Dayler asked.

"There are sixteen energy pattern stabilizers surrounding the photonogrid. You know, the components that look like light tubes affixed to the circumference of the ring. They focus the energy beam to stay within the torus. The energy cone it produces is how space-time was opened for us.

"The problem is related to chaotic inter-modulation distortion somewhere along the circuit path between the processor and the photonogrid. It's been affecting some of the buffer circuits attached to the stabilizers. It causes a feedback loop which affects intra-circuit communications back to the memory buffers at the processor.

"Sorry, I realize this is a long explanation," he added.

"We had this problem before we started our main experiment, but when it happened we simply cut the power to both the photonogrid and the processor and the problem went away. Its occurrence has been unpredictable so we weren't able to pinpoint why it occurred, or when, or even *if* it might happen again. Unfortunately, it's happening again. But we certainly can't shut the processor down while we're here. That would mean we'd be stuck here forever. And once down, that's it, no one would even be able to rescue us either since no one would be able to return to this time again."

"What?" Kallen exclaimed in a panicky voice.

Dayler noticed Kallen's reaction right away.

"Are you saying that once the power is shut down, the portal can never be opened again?"

"Opened yes, but the time and place it opens to is completely unpredictable. Once the power's shut down there's no way to coax the processor to this time coordinate again. It's as if the location of where the portal opens to disappears from the neural-core processor memory buffers. That's perhaps the best explanation I can give you for the moment."

"How could you possibly know that?" Kallen sounded desperate.

"There were some things we didn't brief you all on, since it wasn't important. We energized and de-energized the processor several times when this problem occurred before. Each time it was re-energized we ended up with a portal to a different place and time. It's something we have no control over. Our portal exists only as long as the power is on at the processor level. Previous to this, we saw signs of civilization. Ancient, yes, but populated areas nonetheless. The reason you all and myself have ended up here is because there's no one else around, and this is where we've conducted all of our scientific inquiries."

"That can't be true!" Kallen sounded like his heart was being ripped out.

Dayler was searching Kallen's face. *Why is he so upset?*

Senji's eyes could have burned holes into Kallen's from the way he was looking at him. He wished Kallen would quiet down about this. His concern could easily draw more attention than he cared for. He turned to the major. "Major Montarco, we need to break camp as quickly as possible. We have about an hour. That will give us another hour leeway."

"But-but there's still a danger to us back home. We haven't grounded all the energy yet," Lander said.

"We don't need to be concerned with that anymore. Dr. Katterjay refined our calculations. The converter has grounded enough energy to prevent the storms from recurring. There might be a minor one, but most likely not. Regardless, at this point it won't harm anyone anymore. Our job here is done."

Major Montarco didn't need another second. "Lander, Madsen, Deshara. Start the shutdown sequence on the converter. You can come back here when you're done to pack your gear. Guyez, Lackson. Cover the latrine and disassemble the shower. Stow everything back into the transport containers. I'll assist with camp break down. Craistok, Biggert. Police the area. I want it looking like we were never here. Return here when you're done and assist us. The techs will bring the stroller back in a few minutes and we can start piling everything onboard it. Go."

There was a rush of activity as everyone commenced with their assignments.

Senji pulled Kallen aside. He wasn't sure why Kallen was so upset with the news, but he needed to reiterate another very important point to him. He whispered now.

"Sergeant Deshara, remember our conversation. I don't need anyone thinking we'll ever be able to come here again—which we can't once the power is cycled off. It's better that they all know that opening a portal in space-time was a mistake, a fluke. Frankly, I'm glad we're leaving here sooner than I expected. I'm bored, exhausted, and ready to get back to where we belong. I'm sure you are, too." Senji turned to go.

Kallen returned to the tent to don the rest of his clothing. His head was still spinning, stunned at what he had learned so suddenly. An intruding thought floated upward from his unconscious. The bubble it was contained in broke the surface, spelling it out for him. He tried not to acknowledge what it said, but it was persistent and impossible to ignore.

This was where he belonged.

Not where Senji wanted to go.

Not where the rest of the men wanted to return to.

He headed for the converter, aching inside. The instant he stepped across the temporal boundary, Aaric will have been dead for over six hundred and fifty years. Intense despair cut to the very core of Kallen's being at that knowledge. *I'll never be able to say goodbye to him.*

Aaric's beautiful face, his body, his uncomplicated world.

Everything about him.

Gone.

A fire as hot as plasma burned inside him as he raced toward the converter. These last several days were the only real moments he'd spent in his whole life. How could he go back to his dreamlike future, to an unreal life after what he had experienced here.

After how he was feeling now?

His stomach tightened, lurched. He had to stop moving as the familiar feeling of needing to retch rose up. As he stopped, he remembered what Aaric had said to him just yesterday. The words echoed loudly in his mind, although Aaric had barely whispered them.

I want to live for another six hundred and thirty-nine years.

So I can wait for you to be born.

So I can be the first to hold you.

So I can watch you grow up and be the first to kiss you.

Then be the first to…be with you.

Kallen held his eyes tightly closed as the excruciating physical pain he was experiencing transmuted into emotional pain. Aaric might as well have never said those things. Their meeting might as well have never happened.

No. No!

God damn him!

God damn Aaric Utzman!

Why did I have to meet him?

Why did I have to fall in love with him?

Why did I have to find something I didn't even know I was looking for, only to have it taken away?

Kallen swallowed hard. He felt as if he were preparing for his own death. Once they crossed the portal, the one person he wanted, the one person he needed, the only person he'd ever loved like this…would disappear forever.

Dead.

Dust.
For over half a millennium.

It would be as if *he* deliberately killed Aaric the moment he returned to 2479. How could he keep that from happening?

He had less than an hour to figure it out.

CHAPTER 25

Sunday, June 25, 1820

Dayler was at the converter's vidscreen when Kallen arrived only moments later. He was going through menus, stopping processes, ending code threads, shutting down services. Kallen heard a slightly audible whine. Several LEDs on the side of the panel glowed green. A disembodied female voice spoke. "*Converter shutdown complete.*"

The major came up to them. He had a closed case in his hand. "Is the converter still grounded?"

"Yes sir, we haven't pulled the stakes up yet."

"Good. Discharge the remaining energy from the reservoir."

"Sir?" Dayler asked.

"Use the emergency code. Dump the energy reserve."

Dayler nodded his head. "Yes, sir." He slid open a panel on the side of the converter. Inside the opening was a nondescript square black box with a handle on it. He pulled on the handle and the box slid out—a sealed quantum energy resonator—the converter's power source. He set the box aside, slid the panel shut, and input the emergency dump code. They all stood back while the timer indicated the energy discharge rate.

"Two minutes and counting," Dayler announced. "Sir, why am I doing this?"

"You'll see. Get over there and assist them with the antenna breakdown."

Kallen, Dayler, and Lander trotted over to it and disconnected the guy wires, lowered the antenna, then quickly unsnapped its sections and stacked them on the stroller. Dayler rolled up all the cables and threw them on the stroller, too. They returned to the converter. The energy reservoir indicator was on zero. They pulled the ground stakes up that surrounded the converter and threw them onto the stroller, too.

Kallen watched the major. The major had already opened the case he'd been holding and had been affixing some sort of devices to each side of the converter. The major looked at his wristcomm, adjusted a control on each device, then checked their displays.

Kallen and Lander went back to dig up the antenna stakes, then piled them atop the stroller. Five times they landed with a loud clang, one for each stake.

Now out of breath, Kallen returned to inspect the major's handiwork again. Kallen recognized the devices now. They were thermal detonators. "You're gonna destroy the converter? Why aren't we bringing it back with us?"

"It would take too much time to get it out of here and haul it back through the portal. Besides, I was briefed about the little problem they've encountered. That's why I have these detonators."

He was briefed about that? Kallen wondered. Senji hadn't told him everything after all. A lot, yes. Clearly though, several of the most important parts of this whole time travel mess had been edited out of all their conversations.

A Mark 8 thermal detonator was an extremely efficient device. They were used in scorched earth procedures—something that the NAA military had perfected long ago. Apparently, that policy extended to here and now as well. A Mark 8 worked in two stages. First, an extremely powerful EMF pulse was issued. That would effectively disable every unshielded electronic circuit in a forty meter radius. That took care of electronic components only. Since photonic components were unaffected by an EMF pulse, it was necessary to make that circuitry unrecognizable, as well as unworkable. What better way to accomplish that feat than to melt or vaporize it?

The major had set the detonators to maximum thermal intensity. They not only weren't going to bring the converter back with them, he was going to make sure no one would ever know what the converter was. Kallen was sure of that. A good deal of it would vaporize.

Kallen surveyed the surrounding rocks. With the converter being where it was, almost completely surrounded by a meter of rock, the intense heat of the incendiary effect wouldn't start a forest fire. And, if someone found the slag heap, perhaps years hence, they would have nothing more than an anomalous archeological mystery on their hands, if that.

Lander cut the ropes holding up the tarp over the converter, partially folded it up, and threw it onto the stroller. At the major's behest, he activated the stroller and they walked it back to camp as quickly as the stroller would allow them.

The flurry of activity was continuing. The tents had already come down and been packed up. Their personal gear was scattered all over the place. Everything they had been using in common was already stowed in containers, their tops snapped down.

The idea hit Kallen like a bolt of lightening. He knew it was completely crazy. It couldn't possibly work. He knew he would fail. But his heart said he had to at least try. He didn't care if he'd end up in the brig and with a court-martial.

The medkit. Where's the medkit? Kallen searched the piles of gear for it. There, by the heatstove, almost completely covered by that blanket. No one was looking. Kallen took it and stowed it at the rear of the stroller. His pack was next. He quickly filled it. Canteen, lightwand, water filter, raingear, clothing, kit bag, and the rest of his things. He rechecked his utility belt. His vidPAD was securely snapped into the holster. His pulse stunner and the second energy pack were securely attached at the other hip.

"Ten minutes," Major Montarco announced.

Activity was at a record pace. Kallen looked up at the other men. No one noticed as he knelt down next to the display on the side of the stroller. He quickly entered a sequence of codes. He knew exactly what he was doing. After all, he'd repaired two of these strollers already. He bypassed a redundant backup system, then shut down the primary and secondary rear horizontal gyro circuits. He left the front ones alone. He was finished in less than twenty seconds. No one would realize what he'd done until he executed the next step of his plan.

Craistok came up to the major. He was breathing heavily from exertion. "Sir, the detonators are still counting down and the area is secure," he reported.

"Good. Help them stow the rest of that gear onto the stroller."

No one cared how the pile of gear looked as they continued tossing the remaining containers into it. Without the converter taking up so much room, it was easy to throw things in and let them pile up. Kallen stood at the rear of the stroller, caught things tossed to him, set them down, and made sure the medkit wasn't getting covered up.

"Five minutes," the major announced.

The last container was unceremoniously dumped into the front of the stroller.

"Places," the major said.

The men stood at the left and the right of the stroller, held onto the guide handles, and maneuvered it to within a few meters in front of the portal markers. The major pulled them from the ground and stowed them on the stroller.

Kallen was at the right rear corner of the stroller. He found his mind oddly clear now. Nothing mattered except for his plan. The medkit was on the top of the pile in the very back. It teetered. He had deliberately placed it so it would do that. It started sliding toward him.

The major was directly behind him now as he came around and took his place opposite Kallen at the left rear corner. He pointed. "Deshara. The medkit."

Kallen reached over, caught it, grasped the handle, and held onto it tightly. Step one was complete. His pack, slung over one shoulder, was so laden it was starting to dig into it. He winced.

The major glanced at him. "Deshara, stow those things."

Kallen looked over at him but didn't answer or make a move to do so.

The major re-gripped his guide handle. He looked down at his wristcomm. "One minute," he called off.

Senji was at the front left corner. He glanced back at Kallen. The blood looked like it had drained out of Kallen's face. He was white as a ghost.

Twenty seconds later, the portal that had been invisible since they had arrived, appeared to ripple in the open air like a thin sheet of cascading water. Kallen watched the shimmering transform. Objects came into view, were translucent at first, then became more solid as the image in the wide circular opening grew in intensity. The trees and foliage of their immediate surroundings became completely obscured by equipment from the hydroponics lab.

"Deshara, stow that gear," the major said once again. "Move ahead," he called out to everyone.

The men pulled on the guide handles of the heavily laden stroller. In unison they started forward. Senji and Guyez were through a second later. Lackson and Madsen were next. Biggert was directly in front of Kallen. Opposite Biggert was Craistok. Kallen had half a second left to execute the next step of his plan. He grasped the snaps that held his backpack strap across his shoulder and clenched them together. The pack landed on the ground with a loud thump. It got the major's attention. His eyes grew wide with concern.

"Deshara! Your pack!"

The medkit was still in Kallen's hand. He heaved it off to his right.

"Deshara!" The major released the stroller's guide handle. With strength Kallen didn't know he had, he dug his heels in and pushed the back end of the stroller sideways, skewing its trajectory through the portal. Since the rear gyros had been disabled, his push quickly made the stroller yaw from the rear along a stable pivot point at the front.

"Sergeant Deshara!" The major had stepped to the side to avoid the stroller hitting him. It was completely through the portal now, but with a new vector.

Kallen and the major stood alone on the hilltop only two meters from the opening.

Not hesitating even an instant, Kallen stepped back a few paces then ran forward, ducked his head, and rammed the major as hard as he could with his shoulder. With a loud *umph*, the major went right through the shimmering barrier and slammed against the side of the stroller. His impact caused the stroller to yaw even more before he landed in a heap on the lab's concrete floor.

The rest of the men's hands had been firmly holding onto a guide handle. The stroller's mass, and now the new trajectory from Kallen's push, along with the major's tumble against it, threw them all to the lab floor, too. The stroller continued pivoting, while still moving forward, but now by itself. An a-grav stroller that wasn't guided by anyone, especially one that had this much gear on it and whose gyros were crippled, was a very dangerous object. Unless properly guided or maneuvered, it was pure undirected mass.

Dayler immediately raised himself off the floor in the pushup position. The a-grav stroller slowly reached the far wall of the lab. Its sideways motion had been stopped, but not its forward momentum, as it carved a long deep gouge into the wall before it came to a stop.

Dayler turned his head and looked through the portal. Kallen was on the other side of it, looking like he'd just killed someone. He saw Kallen's pack at his feet. He could see the edge of the medkit off to the left. Dayler held his forehead with a shaky palm. He realized exactly what was going on now. It couldn't be happening.

But it was.

Oh my God, he's gonna stay!

He watched as a wild-eyed Kallen snapped the pack strap together, quickly lifted it onto his shoulder, scrambled to retrieve the medkit, then took off running. He was out of sight in seconds.

Dayler's heart pounded with anxiety and fright. *He's crazy! He's completely fucking crazy!*

He frantically sought out Dr. Katterjay. The doctor was at the console looking confused. No wonder. Their arrival should have been as smooth as their departure. Since it wasn't, the doctor was understandably upset at the jumble of men and the uncontrolled stroller that threatened to wreck the room.

Dayler looked back again. Kallen was nowhere to be seen. *He's actually fucking gone!*

He suddenly realized a very important thing. Once the power to the processor was turned off the portal would never be able to open to that time and place ever again. He heard it straight from Senji's lips. That meant the very instant it was de-energized an entire lifetime's worth of Kallen's influences would have accumulated. Even a year, hell, for all he knew, a *day's* worth of changes to history might be enough to completely change every moment thereafter. The instant Katterjay de-energized the processor, the possibility was there that everything they knew, including themselves, might cease to exist!

Dayler knew exactly what he had to do.

Almost crazed with fear, he dashed toward the console. He saw Katterjay's finger poised over the control to cycle off the power. Apparently, in the ensuing pandemonium the doctor didn't realize Kallen wasn't with the rest of the men.

Dayler shouted. *"Don't! Don't shut down the power. Deshara's still back there! You can't shut it down!"*

Dr. Katterjay was startled to see Dayler's frightened face. His own took on the look of outright horror. There was no way he could let anyone stay behind—but he *had* to shut down the processor. The inter-modulation distortion was steadily increasing. The feedback would eventually cause unavoidable circuit damage if he didn't shut everything off. On the other side of the temporal barrier the thermal detonators were still counting down on the energy converter. When they detonated, the EMF pulse would be powerful enough to affect the photonogrid here in 2479. The detonators couldn't be stopped; there was no remote control.

Dr. Katterjay was panic-stricken. He couldn't shut anything down and strand Kallen in the past. But he had no choice—he had to de-energize the array right now. It was an impossible dilemma. *What am I going to do?*

About the Author

Mark Ian Kendrick is the author of several titles.

Desert Sons is the first of two stories that trace the relationship between Scott Faraday and Ryan St. Charles.

Scott Faraday, sixteen, has no idea that his world is about to radically change. Scott is in a small-town rock band, is fun loving, and out—but only to a select few. When Ryan St. Charles comes to live with his uncle in Scott's hometown of Yucca Valley, CA, they meet and form a tentative friendship. Ryan is a brash seventeen-year old who has just severed a long relationship with a man, but still considers himself straight. As Scott and Ryan's friendship develops, Scott begins to suspect that Ryan might be covering up that he's gay. Scott is sure Ryan has no idea that Scott is gay, so he comes out to him. The result is that Scott transforms their friendship into his first real relationship. Then, Ryan's hidden past comes into view. Scott is not at all prepared for what he discovers. Despite their vast differences, Scott sticks with him, and learns more about himself and relationships than he ever thought possible. This novel spans the summer that forever changed them both.

Into This World We're Thrown is the sequel to *Desert Sons*.

In this dramatic conclusion to *Desert Sons,* Scott and Ryan's relationship takes on new twists and turns. They both come out to those they love and have to confront their responses. Ryan's grandmother, his long-time caregiver, dies, which causes Ryan to re-evaluate his entire life. The band Scott is in might break up. Scott discovers he has secret allies, a schoolmate who's bent on having Scott be his no matter what, and a twisted foe. Will his secret admirer permanently ruin his now tenuous relationship with Ryan? Will Scott's foe turn his life into a living hell? Will Ryan pull himself from the depths of his emotional turmoil? Can the boys remove the bitterness that develops as a rift opens and widens between them? Can they uncover and express their love for one another before it's too late? All of this and much more is revealed, explored, and concluded in this exciting sequel.

Stealing Some Time is a gay-themed science fiction adventure story. A single extended novel told in two volumes, this series follows Kallen Deshara and Aaric Utzman, and their serendipitous relationship.

Part I: World Without You

It is 2477 CE. Much of the world has long since become desertified due to the unchecked use of fossil fuels in centuries past. The world of the 25th century is an advanced one, where technology rules, where ruthless leaders have the upper hand, and where water is the limiting factor for all of civilization. Eighteen-year old Kallen Deshara is entering his obligatory 5-year stint in the North American Alliance's Air Defense Force. While in boot camp, Kallen comes to terms with the fact that he's gay. He even finds his first gay relationship with a fellow graduate recruit, but is dumped almost immediately. While nursing his wounds, he finds his second relationship in a fellow student while in the ADF's Schools Division. This one lasts longer, but he gets dumped again. Once his school training is completed, Kallen is shipped off to his first duty station in the mountains at the edge of North America's Great Central Desert. There, Kallen becomes a force to be reckoned with as his natural talent with photronic software comes to the fore. Another relationship follows. This time with an officer. But it falls short again. When called to Central Security, he's sure he's walking into a court-martial due to being found out. Gay activity in the ADF is a serious breach of military law. Instead, he finds that he's been called for a secret mission to 1820, specifically to post-colonial Kentucky. *Time travel!* He and a hastily assembled team have been called to rectify a problem caused by the very device that opened the portal to the past. Not expecting more than to do his duty, Kallen isn't prepared for what awaits him.

Part II: Chance Encounter

Sergeant Technician Kallen Deshara's mission to 1820 Kentucky hasn't prepared him to meet young handsome Aaric Utzman, whom he literally and figuratively falls head over heels for. Aaric and his entourage are just passing through Kentucky on their way out west. And, while on the mission, one of the scientists who invented the device that opened the time portal, uploads to Kallen the real history of how the world became burning hot. Kallen couldn't be any more ill-prepared for that long-suppressed truth. In addition, before he left, he hacked into the base commander's personal vidfiles. Once he goes through them it brings him face-to-face with the awful truth about the commander, his country's President, and a long abided-by water treaty. Everything he thought he knew about the past, his present, and his allegiance is put to the test. In fact, he's forced to challenge the limit of his sanity as he tries to absorb the truth of the world and of his heart.

Part III: Journey's End

Kallen Deshara now knows his world's origin, nature, and destiny; and has fallen madly in love with young Aaric Utzman. He's grief-stricken at having given up everything he's ever known: his family, his friends, his country, even the era he's from, to stay with Aaric. But he's made his decision. His colleagues who've returned to the 25th century have other plans. They must bring him back before his presence in the past inexorably alters the timeline. They intend to return him even if it means having to kill him. But first they have to find him. Traveling along the Wilderness Trail with his new companion, Kallen is unaware they're being stalked. In the meantime, he realizes what had been missing in his life, deepens his love with Aaric, and sees more free-flowing water than he ever thought possible. Slowly but surely, he recognizes that he has more to offer than he ever knew. In fact, he may even be able to shape the future that should have been! But he learns an even more important lesson. Kallen discovers that love knows no boundaries—not even of time itself.

More information is available at Mark's website at www.mark-kendrick.com. You can contact him from there as well.

978-0-595-27672-1
0-595-27672-5

Printed in the United States
113667LV00011B/152/A